A CLARA MONTAGUE MYSTERY
BOOK TWO

THE
FALLEN

LAUREL S.
PETERSON

THE FALLEN

A Clara Montague Mystery

— Book Two —

For Rebecca —
Enjoy — wherever it falls

Laurel S. Peterson

in the big, glorious
stack of books.

Laurel S. Peterson

Woodhall Press
Norwalk, CT

woodhall press

Woodhall Press, 81 Old Saugatuck Road, Norwalk, CT 06855

WoodhallPress.com

Cover Design: Jessica Dionne Wright
Layout Artist: Zoey Moyal

Library of Congress Cataloging-in-Publication Data available

ISBN 978-1-949116-38-0 (paperback)
ISBN 978-1-949116-39-7 (electronic)

First Edition

Distributed by Independent Publishers Group

(800) 888-4741

Printed in the United States of America

Acknowledgements

Thank you to Christopher Madden and Woodhall Press for bringing Clara back into the world and being patient with my social media skills. Liz Eslami read an early draft and gave me lots of wonderful feedback, as did the amazing students in the MFA program at Manhattanville College. The book Katrina: After the Flood by Gary Rivlin provided context and information about the impact of the hurricane on the city of New Orleans. Finally, there is a real Pasquale's Osteria in Norwalk, Connecticut, and it is worth the trip for good Italian food. When you call for reservations, tell Pasquale that Laurel and Van said to stop by.

For Van, always

CHAPTER 1
Clara

The first time, the dream came in waves of violet, gold, and black, like northern lights reflecting off ice or water. The lights were distant, and I was safe. But they retreated then lunged with greater and greater force, the suck and roar like my pounding heart as suffocating color exploded over me.

I woke, shaking.

Not again.

I pulled the covers to my shoulders, the smooth cotton comforting against my sweaty skin. The crystal clock read 2:15 a.m. I needed to sleep. Tomorrow, I had clients to see and a business to run.

As I stared at the red numerals, they intensified and became shapeless, merging with the images of the dream, waves of color rocking the bed. My breathing grew deeper and faster and louder, the air slashing in and out of my lungs like sails through midnight air. The bed tipped. My body jerked. This time, I woke fully.

I sat up, pressing my back against the raw silk headboard and hugging my knees. I dreaded these warning dreams. In the past, they signaled a death: first Father's, then Mother's. Mother was still alive because, together, we had found the person who threatened our family. But I had failed my father. I'd been unable to reach him in time, and he had died of a heart attack too far from help.

Now, again.

Yellow and black auras signaled power struggles, violence, and destruction. Someone I loved was in danger, but who?

No answer echoed in the darkness.

CHAPTER 2
Kyle

Chief of police Kyle DuPont had asked Clara to join him at Dominick Ofiero's house on a chilly mid-March morning. The boy had been moaning about some disease or other he couldn't identify on his roses, and while she was a landscape architect not a landscaper, Kyle figured it was close enough. Besides, she had a laugh that could blow away cobwebs and fog, a laugh that always made him feel better. He just wished he knew what to think about those dreams she had and her laissez-faire attitude toward her divorce-in-progress. He wouldn't let a divorce slide like that, not over money. He'd get it done, move on.

Dom was a nice kid, a compact Italian boy with bristly dark hair, and Kyle's first hire as police chief after Kyle had moved to Connecticut from New Orleans four months ago. A Bronx native, Dom promised the department wasn't a stepping-stone to the NYPD; he said he liked smaller towns and ones that paid well he liked even better. Besides, his father and sister had left the Bronx for Stamford, so this was close.

Dom had rented a little house about ten minutes from the police station, gotten permission to plant a few things, settled in with a good attitude. It always took a while for someone to prove himself, and Dom took a fair amount of hazing—salt substituted for sugar in his coffee, gum on the seat in his cruiser, various unrepeatable nicknames—but it remained good-natured, and he managed pretty well, which made his insistence on this meeting, away from the office, a little strange. But even though Kyle had arrived first, Dom had just shaken his head when Kyle asked what was wrong.

"After your girl goes," he'd said, turning away, so Kyle couldn't see his expression.

The hazing Kyle had gotten when he'd arrived had been far more subtle, little tests of the authority a black chief would wield over his white officers in a predominantly white town: delayed reports, slight pauses before answering "yes, sir," a few too many officers sick on the same day. He'd put paid to it quickly by demanding performance but allowing his officers a lot of authority. He hated micromanagers and would be damned before he'd become one himself. As long as they acted with integrity, he could tolerate the other stuff, although some of the jokes had already started to get old. How long would it take before he had to assert his authority and risk alienating some of them? And why was that alienation always inevitable?

He sighed, then turned as Clara, a good sport about the whole thing, spun her Porsche Cabriolet convertible into the driveway promptly at eleven o'clock. Showing off a little. The door opened and one red heel met the pavement, followed by the length of her in the beige Armani pantsuit he liked, and finally the second red heel. Her blonde hair was carefully twisted up to accentuate her sharp cheekbones and green eyes. Red lipstick matched the heels. The outfit cost more than Kyle made in three months.

He still couldn't believe they were dating—if that's what one called having dinner with a married woman, while an entire town looked on. A few months ago, when he'd first met her, she'd just returned home from fifteen years abroad, where she'd gone after her father died. She'd come back because of a frightening dream her mother might die and, despite interfering in his investigation and nearly getting herself killed, had solved the mystery of her own painful upbringing.

Now she came to where they waited by the garage watching two new mothers jog by with their kids in strollers.

"Hey," she said, touching Kyle's arm. Shadows darkened the skin under her eyes. They'd been too busy to catch up with each other for a couple of days, and he wondered if things were difficult at work. He knew she felt overwhelmed at taking over her late father's business.

Kyle rested his hand lightly in the small of Clara's back and introduced her to Dom, who brusquely nodded his head in greeting. Did he feel awkward? Kyle hadn't seen him ill at ease before; the kid usually joked his way through the day, endearing himself to other officers and the public. Something was on his mind, even if he wasn't ready to share.

Now that he thought about it, Dom had seemed off the past few days, and Kyle recalled a couple moments, which made sense only in retrospect, in which the kid had started across the room toward his office, only to change his mind and head for the coffeemaker. Kyle wondered if he shouldn't have asked Clara to come after all. Perhaps Dom had wanted a quiet conversation with his new boss. Even now, his shoulders set stiffly as they walked around to the ailing rose at the back of the house. "It's a New Dawn rose," Dom was saying. "My favorite."

Kyle made a mental note to make it up to the kid, soon. Maybe after Clara left they could grab a cup of coffee.

"That cascade of pink blooms every year is heavenly, isn't it?" Clara said.

"Yeah, and the guy who rented me the house, they're his favorite too. Almost dug it up before I persuaded him I could handle it."

"They're pretty hardy, if that's any consolation." She smiled at him. "We'll fix it. Don't worry."

His eyes flickered to Kyle.

Clara went right to the bush, even before Dom pointed it out, ignoring the damp ground's effect on her fancy leather soles. "It looks like canker," she said a moment later, the rose cane between her long, graceful fingers. "The good news is that you should be able to prune it out. I can help if you want." She grinned at him. "It would be fun. But take a piece to a rose nursery first to confirm before we chop it back. Twombley could help you, up in Monroe. Sorry, I guess that means a whole morning to trek there and back, probably the last thing you want to do on your day off."

Kyle saw Dom relax fractionally, his brown eyes gleaming. "Sounds like a great use of my time. What can I say?" He held his hand out to Clara, his posture in his jeans and dusty sweatshirt military straight. "Thank you, ma'am, for coming by. In June I'll send some of the blooms your way with the chief."

Kyle could see how much the gesture touched her. In June her estate would be busting out in flowers.

"I would love that," she said. "And I mean it about the pruning." She pinched the lapel of her suit. "I don't always dress like this."

The three of them walked to the front again, enjoying the momentary quiet, Clara and Dom trading plant nursery names as if they were recipes for excess zucchini. Dom came from a family of Italian gardeners, the kind throughout the New York outer boroughs, with little patches tucked behind their houses, using every available inch of dirt and sun to grow tomatoes, zucchini, broccoli rabe. He said he left the vegetables to his Pops in favor of the flowers. When it got warmer, he said, potted geraniums and impatiens would flank the front door of the small Cape.

"I'll add more color," he said, "but I might have to put in a tomato or two by the garage if my Pops has his way." He ran his hand over the bristly hair. "Pops has his way a lot."

Kyle was thinking that flower gardening would likely lengthen the period of Dom's hazing—although he'd known guys in the NOPD who knit in their spare time, straight guys, guys who would beat you senseless if you suggested otherwise—when the car growled around the corner, squat and menacing.

He'd heard sounds like that too many times when he was patrolling New Orleans, but he never thought he'd hear it here in this town of rarefied greenery, long graceful fences, and purring German machines. No one let their muffler drop off, although every once in a while some disaffected kid pulled it off his car for a couple of weeks until his father took the keys away and paid an expensive foreign car mechanic to return it to its proper place.

This rumble wasn't like that. It wasn't about loud so much as it was about power. It wasn't a parade; it was a warning.

The truck, a lowrider souped up with bright blue paint and shiny chrome wheels, slowed in front of the house. The car's darkened windows lowered a crack and a gun muzzle poked through.

"Sir!" yelled Dom, turning white.

"Down," Kyle yelled, dropping to the ground and pulling Clara with him. Later, he would feel guilty for protecting her first, but it was instinct. Clara was a woman. Dom was police. He should have known what to do.

Kyle heard the spatter of shots and a grunt, the revving of the car's engine; bullets thumped into the ground around them, pocking up divots of grass and puffs of dirt.

He drew his weapon, twisted onto his stomach and aimed, but held off firing, wary of the neighborhood, the consequences. They let loose another volley. Dom groaned. The car disappeared around another bend. Kyle pressed Clara into the ground a moment longer to be sure the car was gone, suburban silence restored, then helped her to her feet, her perfect suit now smeared green and brown. "You OK?"

"I think so." Dirt smudged her pale face like a tear, but she seemed to move all right, and he couldn't see any blood. He holstered his gun and turned.

"Dom? Dominick!"

Dom lay in the middle of his perfect green lawn, blood pouring from a hole in his chest, eyes staring at the green canopy of trees.

Kyle yanked his phone from his belt. "Officer shot at 1070 Dayton Avenue."

Clara ripped off her jacket, bunched it and jammed it against the wound. Even as she applied pressure, blood soaked the jacket and squeezed through her fingers to slide down into the grass.

Kyle dropped to his knees, put his hand on Dom's shoulder. "Dom? Can you hear me?" Dom was grey. He tried to say something but couldn't seem to get air.

Kyle barked into the phone, "He's barely responding. Get someone here now." He thrust the phone at Clara. "Let me."

Clara put her hand on Dom's forehead. "It's OK. Someone's coming." Dom's eyes moved to her face, his lips moved, but nothing audible came out. She said, "They'll be here soon, so you just hold on. And who is stupid enough to shoot a police officer?"

Kyle heard a siren, and an ambulance skidded onto the lawn, disgorging two EMTs in dark blue uniforms. A patrol car pulled up behind the ambulance. The EMTs hurried toward them carrying a flat stretcher, the police officer two steps behind, his hand on his holstered weapon.

Kyle said, "Gunshot wound to the chest. No other damage as far as I can see. His name is Dominick Ofiero, twenty-eight years old, good physical condition. He's stopped responding to stimuli."

"Thank you, sir," the woman said. She was tall, with red hair and a brisk manner that reminded him of a high school gym teacher. The man was short but built like a rugby player. The two of them quick-fired their assessments at each other: mouth and nose clear, breathing shallow and labored, blood pressure low and dropping, pulse faint. They angled his head back to help him breathe.

"Put him in the unit," the man said. "We can stabilize him there, put in an IV line." The woman nodded; they shifted Dom onto the stretcher, then lifted it and jogged it to the ambulance.

"Chief? You OK?" Tall, thin, and blond, Officer Trevor Tremblay's color never looked healthy, but at the moment he was the color of swamp moss. Dom had been good at making friends with the other officers.

Kyle's knees were damp and muddy, his shirt and suit sleeves soaked with Dom's blood. "I'm fine. Set up a perimeter and do everything by the book. I don't want anyone in here who doesn't have credentials. Nobody gets away with shooting a cop on my watch. I'm going to the hospital in case Dom can talk. Get someone out here to do scene-of-crimes evidence collection ASAP, and I'll be back as soon as I can."

"Already on the way, sir. And, sir, it looks like you're bleeding."

"It's Dom's."

He shook his head then nodded and strode toward the cruiser for crime scene tape.

The ambulance siren pierced the air. As Kyle and Clara followed it to the hospital, he radioed dispatch and asked for Detective Joe Munson, his best man, to meet them. Kyle wanted them caught. Dammit.

Clara had insisted on coming, sitting white and silent in the passenger seat. Her hands were whip-stitched together as if she were going to play *here's the church, here's the steeple.*

He said, "Try to remember everything you can. Don't tell me; I don't want either of us to dilute or shift impressions by sharing them. Include every detail—even stuff that doesn't seem important. These fools might be cop-killers and I don't want them getting away with it."

She nodded, unhooked her fingers, steepled them again. She still hadn't spoken. He reached across and briefly rested his hand on her shoulder, surprised that it hurt to do so. He must have wrenched his arm when he pulled her to the ground. "Hang on, OK?"

A long line at the stoplight stretched to the I-95 ramp. He hit the sirens and accelerated around the waiting cars. Cars cleared to the right in front of them, and the miles hurried by, one corporate building after another. Behind him, some asshole raced in his wake. There was always one. At the exit for the hospital, he ignored a yellow light to make a left under the highway, flying up the hill and into the hospital's emergency entrance.

Inside, a nurse directed him through the doors to the treatment area, Clara at his heels.

"Sorry, Chief," said a rangy man in green scrubs, his gloved hands bloody. "He's not conscious. Leave your number with the nurse? She'll text you."

"He's brand new, Doc," Kyle said. *And he had something he needed to tell me.*

No one responded, but he knew they'd heard him. The emergency room coordinator, a nurse in her fifties with white-blonde hair, told him the EMTs had raided the boy's wallet. Dom's family would be here in fifteen to twenty minutes, depending on traffic.

"Where are they coming from?" Clara asked.

"Stamford, east side," she said.

Clara disappeared to clean up, although that suit was probably history. Kyle called the station. His admin picked up. "Hey, Sid. Joe leave yet?" He felt suddenly light-headed and looked around for a seat.

"He just radioed that he's parking, Chief. He'll check in at the scene on his way back." Kyle noticed Clara conferring with a pretty Latina nurse; they vanished around the corner.

"Maybe we can get ballistic evidence. I'll be here for a little while longer, if you need me."

His admin clicked off without answering. Never one to waste words, our Sid. He did a quick skim of Twitter to see if any of the news stations had picked up the shooting yet. Still quiet. That was a relief. Only one text from Joe to say he was on the way, and the email could all be dealt with later. He clicked the phone off, leaned back, exhausted. He would have to do better than that. He had to get back to the scene.

Clara came toward him, holding an ice bag.

"What happened?"

"I landed funny on my wrist. The nurse thought ice might help."

Had he done that when he pulled her to the ground? A sprained wrist was better than getting shot, but he hadn't meant to hurt her, hadn't been thinking about the damage he might do protecting her.

"Should you get it X-rayed? Make sure it's not broken?"

"I can still move everything, Kyle. The worst it might be is a sprain. If the ice doesn't solve it, I'll see the doctor. Promise." She smiled, shaky still. Her pants and blouse were damp from where she'd tried to sponge off Dom's blood. "How are you? What's happening?" she asked.

He told her he was waiting for Joe and for Dom's family.

She studied her wounded wrist. "I'm so sorry about all this."

Why did people always apologize for things that were far beyond their control? He understood, of course, that it was a manner of speaking, but he was tired of saying he was sorry for someone's loss, when it was impossible to salve their pain. No one could ever salve another's pain; most people could barely manage their own.

As they turned toward the waiting room, Clara said, "Kyle, I need to tell you something."

She looked pale and a thin line of sweat pearled along her hairline.

"What's the matter?" He gripped her arm, guided her to a chair.

"I had a dream. I—I didn't know it was about Dom. I couldn't tell… it was just colors." The ice bag crackled as her fingers dug into it. "I'm so sorry," she whispered.

His arm sent out a stab of pain. *What the hell.*

Joe walked through the sliding doors and scanned the room. Thick-bodied and a little stooped, Joe looked fatherly, but was as benign as a polar bear. A local man with forty-plus years of contacts in town, he was one of the few officers who had never participated in the racial hazing.

Kyle patted Clara's arm, trying to stay gentle. "This is going to have to wait, sweetheart." *Sweetheart? Where had that come from?*

Joe planted himself in front of them, nodding at each in turn. "Boss. Clara. Any news, Chief?"

Kyle shook his head. "Too early to know."

"All right then. Let's do this." Joe asked Clara to wait out of earshot while he took Kyle's statement.

Twenty minutes later, having given Joe everything he could think of, Kyle stood, feeling the crime scene like a pressure in his gut, his need to get back to see what Trevor had found, to interview the neighbors, almost painful. Joe would stay at the hospital to interview Dom's family.

As Clara moved toward them, Kyle pulled out his car keys. Her step hiccupped, then she recovered, her smile pale like November sunshine.

"I'll see you later?" He couldn't help it. He had to get back to the scene.

Her eyes squeezed shut, opened again.

He brushed her hand, quick and light, and then the world spun and he felt himself fall.

CHAPTER 3
Clara

Within seconds, ER staff surrounded him, yanking off his jacket, opening his shirt.

"He's got a gunshot wound to the triceps. How long has this been bleeding?" one of the nurses shouted.

"We came in about twenty minutes ago. Maybe twenty minutes before that?" I stumbled forward, felt myself pulled roughly back. Staff manhandled Kyle onto a gurney and rolled him toward the ER.

Joe guided me to a seat, well away from the action, where the two of us sat, despairing. Rorschach-like stains bruised the beige wool of my suit, and I smelled as if I'd been dropped in sharp-sweet vinegar. My car still sat in Dom's driveway. I couldn't go home and change. I had to sit here, bloody and awful and cradling my wrist.

Joe said, "You OK, Clara?"

"You think I would be?" I gestured at my clothes, still discolored despite my efforts with cheap paper towels and cold water. Was it cold water?

Maybe it was hot that took out blood. I plucked at the fabric. Maybe I should go back to the bathroom, try again. *Stop it, Clara.* Before I could stop them, tears escaped down my cheeks. "I... I could have stopped it."

He looked sharply at me. "You couldn't have done anything."

"I had a dream." I barely got it out. Waves of purple, gold, and black threatened the edges of my vision.

He shook his head. Joe knew about my intuitions. He was even more of a skeptic than Kyle, who at least had experience of voodoo from New Orleans.

"A dream?" he growled. I suppose he meant to be sympathetic.

My dreams haunted me until I figured them out. If I ignored them, which I'd tried to do in the past, I dreamed with increasing frequency and intensity until it was as if I were living a psychotic nightmare, unable to escape the slashes of imagery cutting into what remained of my conscious and rational life. Once, ignoring my dreams had ended with me in a Swiss sanitorium.

But I hadn't ignored this one. I just hadn't known what it meant. Usually, I had more time before something happened. How could I have guessed that the curtains of gold and black would have to do with Dom? Or with Kyle? Was he the target? My dreams had always connected to someone I knew intimately—father, mother, friend.

Now, I kept seeing that gun nosing from the car, hearing the pops, watching the blood thump out of Dom's chest. That bullet could have hit me as easily as it hit him. It's not that simple to shoot accurately, especially not from a moving vehicle. I knew. I'd done some shooting in my life. Most people with estates our size learned to hunt. Idiots used automatic weapons so they didn't have to be competent shooters. Spraying all of three of us guaranteed they got their target.

Joe handed me a neatly folded handkerchief. I blew my nose, and he took me through my statement. I kept looking around for someone to tell us what was happening with Kyle.

"They'll come tell us when they know something," Joe reassured me repeatedly. It didn't help.

Fifteen minutes later, two people with dark frizzy hair steamed through the door. The man marched toward the nurses' station, his prominent nose leading the way. "You have my son here?" I heard him say.

"Bianca!" the nurse exclaimed, slipping from behind the desk to hug the woman. "I'm so sorry about your brother."

"Can we see him?" the man asked.

The nurse shook her head.

Joe and I crossed to them. "Mr. Ofiero?" Joe said.

The man nodded.

"I'm Detective Munson and this is Clara Montague. I'd like to talk to you about your son."

"You were with him when he was shot?" The woman looked at my ruined suit, tears rimming her eyes. She grabbed the man's hand.

"Yes." I again felt the jolt as Kyle yanked me to the ground. I'd only sort of heard the car. Dom and I were having too much fun talking about where to get beautiful, glazed plant pots. "Gilbertie's," I'd just said. "Reynold's Farms." And then the bullets.

I held out my hand, but she averted her eyes. I wouldn't want to touch the woman covered in my brother's blood either.

"I'm so sorry. I—I tried to help," I stammered. "We were looking at his roses." I felt tears rising and turned to wipe them away. I felt a hand on my arm, and when I turned back, the woman gave me the barest of smiles.

"Thank you," she said, then the lightest squeeze, like a bird's heartbeat.

"Please, come sit down." Joe led them toward the rows of blue chairs, gesturing that I should make myself scarce.

I found a chair just within earshot, but far enough away that Joe would think I was being a good girl. I put a magazine in my lap, and flipped it open, and pretended to read, while glancing occasionally at their little group to match voices with words.

They arranged themselves, Dominick Senior across from Joe and the woman, Dominick's sister, Bianca, who had patted my arm, next to him.

Dominick Junior had inherited his compact size and shape from his father. Senior had a head of thick silver hair, cut short and parted on the side over a pair of fading but sharp blue eyes. His hands were strong and weathered, the hands of someone who loved the outdoors. He wore a heavy wool sweater and a scarf, but no coat, and every couple of minutes he gave the scarf a tug.

His daughter Bianca was slender and fine-boned, with her father's heavy, dark hair, blue eyes. She wore stretchy black pants, a yellow-collared blouse, and a plain watch with a flaking pink leather strap. A simple gold cross hung in the V of her throat.

"What happened? Who shot my son?" Dominick Senior asked. Bianca hugged her purse on her lap, as if it were a baby, her cell phone clutched in her hand.

"Is there anyone who held a grudge against him? Anyone he'd recently fought with?"

Bianca flipped her phone from one side to the other. Senior shook his head, as if such a thing were as incomprehensible as the world being flat. "My son is a good boy," Senior said. "He never got into trouble. All he ever wanted was to be a cop."

Bianca looked toward the nurses' station. I thought about the nose of that gun peeking through the window crack.

"Tell me about your family. How long have you lived in Stamford?"

"I bought a three-family house two years ago," Senior answered.

Bianca said, her face pinched and tired looking, "I'm on the top floor and my cousin Nikki rents the basement apartment. Dom and I were probably closest."

"Do you have other family here?"

Bianca said something about aunts in the Bronx and in Italy, her voice nearly on mute. For a moment, I remembered golden light on Roman limestone; then I looked down, rubbing my suit sleeve between my finger and thumb.

Joe said, "What else can you tell us about your brother? Friends? Disputes? Hobbies?"

"All he cared about was family," Senior said. "He wanted his own, couldn't find the right girl, worked at being the best *zio* to Bianca's little one."

Bianca smiled slightly at her father's words, like a curtain lifting to let a sliver of light through, and suddenly I saw the light around her, her aura, was a grey-brown haze like polluted sunshine, how L.A. used to look when flying in over it on a July afternoon.

The phone rang. She started, hit "ignore." A wave of red burst around her heart, then receded. It prickled in the center of my chest, and I rubbed my breastbone before I remembered my wrist and sucked in the pain. Bianca heard me and her eyes caught mine.

Grey-brown auras indicated depression, insecurity, negativity, all of which could be explained away by our presence in an emergency room. Maybe. But the red? Was it anger? Passion?

I wished I knew more, but I'd spent so much time in a push-me-pull-you relationship with my gift. My healer friend Paul had chastised me more than once for shoving it aside for more practical pursuits like running my father's business. Living in the swirling colors and thick emotions of the visions exhausted me. Avoiding the visions exhausted me. I couldn't win. Even now, I could feel her haze sliding my way.

Let her in, Paul said, his teaching voice ever present in my head. *Just protect yourself with turquoise light. And breathe.* So I imagined myself with a field of turquoise and white light around me, thick but clear. Whatever came into that space I could handle. I invited in the wisp of Bianca's aura; it retreated. I took in a long breath, let it out.

The pretty nurse rested her hand on Bianca's shoulder. She was slight, no makeup, loose white pants and top. "Dom has been taken into surgery. It will probably be a while, if you want to get some coffee or something to eat after you're done with Detective Munson. We'll page you when the doctor is finished."

"Is he going to make it?" Senior tugged again at his scarf.

She pinched her lips together, then repeated, "We'll know more when the doctor has finished."

"But it looks good?" he pressed.

"We don't know, Mr. Ofiero. Best just to see what the doctor says." The nurse patted Bianca's shoulder, then turned away. Bianca's aura had gone almost black. How could I help her?

Bianca watched me as I stood and went after the nurse. "May I have another ice pack?" I asked. "Would you mind? This one has melted."

She nodded, and I followed her down the sterile corridor to a treatment room. She took the ice pack from me, then frowned. "This is still cold."

"I'm sorry, I know. I… is Bianca OK?" I stopped. I couldn't tell her about the aura. She would think I was crazy.

"I doubt it. Her brother was just shot." She leaned against the treatment table, her arms folded across her chest.

"She seems, I don't know, like something's going on with her." I hadn't thought this through. Prying like this was the reason Kyle and Joe got angry with me.

"Seriously? I have sick people here. I know anything, I'll talk to the detective."

"It's just…I know I'm overstepping, but in case there's something… say, something she doesn't want to talk to the police about, well…."

She looked me up and down, her eyes lingering on the bloodstains. "Leave the investigating to the cops. You already look like you're in over your head."

I fumbled through my purse for a business card, held it out to her, dug down for some Montague backbone. "Someone shot the police chief and Bianca's brother in front of me, and I'm covered in his blood. Dom—he seemed like a nice young man with a good future in front of him." My voice sounded like the twang of a steel wire. I took a breath, slowed down. "The police will find the shooters, I'm sure, but that won't ease Bianca's pain. I want to help."

She stared at me a moment longer, then pinched the card from my fingers and tucked it in her pocket. "I'll think about it."

"How do you know Bianca?"

"Community college." She paused, looked me over one more time. "But I don't know nothing about her boyfriend." She handed me my ice pack, the same one, and marched back to her post.

CHAPTER 4
Clara

It was dark when I arrived home around seven, wanting nothing more than a shower, a glass of wine, and more ice for my wrist. My insides still felt as if they wouldn't stop vibrating. I couldn't shake the images of Kyle's blood-covered hands, his desperate eyes, as he worked on Dom's inert body—and then the doctors rolling him away. I hadn't considered before the weight of responsibility he must carry, not just for his officers, but for every person who lived in his town. Maybe he couldn't think about it too much or it would paralyze him. Maybe that's what training was for.

Joe had called the office late in the day to tell me that Kyle had been sideswiped by one of the bullets, but it wasn't life threatening. They'd patched him up, pumped him full of fluids, and then Kyle insisted on checking himself out, against medical advice. I could hear Joe's frustration.

"He insisted on getting back to the crime scene?"

"We'd cleared it by then. Nothing for him to do. I took him home. He's probably sleeping off the meds."

I left the Porsche in the garage between the Jeep I usually used for work and Mother's prized Jaguar. We were so fortunate. And on this night when the Ofieros had lost so much, it felt distasteful, obscene. I needed to find a way to help them.

How did other people handle trauma? I had spent the afternoon at the office, trying to check off items on my to-do list, but every time the activity slowed, a shot of adrenaline crossed my heart, like two broken electrical wires kissing. Every grumbly car from now on had a gun barrel poking out its window.

I walked through the low-walled kitchen-garden toward the back door, where a lone light threw out a few rays. My heels clicked on the slate walk, and one of the roses that bordered the vegetable patches grabbed my suit sleeve. I paused to pull the thorns free, thinking about Dom's shrub. He might not make it to Twombley Nurseries. The doctor had only been moderately hopeful when he exited surgery. "He sustained a lot of damage," he said. "We'll know more in twenty-four hours."

I knelt down and stuck my hand into one of the newly turned-over beds, bringing some of the dirt to my nose: moss and metals, worms and rain. The loveliest stuff in the whole world. We would plant lettuces in it this weekend. It had been a while since my hands worked the ground, but I had been planning all winter, sorting through seed catalogues, and consulting with our gardener Gerry over cups of tea in the kitchen. We had a list of vegetables and herbs: heirloom tomatoes, zucchini, cabbages, onions, kale, scallions, arugula, Black Seeded Simpson lettuce, lemon thyme, ruffled purple basil, apple mint.

I hadn't earned these pleasures. I was lucky only by birth—and where I'd been standing this morning. Dom, so happy to puzzle over a gardening problem with me, now fought for his life. I would make the drive to Twombley. I would care for Dom's rose until he could again. Tears collected at the back of my throat and I stood, brushing my hand off on my suit jacket.

Two more strides brought me to the back door. As I stuck my key in the lock, someone stepped into the light, dark and solid, and reached for me. I screamed, abrupt and sharp.

Kyle.

I couldn't stop myself from slapping my hand over my heart. It was better than slapping him.

"What are you doing here?"

He tucked his hand under my elbow, as if to push me into the house. "You need a better lighting system. I've watched you for the last several minutes, and you didn't know I was here."

I stared at him.

"Let's go in," he said. "I want to talk to you about this morning."

I shoved open the door, freeing my arm, and stepped into the kitchen. I switched on lights and dropped my purse on the counter. "I am having a glass of wine. After today, that and a shower are about all I want." I started toward the dining room wine rack, then turned. "You watched me? That's creepy."

He brushed a hand over his forehead. "I'm sorry. I was waiting and forgot you couldn't see me. I didn't intend to frighten you."

He looked drawn, as if the meds weren't working or he wasn't taking them. One arm rested in a sling, with a bandage up near his shoulder. He opened his other arm, and I pressed myself into his bulk as if he were the one thing that could keep me from drowning. I felt his lips on my hair and lifted my face to his. He ran his hand down my cheek and ran his fingers across my lips. Then he shook his head and pulled away. He'd been coming close then pulling away for months now.

I pulled two glasses from the cabinet and fetched a bottle of red from the dining room wine rack. "Red or white? I have white in the refrigerator. Or should you not drink? Did they give you pain meds?"

Kyle was standing at the kitchen counter staring at my bag. Some of

Dom's blood had stained it. "Pick what you want, Clara. It doesn't really matter."

I set the bottle on the island, twisted off the cap. No corked bottles tonight, not with his damaged arm and my sore wrist.

I poured red; then I took him down the hall to the solarium. Collapsing onto my favorite couch, I set my glass on the end table and pulled the cashmere blanket that rested along its crown around my shoulders. He sat in the chair catercorner to me, the wall of glass that looked out across the lawns opaque in the darkness behind him.

"Please come sit next to me." I wanted human comfort. Mother, who had allowed me to share the family home until I got the divorce sorted and decided my next step, was away in Montana, seeing Vance, her political operative beau. They were probably dreaming up campaign schemes over Pinot Noir and fancy cheese. Even if she had been present, a perfunctory hug was her outside limit for affection.

Kyle hesitated, then slid from his chair to my couch. I breathed in his scent of herbs and leaves, leather, good wool. He sipped his wine, then set the glass on the end table, turning his body slightly away from me.

"What did you want to talk about?" I needed to distract myself. Anything would do.

"Are you OK?" he asked.

"What do you mean?"

"You had a rough day."

"Yours was worse."

"I'm a cop."

I shook my head, but it felt like I had cold honey for brains. "I keep going over and over it, as if there were something I could have done to change the outcome." What if we hadn't walked out in front of the house at that moment? What if we had made the date for another day? What if I had pressed harder on his wound or heard the car coming sooner?

What if I had shared the dream? Maybe we could have avoided the bullets. The questions ran over and over, like the streaming news ribbon at the bottom of the CNN screen.

"That's normal, Clara. Keep telling yourself there was nothing you could have done. It's true."

"But the dream...and you..." The back of my throat constricted.

"Unless it gave you a name, date, and time, Clara, you're off the hook." He tried to smile, but it looked more like a grimace.

I wondered how many shootings he'd seen and what it had been like for him after Katrina, dealing with the dead bodies, the people left in their wheelchairs or by the side of the road or in their flooded houses in the heat because there was no one to come pick them up. What was this shooting multiplied by fifty or one hundred? How did a person carry that without fracturing?

"You've been through this before," I said.

"It doesn't get easier."

As I watched his clasped hands, beautiful and dark against my cream-colored furniture, I wondered what it was to be a black man in this town. Black culture had made a home in Fairfield County, but it was a long way from the South. What did he feel when he looked at all those white faces and their largely petty concerns, after dealing with a big-city job where lives were on the line daily? Even though he was chief, did it feel like a comedown? Did he feel he had sacrificed his career? And why had he come? He hadn't told me yet, even though I'd asked, and asked again, and I wondered how much violence the story contained.

"I could have lost you today."

"But you didn't."

"I'm sorry I'm so..." I shook my head, unable to finish. I meant it about everything: all the possible dreams he had left behind in New Orleans, all my indiscretions and impetuousness, all the gaps human beings had that were impossible to fill. I felt it for everyone, not just us, but the fallibility and imperfections of all humankind, so unable to give others or themselves the very things they needed most. I laid my hand on his arm, and it broke something open in him. He turned and put his hand behind my head and pulled me to him, kissing me hard at first, and then softer. I wrapped my arms around him, holding tight while trying not to hurt him. He didn't break away. I didn't break away. Then we did. "Come upstairs," I said.

At first that night, his presence guarded me from the dreams. I slept without them until dawn, and then I woke screaming. It was a new dream, a dream I wished I hadn't had. I always wished I didn't have them.

I lay there, the darkness pressing around me, trying to forget, trying to remember. In the dream, it's dark at first. I'm on foot in the forest, trees packed densely around me. There is no moon. I feel my way, hands stretched out like a sleepwalker.

Then, a twinkle, something that could seem hopeful if it didn't feel so ominous. I hear a sound like wind chimes, but more sonorous; the trees part, ringing a fairy dell, the perfectly round space in the forest where, in my childhood imagination, fairies danced. Each thick-limbed oak brandishes multiple muscular branches. Amidst the green and luxurious leaves hang glittering knives, sharp as loneliness. When the breeze moves, they kiss each other, edge chinking softly against edge in the dark, reflecting light from some hidden source, almost as if a lit candle burned in the center of each tree.

It is only when I move past their barricade that I see the man lying on the ground circled by staves, as if ready for some voodoo sacrifice. A sword through his chest pins him to the dirt. He is still alive.

Kyle pulled me into his shoulder. "Clara, it's OK. It's me."

I realized I was clawing at him. I balled my hands into fists and dropped them to my face.

He pried them off. "What's the matter? What happened?"

I turned my back to him and curled in as tight as I could, drawing his good arm around me. I kissed his wrist.

"A dream?"

"Yes." He let me cry, and when the tears abated, asked if I'd dreamed about Dom. I shook my head, wondering if he could see me in the dark. "I don't see anyone specific at the beginning. It takes a long time to put the pieces together."

"It couldn't just be the residual from the day? After Katrina…" His voice drifted off. "They were pretty awful for a while."

"Oh, Kyle." I turned to face him, the bare light of morning just touching his features and creeping greyly across the carpet. My hand traced his cheekbone, the line of his jaw. "I'm so sorry. I—I can't imagine."

He wrapped his hand around mine and pulled it to his chest and holding it there. My fingertips pulsed with his heart's muted thump. "What happened during the storm?"

He rolled onto his back, staring at the ceiling. "Nagin waited too long to put out the evacuation order, a full day after Barbour and Blanco, so we scrambled to get people out or to shelter. Some still wouldn't leave; there are always fools who think the storm won't be as bad as predicted, or who have ridden out some previous 'big one' without any harm. Makes them think they're invincible. And then there are the ones without resources: nowhere to go, no way to get there, no money to pay for it." He stopped.

The heat cycled off, and I pulled the blanket up across his chest.

"It was a mess. We couldn't get water or food in fast enough; we couldn't get buses to get people out. FEMA didn't know its ass from its elbow. People were desperate, looting for medicine and water and food, along with the idiots who thought this would be a good time to stock up on DVD players and PlayStations.

"We were short staffed, and we're trying to keep order, get people to safety, and figure out what the hell was going on. Communications were down, huge portions of the city were impassable because of the flooding. It was a war zone, Clara. I've never seen anything like it."

He stopped. I waited, but whatever it was didn't come. "I can see how that might stay in your dreams for a long time," I said.

He rolled to face me again. "Are your dreams like that?"

I shook my head. "I've had dreams like what you describe, especially after Father died. I kept reliving the funeral, willing him to step from the casket, resume his life. But these dreams, like the one tonight and the ones before he died, they... I don't know how to explain it. They have a certain resonance, an archetypal quality. I know I'm not going to find someone lying ringed by trees in the woods—not literally. The images mean something, and I need to connect them. I don't know how else to explain it. But they aren't the replaying of trauma like you're talking about. Do you still have dreams about Katrina?"

"Sometimes."

"I'm sorry." I stroked his cheek again, feeling its rough morning bristle.

"Me too."

We let the quiet linger. His dark eyes studied me. "Thank you for last night, Clara. It felt good to hold you. I've wanted that, wanted you, for a long time. Being with you patches me up somehow, keeps me whole. Last night made me aware of how much I need you."

"I need you, too. You ground me."

He laughed. "Yeah. When you're not getting me in trouble."

"I wish I could magically heal your arm." I ran my fingers lightly over the bandage. "Does it hurt a lot?"

He shrugged, winced.

"It scares me, you know, that I could lose you."

"When I interviewed, the town council told me this was a quiet town, which apparently it was, until you got home. Maybe hanging around you is what's dangerous." He waggled an eyebrow at me, then reached for my hand.

Uh-oh.

"I don't think we should do this again for a while, as great as it was."

"People already know we're interested in each other," I said.

"That's not this. This changes things."

"It will be all over town in twenty minutes whether one of us opens our mouth or not." He should know that, but maybe he hadn't been here long enough yet. Maybe the big city didn't work that way, but most of the ones I'd lived in had networks just the same. Once you were on that party line, your business was broadcast like *Extra*.

"You're still married," he said. "Most people consider it a moral crime. I can't be seen in that light."

Oh, I really didn't want to deal with *that* right now. "Adultery laws were repealed in Connecticut in 1991, as if that late date isn't shocking enough. And I've been separated for a year."

"It's not about law, it's about perception."

The man had come here last night. He was lying in my bed. He had kissed me. He wanted to get righteous now? "You know Palmer is holding things up," I protested.

"By not agreeing to your demands?"

"By demanding unreasonable things."

"Too much money." He looked around my spacious bedroom, far larger than the living room in his house. It had its own private bath and a closet with a built-in dresser in the center that Mother had commissioned for me when I was fifteen.

"It's not Palmer's money to spend." I sat up, clutching the sheet to my chin.

He reached for me. "I'm not telling you what to do, Clara. As if I could. I'm only telling you how I could be perceived. I'm a black man, stuck with a different standard. It doesn't matter what the law says if people perceive I'm breaking some taboo."

"The taboo about the black man defiling the white woman?"

A look of distaste crossed his face, and I knew I'd gone too far. But before I could correct my mistake, his phone buzzed. He reached for it and flicked his finger across the screen.

"Dom's awake. I've got to go." He slid from under the covers, already reaching for his clothes, his mind already beside Dom's hospital bed. I flopped back on the pillows, disgusted with myself, again.

CHAPTER 5
Kyle

Kyle walked onto the ward fifteen minutes after leaving Clara's, trying not to think about her last crack, and instead to think about the case. How long would the nurses allow him to talk to Dom? How much stamina would Dom have to speak? He had to ask the right questions and hope Dom had answers.

But her words kept reverberating. Black men had been lynched for looking at white women; didn't she understand the impact of that image?

He approached the nursing station. A blonde who looked as if she were ending a twenty-hour shift dropped her pen on the counter and sat back in her chair. "Help you?"

"Dom Ofiero?"

"You family?" She raised an eyebrow, reached for her coffee mug. An inch of filmed liquid slopped against the sides.

"He's asking for me. I'm his boss."

"The cops." She shrugged, typed something into her computer. "Room

517, down the corridor to the left, with the officer you guys left to babysit outside his door. I don't see you again in five minutes, expect me to come boot you out."

Five minutes? What could he get from Dom in five minutes?

"How's he doing?"

"He needs to rest."

He took her point, but he would do what was necessary to put those shooters in prison, even if it meant making Dom tired. He started down the hall, checking room numbers and fuming a little. Everyone had their job. Why didn't anyone ever understand he was just doing his?

He thought back to yesterday morning at Dom's place. What had the kid wanted to tell him? If it had only been a gardening question, his Pops could have helped him with the rose; he didn't need Clara's intervention. Had it been a way to get Kyle out of the station, somewhere more private to talk? Maybe Clara had arrived too quickly. He shook his head. Blaming her wouldn't help.

Room 517's window looked out at the parking lots and a grey morning sky. The window provided the only light, but the white walls, floor, sheets, equipment gleamed dimly against that corduroy backdrop. Dom lay with his eyes closed with drips for hydration and food and pain meds arranged around his bed, like so many spider legs poised to land. Kyle paused in the doorway. Should he wake him? He only had five minutes. He moved toward the chair, pulling it close to the side of the bed. Dom opened his eyes at the noise.

"Hey, boss." His voice scratched like thin wire on slate, barely as loud as a whisper.

"Hey, Dom. How you doing?"

"Pretty bad. This getting shot thing isn't all it's cracked up to be."

Kyle gestured toward his arm. "Tell me about it."

"Sorry," Dom rasped. "You OK?"

Kyle nodded. "You should take as long as you need to get well. We just want you back whole and healthy."

Dom's face moved in what Kyle assumed was an attempt at a smile. "Boss, have to talk to sister. She knows."

"About?"

Kyle waited. Clearly, Dom's situation was desperate, based on the number of machines and drips and the fact that Kyle had only five minutes, two of which he'd already used. Dom looked ashen with pain and exhaustion. He had barely enough energy to propel words from his mouth.

"Who was in the car?"

Dom moved his head on the pillow. A no?

"Not the car?"

Dom dipped his chin.

Did that mean yes to the car or yes he was right that it wasn't the car? "What then?"

"You. Roses. Needed to tell."

Kyle watched as Dom's face grew greyer, his breathing labored. Did he have an infection? What kind of damage had the bullet caused? Maybe Bianca could tell him.

Dom seemed to be waiting for Kyle's response, but Kyle didn't know how to respond. "Needed to tell me something?" he said finally.

Dom's hand lifted fractionally off the coverlet. "You," he whispered again.

"Time's up." Kyle turned as the nurse strode toward the bed to check Dom's vitals.

"I just need another minute."

"Absolutely not. Can't you see how much pain he's in? He refused medication this morning in order to talk to you, and now that's done. Out."

She might be finishing a twenty-hour shift, but Kyle didn't doubt her ability to have him hauled off the ward. He stood, touched Dom's hand. "I'll talk to Bianca," he said. "Then I'll be back, OK? You just get better."

Dom gave him a desperate look as the nurse hit a button and pain medicine surged through the tubes.

"It's OK," Kyle reassured him. "I've got this." But did he? He had no idea what Dom wanted him to do. At the house, if Clara's presence kept Dom from telling Kyle something, what was it? If Dom didn't know who the guys in the car were, then why had they shot him?

He watched as Dom fell asleep, and then walked out with the nurse. His eyes took a moment to adjust to the bright hall light. "Is he dying?" He saw the babysitter's eyes shift suddenly his way.

"It depends on how strong his immune system is."

"Is there infection?"

"Not yet."

She wouldn't say any more.

Kyle worried over it all the way down the elevator and out into the parking lot, turning Dom's words around in his mind and looking at them from every angle he could conjure, but nothing made them any clearer.

CHAPTER 6
Clara

As I stepped into the reception area at Montague and Brown, late already and still agitated about my screw-up with Kyle, Shona looked up from her desk, braids rattling across her bony shoulders, proud as an empress. This week's beads were neon green.

"Good morning, miss." Shona refused to use my first name, even though I had asked her to repeatedly. "There's someone waiting in your office. I, uh, didn't know what else to do with her." She shrugged. *Your problem.*

Yeah, she and I were going to have a conversation about whose problems belonged to whom—and shortly. *Whew. Had to back off that.* She was only being herself. "Who is it?"

"A woman. Bianca Ofiero. She's got a little kid with her."

Dom's sister. So she'd come. I had intended to work on the boyfriend angle this morning—after I attended to some real work. My anxious partner Ernie was bugging me about soliciting new jobs, and I needed to make some calls. I didn't have time for this.

"Thanks. Can you bring in coffee for us?"

"Um, before you go, your husband called again, and you have an appointment for later this morning with Mrs. Fruchtman." She twitched an eyebrow at me.

I ignored her and took the pink slips from her outstretched hand. Everyone else had their messages forwarded to their email, but if I didn't have that little piece of paper to remind me, lots of things got forgotten.

"What did my *ex*-husband want?"

"He didn't say, miss." She grinned, then let it fade, as if she'd realized that wasn't the right response.

When I opened my office door, I saw the child first, a little girl with pink-barretted brown hair. She clung to Bianca's hand, her other arm wrapped tightly around a faded blue terrycloth bear. They turned from their huddle at the window, looking down from our twentieth floor at the tiny cars and people on the street below. Even against the backlit window, I could still see Bianca's dark aura.

"How is Dom?" I asked, tensing.

"Not so good. He's still in intensive care and the doctors only say *wait and see*. It's hard for my father."

I nodded, but she was squeezing her hand into a fist, the knuckles whitening.

I said, "It's a first-rate hospital."

"They don't look very confident. They look tired and watchful. My friend, she keeps shaking her head."

"The nurse I met."

"Leila. We got to know each other in nursing school."

"Is this your daughter?" I squatted down at the little girl's level and asked if we could get either of them something to drink.

"Maybe some Coke for Therese?" Bianca tilted her head at the child, who nodded shyly. "It's a big treat."

Shona, hovering in the doorway behind me, indicated she'd only be a moment and shut the door behind her.

I gestured to the corner by the window where two couches fronted a low coffee table. Therese climbed up and tucked herself under her mother's arm.

"How old are you, Therese?"

She stared at me, clutching the bear.

Bianca said, "You can tell her. How old? Show her with your fingers." Three tiny brown fingers unfolded from the safety of the bear and just as quickly disappeared again.

"Three. Wow. That's pretty big. Who's your friend?"

Bianca laughed. "He's Mr. Bear. Hard, no?"

"That's a perfect name," I said. "Easy to remember." I smiled at Therese, who hid her face.

There was a tap at the door, and Shona slid in with a tray. On it rested two Cokes and two glasses of ice, and a mug of coffee doctored with cream and sugar. She'd even managed to find some chocolate cookies, probably from someone's luncheon hoard, maybe even her own.

"Thanks, Shona. That's perfect." I smiled at her, got a nod in return.

Bianca cracked open one of the Cokes and poured a small amount for Therese. She handed her daughter the cup and watched to make sure none spilled on my black and white zebra coverings. "I'm sorry for showing up like this."

"Not a problem." I picked up the coffee with my good hand, letting the silence settle.

"Those cops, they aren't going to believe Dom is innocent. They're going to think this was retribution for something." She flapped her hand like a flag in the breeze.

"Why?"

"It's his best friend, Teo." Her face softened, so fast I wasn't sure I'd seen it. "Him and Teo, they've been friends from when they were Therese's age, playing soccer and racing bicycles."

"Why would having Teo as a best friend be a problem for Dom?" Bianca shook her head, and I felt frustration well up. She'd come here. I had work to do.

Was I supposed to magically intuit what she wanted? I took a breath. What was wrong with me today? First the crack at Kyle, and now this? It was like my nerves had been unsheathed and every stimulus tripped a reaction, like a circuit breaker snapping off.

"You came here, Bianca. I can't help if I don't know what you need."

The fist formed again. "Sunset Boyz."

"Which is what?"

"Teo's new…friends."

"What's wrong with Teo's new friends? Didn't Dom like them?"

"Dom, he hates how they changed Teo, made him harder and angrier."

"What kind of people are his new…friends?" I was missing something; I just didn't know what.

"Teo, he just feels rage. My Pops tried to help. Teo lived with us for a few months, but Pops finally kicked him out. Those friends were his new family. I just wish it could be us. I know Dom wishes that, too." She smoothed her daughter's hair back from her forehead, but the little girl flinched.

"This Teo, he's still around? He and Dom are in touch?"

"They're friends. No, no, brothers."

Therese looked up at her mother and held out her cup.

"Sure, baby." Bianca poured another breath of Coke over the ice.

"So what are you really worried about, Bianca?"

"I want you to find out who shot my brother and why."

Never mind that I didn't have the expertise, Kyle would never speak to me again if I agreed to help her. I hadn't really thought through what kind of help she might need; I'd assumed her aura was emotional pain; I could help with that, not with police business, but they were so intertwined that dealing with one meant dealing with the other. "The police—."

"No. You. The police will say it's just some gangbanger shooting." It slipped out before she could stop herself. She turned frightened eyes on me. "Leila thinks I can trust you. You told her you'd help me. And my Pops—he loves Dom. It would break his heart if he had to live with people believing he raised a dirty son." Her aura flared red, like a corona around the sun.

Did she really believe people would think Dom was involved with a gang? "When Dom wakes up, he can speak for himself. Shouldn't we wait to hear what he has to say?"

She shook her head. I wondered what the doctors had told her. I had seen the blood pour out of Dom; I'd heard the rigid control in the EMTs' voices, but it was impossible to tell who would live and who wouldn't.

"I'm not sure what you think I can do. The police have resources, and they know how to investigate."

"You solved a crime already."

So she'd Googled me.

"Yes, but that was my family."

"And this is mine!" She stood, her body straight and rigid. "Is your family more important than mine?" Therese whimpered and clambered to her knees on the couch, pulling at her mother's arm.

"That's not what I mean, but—." I didn't have time for this. I had a business to run, dreams to decode. My impatience reasserted itself, and I tried to shove it back down.

"I see this was a mistake. You don't want to help. Fine." She swept her daughter into her arms.

I let her loom over me. "All I meant was that I knew the people to talk to. I don't know your family or your connections." I gestured at my Chanel suit. "I'd be completely out of context."

It was clear from her expression that she didn't understand what I meant by context, but she did understand my denial.

"The Sunset Boyz—those are his friends. In Stamford, they are run by a rich businessman. They do nothing without his say-so. You have perfect—" she waved her hand at my suit in a parody of my own gesture—"*context* to find out why he wanted my brother dead." Her aura darkened, crimson to garnet.

I held my hands up in surrender, wincing as my wrist pinged a warning. "OK, OK. I know my town's police chief. He was with me when Dom was shot. Let's start there. He can find out if Stamford police officers are looking at your brother's gang ties. If they are, we don't have to do anything; we can let them find the shooters. If not, then I'll see what I can find out for you. OK? Meanwhile, maybe Dom can answer all these questions himself."

She nodded, her body still stiff.

"How can I get in touch with you?" She clung to Therese, and the little girl squirmed.

"To let you know what I find out."

"Oh. You got a piece of paper?" I snagged a pad and a pen from my desk. She wrote her email address.

"No phone number?"

"I don't want Pops knowing what I'm doing. He can't have me suspecting Dom, too. He's not in such good health."

The man I'd seen the day before looked robust to me. I wondered suddenly how much of her story and its accompanying drama had been concocted for my benefit. How much had she left out? What did she think would make me say no?

For a long time after she'd gone, I thought about the businessman and Teo's friends. Bianca said Dominick's friend Teo was part of the Sunset Boyz. Who was this group?

I turned to Google to answer my questions, even if I felt guilty every time someone passed my office, as if I were sneaking peeks at my Instagram feed. Scrolling through Wikipedia's entry indicated the gang originated in Chicago in the 1940s, expanding since then throughout the U.S., and into Latin America and Europe. Since the grammar was wrong, I had some doubts about how accurate the numbers were. The entry also talked about the gang's attempts to "legitimize itself as a pathway for minority empowerment." Someone had read a sociology textbook. Members, it said, joined because they felt disrespected by the culture for racial or economic reasons. But that empowerment came at the price of murder and drug trafficking.

When I searched Sunset Boyz and "Stamford, Connecticut," to see if the gang had infiltrated the suburbs, Google spit up pages of references about members and their activities in Stamford, Norwalk, and Bridgeport. One alleged member worked at the local aquarium as a security guard, answering little kids' questions about the marine mammals and making sure no one got hurt crossing the street. During smoke breaks, he phoned his buddies, arranging drug buys and a gang war. The article suggested the gang had expanded into "bedroom communities," like mine, which was more than a little disturbing.

One of the Google articles concerned a Hartford police officer accused of working with gang members to commit robberies and extort money. He'd even allowed a member to pose as a police officer.

What if the real story was a bad story? Had Dom been involved with the gang after all, like this cop in Hartford? Maybe he knew something the gang didn't want him to know? Could that be a motive for murder? What did I know, rich little suburban white girl like me?

Well, this little white girl wasn't going to talk to any gang members, that was for sure. That was police territory.

I shook my head but hesitated as I reached for the phone. I should tell Kyle about Bianca, the businessman, the Sunset Boyz. Maybe it would help bridge the morning's awkwardness.

The call would take, I thought, about three minutes, and then I could wash my hands of the whole situation.

"I was just going to call you," Kyle said when he picked up the phone. "Dom's gone. Blood clot."

"Oh no! No." The scene ran through my mind again: the car, the gun, the grass, the blood. Adrenaline rushed my system, and the world went black for a moment. I grabbed the edge of my desk, something to hold on to, and I realized I couldn't turn my back on Bianca. I would check out the businessman. I could do that much for her.

"Doc told the family. I'm going over to see them. It's a murder now, so things are going to be crazy for a while, Clara. I don't want you to think it's because of…what we talked about this morning."

"I'm sorry," I blurted. "I didn't mean it. I was angry and frustrated."

"I know. It's not OK, though, but I can't talk now. You understand?"

"Yes." The part of me that was three years old thought it was all a little too convenient. "Can I come? Would you mind? Bianca was just here with her little girl." As I said it, I realized what he would think.

"Clara, stay out of my investigation. I mean it. You cannot involve yourself in a cop shooting. The other officers will crucify you if you screw up their ability to get a conviction."

"She came to ask for my help." I left out the part about my business card. "She left, literally, five minutes ago." OK, maybe fifteen. "I called you first, and I'm telling you all about it. Right? I'm doing the right thing."

He grunted, unmollified. "What did she want?"

"She thinks the officers investigating her brother's shooting might be distracted by a gang connection she claims he has."

"What gang connection?"

"Dom's best friend, Teo Welles, is a member of the Sunset Boyz in Stamford. I think he's Bianca's boyfriend." I would tell him about the businessman when I knew more.

"We'll check it out."

"She knows me now, and if I introduce you as a friend on the force, she'll see you as someone with a personal interest in her brother." *Then she won't think I betrayed her.*

He made me wait for an answer, drawing out the silence, and in that space flashed the image from my dream, the faceless man, impaled, blood running down his chest.

CHAPTER 7
Kyle

The Ofieros lived just south of I-95, outside Kyle's territory, but Chief Rosica Videz and he knew each other pretty well by now for reasons that included more than the chief's being the first Latino to lead Stamford's police force. After Katrina, Kyle had had to learn to trust his fellow officers again, and while being the boss gave him some control, being a black boss in a white town felt like the same old same old. Rosica Videz understood.

The thought bothering him as he drove the cruiser down the Ofieros' street was that he had missed something when he'd hired Dom. Had the racial hazing distracted him? Had he, as in NOLA, missed the darkness? Could he trust his judgment anymore? Maybe he couldn't trust Clara either. Maybe his officers didn't really have his back. What darkness did he himself carry that made him blind?

The Ofieros' street led to the beach and Cove Island Park, which housed a skating rink, home to the local youth hockey league. The park looked out over Cove Harbor, a large inlet off Long Island Sound. Usually, water access would make it an expensive area, but these neighborhoods below the interstate were mixed, Stamford and Norwalk emphasizing mostly industry while Darien and Greenwich housed big estates with private beaches.

The buildings surrounding the Ofieros' home were multi- and single-family houses with small garden patches and narrow driveways, a few two-story condominiums, some light industry and mom-and-pop stores— grocery, liquor, laundry. Their three-family had a cement walkway to the front door, a bricked face, and a peaked roof with, of all things, a copper pig weathervane. It was lined up east to west, as if a storm were headed in. The dirt in the small front garden was turned over, ready to plant. Daffodil stems poked from the ground like spiked fence tips. Dom would have planted those in his front yard, too. Kyle looked away.

Bianca answered the door to the first-floor apartment. She inspected Clara, and then him, appraising the sling that held his wounded arm. Stamford officer Iannotta, who had joined them as a matter of protocol, lingered on the bottom step. "What's this?"

"I'm Chief Kyle DuPont, Dom's boss. We need to speak to you and your father, please," he said. "It's important."

Her eyes were red and puffy, and her sweatpants and tissue-thin t-shirt left little to the imagination. A toddler hung back behind her, holding a stuffed bear. "We know about Dom. The doctor already told us. My father, he is resting. He doesn't need any more news today."

He said, "We're trying to find your brother's killer."

She looked at Clara, anger flashing like lightning. "You told him?"

He felt Clara flinch.

"He's a friend, Bianca. He'll help, and he was wounded, too."

Bianca's lips pinched together, as if willing Clara to keep her secrets. But there would be no secrets, not in a murder investigation. Later, Clara would explain to him exactly what she had left out. She always left out something, which made him wonder again why he trusted her.

Bianca looked back and forth between them, raised her chin slightly in acknowledgment.

They walked down a narrow hallway to the kitchen, a pleasant space that opened to the backyard through a pair of French doors. The still-raw March weather kept them inside, but he could see the beginnings of work on some fifteen vegetable beds, with crushed stone walkways between, and a garage at the end of a driveway that slid up the right side of the house. A sturdy fence kept out neighboring animals and children, but a fancy swing set with an attached slide and a small tree house took pride of place in the corner. Grandpa obviously adored his granddaughter.

"From now until November, my father is out there every day." The skin under her eyes was smudged dark, as if since yesterday she'd missed three nights' worth of sleep. "Keeps us in vegetables. I hardly have to shop at all."

"Are you the cook?" Maybe she would relax talking about the familiar.

"Pops is a great cook. He's done most of it since Mama died twenty years ago, but I do some. He gets more tired these days." She gestured toward the kitchen table and asked if they wanted coffee. They accepted, and she turned to pack the espresso filter and twist it into its slot. The little girl hung onto her mother's leg, watching as Kyle and Clara sat, and Iannotta stationed himself just inside the doorway.

"How old is your father?" Kyle asked.

"Seventy-two in September."

"Retired?"

"Yes. He trained as an engineer but worked most of his life as a tool and die designer."

"He emigrated from Italy?"

She handed the first espresso to Kyle, pushing the sugar bowl in his direction. "What do you really want to know?" She turned to the machine, avoiding his eyes.

He said, "When you're done with coffee. No rush." He wanted to see her face. He could read faces—or thought he could until Jonah.

She tapped out the filter and refilled it three more times, serving Clara, then Iannotta, then herself. Clara asked the little girl about her bear. Iannotta drank the coffee black and set the cup on the table, as if he couldn't be distracted. Kyle pushed back in his chair, noting the cheerful green curtains and tidy countertops, wiped clean of crumbs. Dishes were stacked in glass-fronted cupboards; the refrigerator held a collection of primitive artworks heavy on stick figures and crayon. How did someone who came from this get hooked up with a gang member? What would have attracted Dom to Teo in the first place, when they were children? Kyle had studied psychology undergrad, before he joined the police force, mostly because he didn't understand human motivation. Being a cop tended to make a person think in black and white, but no human he'd ever met was as black and white as the judgment others foisted on them. Even now, in this homey kitchen, some thread that led Dom toward Teo's darkness must linger, even as Kyle knew he himself had been led astray by another's darkness.

When Bianca finally sat with her own cup, Kyle said, "I understand you are concerned we won't investigate Dom's death seriously. Something about an old friend?"

The sun slanted in the window and illuminated the vase of forsythia on the table, making the yellow flowers glow, like a stalk of little candles. Bianca slumped in the light like a melting shadow. "My brother was *not* a Sunset Boyz member."

"That's what Dr. Montague said."

"He wanted to be a policeman because of his friend Teo Welles. He wanted Teo out, and he wanted to shut the gangs down."

"I remember that from his job interview."

"You don't think he's gang?"

"We never did, ma'am. His background check came out clean. Had Mr. Welles and your brother been in contact recently? Would the gang, or Mr. Welles specifically, want to harm your brother? Did his joining the police force threaten them in some way?"

She shook her head slowly, reaching out to touch some of the forsythia flowers. Her finger shook, and one flower dropped to the table. She twirled it in her fingers. "I can't think what that would be."

"Have you seen Mr. Welles recently?"

She crushed the blossom to a smear and reached for a napkin to clean her fingers, avoiding Kyle's eyes. "They talked all the time. They were like brothers."

That wasn't his question. He let it slide. "Brothers argue." Friends you thought of as brothers argued. He pressed her. "Had they argued in the past few days?"

She held her fist to her mouth, her other hand holding her wrist, as if creating a body block against them. Whatever she knew, she was afraid it would hurt someone, and she didn't trust the police to do right by her secrets. People forgot their secrets looked like everyone else's: love, money, sex. Most humans weren't creative in damaging each other.

Finally, the story spilled from her like coffee into the espresso cups. Teo and Dom had been hanging around the backyard last Saturday drinking a lot of beer. She'd come out to ask if they'd run to the store for extra ground beef for dinner, but they'd been arguing so intensely they didn't hear her walk onto the porch. When he saw her, Dom yelled at her for creeping up on them, and he never yelled at her. She hadn't even heard anything, she'd barely been standing there a moment, only the words *righteous, homeless, car, fire*, which didn't make sense anyway. She'd seen their fists clenched, their arms raised, muscles straining. She'd never before seen them angry enough to raise a hand toward each other.

She hadn't thought about it again until her brother was killed by gang bullets. Maybe, she thought, they'd been talking about something the gang was going to do; maybe Dom had tried to talk Teo out of it or had threatened to tell someone. But she'd scanned the newspapers for the last week and she hadn't seen those words. Now she worried the gang's plans were still in the future.

Homeless? Car fire? It couldn't be.

"Are you absolutely sure those are the words you heard? It's important." He saw both Clara and Iannotta look at him and tried to dial down his intensity.

"Positive. I've been thinking about them all week."

"Would Teo or his gang kill Dom to keep him from stopping their plans?"

She snatched up her cup and drained it, looking at Clara. "Teo would never hurt Dom. Never. They loved each other, even if Dom didn't understand why Teo stayed with the gang. He was *family*."

Family could foster the most intense hatreds, hatreds that spawned terrible, irrevocable actions. Dom had claimed in his interview that he rarely saw his friend from the gangs, but Bianca made it sound as if they saw each other all the time. Which version was truth?

Therese, hearing the tension in her mother's voice, tugged on her sleeve. Bianca picked her up and set her on her lap.

Kyle asked, "Was your father home when they were talking? Might he have heard the conversation?"

"Pops attends a garden club meeting on Saturday afternoons; then they all go for pizza. He wouldn't have liked Teo being here."

"Why?"

"He thinks Teo brings bad influences." She turned sharply to look out at the garden. "Like a drive-by shooting." Shadows crept across the beds. "He doesn't want him around Therese at all." She ran her hand over her daughter's hair. Therese was having a whispered conversation with the bear, her face pressed to his.

"Where would we find Teo? I need to talk to him."

Bianca looked at Clara, tears spilling over her cheeks like a thin sheet of water over sand.

Clara reached for her, then drew back, as if realizing her comfort would be rejected. She said, "After Chief DuPont confirms Teo's alibi, he can move on to other suspects."

"Other *suspects*? I've already told you Teo wouldn't kill Dom."

Therese looked up at her mother, her eyes filling with tears at her mother's tone. Bianca hushed her. "No, no, baby. It's not about you. You're a good girl." She rested her chin on Therese's head.

Kyle had seen this before; Bianca was willfully ignoring Teo's multiple acts of violence to prove his loyalty while working his way up the gang hierarchy. Nothing her father or anyone else said about what he might have done would change how she felt. She thought she was in love. Women who chose a gang member often came from chaotic or dysfunctional backgrounds. Dom's family looked loving and supportive, but who knew? Maybe the old man's anger went deep. Maybe because she'd known Teo for so long, she couldn't accept that he might not be who she thought he was. Maybe she thought she could handle the darkness without being touched by it. Kyle figured Teo's feelings of inferiority were too well entrenched by the time Dom's father took him in, and inferiority made people do all sorts of stupid things. He knew that from personal experience. His own father. He stopped himself. Not now.

But Kyle couldn't worry about her feelings. Teo had had an argument with Dom, where they almost came to blows. Three days later, his officer was dead—and Kyle hadn't paid enough attention. So once again, he was culpable for a man's death.

"Where do I find Teo?"

"He'll be at the funeral. He won't tell me where he lives."

"You must have some idea." He nodded at Therese, acknowledging the unspoken assumption that the girl was Teo's. "If not, maybe your father knows."

"Teo hasn't done anything wrong." She set Therese on the floor and swept the coffee cups off the table. "If you want to talk to my father, you can come back another time. I think it's more important he rest. Anyway, he doesn't know anything about Teo. We kept it from him."

"Kept what from me?" Dominick's father stood in the door in soft, faded khakis and a white t-shirt, his face creased from sleep. He carried a pair of gardening gloves.

"Grandpop!" The little girl ran toward the old man. He held out his arms to her and swooped her up.

"Pops, it's too late to garden," Bianca said. "Look, the sun is already setting."

"Don't change the subject."

Bianca looked at them, her face plaintive.

Kyle shook his head. "I'm sorry, but this is a murder investigation. No information is sacred. I'll protect you if I can, but you need to talk to your father." He turned to the old man. "Sir, we need to know about your son's relationship with Teo Welles."

"Teo." The old man set the girl down, suggesting she go get her doll. He waited until she left the kitchen, then shoved his feet into a pair of rubber gardening clogs. "I tried everything, but his rage… You have to murder someone to get in that gang. And my son, he defended Teo. Her, too." He pointed at his daughter. "Said Teo was doing his best. Murder? After his parents died, I offered him a roof over his head, food, counseling even. Instead, he quit school and joined the gang. And now, violence has harmed our family, just like I said it would." He shook the gloves at his daughter.

Clara stood, held her chair for him. "Please, come sit down."

"I've told you all I can."

Kyle said, "Thank you, sir, Bianca. If we need anything else, we'll be in touch."

Bianca walked them to the door. Iannotta went out first and waited at the foot of the steps.

"You've made it hard for me," she said, looking at Clara. "My father won't trust me now."

"I want justice for your brother, like you do. Chief DuPont is your best hope for making that happen."

Kyle pulled out a card and gave it to her. "If you or your father thinks of anything else, please call me, especially about the words: righteous, homeless, car, fire."

She nodded, but the door snapped shut behind them.

"Who is this gang?" Clara asked on the way back to the station. The day had turned gloomy and damp, a grey mist drifting in from the south that coated the car like a fine sweat.

"I'm going to have to follow up with Stamford's organized crime and gangs unit. We're so small, we haven't had to face it before." He'd already started rehearsing the phone call.

"So has it moved—literally—into our town? Or are they coming only to do business?"

"Not sure, Clara. Rich kids have plenty of money for drugs, but they usually go to the dealers rather than the other way around."

Car fire... He wondered if he should call his buddy Oz in NOLA. His only remaining friend on the force.

She ran her finger along the bottom of the window to collect the condensation. "So when they move in, they establish a sort of safe area? Surrounded by people who are on their side?"

What was she talking about? "I've never met anyone outside a gang who was 'on their side.' You're either in the gang or you keep your mouth shut. They hurt people who get in their way, fingers cut off, tongues cut out, ears severed from their heads. It's not something to toy with, Clara." He shook his head, tried to think of how he might approach Oz. They hadn't kept in touch.

Silent, she stared ahead at the line of cars.

"Do they own property? And if they don't, wouldn't local business or civic leaders have to look the other way while the gang operated in their neighborhood?"

He tried to focus on what she was saying. Real estate investing for gangs? "What's this about?" He caught her profile in the corner of his eye, traced it, noting the full lips, the deep-set green eyes. Even as one part of his brain kept track of her questions, parsing their source, wondering what she hadn't told him, because there was always something she hadn't told him, another part kept falling for her, even though the timing was all wrong. God, could his thoughts get any more scrambled?

He would never make in a lifetime what she had stashed in one investment account, but he couldn't imagine being anything other than a police officer. She brought to her life the same kind of intensity he brought to his job. In that sense, they were a good match. But the puzzles she'd encountered since he'd met her could have left her injured or dead. Gang members wouldn't consider her bank account protection. No one but rich people considered a bank account protection.

And they still had to talk about last night, which had been a mistake. He had just needed her warmth. All mistakes should feel even half that good. He was so tired of losing people, of being afraid for himself, his family, his officers. And then, to lose Dom so young. The boy had barely started work. So much senseless waste.

He maneuvered up the on-ramp for I-95 and let the cruiser accelerate. He signaled for the left lane and watched the cars clear in front of him.

"That amuses you, doesn't it?" She had avoided his question, now asked her own. "What did those words mean to you? Righteous? Car? Fire? Homeless?"

He could never forget how sensitive she was. "They might connect with another case." He'd almost slipped and said an "old" case. He'd only been here six months; all his old cases still lived in New Orleans, and he wasn't ready to tell her about the one that haunted him, the case with a car fire in it. He wasn't even ready to think about it himself. It couldn't be connected. How could it? He was thirteen hundred miles away. No one here even knew.

He slowed the cruiser for the exit and turned left under the highway to the police station, parking in the chief's spot by the back entrance. They got out, and he looked around again at his new home. When they'd interviewed him, they asked why he wanted to come north. *For a change,* he'd said, avoiding his real reasons. *But will you stay?* He'd said of course, but who ever knew what directions life would take? He had never expected to end up here, nor with this woman. Everything these days felt a little like limbo.

"Clara, asking questions about gang members will get you into real trouble real fast. No one will burst in at the last minute to save you, and then I'll be without you." He came close to say this last. She sucked in a breath and looked up at him, but he couldn't kiss her here. Too many eyes.

"Will I see you tonight?" She didn't come right out and say she intended to ignore his admonitions, but the message was still clear.

He flexed his hands, felt the wound in his left arm twinge. "I can't. We need to follow the leads while they're fresh."

She shook her head, but said, "Sure."

He turned and jogged up the stairs and through the station doors, back to the routine that staved off this feeling of brewing trouble.

CHAPTER 8
Clara

Richard and Paul were balm for my frustration. They knew it, poor things, and put up with my random appearances with all the graciousness of old and dear friends. Occasionally, I was even allowed to take care of them.

Tonight, I persuaded them over an early dinner to take me clubbing. I hated clubbing, but Bianca had said a businessman who ran a string of clubs was masterminding the gang drug business. Since Dom could no longer speak for himself, and Kyle had shown me this afternoon that he was taking the gang connection seriously, I was determined to live up to my promise to help her. Besides, I needed to redeem myself. I'd betrayed Bianca's trust by telling Kyle about Dom and Teo's argument; the least I could do was check out her mysterious businessman. Visiting one of his clubs seemed an easy place to start—if I could figure out who he was. And, if I could shake his hand, I might get an image, a color, something that would provide a motive for Dom's death. Kyle's warnings about gangs scared me, but how much trouble could I get into surrounded by a crowd of people?

Richard said only two guys were real possibilities. "You know the owner's not going to be hanging out in one of his clubs, right? It's not like some Vegas movie, where he's in back smoking noxious cigars with blondes draped over him like cashmere scarves. He's at home with his wife and three kids watching *Dexter*."

I waved his objections away. We'd see something. We had to see something.

Richard figured if anyone was running gangs in Stamford, it was Vlad Espejo, nicknamed Vlad the Impaler, because he allegedly liked to use a long knife to terminate employment contracts. So much for my idea of nonviolent businessmen. Because I was an idiot, this still didn't scare me enough.

"Oh, he doesn't do it himself," Richard said. "He has employees for that." Paul, a shaman and therapist, suggested our going clubbing was a stupid idea, but when I said I would go alone, he tagged along to keep an eye on Richard. And me. Someone had to call the cops if it all went off the rails.

The club sat a couple blocks off Washington Boulevard, near UConn Stamford and north of I-95 and the train tracks in a seemingly respectable neighborhood. When we stepped from the car, the smell of the Sound rushed to meet us, rank with salt and sewage and damp; it was overlaid with diesel must from the highway and an asphalt tang, the fragrance of unforgiving steel, glass, and fumes.

My Jimmy Choos clicked on the concrete sidewalk, and Richard grabbed my hand, his bear shape and size like a stone wall between me and my unease. I hadn't been clubbing in years. Now, I was fifteen years too old to be here, my clothes too expensive, my eardrums too fragile, and my dance moves out of fashion, never mind that my shoes wouldn't be good for running, something that had just occurred to me. But I wasn't the target. Dom had been the target. Or Kyle. Kyle had pulled me out of the way. Could the bullet that hit him have hit me?

The realization came as if the round had just slammed into me. Only one person might want me dead: Palmer. The sidewalk wobbled for a moment, and I almost fell, but Richard's hand steadied me.

"You OK?"

I nodded, even though I wasn't sure I could move. I'd tell them later, get their take. It couldn't be. Palmer didn't have the guts. But he did want the money. Oh-so-desperately he wanted my money. I shoved the thought away, trying to focus on gangsters instead.

The line prattled with information about manicures, celebrity purchases, bitchy sluts who would sleep with any guy, especially another girl's, and the relative fatness of each of the clubbers. Why did women allow themselves to be stupid? I knew they weren't. It just wasn't possible that every girl in that line had an IQ lower than a Labrador Retriever. The boys seemed indistinct, a mass of rough denim and cologne, watching silently, or sliding their arms over silky, bare, chilled skin.

Richard cut to the front. He knew the assistant manager from way back in his clubbing days, something that caused Paul a small hiss. Richard asserted the casual nature of the connection; Paul let it go. Everyone had a past.

Maybe the assistant manager would talk to me. Maybe he would shake my hand. I often got images when people shook my hand.

The bouncer reeked of Paco Rabanne. He let us in, pressing open a heavy door as silent as the well-oiled hinges of a bear trap. The fussing from the line at our privileged entrance faded as it swung shut again, the rough exterior stone walls giving way to paneling as smooth as glass and then a wall of lock boxes for purses and keys that rattled open and shut like a train rocketing off its tracks. The stench of spilled alcohol, sweet and rotten at the same time, like the bouncer, flowed from the passageway, as if it were a swell of California fog, and mixed with the dizzying scents of competing hormones: rage, fear, desire. Maybe management sprayed the air with pheromones every night before opening to guarantee repeat customers. Not that twenty-year-olds needed an excuse.

We clacked down the hall into the main room where big-screen TVs hummed and pulsed above the dance floor, showering the bodies below with wave after wave of light. Skin and textures pressed around us as we moved toward the bar—satin, velvet, cashmere, denim—all those bodies kissing, sucking and sliding against each other, the colors swirling behind my eyelids as I brushed hands or torsos or arms in passing. The air was sticky with hair product.

"Drink?" Richard shouted over the pounding bass. I couldn't even identify the music; I was so out of touch. When had electronic music become the go-to sound for dancing? It was nothing but throbbing and sliding, aural sex. The electronic line ran like a thread and needle piercing the back of my eye over and over.

"Cranberry and seltzer," I shouted back, not wanting to risk alcohol dulling whatever I might pick up, even though I dreaded picking up any more images like my dream images. If someone here had a hand in Dom's death, then I wanted to be clear enough to notice it. Richard handed me a cool plastic cup, chattering with ice and liquid, which had already started to sweat. Water coated my palm. I switched hands and rubbed the damp across the back of my neck, feeling it as a breath of air, soon extinguished.

"Omar should be around here somewhere," Richard shouted. "He's usually close to the bar, so his people can find him. Let me look, and I'll be right back."

I let go of his hand and grabbed Paul's, and we found a wall to press ourselves against. I could feel his tension like tiny whips serrating my skin. Green pulsed like an aura around the dance floor. Afraid of his reaction, I refused to look at Paul. Why had I dragged them into this? Finding out anything over this rage of music would be nearly impossible.

On the dance floor, both genders were half naked and gyrating, doing their best to imitate clothed sex to prove their prowess at the real thing.

The crowd seethed like mud with something unseen moving under it. The longer I stared, the more I noticed patterns. There were two, maybe three guys, built like they'd been working out in a prison yard, their arms and necks tattooed in purple and gold crosses. The one closest to me had a round medallion on a chain hanging around his neck with a highly stylized design of a setting sun on it. Around it were those same purple and gold crosses. Prison chic. People moved toward and away from them, briefly, and with little to no communication other than a look and a touch.

Suddenly, someone next to me pressed something small, round, and hard into my hand. Rippling purple lines flashed across my vision. "If this is what you and your swish friends are looking for, it's available," the voice whispered. "This one is free. After that, you pay." He dragged out the A, as his lips touched my skin, their wetness a deliberate smear. I jerked away, looking, but he was gone, only someone with dark, shiny hair parting the crowd, a smoky purple trail behind him. I opened my hand. It weighed nothing but would punch me into darkness and dreams. Briefly, I wondered if drugs would enhance the visions. "Paul, do you know what this is?"

He shook his head. "Probably Ex. I can't see it clearly enough in this light. Where did you get it?"

"Someone just gave it to me. Do you think Kyle could tell me?"

"If you want to get arrested for possession."

"He wouldn't do that."

"He's a cop."

I dropped it onto the floor and crushed it, felt its pill shape give way to powder through the thin sole of my shoe.

A minute later, Richard came back. "Omar's not here. His night off." He shrugged, apologetic. "The manager will talk to us."

"OK. Let's go." I held on to Paul and Richard grabbed me, and we snaked our way through the heaving bodies. The scent of one perfume morphed into another, morphed into a gasp of beer, a hit of stale cigarette breath. I tried to ignore the shivers of colors, the little pinpricks of energy that stung me at every unintended touch. My pain paled beside Bianca and Pops's.

Behind a dark blue muslin curtain was a plain wooden door. Richard knocked once, and then opened it into a plain office with neon lights and a metal standard issue desk.

"C'mon, c'mon. Don't want the plebes knowing where I hide." A man sat with his feet on the desk, smoking a cigar and flicking the ash onto the floor. His voice had the whisper of a drawl in it. "Siddown. Whaddya need?" He was about forty and a red scar gleamed on the left side of his jaw.

Richard shut the door and looked at me. The room was smoky and stifling, and for a moment claustrophobic blackness folded in on blackness.

"She OK?" I heard him ask as I touched the rubber edge of the desk to steady myself.

"Sorry." I pulled myself back. "Someone I know was shot yesterday. I probably shouldn't be out."

His small eyes, like gleams of yellow in blackness, shifted from me to Richard and back. "You think I know something about it?" His voice's Southern softness muted his tone. In my fog, I didn't catch Richard's warning glance.

"Do you?" Feeling faint made me sound aggressive.

His eyes burned through my dizziness, taking in the skin exposed by my silk blouse, my gold watch, all of it a slow cataloguing of assets. His lower lip glistened, and the stub of the cigar was wet from his saliva.

"It's a nice club," I stammered. "I haven't been out in some time."

He snorted, then picked a bit of tobacco off his lip. "Yeah, you're ancient for this crowd. We gotta nicer place over the Hyatt. You oughtta try that some time. Plays better music and you can hear yourself think," he drawled.

"Actually, I'm, uh, interested in the drugs." In for a penny.

He slammed his booted feet on the floor and the sound hurtled around the room like a swung baseball bat. "If you thought you could score because you're grieving...." His sarcasm burned like the red poker end of his cigar, which veered toward Richard's hand.

"I—I don't mean to buy. I mean the guys selling on your dance floor, I just want to know what gang they're in." I stumbled through it, realizing as each word fell from my stupid mouth that I was doing exactly what Kyle had warned me against. *Vlad the Impaler. He has employees for that.*

The manager—had we ever gotten his name?—leaned his elbows on the scarred desktop and blew smoke straight into my eyes. "No gangs here, little girl."

For a moment, I questioned what I'd noticed on the dance floor. Did I really think I could pick out drug dealers? I could spot pickpockets in Paris and Madrid, call girls at the Ritz, room service waiters on the take, but drug dealers were new to my turf. Then, I saw Dom bleeding on his beautiful green grass, shot by cowardly thugs, and Kyle rolling away from me on a gurney, and felt a spike of rage. "Want me to show you the dealers? You've got at least three of them out there, guys with purple and gold tattoos. Are those gang colors?"

Paul gripped my hand so hard I felt his nails dig into my skin. The assistant manager stood and let his jacket fall open to reveal his gun. "Anyone who pays the cover charge can dance and drink. I don't care who they are."

Paul gripped harder, pulling me to my feet. "Sorry to have disturbed you," he said.

"No problem. But next time," he slapped both hands on the desk and leaned across it to get in my face, "fresh-faced suburban matrons like you with their gay friends"—he stuck his chin out at Richard and Paul—"really belong at that club at the Hyatt. This isn't your kinda place." He adjusted his jacket and sat down, with his feet back up on the corner of the desk, and blew a cloud of smoke that followed us as Richard opened the door and we stumbled out, trying to maintain dignity all the way to the street.

"Did you get what you wanted?" For Paul, this was the equivalent of shrieking at me. He stopped to face me, his body as rigid as a police baton.

"I'm sorry." I backed up a step, felt my Jimmy Choo quiver.

"You're sorry? You didn't know what that guy would do. You're not invincible, Clara, yet you just kept pushing." I felt it like a slap.

Richard blew out a breath that steamed like smoke in the night air.

"We just have to leave it alone. They won't bother us if we leave it alone." I opened my purse and then shut it again.

"Which you do so well." He turned away slightly, stared at the highway. Maybe he wished he were on it instead of here with me.

I touched his arm, but he pulled away. "Paul, I'm having dreams. What am I supposed to do?"

Paul understood that reason, but was what I'd gotten worth putting us in danger? What had I learned anyway? Wouldn't there be drug dealers in any dance club? Did that necessarily mean Espejo allowed them to peddle there? Was it possible he knew nothing?

"With a nickname like Vlad the Impaler? He knows when someone chews a fingernail in one of his clubs. Count on it." Richard this time.

One of the bouncers touched his earbud, then made his way toward us. A tall young man slipped out the club doors behind him, headed down the street away from us, slouched and wearing a purple hoodie with "85" on the back.

"You folks need me to call you a cab?" The bouncer parted his coat so we could see he was carrying too.

We waved him off, started walking toward the car.

Richard claimed that owners who didn't want drug trade in their clubs worked hard to keep them clean. Some clubs had good reputations, but not this one. "So now you have your next step, right?"

"Which is?"

Richard put on his simpering girl, probably hoping to break the tension: "Oh, Mr. Espejo. I was in your club on Thursday night and this young man tried to sell me some Ecstasy. I was so upset, and I just thought you should know."

Paul stared straight ahead. I hugged my sweater around my shoulders. "I'm supposed to walk up to him in the country club and say that? No way."

He shrugged. "Why not? It's safer than what we did tonight."

"And he's going to say, 'Oh, yeah, the gangs distribute for me'? I don't think so."

He beeped the car open and we piled in, me in the back. Paul looked at Richard. "You're not helping."

"You know we can't stop her." Richard started the car, twisted the heat to high.

Paul sighed, then asked if my gift had given me anything. "What was that moment about in the office?"

"Just blackness."

"Like inside a coffin?"

I shrugged, let him have his dig at me.

"Maybe then," he twisted to look at me, "the best choice is to leave the investigating to Kyle."

I tried to hear the kindness and worry under his anger as I eased off one of my shoes and rubbed my toes. Why couldn't I leave it to Kyle? Dom and Kyle had been shot in front of me, and his sister had begged for my help. I leaned back against the seat and shut my eyes, letting the tears come.

As Richard accelerated onto I-95 and the air brakes of the tractor trailers rumbled around me, I felt myself lift out of the car and into the darkness, as if my tears could float me up. And then, there it was again, that purple line, snaking like a long ribbon through a tree of knives, caressing their blades. In the middle lay the man, the purple ribbon tightened around his neck, and at the end of the silk, a medallion of the setting sun. As I looked, he opened his eyes.

It was Kyle.

CHAPTER 9
Kyle

By the time Kyle arrived, the car was already a burned-out hulk. Only traces of the bright blue color remained. It was a two-door, the trunk popped and burbling smoke, a thin stream of water still washing down the body to cool it, so the tech could work.

Two brittle bodies were propped in the front seats. He could see their charcoal-smeared leather faces from where he stood with Joe, about twenty feet away. At least they didn't look like they'd died screaming. The breeze was blowing off the land toward the water, taking the stench with it for once. God, he hated fire scenes, couldn't think of a way he'd less want to go, except maybe drowning.

The car was in the lot next to the Maple Market, which backed up to the estuary. Dry-docked boats from the marina shared the space, their riggings still in the middle of the night, their bell-like clangings waiting for the morning breeze. On the other side of the lot, a small park extended up a dark hill where, Joe said, a local theatre company performed Shakespeare for picnicking crowds. The lot was small and cramped, and a few cars had been left overnight. There was another marina down the street and lots of fancy new construction, including condominiums that overlooked the inlet. The streets were narrow and winding, tree- and stone-wall-lined, almost claustrophobic.

The firefighters had cordoned off the scene, waiting for the car to cool. Everyone was standing around drinking coffee, including a bunch of the neighbors in their pajamas or hastily donned clothes. One guy wore a pajama top with a sweater tied around his shoulders, like some kind of sleep-deprived GQ ad.

Joe gestured at the guy, grousing about the changes in the neighborhood. "Place used to be great up until about twenty years ago, when the fishing shacks and grungy old houses were restored"—he used his fingers as quotes—"by yuppies. Now, it's filled with blonde mamas and their perfect babies in thousand-dollar strollers." He shook his head as if improving real estate were a crime against humanity. "We're gonna spend the next three weeks fielding phone calls from New York lawyers throwing their weight around. You wait." He sipped at his coffee. "Gotta go check in with the tech. Be right back, boss."

Kyle walked over to Trevor, who was managing the small crowd. "How you doing?" Kyle rested his hand on the young man's shoulder for a moment. He'd only seen him briefly since Dom's shooting.

"Boss."

Kyle searched the young man's face, looking for signs of stress. "What have we got?" he asked.

Trevor nodded. "You might want to talk to that lady over there—Miss Hilary. Says she saw the whole thing."

"Thanks. Any more coffee around here?"

"Stuben's gone for it."

"Radio him—ask him to grab one more for the witness."

Miss Hilary looked to be about seventy-five. Her face, yellowed by the glow of the lights, was cratered with life experience, but at three in the morning, she was fully dressed in designer jeans and a thick sweater.

"Would you like to sit in my car, ma'am? It's cold out here, and I understand you have some things to tell me."

Did she ever. Hilary had complaints about her neighbors' dogs and their incessant barking, and another neighbor's tendency to blow his leaves onto her lawn, never mind that it was his tree she had to clean up after in the first place, and those boys who raced through town in their fast cars thinking they were invincible just because they drove BMWs.

"Tonight, ma'am? Did you see anything?"

She certainly had. She'd been reading. She liked to read in the evenings when it was quiet and she could concentrate. Tonight, she'd been reading *War and Peace*; she'd never read it as an undergraduate, can you believe that? And at a school like Stanford in the 60s. You would have thought.

Kyle knew he shouldn't judge reliability by someone's education. He'd learned never to underestimate a witness and even old ladies who rambled, according everything equal importance, could be well-educated. But *Stanford* changed how he listened to her. It changed his level of respect. Even as it did, he knew it was everything he hated. "What time was this?"

"Around one-thirty. I know because I'd just looked at the clock and thought I ought to go to bed. I tend to get carried away and then I stay up too late, can't get to sleep because I'm too wrapped up in what might happen next in the story." She grinned at him, and he suddenly fell in love.

"Anyway, I looked out the window because I heard cars revving, like they were about to drag race again."

"You've heard them drag racing here before?"

She nodded. "The streets are empty this late at night, but they usually save the racing for the weekend."

"It looks winding and narrow. How do they get up any speed?"

"They like that it's flat down McKinley for about a half mile or so to Highland, and they turn there, by Graham Capital, and race back to Wilson. They have to slow down on Wilson, but it brings them full circle back down to Rowayton, where they can pretend to have beat each other and start all over again."

He held his laughter. She had the whole route down as if she'd been out there one night with a stopwatch. She tweaked an eyebrow at him, as if she knew what he thought and knew he couldn't prove it one way or the other.

"Did you hear them speaking?"

"I heard some shouting. My Spanish is a bit rusty, haven't practiced much since the two years we lived in Venezuela, but it sounded like they said, and I'm translating here for you, *That's for being stupid.*"

"Just to be sure I'm understanding you: there were two cars?"

She nodded.

"How many people?"

"Four. The two lying out there now," she gestured at the burned car, "and two more, both with guns. After the yelling, the taller one shot the two in the car, while the shorter one doused it with gasoline and threw a match. Then they left."

"Were the two men in the car when they were shot?"

She nodded.

"Did the men have an identifiable race? Clothing? Posture?"

"They weren't black, Mr. DuPont, if that's what you're asking."

He let his title slide, figured she was owed it due to the hour and her age.

"Their hair was under ball caps. The language was the only identifier. The men faced away from me. One was about six feet tall, the other around 5'5 and slender. The taller one had broad shoulders and big hands. I could see them when he lifted the gun to shoot." She paused. "I did get the license plate."

72

He took it all down, asked her to come in again the next morning to review and sign her statement.

One of the firefighters shouted in his direction.

He said, "Please, excuse me, ma'am. I need to go. I'll see you tomorrow."

Outside the cruiser, the man held up a piece of metal. "You'll want to see this, Chief."

It was a medallion of some kind, bent and warped by the heat, but Kyle could still make out a design. A setting sun? "Ring any bells?" he asked the tech.

"Looks familiar, but I'd have to do some research." The guy shrugged.

Kyle took another look at the car and mentally kicked himself for what he should have noticed right away: its bright blue color, the same color as the car in the drive-by at Dom's. Why would a couple of guys involved in shooting a cop yesterday be found burned to death in their car today? Was this connected to Dom and Teo's "car fire"? He didn't believe in coincidence. Were these rival gangs? One who set out to kill his officer and the other who took issue with it? Why would one gang want to kill a cop in the first place? They liked to steer clear of law enforcement. "The witness got the plate on the other car."

"Sweet. No plates on this car," the tech said.

Kyle headed back to the cruiser to run the plate number. He didn't recognize the names that came up, but Joe could follow up. He was pretty sure someone else had gotten to Dom's killers before he had.

After three hours of sleep, Kyle rolled out of bed and into the shower. He was usually at his best in the morning, but that depended on a decent night's sleep. He hadn't gotten to bed until nearly four, and his injured arm made getting ready more cumbersome.

If only he knew more about the gangs in this area. With all he'd had to get up to speed on, and no real gang activity, he'd left it for later. Later had arrived.

He brought coffee for the detectives. They had a pot in the office, and Sid made good coffee, but everyone had a favorite and he brought them their specialties every time they put in some extra effort for him. He included a box of muffins and scones with it.

"Really? No doughnuts?" Joe kidded him, reaching for his favorite blueberry scone.

"I'm trying to get all you lazy sluggards to work out." A room full of trim officers looked up at him, grinning. He set a meeting for ten minutes, giving himself time to check messages, scroll again through Twitter. Only the briefest mention of the shooting and fire. No hysteria. Good.

"What have we got?" he asked, stepping out of his office and into the bullpen, where his officers' desks littered the open space.

Joe spoke for the group. "That gang medallion is used by the Sunset Boyz. They are affiliated nationally—loosely. We don't know if they dropped it intentionally by the car to make a statement, or if it was a mistake. And we don't know which set of guys it belonged to—the crispy ones or the shooters. They could be rival factions of the same gang. Somebody sure wanted those two guys deader than dead, but we're not sure why. I've been on the phone with the gang expert from Stamford, and he says everything is quiet. Everybody's hanging out in their territories, doing business. No one has poached anyone's girl, territory, or product recently. The only anomaly is Dom's shooting. No one can figure that, sir."

"We any closer to motive?" Local motive, preferably.

The room remained silent until Trevor said, "Could it be that Dom wasn't the target, sir?"

The room got even more silent. He raised his eyebrows at the kid.

When Joe jumped in, Kyle knew he wasn't going to like this theory, whatever it was. "We considered the possibility that it could be a race thing."

He'd wondered how long it would take for his blackness to be the conversation. "Because I'm a black police chief in a white town?"

"Yes, sir." Trevor again. Courageous. He'd have to remember that. He nodded at Trevor, to let him know it was OK, shifted a little on the desk and adjusted his jacket.

"OK. Who is behind it and how they did know I would be at Dom's? And why now?"

"Could have followed you." The officer followed his comment with a bite of scone.

"Other theories?"

"Maybe the target was Dr. Montague?"

"Motive?"

The officer shrugged. "We'd have to check it out. As for the other theories, the main guy running gangs around here is Vlad Espejo, a Stamford businessman. Owns a bunch of clubs where lots of drugs change hands. Any chance you've met him?"

Kyle thought a moment, then nodded. "Some meet-and-greet when I first arrived, was getting ferried around to all the other cop shops and mayors' offices. Kind of dramatic dresser, as I recall."

"Doesn't have your taste, sir."

He cocked his head at Trevor. "You dissin' me, son?" His custom suits, made by a friend of his mother for cost, were a source of amusement for his officers.

"No, sir." The kid grinned; forgiveness made him light.

"OK. So you think this Espejo has some issue with a black cop and sent his gang kids to solve it? Or that he had an issue with a white woman dating a black cop?"

They stayed silent, waiting for him to think it through.

"Is it really that prejudiced around here?" He thickened his drawl. "I thought the Northeast was a bastion of open-minded liberal thinking, unlike the South where I hail from."

"Don't know what made you think that, sir." Laughter sprinkled the room.

"So Dom's a mistake?" He tamped down the rage he felt rise as he said it. He would deal with it later. "And those kids last night? Why them?"

"Maybe they were covering their tracks, getting rid of the idiots who screwed up."

"Find out."

"Stamford said they've got a couple of informants."

Joe said, "What about Espejo?"

"I guess he's mine," Kyle said. He went back to his office to research his quarry, as well as the words "car fire," "righteous," and "homeless" in conjunction with each other and the local geography. Gingerly, he shrugged off the sling and started typing, but no matter how he combined the words or rephrased them, he came up empty. He couldn't really believe it was about race or Clara, but how would Dom and Teo have known about his past? Those court records were sealed, although there was probably reporting from Katrina that might have mentioned his betrayal.

And what did it mean that his officers thought this might be a hate crime? His mother had raised him to be polite, to use conventional language, to dress properly, but no matter what he did, people still saw—or didn't see—him based on his skin color. It made him so tired. He couldn't just live his life—he had to live his life *and* be black. He was always negotiating something: *no, you don't need to be afraid of me; yes, you need to be afraid of me; yes, you need to take me seriously; no, you don't need to cross the street to get away from me; yes, I can wear a hoodie when I jog down the street, and, no, you don't need to be afraid because I am not running after you. I am simply running, like you are, with your little girl in the stroller. Yes, you can smile at me, and I won't think that means you're coming on to me. If you don't smile at me, that doesn't mean I think you're a racist.*

He knew racial violence, had witnessed it on the NOLA force. He knew, even though the judge let them off the hook, that the residents of Gretna Green had been frightened because the people getting off the buses, in need of food and water and medical attention and shelter, were black and poor. Or maybe it was just poverty that frightened them, people who *needed.* God forbid, anyone in twenty-first century America should have to face another's need and feel compelled to respond.

He knew he wasn't fair. Lots of people had helped after Katrina, even more than Brad Pitt and his fancy houses. Community organizers. Local homeowners driven to make their communities better, because no one else was doing anything to help them. But this was a small town. People here weren't immune to racial prejudice—he saw it in their scared white faces every day. But enough hatred to come after him with a semiautomatic weapon? Why?

And how would Espejo fit into the scenario? What would a Connecticut gangster have to do with Kyle's own past? What would he hope to gain by shooting either Dom or Kyle himself? Or Clara?

He shoved aside the paperwork that always threatened to engulf his desk, and searched Espejo in the database. No arrests, but the man had a federal file, which probably meant he sold or bought product across the state line in New York. He called up Nate Jones in the New Haven FBI office. Kyle had met Nate at a conference on profiling a year or so ago, a few months before he'd moved north.

After the preliminary catching up, Kyle asked Nate about Espejo.

"You got something on him? We'll take all the help we can get," Nate responded. Kyle heard his chair creak back.

"Actually, I don't know what I have," Kyle said. "It's early days, and I'm looking for context."

"Context." He heard the flick of a lighter and a first quick inhale. Kyle wondered how Nate got away with smoking in the office. "The guy presents as a slightly eccentric businessman: nightclubs, construction company run by his son-in-law, couple other smaller businesses he can launder money through. We can't make any direct ties to the gangs, but they do business on his premises. Last year, we almost had him—some dissension in the ranks, I think. I'd have to check the file. Anyway, we just couldn't get enough evidence." Kyle heard another inhale. "Your turn."

"I've got a police officer shooting, a two-victim shooting, and a car fire. One of the officer's family members has a gang connection, and that gang has ties to Espejo."

"Territory dispute? It's always the place I start with gangs."

"Not sure. Both incidents occurred outside their normal territory. And why would they shoot a cop?"

"You think it's about expansion?"

"Heard anything?"

"Nope. Could be the info just hasn't worked our way yet. I'll check with my CIs."

"Thanks, man. I owe you."

"You do!" Jones laughed. "Come up to New Haven and have a beer with me some night."

"In that traffic?"

"You got a cop car, man. Isn't that what it's for?"

Kyle laughed and hung up without committing. He didn't even know how long he would keep this job. This thing could blow up in his face, reverse any positive changes he'd made for himself.

Plus, now he knew he couldn't escape going home to New Orleans. He would have to be sure those words weren't connected to his past, even as his officers ensured they weren't connected to his present. He called Joe into his office.

"FBI wonders if it might be a territory dispute. The thinking is maybe Espejo's trying to expand and some other gang doesn't like the idea—or one of his own guys wants to expand. See what you can find out, will you?"

Joe nodded. "You don't think the race thing holds any water?"

He shrugged. "Do you?"

Joe leaned back in his chair and scratched his neck. "I guess we should investigate every plausible theory."

"But who?"

"The kid"—referring to Trevor—"wants to work it."

"OK." He spun his cell phone on the desk, leaned back and then forward again, before Joe shot him a look. "Listen. I have to go home for a few days." He gestured at his arm. "I'll take a medical leave. You're in charge while I'm gone, OK? I'll make an announcement."

"What for?" Joe's dark eyes didn't miss a thing, and right now he looked a little pissed. Kyle couldn't blame him; he'd be angry too if his new boss suddenly took off, especially when the squad was working a case that could potentially explode.

"I'd rather not say until I know more." Joe drew in a breath to protest, but Kyle waggled his cell phone. "You can reach me 24/7. Promise."

Joe stood, hesitated a moment. "You know you can trust me, right? That what you say to me won't get spread around?"

Kyle leaned back and looked up at his second-in-command. "Yeah. That's why I'm leaving you in charge."

Joe shook his head once and left the room. Kyle picked up the phone and dialed United.

CHAPTER 10
Clara

I didn't sleep well after the night at the club. I would drift into REM sleep, only to end up at the foot of that tree again, staring at Kyle and his pleading eyes, and jerk myself awake. I couldn't keep this up. Sleep deprivation resulted in hallucinations and hospitalization for me.

But if the dreams predicted death, as they usually did, and Kyle was targeted, why had they shot Dom? Had they missed and hit the wrong man? It couldn't be about me. The dreams didn't make sense then. My heart raced and I made myself slow my breath, like Paul had taught me. Should I tell him? I hadn't told my father, and he'd died. When I'd told my mother, she'd refused to believe me, and she'd almost died. I'd just found Kyle; I didn't want to lose him, but would he believe my dream?

Kyle called around eight, after I'd given up trying to sleep in favor of grimacing over an espresso in the solarium. Dom's killers had been found, he said, by someone who had acted as judge, jury, and executioner. He didn't say much else, except that he missed me.

"Will I see you tonight?" I couldn't tell him what I believed over the phone.

"I'll text you later. Maybe."

I asked if he planned to attend Dom's funeral later that morning, and he confirmed the entire department would be there. It was just stupid I didn't mention the club and the drugs. The dream and the new murders blew it out of my mind until after I'd hung up the phone. I would tell him in person later, I thought, but maybe it set in motion my keeping things from him again.

I wasn't the only one keeping secrets. Kyle, as I was to discover, was the master.

The morning was bright and sunny, welcome at this time of the year, as it portended the summer weather I longed for. A cool, damp shimmer on the road kicked up a fine spray on the windshield. I turned into the church parking lot and found a spot near an exit. The hearse, parked by the steps to the double doors that opened into the sanctuary, gleamed for Dom's final journey.

Inside, my eyes took a moment to adjust to the dim sanctuary. Uniformed police officers filled the right side of the church. I would never find Kyle in that mass. I slid into a row in the back and located Bianca and Dom's pops in the front. They were alone. If Teo was coming, either he hadn't arrived or lurked anonymously farther back. That many cops? Intimidating. I ran my eyes methodically over the rows, searching.

"Excuse me."

A young man in a cheap black suit and a purple t-shirt gestured to the seat next to me.

"Sure." I nodded and slid over.

A tattoo crawled up his neck. A slight crescent-shaped scar marred the skin under his left eye. From the right pocket of his jacket, a small furry head peeked out.

"I'm Teo," he whispered. "Bianca said you wanted to talk."

I stared at him.

"I need to tell you Dom was clean. He didn't do nothing."

How had I gotten myself into this? "I know that."

He hissed, frustrated, and the kitten gave a tiny yelp. He pulled it out and rested it on his lap, his hands moving gently over the tawny fur. The kitten's claws kneaded his leg, but he didn't seem to mind.

"Who's this?" I asked.

"I found him behind the church near the dumpster. I couldn't see the mother, so I took him. Poor little guy. Tough to be abandoned."

A little projection there, I thought, despite the intensity I felt rolling off him like a thick cloud of iron filings. "Can I buy you a cup of coffee after this is over?"

"I make people in Starbucks nervous."

I bet. His shoulders rippled under the jacket like a little earthquake. What did he want? I couldn't do anything, and Bianca certainly knew that by now. But he had come, at risk to himself.

He said, "He never was involved in anything unlawful, not even when we were kids. He was a boy scout."

"Then who killed him? And who killed the boys who killed him?"

He leaned toward me, crowding me. So sensitive, this boy-man; everything a possible slight, every sentence parsed to be sure the speaker was taking him seriously. "Boys?"

I said, "No disrespect intended. I'm trying to find out what you think I can do for you. It's the police who are wondering if you were involved in Dom's killing."

He leaned back. The kitten had started purring, its whole body vibrating with rumbles. "Yeah, see, that's why I can't talk to the police." We were still whispering, his voice so low the kitten was almost louder. "Police won't believe me, and then they'll lock me up just 'cause they feel like it."

"OK."

"Listen. Dom, he was my brother, you know?" He touched the center of his chest with his fist, tattoos black across his knuckles. "We grew up together. Went different ways, but he never disrespected my choice. He understood."

I doubted that. "And why did you *have* to become a gang member?"

"Family," he said. "I got none." The chin lifted.

"Mr. Ofiero says he offered you a home, a chance at finishing school."

"Mom died of a drug overdose. Didn't know my dad. Don't got no other family here but an aunt; she's busy working. She tried, but she already had two kids, just barely getting by. The gang, they helped out with money and food and stuff. Mr. O never got why I had to pull my own weight, couldn't let anyone do for me."

"You were how old?"

"Fourteen." One shoulder hiccupped a shrug. *No big deal.*

Music began to stream from the speakers, Elgar's *Nimrod.* I wondered if Dom liked classical music.

"A fourteen-year-old boy needs to pull his own weight? That seems pretty stern." I waited. My body felt stiff, and I tried to home in on what the intuition was telling me. It wasn't fear that I felt, but his loneliness.

He smoothed the front of his t-shirt with one hand. That purple: where had I seen it before? He said, "Stern, yeah. I see you don't understand either."

A woman across the aisle started pointing at the kitten and whispering to her husband, as if Teo had committed some breach of etiquette. Teo turned to look at her. She shut up and shrank back. My sore wrist twinged in sympathy.

I said, "It's hard to do things on your own. I ran away from here at twenty. It was hard for me and I had money. I can only imagine how hard it must have been for you."

"You white ladies think everything's going to be fixed by education." I started to protest, but he grimaced and snapped his fingers to cut me off. "Community college doesn't mean I'm going to make any money or get that nice middle-class, middle management position you all want me to have. Who do you think is going to hire me? Yours is a world of privilege that let you run away to Europe. Lucky you. I can't run away. Where would I go?"

I deserved that. "Except Dom was your support, right?"

"Dominick, he always studied hard, never partied. Wanted to be a cop for as long as I knew him." He looked at me. "Cops won't believe I wouldn't hurt him—but I didn't."

"Did knowing you hurt him?"

"You mean hurt his rep?"

That's not what I meant, but we could start there. "Yes. His reputation."

He looked annoyed. "Could be, I guess. He didn't talk none about stuff outside the family."

"You know the chief of police was there yesterday morning when Dominick got shot. He thinks this was a gang shooting. Do you know why the gang might want Dominick dead?"

"If there was a problem, they would've told me."

I didn't understand what he meant, but it wasn't what I wanted to know anyway. "So if Dominick was as straight as you say, why is he dead? Why are two other men dead as well?" Then I remembered where I had seen that color: last night, coming out of the club. A young man in a purple hoodie, walking away. Had that been Teo? Was he one of the dealers? I was so disturbed by the possibility that I nearly missed what he said next.

"Maybe Dom wasn't the target."

All the air left my lungs.

Before I could ask another question, he'd tucked the kitten in his pocket, slipped out of the pew, and vanished from the church.

Bianca and her pops had been swarmed by cops and condolences after the funeral, and my questions for them could wait. If Kyle was the gang's target, that made contacting Espejo my next priority. He beat me to the punch. He called as I stepped into the office, still quivering on my heels and needing nothing more than five minutes to catch my breath and get a cup of coffee.

Shona transferred the call to my office. I picked up the receiver and sank into my chair, kicking off my shoes. "Good morning, Dr. Montague. I'm redoing my daughter's property. I'm wondering if you would be interested in looking at the job." The voice wasn't a stereotypical gravelly gangster's voice, at least not as played by Marlon Brando. What he said vibrated for a couple of seconds between his ears before it came out his mouth, like loud hummingbird wings. Almost hypnotic.

I slid my feet back into my shoes. It felt wrong to be unclothed—as if heels could protect me. I wanted nothing to do with his property or his daughter's. If I never had to meet him, that would be a good thing. I just wanted to ask a couple of questions, preferably over the phone where he would never see my face. I wondered if he'd called because I'd suggested someone was dealing drugs in his club. Would I get to his house, be surrounded by armed thugs, and drowned in the swimming pool?

"What's the address?" I pulled up Google Maps to look. Nope, no swimming pool and no big hole in the ground the right size to drop a landscape architect in—if the satellite photos were up to date.

We set a time, against my better judgment, for that afternoon. I'd promised Bianca, and besides, the firm needed the work. I disconnected, then dialed Kyle, but he was out, probably still at the funeral luncheon. I tried his cell but he didn't pick that up either, and I didn't feel right leaving the message that he might be a gang target without explaining about Teo. It would have to wait. I texted: *Have to talk. ASAP.* Maybe that would get him to stop by tonight.

At two o'clock that afternoon, I parked in Evangelia Moscarelli's circular drive. Her husband was at work, she said as she ushered me through her cool, blue-tiled foyer toward the kitchen at the back of the house, but she had been making all the landscape decisions. Unfortunately, since her father was funding it, he insisted on being part of the process. She hoped I didn't mind, but he was waiting for us. She gestured toward a smaller, library-like room off the kitchen and led the way. I minded a lot, and wondered why the husband wasn't paying, but I'd accepted the appointment. It was too late now.

Evangelia looked like every other wealthy Stamford mom. Designer jeans and flats and a Tiffany gold bracelet on the same wrist as her watch. The marriage diamond was yellow but half the size of a shot glass bottom. Daddy paid hubby well.

The room was intimate for the size of the house, but still not small. All four walls were lined with bookshelves, except for the fireplace complete with lit wood fire, at the center of the wall opposite the door. Plush burgundy couches bracketed a large square coffee table. A girl of about five or six changed the outfits on a Barbie doll in front of a muted television. Espejo sat near the little girl, admiring her sartorial choices. He looked up at his daughter's entrance.

"Papa, this is Dr. Montague. Dr. Montague, my father, Vlad Espejo."

"Mr. Espejo, a pleasure," I lied.

"Vlad." He extended his hand. With his high cheekbones and grey hair, he looked like any Wall Street tycoon, not unusual in these parts. But the neon green pants and the pale-yellow button-down dress shirt with a red silk pocket scarf made him look as though *Vogue's* and *Golf Digest's* art directors had reconstructed their magazines after a gas explosion.

I shook his hand, got a jolt. Something. A color. Purple? Maroon? "Clara."

"Yes." His hand lingered in mine, assessing. Smooth and almost hairless except for a few wiry specimens, like a white grub lingering in dirt. When I pulled my hand away, he smiled. "I understand you know my good friend Darren Tornow."

"The Stamford mayor. Of course. My mother knows him better than I."

He picked up a tiny coat, offering it to the little girl. She shook her head, chose one with silver sparkles instead, pulled Barbie's tiny arms through the sleeves, then rejected the look, tugging it off again.

"He keeps a close eye on things; I like that in a mayor."

Was that a warning? Why couldn't people just say what they meant? Supposedly this was a man who killed people with a long knife—or had it done—sitting here, in the afternoon sunshine, in a well-appointed library discussing landscaping plans and playing dolls with his granddaughter—which, now that I thought about it, effectively kept me from asking uncomfortable questions about murder.

"Do you do most of your business in Stamford?" I wondered how much information he would give me. Maybe I could just ask him if he'd had Dom killed, and then I could go back to being just a landscape architect and not a spy. I hated being a spy.

"All of it." He handed the little girl another jacket choice, watched her hold it up to the doll. "I'm a territorial guy." His lips stretched into what I assumed was a smile.

Evangelia looked at him and said, "Oh Papa, stop. You'll scare her." He slid her a cold look, but she didn't seem to notice.

"Please, sit." Evangelia folded herself onto one end of a couch, left foot tucked up under her. "These are some of the plans we've gotten so far, and here is a sketch of some of my ideas." She pushed a delicate watercolor rendering at me.

Perhaps the daughter wasn't involved in her father's business, other than doing his bidding when he suggested a landscape architect. What kind of child painted like this when her teachers and friends knew her father was a gangster? Perhaps the art had been her retreat from reality. And how much did she know? How did you tell your child what you did for a living, when what you did for a living was to get her classmates addicted to drugs? I turned off the questions, focused on the problem at hand.

I picked up the watercolor. "It's lovely."

"Thanks. I dabble." She smiled as if she could read my mind.

The painting showed a flower border against a rock wall, with a water feature about a third of the way down its length. It looked as though it were built into a hillside; steps curled down to the right of a fountain to a patio abutting a large swimming pool.

"How much of this is already in place?"

She laughed. "None of it. My husband is appalled at my plans—he's afraid of the water, can't swim. But I don't care. I've wanted a swimming pool since I was a little girl, and my father," she rolled her eyes at him and he grunted, his eyes on his granddaughter, "would never agree."

I looked at Vlad. "Don't you have contacts in construction? Someone who could do this job more cheaply than I?" Could I talk myself out of this job?

"But you're the best." Evangelia cocked her head, and I wondered how much was an act. "Besides, some construction guy won't understand land. Ask him to put up a pool house, and it would be beautiful. But moving dirt around? Uh-uh. Those guys—totally different way of looking at things." She shook her head and the hair in her ponytail floated like willow branches.

"Evangelia, can you walk me around the property, talk me through what you want to do?"

"Oh god, call me Lia. No one can manage my name."

Her father snorted.

French doors led from the kitchen to the outside deck, and from there onto a graveled patio. "Hideous, isn't it? That's the first thing to go. I want a kidney-shaped saltwater pool here, with a hot tub to the side, and then gardens and a slate terrace with a pool house, there." She pointed to where a magnificent spruce shot gloriously up into the spring air.

"You want to take that beautiful tree down?"

"It's in the way. You know, sunshine at the pool and all that."

I nodded. "I can see that. However, it would also provide you with shade, at a time of day when it might be welcome. Think of shaded late afternoon drinks in July, or a patio supper with that lovely scent in the background. I'd recommend working around it if you can. Trees like that are hard to come by and expensive."

She smiled as if I'd passed some test she'd dreamed up. She crossed the gravel to the edge of the patio and indicated a long slope of land that ran down into woods at its base. A spectacular meadow, it would provide wildflowers all spring and summer. She agreed, but said wildflowers weren't really her favorite thing, and she'd much rather turn it into a formal garden, like one of those lovely European palace gardens with walkways, structured beds, clipped trees. Something controlled, you know? Something one could walk in at leisure, if a person could ever get some leisure. The way it was now, well, the children couldn't very well run in that, could they? Not with deer ticks and mosquitoes and all. As if turning it into a miniature Versailles would rid the landscape of mosquitoes and deer.

I said we could do it, but it would cost a fortune, since that was several acres of land she was talking about redoing. It would also be a long-term, several-stage project. Was she sure she wanted to undertake something of that scale?

Oh yes, oh yes.

Well, OK.

I loved it when people decided they were going to spend a whole lot of money with my company. I liked it a lot less when they spent it in ways that didn't make sense. Wherever possible, I maintained as much of the natural landscape as I could. Adding gravel meant it would have to be weeded by hand or sprayed with weed killer. Animals lost habitat—rabbits, foxes, chipmunks, squirrels. It contributed long term to global warming. But she was not to be persuaded. Landscape architects tell themselves that if someone is going to do it, better it be them, so they can build in whatever preventative measures they can. That would be me, anyway.

Then, she surprised me. "I want to use as many native plants as I can, and I'd like the walkways to be grass. That way, we can just mow, and we won't be spraying all the time. I'm concerned about the environment, you know. I just want to bring it a little under control, make it more *accessible.* You do understand, don't you?"

Sure. Sure.

I made some rapid sketches of the landscape as it was, and then made a few more sketches of ideas, ways we could arrange beds to cascade down the hill, add a water feature for natural drainage, where I might put fruit trees, flowering trees, paths. I would have to think it through more care-fully at the office, but I also had to survey the property. Back at the car, I extracted a pair of rubber boots from the trunk to tuck my pants into. I spent the next hour walking the meadow, evaluating the dry and wet spots, the different kinds of plants that were growing and where, and wondered if I could persuade her to keep some of these if I invoked the Highline Park in New York.

Meanwhile, another part of my brain still mulled over why Vlad had offered me this job. What had he meant by what he'd said to me? Had Vlad ordered the hit on Kyle? He'd said he was a territorial guy. Did that mean he wouldn't stray from Stamford? Or that anyone who strayed into Stamford would be a target—like me or any out-of-town cop that stuck his nose where it didn't belong? Why would his gang kill outside its normal territory?

All the questions made me want to lie down in the grass and take a nap. Instead, I trudged back up to her gravel terrace, where I shucked my boots and knocked on the French doors. She was sitting at the kitchen counter doing something computery on the kitchen island. Vlad was gone, and the little girl, propped up on a stool at the counter, was eating a sandwich. Lia waved me in, and we agreed on two weeks for preliminary designs and a rough estimate. She put out her hand, and we shook. I was officially employed by a gangster who'd warned me off. But I knew someday soon I would find a way to ask Vlad why his gang wanted Kyle dead.

CHAPTER 11
Kyle

The flight attendant set down a glass filled with ice and a can of Coke, and dropped a couple packages of pretzels next to the drink. "Anything else?"

He shook his head and poured some soda over the cubes. "Thanks, though." They'd taken one look at his ID and his sling and upgraded him to first class.

Out the window, clouds formed a burnished pink mat that stretched to the horizon. He wondered what Clara was doing, wished he could stop thinking about her, wished he didn't have to think about where he was headed or what he was headed into, wished he could let those clouds stay where they were, a barrier between him and what he had to face, finally, in New Orleans.

What he could never fathom was how it could have been Jonah.

He remembered the day they'd gotten their shields, the day of graduation from the police academy. Alphabetical order, so Kyle walked first, the academy director handing him his certification, shaking his hand.

And then the superintendent—Jonah's father—a little farther on, presented his badge. Finally, something he could hold in his hand, something that demonstrated his competence, authority, hard work. The law classes, the early mornings at the track running sprints, the semester he sweated through foreign language training so he could speak enough French to get by in Cajun country—he'd done it. And Jonah had sweated it every bit as much as he had.

Jonah followed him across the stage, and after all the new recruits were sworn in, their families swarmed around them to pin the badges on. He remembered glancing away while his mother tried not to stab him, seeing Jonah's father's face, pride radiating like heat off summer grass, Jonah looking back as if he'd been working his whole life just for that expression. His arrogance, his belief that his own destiny would protect him, proved his undoing.

Kyle rattled the ice in his glass, looked out the window again, wondering if he could ever see clouds without thinking about Katrina.

Oswald Intriago was probably his one remaining friend in the New Orleans Police Department. Short and burly, he arrived five minutes late for breakfast downtown the next morning, wearing his trademark soft felt hat and carrying a file folder tucked inside a leather portfolio. Kyle had grabbed a booth in the back corner, where he could watch the door. Oz had insisted on meeting here, but Kyle hoped he wouldn't run into any of the other officers who frequented this shop.

"What's up, man? We miss you around here."

"I doubt that."

"OK, I miss you around here."

"I doubt that too." Kyle grinned.

"You're a pain in the you-know-what. Try to give you a compliment and it's just deflect, deflect, deflect, like you're some girl." Oz gestured to the waitress, who came bearing two heavy mugs and the coffeepot. After they'd ordered, Oz slid the folder across the table.

"Seems your boy took up with the bad guys. This fairy tale you spun me about a hit on you seems more plausible. Never mind the faked drama of your arm in a sling."

Kyle flipped open the file. These were his case notes and the notes of the few guys who'd worked with him, although he'd done most of it alone. He knew what happened to cops who worked with internal affairs, so he figured if he was going down, he should go down alone. Now he refreshed his memory with the details and addresses. Media targets, like Jonah and his family, tended to move and leave no forwarding address—something the media might allow, but not the cops. He located the page, jotted down the information, slid the folder back across the table.

"Any of our fellow officers visit Jonah in the federal pen?"

"Couple."

"Anybody I should be interested in?"

Oz named a couple of names. "There's still a lot of ill will toward you, man. No one wants to understand what you did. Those were good guys who stuck around after the storm. Not right to pillory one of them."

"Pillory? You look that up in your off-hours?"

"Shut up."

The waitress set their breakfasts in front of them: pancakes, eggs, and ham for Oz, three scrambled and toast for Kyle. Behind her lumbered Buzz O'Reilly, all two hundred and fifty menacing pounds of him.

"DuPont. Thought we threw you out of our fine city." His face was red, but it wasn't clear if that was its normal color, the walk, or his anger.

A room full of eyes turned in their direction.

"Hey, O'Reilly. Just passing through. Gotta couple of loose ends need tying. Why'n't you sit and have some coffee?"

"Glad to see you hurt your arm."

Kyle let the insult pass. A bully of a man, O'Reilly had threatened Kyle more than once. He'd hooked himself to Jonah, Kyle sometimes thought to Jonah's dismay, as a sort of informal bodyguard and promoter. He curated a small crew of equally thuggish cronies, all of whom had thrived and profited after Katrina. If Kyle had worked IA, he'd open a file on O'Reilly. No way he wasn't on the take.

"Good to see you too."

"Don't let me see your face here again." He snapped out the cliché as if he thought it original. Kyle just stared until he turned and stomped back to his buddies in the take-out line.

"Told you we shouldn't have come here."

Oz shrugged. "You never did tell me the whole story."

"Less you knew, the better."

"We're almost three years out. Besides. You say someone's gunnin' for your ass. Maybe having help wouldn't be so bad."

Echoes of Clara. Kyle scraped some butter onto his toast. "You know Jonah wanted superintendent, right?"

"The man practically wore a sandwich board."

"It's the only motive I can think of."

"Wait, so he kills a guy, then burns him up in an abandoned car, just so he can become police super? C'mon, Kyle. No one would buy that."

"Right." He forked up some eggs. "I didn't either. But what possible motive would he have for killing some guy in the Ninth? And how did he find him?"

"Coincidence?"

"Yeah, cuz we all believe in coincidence." He glanced at Buzz and his buddies in the coffee line, hoping their antagonism didn't morph into action. So far, they seemed content with throwing glares his way.

"Hey, stuff happens. Can't control all of it."

Kyle sighed. "As Jonah told it at trial, he was patrolling, had sporadic radio communications, and hadn't slept in three days. The last time he'd seen his commanding officer was the morning before at Harrah's."

"Right. Great choice for command post."

"Everything else was under water. Anyway, you remember everyone was stretched to their limits. Too much coffee, not enough sleep, too much adrenaline. Jonah says he's in the Ninth when he hears a noise in the rubble behind him."

"Weren't you partners?"

"Command paired him with some rookie from traffic, not enough experienced men to go around. Anyway, his partner was a block in the other direction, too far for help. Jonah said he called out *show yourself*, and *NOPD*, but nada."

Kyle remembered the floods had punched through there like God's revenge, leveling whatever structures and objects humans had asserted against the darkness, including the streetlights. During his own patrols, mosquitoes rose from the residual water and mud, buzzed his ears, their high whine a distraction from other sounds. The bugs, the fear, the smells—any of them could send a man over the edge. He rubbed the back of his neck, O'Reilly's presence akin to that patrol.

Jonah said he kept to the shadows, watching. The person couldn't have been more than fifteen feet away, but it was hard to distinguish a human form among the jagged debris. Then, another flash.

"Show yourself! This is the New Orleans Police Department."

The man popped from a shadow, holding something shiny, moving swiftly. Jonah swore the shiny was a gun. Cops had been shot by looters, so Jonah fired, intending a warning. The shadow cried out, crumpled. When Jonah reached him, the man was dead. Unintentional, he said. Hard to shoot accurately in the dark, he said.

"Yeah, but that wouldn't have sent him to jail," Oz said.

"He claimed he panicked. He said, and he was probably right, that the media would have interpreted this as more white-on-black violence, excessive force, another out-of-control cop." Kyle circled his hand with each additional description, as if indicating the media was a mouse on a never-ending cop-bashing wheel. "Jonah figured that even if he survived the inquiry, it would tarnish his reputation, maybe keep him from the top cop job."

"That's right." Oz snapped his fingers. "He claimed the *rookie* suggested they burn up the body. Even found a car they could torch. Nice touch, that."

Car. Fire.

"If he was lucky, we would never have noticed. Just one more car fire after Katrina. But the rookie denied it."

Kyle had never believed a rookie would suggest a horrific crime to the son of the police superintendent, could hardly believe Jonah had masterminded it. He'd gone home half-sick for weeks, using bourbon and ESPN to numb himself.

"Anyway, that's not even what got him." Kyle ate the last of his toast and pushed his plate aside. "Place still makes the best scrambled eggs in town."

"Aw, you missed us after all." Oz grinned. "Didn't your dad help you solve it?"

If only he could forget what had fractured his family. Jonah had also killed a witness, a homeless man, as if they all weren't homeless after the storm. His father had come to him, asked him to look for his friend, and Kyle had ignored him, as if his father were just another homeless drunk. If his father hadn't insisted, kept coming around until Kyle paid attention, Jonah might have gotten away with it all. Sickened at his failure, Kyle turned over everything he had to the feds, let them finish the job. He rode out the long shunning from the other officers and the trial, then packed it in and headed north, but not before he made sure Jonah would do real time in prison. Justice mattered.

Oz pushed his empty plate aside. "Lotta cops were pissed at you, said you'd ruined a good man in favor of some homeless vagrant. As we've seen," he waved his hand vaguely toward the coffee line, although Buzz and his buddies had gone, "I'd venture those who remember still haven't forgiven you."

"Should I have ignored that he'd killed two people? No one seems to care that I'm stuck in some little Connecticut town making sure old ladies don't get run over crossing the street and dealing with the same old politicians as everywhere. Getting my department funded is a quarterly lesson in Broadway drama. You'd think the people who lived in the multi-million-dollar homes on Long Island Sound ate bread and water, for all they complain."

"I know you. You'd do it all over again."

"I'm a glutton for punishment. And now, some idiot gang member says 'car fire,' 'homeless,' and 'righteous' to a member of my department and the next thing I know, the guy is shot right in front of me. The only car fire in my jurisdiction happened after the shooting, and the only homeless people live in the next town. God forbid." He wrinkled his face up as if he were an old white lady sucking the lime in her margarita. "This case is the only connection that makes sense. Guys inside get messages out all the time, and some clown is always available to do the dirty work."

"Chill, man. You know I'm on your side."

Kyle dry-rubbed his face. "Sorry. Too much coffee, not enough sleep." He'd forgotten New Orleans could make him feel like an aquarium fish. Round and round and round, with all those eyes looking.

"I imagine being the target of a hit would do that to a man."

"One more thing." Kyle pulled the picture of the medallion from his inner jacket pocket. "Ever see anything like this down here?"

"Who torched it?"

"Not sure yet."

"Can I show it around? It maybe looks familiar, but I'm not positive."

"Thanks, Oz. I owe you."

"Yeah, you owe me a follow-up. And not some phone call a month after you get home. You keep me posted now, because this is my patch, and if something happens, it's my ass in a sling."

"No problem. Now tell me about that gorgeous wife of yours." Over a coffee refill, they caught up on each other's lives: wife, maybe-girlfriend, policing the big city versus a small town.

Oz shook his head as Kyle described his first Connecticut case and the small-town politics. "You'd think it wouldn't be as bad, but it is, isn't it?" he said.

Kyle glanced at his watch, gestured for the check. "Gotta go. I'm supposed to be working up there, but instead I'm down here. I need to make every minute count. I'll call you, promise."

Oz rolled his eyes.

Before doing anything else, Kyle headed back to the hotel. While scrolling through Twitter on his tablet for news from home, he called Clara. He knew she dawdled over the *Times*, convinced heading into the office too early was uncivilized.

"Got your message. Sorry I didn't call last night; I arrived late and went straight to sleep. I'm, ah, in New Orleans." Online, all seemed quiet.

"What?"

He sat on the bed, staring out the plate glass windows at the city below. The television informed him the morning was sultry and humid, but he already knew, having walked back to the hotel in it.

"Isn't now a bad time for vacation?"

He nearly laughed. "It's not a vacation, I promise. If I take one of those, I intend to go with you."

There was a crackle as she closed the paper. Maybe he was forgiven.

"Listen," she said. "I'm worried about you." She told him about Teo's claim that Kyle was the target of the hit.

"You went to the funeral?" He tried to tamp down his irritation, didn't mention his officers agreed with Teo's assessment. That would frighten her.

"I think I saw him in the club the other night too."

"Club? What club? You were in a club with gang members?"

He braced his hand on the side table, clenching the muscle in his good arm, as if directing his frustration there would quell it.

"Buying my weekly stash. What do you think?"

He stood up and paced to the desk, grabbing the notepad the hotel provided, bringing it back to the bed. He couldn't forget she would do what she wanted. Always. She'd started young, and it wasn't like he would change her. "Coke or Ecstasy?" He forced his voice to lighten.

"Ecstasy, of course. I'm saving it for when you come home." He let the innuendo slide, despite feeling its heat, and asked her to describe the colors and tattoos, listing the details on the notepad, seeing the connection to the medallion they'd found at the car fire take shape as she talked.

"Is Teo reliable?"

"He's a twenty-five-year-old gang member, angry and frightened, who thinks he's responsible for his friend's death."

"Why doesn't he believe Dom was the target?"

"Teo thinks the gang would've told him first. An honor thing. I didn't really get it."

Kyle explained.

She asked, "They let you kill your own friends rather than having someone else do it? And that's a good thing?"

"It ensures someone you care about doesn't suffer."

"That's sick."

What could he say, that it wasn't true? "Thanks for telling me, Clara." She needed to be needed, this woman, despite all her efficiency and money. He sometimes wondered what she saw in him, when she could have a Wall Street trader or some old-money boy with a yacht and thirty pairs of deck shoes.

"Why would a gang put a hit out on you?"

"I'm in New Orleans to figure it out." He hooked his suit jacket off the back of the desk chair where he'd slung it after breakfast, squeezed the phone between his shoulder and ear, slid one arm in and then his injured one, gingerly, adding the sling last.

"It's that thing you won't tell me about, right? That image I get of you surrounded by mud."

She'd told him about that image shortly after they met. "Something like that." He couldn't tell her over the phone that the image came from a nightmare, not reality, that she'd penetrated beyond his thoughts into his dreams. The intimacy made him vulnerable, wary.

"People there can help you?"

"Some. Yes."

"You did something to alienate the department, didn't you?" She was too damn perceptive for her own good.

He shrugged the jacket straight, checked himself in the mirror. "I have to go, Clara. I need this resolved quickly, so I can come back to Connecticut. If you hear anything else, you'll tell me please? I promise to respond as long as I'm not in the middle of something. Deal?"

"Next time, I'd appreciate knowing before you left. And I'm still going to worry." He wasn't forgiven after all.

"How could I stop you, love?" He froze. He hadn't meant to say it.

She laughed and hung up.

Had she heard him? He sighed. She wouldn't stop looking for answers, and he couldn't protect her from here.

CHAPTER 12
Kyle

Even as Wendy Harris opened her front door, Kyle knew Jonah's sister wouldn't tell him anything. He'd been prepared for it, but not for how it would hit him, how he had counted on her being reasonable, at least. Instead, her pixie face, creamy white and dotted with bronze freckles, hardened when she saw him. "Go away."

"Please, Wendy. You know I wouldn't have turned him in without incontrovertible evidence."

"They're my family, Kyle." She shrugged. "Come up with a good reason I shouldn't slam this door."

But she hadn't slammed the door. That was encouraging, even though there was uncertainty in her face.

"Someone is trying to kill me."

"A reason my family wouldn't celebrate." She allowed a half smile at that, her thick red lips barely curving.

"Not funny. Someone killed one of my officers in Connecticut.

Shot him in a drive-by right in front of me. What we've discovered so far indicates it should have been me bleeding on the ground."

Her fingers clenched tighter on the door frame, and she turned her face away.

"I have to go. I'm sorry." She closed the door gently, as if its quiet retreat into the frame wouldn't be so bleak. He stared at the bright teal paint for a moment, noting the slight ridges the paintbrush had left. Around the peephole, she'd hung a grapevine wreath studded with silk flowers. In this humidity, it would mildew, but maybe she didn't care. Maybe the color gave her hope. Maybe rotted things were just the norm here.

She had been like a sister to him, when he and Jonah had been close. Sometimes, she'd joined them at the bar after work, or at their Sunday afternoon barbeques, soaking up cop stories as if she understood. After all, she had started her career as an ER nurse. But he understood why she was angry now. Almost everyone he knew in New Orleans was angry with him, even if they understood why he hadn't been able to let anyone get away with murder, not even someone he loved as much as he'd loved Jonah.

He turned from the door, stumped. He knew Wendy visited her brother at Pollock. She drove all those hours once a month. She would answer his new friends' questions about pains and infections, insinuate herself into their lives. She would understand Jonah's mood. After all this time, was he vengeful? Resigned? If Jonah no longer cared about Kyle, then he should go home to his job and his life, let his officers pursue Dom's murder.

How else could he find out? Back in the car, he opened and flipped through his notes, but the information hadn't changed since last time he looked, and the time before that and the time before that. Cops say most police work is details—writing up reports that record the evidence that makes sure the perps end up where they should be. Most of the time, they are so stupid that they are easy to catch. But if Jonah hated him enough to try to kill him, he would know how to cover his tracks. Would Wendy help by passing messages to someone outside? He had a hard time imagining it, but then he'd had a hard time imagining Jonah was dirty. Maybe he lacked imagination.

He checked his Twitter feed for Connecticut disasters, and then his email for Joe's update. Everything seemed quiet, except Joe said he thought the gangbangers in Stamford were trying to one-up each other: an exchange of gunfire last night had sadly—Joe's word—left none of the idiots dead. And, of course, none of them would talk. No progress on Dom's death. No progress on the car fire. He'd keep Kyle posted.

Kyle texted back a quick reply, then laid his head back and stared out at the morning. The humidity had started to climb. It averaged eighty to ninety percent in this city year-round; good for the complexion, the women said, but not much else. You could see it in the air, a slight haze that clung to skin and clothes, weighing a person down. He'd never realized how much it calmed him until he didn't have it anymore. When Northerners complained of humidity, they had no idea what they were talking about.

Wendy's street was quiet. A weak breeze stirred the flowers that crowded her fence, and someone's half-open gate squeaked slightly as the air pushed it back and forth. A woman was walking from the corner, her pregnant belly so evident he figured she must be late in her term. Her short dark hair was greased back. She wore stretchy black leggings topped by a plum football jersey, and high-top gold sneakers. Large gold earrings swung from her earlobes and a gold chain dangled around her neck. She pushed through Wendy's gate and lumbered up the steps. Wendy opened the door and pulled her inside, pausing briefly to note his presence still across the street. He could see the anger on her face, even from this distance.

Did she think he was watching her? She could have anyone to her house that she wanted. No law against that. He was just sitting here because he didn't know what to do next, because he was exhausted suddenly of being himself, of thinking Dom's death might be his fault. What should he have done? He'd been welcoming the kid by getting Clara to help him with his flowers. *Flowers.* He and Clara had almost been killed because they were looking at flowers. He shook his head, disgusted.

What now?

He looked through his notes once more, this time searching for information on Jonah's family. What had he forgotten in his months away? How could he have forgotten any of this?

There, on the fourth page: Wendy was an obstetrical nurse at Tulane Medical Center. He'd definitely forgotten that—or maybe he'd just never thought much about her specialty after she left the ER. Was she seeing patients at home? Or was this a friend, dropping by for coffee? The girl didn't look like someone Wendy would know, but then Kyle had started to think his judgment about people was slipping.

He started the car and swung it around, pulling into a shopping center at the end of the street. This time, he waited with purpose, running the car only when the heat got unbearable.

Forty-five minutes later, he watched from a distance as the girl exited, looking worriedly in both directions before trudging back the way she'd come, directly toward him. He turned the car off and cracked the door. The smells from the shopping center drifted in: coffee, fried chicken, exhaust, garbage. All hung thick in the air.

Across the street a signpost marked the bus stop. The girl reached it, breathing heavily, and put her hand on the pole to steady herself. Carrying all that extra weight in this heat must wear a person out. He was out of the car and by her side before she looked up. She panicked, her face contorting as if she were readying a scream.

"I just want to talk." He took a step back, held his hand out as if he were offering her something.

She swallowed the scream, grumbled. "She said not to, cuz I could get us both in trouble." She rubbed her hand over her belly, fingers rippling like she was playing scales.

"How could you get me in trouble?" He deliberately misunderstood her. Maybe she'd let her guard down a little.

She sneered. "No, her and me. I don't care none about you." She gripped the pole harder, as if she could use it as a weapon against him. As if this little bitty girl could take him on.

"In trouble from who? I'm a cop."

"Not here you ain't. You some Northern cop, come down here, goin' to mess up my life. Mess up my baby's life, just like you messed up her brother's life. You just leave us alone."

He shook his head, thinking she knew an awful lot about him and Wendy for a patient. "How do you know Ms. Harris?"

"She helping me with baby stuff. Even though it's none of your business."

"You mean checkups?"

She nodded, just once, slowly, watching him as if he were a fly she was trying to swat.

"Why not go to the hospital or a clinic?"

"You think they goin' to take me? Someone with no medical?" She shook her head at his stupidity, and he figured maybe he was. He wondered what Wendy was charging, doubting her in-home clinic was even legal.

"How did you meet?"

"Friend of a friend." She folded her arms over her belly. He heard the diesel rumble of the bus coming down the street. He fished a card from his wallet. "Here. In case you change your mind."

The bus huffed to a stop, opened its doors with a wheeze. She took the card, stepped up. "I won't."

"What's your name, in case you do?"

"Jewel Willis." She answered without thinking. "Even though it's none of your business." The bus's doors hissed shut behind her, and he watched her collapse into the first seat. The bus rumbled back into traffic.

He allowed himself one second of satisfaction, then, back in the car with the AC cranked to high, called Oz for another favor. After a moment on hold, Oz gave him what he wanted, with a little frosting. "She's been picked up a couple times for soliciting."

"She Craigslist? Or pimp?"

"No evidence on Craigslist."

"Any idea who the guy is?"

"Xerxes Fournier."

"Xerxes? Where'd his mama come up with that?"

"Ancient Persian king. You know how it is."

He did. He'd seen rashes of names from mythology, culture, religion—all attempts to make children feel proud and special. It certainly singled them out, and he didn't know if that was good or bad. Maybe it depended on the child.

"He have a sheet?"

Oz ran it down: possession with the intent to distribute, weapons charges, several assaults. He hadn't graduated to murder—yet.

"Gang affiliation?"

"Sunset Boyz—and he's management. In your fairy tale, that means he gets to tell the other boys—inside and out—what to do."

The image of the medallion with its purple and gold decoration reasserted itself. Jewel was wearing those colors, too. Was she gang-affiliated? If so, she could have passed a message from her boyfriend to Wendy, who might have passed it along to the boys who shot Dom. A lot of *ifs* and *mights*.

"You have that gang down here? I think that medallion I showed you is theirs."

"Unfortunately. After Katrina, we had a lot of opportunist street gangs, you know, made up of guys who were just trying to survive and had found themselves a weapon or two. Now they're institutionalized, got themselves affiliated. Like that's a good idea."

"So if the girl was wearing purple and gold?"

"Be careful. Those boys don't like anyone messing with their women. Where you at, anyway?"

Kyle told him.

Oz laughed. "You think she'll talk to you—if you can even find her now? Unlikely, brother."

"Gotta start somewhere, right?"

Wendy's treatment of Sunset Boyz' girlfriends didn't mean she condoned murder, did it? How could she? How could she have anything to do with Dom getting shot? Unless, as Trevor and Clara both suggested, he was the target rather than Dom. Unless Wendy were taking revenge for Jonah. Did she hate Kyle that much?

He couldn't see it, but then he hadn't seen Jonah's betrayal coming either. "Where does Xerxes rest his kingly head?"

"Federal prison. Drug trafficking."

"Would that be the same prison where Jonah Harris resides?"

"Yessir, it would." Oz hung up.

CHAPTER 13
Kyle

Kyle turned the rental car around and parked again in front of Wendy's house. She didn't look happy to see him, but she'd opened the door. Time to take off the gloves.

"I know who your visitor was."

"Bully for you."

"Why was she here, Wendy?"

"I don't have to tell you, Kyle. Go away and leave me alone." He stuck his foot in the door as she started to slam it. He felt the sting, knew his foot would bruise.

"Do you want to have this conversation on the porch? She's pregnant. She's a gang girl. Some gang in Connecticut tried to take me out. Jonah's in the same federal prison as her boyfriend. I need the dots connected or you get my death on your conscience." Whether she cared would tell him a lot.

"There's a lot of space between those dots." But she pulled the door open and gestured him inside, suddenly slumping against the frame.

He wondered what it had been like for her during and after her brother's trial. It's not as if the family escaped the spotlight. The newspaper wrote stories on Jonah's decorated father, on his mother's charity work, on Wendy's service as a nurse. They asked questions about how someone like Jonah could have come from such an upstanding family. They asked psychologists to weigh in, talked to neighbors and schoolmates, interviewed other cops and nurses, the mayor. The judgment, implicit or explicit, always skulked between the lines: something in Jonah's past had twisted him into a killer, and his family had been oblivious. *Shame on them.*

While Kyle could never say so, he understood that shame. He accepted his guilt for not seeing Jonah's flaws sooner. And yet. How did anyone ever know another? Kyle was paid to make those judgments based on evidence, and the evidence he'd seen, right up until Jonah killed two men, was that Jonah was as righteous as they came. Would Wendy turn out to be the same? Were the armchair analysts right that some flaw in this family created killers of its children?

Wendy's front room sported white-painted paneling hung with framed prints of Louisiana coastline and flora. The cushions on the wicker furniture were covered with garish flowered prints in yellows and oranges, and brightly polished brass planters held silk flowers and ferns. The window air conditioner spit and fumed, but the room remained stuffy and warm, a condition the sling only seemed to enhance.

She gestured at the couch. He sat at its edge.

"Coffee?" She'd moved to stand tensed in the doorway between the living room and kitchen beyond, her body a thin line bisecting the light coming from the window above her sink.

"I don't need anything. Relax, will you?"

"Funny." She was almost vibrating. Rage—or fear?

"I won't share unless I have to."

"Look how well that worked out for my brother."

"Your brother killed two people."

She flung her head back and shut her eyes, as if bracing.

"You should go see him," she said.

"No."

"He was your best friend and your partner. You should stand up to it like a man, not run away to some new life." She pounded her right fist into her left hand as if she were hitting him.

He stared at her, stunned. "I was forced out."

"He needed you, and you abandoned him."

"He abandoned all of us when he murdered those men, Wendy. Maybe the first death was an accident, but the second one was as deliberate as they come." Jonah had murdered a witness.

She shook her head but slid down into the wicker chair across from him.

"You think I'm wrong? Give me a reason."

Something flashed in her eyes, but she dropped them quickly and ran her fingers over the ribs of the wicker, tracing the design. "I know you're not wrong. I just think he never thought he would lose you."

Friends forged in the intensity of police work were hard to replace. They always had your back, on the job and off. They knew you better, sometimes, than you knew yourself. Knew what you were likely to do, who you might fall in love with, how you usually got yourself into trouble—and they watched out for you, got you out of jams. The moment Jonah put himself first, he abandoned that brotherhood.

In a flash, Kyle understood what held him back with Clara: loyalty. If she was as interested in pursuing a relationship with him as she claimed, then why hang on to her marriage? What did she still feel toward her husband? It couldn't really be money, could it?

"Kyle?"

"He thought he could betray our friendship, but I would stick by him? That's crazy thinking, Wendy." He unbuttoned his cuffs and rolled up his sleeves. Had he already adjusted to the North?

"He wasn't betraying *you*. It was always and only about the job. That's all he ever cared about."

Now Kyle had the job Jonah had wanted, even if it was in a Podunk town in Connecticut. The competition that runs inevitably between siblings ran like a fault line between him and Jonah.

"He betrayed the job too. He betrayed everything he said he believed in." The words caught in his throat; he stretched out his neck as if that would release them. "Are you saying he wants to see me?"

"I have no idea if he would see you or not."

"Have you seen him?"

"Once. It's hard to get out there. I work a lot."

He'd been wrong. "So this is about your guilt rather than mine."

She shrugged. "Does it matter?"

Everything mattered, he thought, and he was tired of being told his morals were too high and mighty for everyone else to live up to.

He sighed. She'd stalled him dangerously long already. Who knew what Jewel was texting even now? "Two families—three, if you count mine—have been damaged by his behavior, Wendy. If I'm murdered, you'll carry that. Just tell me and let me get on with it."

"What is it, exactly, you want to know?"

"Anything. Everything. You were always close to Jonah. Does he want revenge? Has he hired someone to kill me?"

"I don't know. You'd have to go see him to find that out."

"So what do you know?"

She studied him, or maybe it was her version of the hundred-yard stare. What she said threw him completely off course.

"I know why he killed the first man."

"You withheld evidence."

"He's my brother."

"You could go to prison."

She shrugged again. "Sure you don't want coffee?"

"I could give this information to the prosecutor for a new trial."

"I've been holding this secret for a long time. Maybe when you hear the story, you'll understand that I have a new opinion of my brother, one more akin to yours."

He said, "So you think he wants me dead."

"Prison has done nothing for his moral compass."

"Yes, I'll have coffee." The ritual would provide normalcy, something to do with their hands while she told him her long-held secret.

She got up to make it, and while she was gone, he surveyed the room again, looking for details he'd missed the first time around: a Cover Girl makeup compact; a purse on the floor with cracks in the leather; a small old-style television. No flat-screen here. Nothing new or shiny, everything well-worn and simple. He knew life hadn't been easy after Katrina. Rebuilding had been hard and expensive. Did she own the house? Did she need money? Wouldn't her father help her, or had the family put all its resources into Jonah's legal defense?

Wendy carried a small tray into the room and set it on the trunk that served as a coffee table. A French press steamed next to two mugs, a jar of sugar, and a small carton of milk. "We'll give it a minute." She sat back in her wicker chair.

He made himself relax, softened his shoulders, unclenched his jaw.

"My brother wasn't as righteous as you saw him, you know."

"I don't suppose any of us ever are."

"Yeah, well, our family knows how to keep secrets." She used one thumb to rub at the base of the other. "Jonah got into some trouble in college. He, um, forced a girl." She stopped. "I sound so cold."

Kyle felt himself go still, revulsed. Not only murder, but rape too? How could he ever have taken Jonah for a brother? What did that say about his character judgment? "How old were you when it happened?"

"Seventeen? Something like that."

"How awful to find that out about your own brother."

She shook her head, as if she still couldn't believe her own family. "My father got involved too. Don't you wonder how my brother became a police officer? Unlikely the department would hire a rapist, even if he was the son of the police superintendent." She forced the plunger to the bottom of the coffeepot, poured and handed him a mug, gesturing toward the sugar and cream. "My father, from his lofty position, persuaded the girl and her family that going through the courts would destroy her life. As incentive, he offered a big bundle of money. It's no wonder my brother thought he could get away with murder."

Kyle sipped the coffee, savoring its chicory flavor.

"How do you know all this?"

"I overheard my parents talking, snooped through my father's desk, figured out my brother's computer password. The tension was unbearable."

A sick kind of glad rushed through Kyle. Sometimes, he had wondered if Jonah's flaws should be overlooked, but Wendy's story confirmed his true character.

"What does the rape have to do with the murder during Katrina?"

"The girl's brother wanted revenge. The three of them attended the same classes, drank at the same pubs—friends until the rape."

"Wait a minute. The brother contacted you?"

"Shannon emailed Jonah—I found the emails on his laptop. He blamed Jonah for his sister's suicide, claiming she'd never recovered from the trauma."

Kyle shifted back into cop-think. "Now his sister's gone, and Shannon thinks he can pursue the matter? Jonah killed the witness." His father's homeless friend.

"I don't think the courts were the kind of revenge Shannon had in mind. Public shaming would be sufficient. He was a journalist. Even if he couldn't prove the rape, the story would still damage Jonah's career."

"Why kill Shannon in the Ninth after Katrina?"

"Jonah told our father that was coincidence. He figured Shannon was scavenging—canned goods, tools, whatever. The family lived in New Orleans East, which suffered severe damage in the storm, although the media didn't talk much about that." She shook her head. "What am I telling you for? You were here."

"So he sees some guy rooting around in an abandoned house, realizes it's the guy who's going to ruin his reputation, and shoots him? Just like that?"

She crossed her arms. "It's only what I've been able to piece together."

Kyle thought for a moment. Could Jonah have arranged the meeting? Maybe Jonah had followed Shannon, looking for an opportunity. Add stalking to the list of his transgressions.

She picked up her cup. "You're right, you know. He's turned strange in prison, embraced the culture of it. It's like he's decided that if he can't be king on the side of the law, he'll be king on the side of the lawless."

"You don't trust him anymore?"

"It's hard to see someone you love change—or at least become who they've been all along, underneath, where they were hiding from you. Why?" Her cry made him ache.

He set down his cup, leaned across to grab her hand. "He did it to me too. You understand why I don't want to see him?"

"Yes, but if you went and saw what I saw then I would know I wasn't crazy." It burst from her, as if she'd been waiting for years to say it to someone who would understand.

"Oh, Wendy. I am grateful someone outside the department sees Jonah like I did."

She started to weep, and he looked around for tissues. Nothing. He stood to try the kitchen, but she stood with him and stepped into his arms.

"No one understands because they don't know how much he's changed.

All his cop buddies, they've stopped visiting him. Who can make the trip? It takes hours to get out to Pollock."

She sniffled into his suit, and he thought about dry-cleaning bills, then chided himself.

He stepped back and she let him go. "If I visited, what would it accomplish?"

She took a big, raggedy breath and sat down again, the wicker creaking slightly. "He's got some deal going with the gang out there. Sunset Boyz, right? That's who you want to know about?"

Kyle nodded. She looked down at her lap, twisted her hands between her knees. "Pieces of garbage. Their girls come to me now—without payment, of course. In return, my brother gets protection."

"They're forcing you to give care?"

"How can I deny him protection?"

"Does he deserve it?"

She looked up. "He's my brother."

Loyalty of a different kind, Kyle thought. People did stupid things in the name of family—or perhaps, stupid things were expected.

"If he's involved with the hit on you, then one of the gang girls is passing messages. A couple have let slip that's the system. They meet here pretty frequently for their 'appointments'—and they're always whispering about something. I try not to get involved. I'm already in way over my head."

He would have to tell Oz. Never mind that it wasn't his jurisdiction; he was an officer of the court. But for now, he would keep it to himself.

As if she could read his mind, she said, "I know you're going to report this, Kyle. You're too righteous."

Her use of the word from Teo and Dom's fight brought him up short. Suddenly, he reassessed her. Was she playing him? If so, why tell him about Jonah's raping the girl and murdering her brother? Did Wendy have some payback in mind? Or was she trying to get out from under a relationship with the gang that didn't suit her? How much of what she'd told him could he believe?

And how would this story help him? It reconfirmed that Jonah could be behind the hit, but the question of why it was happening now remained. It had been almost three years since Katrina. Jonah was in prison. Kyle had a new life. The woman Jonah had raped, along with her baby and her brother, were dead. No more justice could be squeezed out now. It boiled down to saving his own life—and he could only do that if he knew who wanted to kill him.

"Where's the girl? The one who was here?"

"She was frightened. She…had been warned about you."

"By who?"

Wendy shook her head. "Wouldn't say. But." She sighed, shook her head again, as if negating her own resistance. "I sent her to the bayou, to a woman I trust. Fredericka is a safe haven for abused women."

She rose from the chair and went across to a white wicker desk in the corner. She wrote something on a memo pad, then tore off the sheet and turned to hand it to him. "Here's the address. Tell her I sent you. Then, maybe, she won't shoot you."

CHAPTER 14
Clara

I had another dream that night.

I figured I might not fall asleep from worrying about what Kyle had omitted about his trip to New Orleans, never mind that I could still hear the bullets thunk into the dirt, the tires shriek as they spun away from us, the shouts of the boys inside. I was afraid those shrieks would meld with the shrieks I imagined from inside the burning car. Far too vivid, my imagination, and those images I could live without. Once they nested in my brain, they never left.

Beautiful at first, my dream showed Vlad's granddaughter, the little girl I'd met at Evangelia's, as a grand*son* who rode horses, painted watercolors, played hide-and-seek in the tall grass of his mother's meadow.

Then, it shifted, as dreams do.

The walls narrowed to a long hallway filled with doors. Each door revealed a different horror. In one room, the grandson beat a man, snapping his head from side to side, blood spraying from his nose, his flayed cheeks.

When I opened the door, the boy turned and held his bloody hands out to me.

Behind another, he stood in a convenience store, gun pointed at the clerk, demanding cash. The man's hands shook as he emptied the register, and he dropped some of the bills on the floor. He knelt to retrieve them, but the grandson shouted for him to stand up. As the man's head breasted the counter, the grandson shot him. The clerk's head bucked back against the rack of cigarettes, smearing them with his blood as he sank from sight.

When the dream switched again, the grandson stood in the hall of an elementary school, his bloody hands filled with pills. Toddlers crowded around him, clamoring. The first one—I could just see her pink pants and flowered sneakers—was Vlad's granddaughter. "Don't you worry, honey," he said, as he dumped a handful of pills into her outstretched palms. "These will make everyone feel better." I forced myself awake, screaming hoarsely.

I walked in the gardens with my morning espresso to try to shake the dream. Anything that got me out of the house and somewhere green would have shrunk the anxious pit anchored in my heart.

I used my walk to tour our progress on the kitchen garden, pleased to see the dark earth overturned in preparation for lettuce and arugula, the snow peas just beginning to poke through the surface, planters out and cleaned, ready for potting soil and flowers. How lucky to have a place that calmed the shakes, sent the demons retreating. But not even the garden could pull me from the dream images, and I circled back to what they might mean. Was this a portentous dream, or just something bubbling up because I was afraid of Espejo? Was it he I was seeing in the dream, dealing drugs to children? To his own grandchild? The idea made me ill.

I still didn't have enough information to give the dream context. Life would have to catch up with whatever my intuition had picked up. It would come in its own time, but I worried that somewhere out there, someone was gunning for Kyle, and if I couldn't figure out who, I might lose him—if I even had him.

To add to my misery, when I reached the office that morning, Shona handed me a pile of messages, most of them from Palmer, my hopefully soon-to-be ex.

Oh yeah, that's what I need.

His messages made it apparent that he had decided to move our divorce along. Maybe he had found himself a new girlfriend—please, dear God. More likely, he realized how hard life became without all my lovely money, and he was amping up his demands for a piece of it, a piece I adamantly refused to give him. He would cave eventually, or we would go to trial; I didn't much care which. No judge would give him any money; he was able-bodied and trained as a CPA.

Palmer had realized he was getting old when he could feel his scalp through his hair at the back of his head. That freaked him out so badly that he bought a $15,000 bike that he proceeded to wreck almost immediately coming down a hill during a training run in Girona, Spain. After I'd discovered he was having an affair with his trainer, I'd packed my bags to head to Paris, but before I could get there, dreams about danger to my mother forced me home. And here I remained, ensnared by circumstance or love or both. It was too soon to tell.

Palmer and I had met in Madrid. I was standing in the Museo Thyssen-Bornemisza, staring at Hans Holbein's portrait of Henry the Eighth. After seeing it so many times in books, I had almost forgotten it was real. I hadn't known the Thyssen-Bornemisza owned it. And Henry himself, so fat and full of his own power, sure he deserved an heir, faulting his wives for leaving him with only a sickly male heir. I loved that Holbein captured him so fully, left for us, five hundred years later, a portrait that brought the character into the room in all his pompous sovereignty.

Palmer interrupted my awe, loping into view, slightly balding already, in plaid shorts and polo shirt, camera strung around his neck on a thick leather strap. "Oh wow," he said. "Henry the Eighth. Cool. I didn't know this museum owned that painting."

What had I seen in him? Stability, maybe. An easy smile and way with people. Need. No one had needed me for a long time.

Madrid is not the most romantic of cities, so it didn't take us long to migrate to Paris via Bordeaux and Champagne. Palmer had taken the summer off from his job, a sort of sabbatical he said, to see Europe the way he wished he'd traveled after college—with a backpack. I found backpacking tedious and far too intimate with the insect kingdom. Palmer was more than happy to ditch it for my version of things, which included rented cars and upscale hotel rooms. Not until two years later, after we'd been married a year, did I perceive this as Palmer's finding a good thing and sticking to it like a leech.

It saddened me that I was so gullible or lonely. We enjoyed each other at the start. Palmer was funny and intelligent, knew a lot about art and literature, liked to walk a lot. But then cycling became the obsession. He wanted to win, and he wanted to win big. I tried to tell him that those medals went to much younger men, but he insisted he could win in his age category. Even as I'd stuck it out, hoping, I'd known the relationship was over. Now he wanted my money, and I thought he could get off that bicycle and make his own damn living. How could I not have seen the real Palmer? Had our relationship, my money, something, changed him or had his self-centeredness been present all along, hidden under his smile? And was there any chance he was behind that first shooting, no matter what Teo said?

I called him back. Take the pain first, and everything after that is easier.

"Clara." Already whining. "We need to talk."

"Have your lawyer call my lawyer."

"If we could just talk like human beings, it wouldn't have to be so nasty."

"You mean the nastiness of lawyers?"

He harrumphed. I didn't think people still did that. "Why are you so angry?"

"I'm not angry. I just think it's unreasonable that you want to spend my money to play and sleep with other women." Well, OK, maybe a little angry.

"You should have thought of that before you made me dependent on you."

"I'm sorry, I made you *dependent?*" I twirled my letter opener on the blotter, wondering if I could throw it hard enough through the phone to kill him, wondering if he'd used my money to send a bullet my way.

"We moved from country to country, depending on what garden you wanted to study. You never asked what I wanted, never stayed anywhere long enough for me to settle into anything, and you would never talk about coming back to the States, where I could have worked. You owe me."

"I *owe* you? You didn't want to come home. You didn't want to work. That's what you said."

"You would have heard anything different if I had said it?"

"You should have tried. Married people talk to each other about the things that matter, not sneak off and have affairs."

"Speaking of, I hear you've got a new boyfriend."

How had he heard that? Some idiot had probably tagged a photo of us on Facebook. I'd have to change my privacy settings. "Not really."

"I'm not stupid, Clara, even if I don't have your money."

"What do money and stupid have to do with each other? I never treated you as stupid."

"You treated me as stupid all the time. Every time you made a decision without consulting me, you treated me as stupid."

I tested the point on the letter opener.

"When did you take up with him?"

"I haven't *taken up* with anyone," I lied. I didn't have time for this. "I have friends. Some are male, some are female. Anyway, it's none of your business what I do."

"Whatever my *wife* does is my business. You'll be sorry if you don't pay up."

"I'm hanging up now." I slapped the phone back into its cradle. Seriously? I hadn't even met Kyle until I'd come home. A court would never take our relationship into consideration, would they?

I growled. Palmer and I were both stubborn enough to make the debate last far beyond the point of no return. Maybe I would have to settle at some point, assuming he hadn't hired a hit man.

I just wasn't ready. Why I wasn't ready was another question. I had left him behind, emotionally, long before I came home, and moved on to a new and potentially wonderful relationship with an interesting, if absent, man. A man who wouldn't tell me about his family or his past, who had reservations about my gift, and who had disappeared yesterday without telling me where he was going. What did I not see under his surface?

I stabbed the letter opener back into my pencil jar, heard it grind into the glass bottom. Something else damaged. Oh wonderful.

I turned to Evangelia's landscaping problems. Those, at least, I knew how to tackle. She would need to manage water if she intended to remove a hillside's worth of plants. Figuring out how to direct the flow and avoid having the entire hillside end up in her neighbor's backyard took me most of the day. Once I sketched my ideas, I gave them to one of the interns to draft; we could review them with my partner Ernie to identify any pitfalls.

Even with a head full of water, gravel, dirt, and dreams, I couldn't get Palmer, Kyle's absence, or poor Dom and his family out of my head, so when I finished the design, I called Bailey and persuaded her to meet me for drinks and dinner at The Swan, a new bar and grill just off Route One downtown. It didn't take much, and her voice had an unusual lilt to it. Maybe my best friend and I could just unwind and have fun. I needed some of that.

CHAPTER 15
Clara

I parked behind the CVS in the public lot and walked up the slate path past the still-dormant gardens. Lilac and forsythia would bloom there in a month and a half, but now, the damp cool air kept everything in hibernation.

Early as usual, Bailey sat at the bar with her martini already partly gone, and a new pair of red glasses sliding down her nose. Her black raw silk suit jacket decorated the back of her bar stool, and her red blouse draped artfully around a tasteful diamond pendant. Matching diamond earrings twinkled from her ears, and she was a little flushed, although that could have been from the drink. What looked like a legal brief rested on the bar next to the martini. "Hey, girl," she said. "You look run down. Traffic bad?"

I gave her a one-armed hug, still favoring my wrist, then claimed the seat next to her. "Just the usual from Stamford. You know the drill."

I-95 was a parking lot from Greenwich to Guilford every night from four o'clock to about seven thirty. If you were lucky, summer construction didn't halt traffic at midnight or five a.m. as well.

"It's everything else that's got me crazed." I set my phone on the bar where I could easily see it, in case Kyle called, if he ever stopped shutting me out. *Getting divorced might help,* a little voice said. I shook my head and Bailey raised an eyebrow at me. Would he ever tell me what was really going on?

"Fill me in," she said. She packed her reading material into her brief-case and stowed it on the floor behind the brass foot rail, then gestured at the bartender for another martini for me.

I started with Dom's death and worked my way forward. The martini arrived, little ice crystals on its surface. We toasted. She was on her second martini by the time I had finished with Kyle's trip to New Orleans, Palmer's phone call, and last night's dream of the shape-shifting grandson/granddaughter. I wouldn't use Vlad's name in a public place, but she got the idea.

The bar had filled by then, too, with after-work commuters and a couple of professors from the local community college. I could tell by their terrible shoes, flat things with hunks of rubber for soles and wide stretchy straps across the instep. Why did they wear that crap?

"God, Clara. I let you out of my sight for a few days and you're up to your neck in it again. Are you OK?" She'd lost a little of her earlier glow. "I worry about you."

So much had happened that I hadn't thought about whether I was fine. On the one hand, not thinking was good. I didn't want to think about Dom dying or bullets flying randomly from cars or Kyle in New Orleans not telling me what he was up to. On the other, I was pretty sure I wouldn't be sleeping well for some time to come, especially since everything I didn't want to think about found its way into my dreams.

"Thanks, sweetie. I worry about me too. But I'm more worried about my dreams."

She asked what I thought they meant.

"A man in a clearing with knives all around him is a clear image of threat, but does that even connect to the second dream? Knife man bears no resemblance to drug pusher boy, and as far as I know, Mr. Gangster doesn't have a grandson."

"So…two separate problems?"

"Do you think, well…could it be Palmer? I mean, it couldn't be, right?"

"There's a lot of money at stake."

"I just have a hard time imagining him arranging for someone to *kill* me."

She shrugged, seemed almost uninterested. "Paul's better at helping you with the dreams than I am."

"He's pretty angry with me right now for my screw-up at the club. I don't think he's going to be willing to help for a while."

She turned her head away. "Have you considered apologizing?"

"No. What a shockingly good idea. I'd never have thought of that on my own, so thank you, dear."

She winced.

I took another sip of my drink. "Sorry. That came out sharper than I intended." Too much blood in my dreams. The violence made me edgy, as did Kyle's silence.

"You know, Clara," she adjusted her martini glass a millimeter, "it's not just danger that concerns Paul. Richard's health?"

"Oh god. Has something happened? He's been at work." Richard was our IT whiz. I'd hired him after some HIV-related bullying made his previous employment untenable. Easier to leave than file a lawsuit—the truth all bullies rely on.

"No, nothing. Not the point. You have to *think*." She pressed her finger on the pendant as if it were a talisman.

"Well, then, you're going to be really pissed at me because Kyle and I slept together last night." Best friends had certain rules about what they could be left out of, and love lives were definitely not one of those things. Kyle might be upset if he found out I'd told her, but he didn't need to find out. Best friends also kept their mouths shut.

She stared at me.

I plowed on, disconcerted by her lack of reaction. "Then, he called this morning and tried not to be angry with me for checking out the club and meeting a gang member at Dom's funeral."

She fingered the pendant at her throat. "Sometimes we have to do things we don't want to get what we do want."

"What do you mean? The pendant is beautiful, by the way. Is it new?"

"I made partner."

"Oh my god! That's great news. Right?" I hopped up to hug her and she patted my back. Surprisingly lukewarm.

"Of course, it's good news. I just… I was thinking more about you."

"Things I shouldn't be doing? Like what?"

"Like staying out of investigations we've been told to stay out of to keep the police chief from looking like he can't control his own girlfriend. Like finalizing a divorce so the police chief doesn't have to worry about public perception."

"Say that a little louder, why don't you."

She shrugged, frowning, her shoulders like the warning flap of a flag in a bullfight.

I said, "If you had seen Dom murdered in front of you and the family asked for your help, could you walk away?" She had always been on my side. What was I missing?

She ran the pendant along its chain and back again, then dropped it and tucked her hair behind her ears. "Gangs, Clara, are not nice people who play by your rules of polite society, where cutting someone off in traffic or arranging to put a thousand people out of work is a successful day. That gangster does not care about your pretty car and your nice house and your security and privacy. All he cares about is money and power."

I laughed. "Oh. They're lawyers."

"Very funny." She wrinkled her nose at me, started playing with her pendant again.

"I haven't done anything. I don't know anything about gangs." I stopped. "I just want Dominick's murderer caught. For Dom to retain his reputation."

"He couldn't have had much of one. He was only a police officer for about ten minutes."

"Bailey."

"OK, whatever." She swiveled around on her stool and scanned the room.

"Why does this bug you so much?"

She swiveled back. "I don't know. Every time we get a little space where we might do something fun, like go to the movies or take a weekend away, you're up to your neck in dreams and blood."

I stared at her. Surely, she couldn't be annoyed that I'd saved my mother from jail time. "We just spent Fashion Week in Paris." I'd gotten tickets from a friend, taken Bailey with me. We'd shopped and eaten and looked at the ridiculous and fabulous creations, and even bought a few of our own.

"Yeah." She waved at the bartender for another round, her third. We needed to order some food. "Do you ever think about marrying again?" she asked.

The wild shifts in topic were wearing out my already fragile hold on this conversation. Marriage? Bailey was the most self-contained person I knew. She was driven and ambitious, never one to turn down a case, or worry about working through the weekend. Her Monday-through-Friday routine involved an hour at the gym between five and six a.m., a quick shower, take-out coffee. She was at her desk by seven. I could seldom drag her away before seven in the evening, and sometimes she would return to work after our drinks or meal. I couldn't see her giving up her workouts or long days to tend to a husband or raise children.

"I have been married. It's not something I recommend, especially to excessively independent friends. That said, who is he?"

Someone screeched a laugh. The community college professors were getting raucous. The tall one, with the long string of fake pearls, wobbled up to get another round of cosmos.

Bailey shook her head. "Not me, you."

"You think I want to marry again? I'm not even out of my current one." I laughed but it sounded like a blue jay on uppers.

She looked at me sharply.

I pushed some hair behind my ear. "By the way, no one is supposed to know. So no sharing, please?"

"Because?"

"We were supposed to have dinner and talk about it, but then he flew away. Literally."

"He is a cop."

"I get it."

"You don't get it. He's a black chief of police in a mostly white town, and you're still married."

The bartender set the two new martinis in front of us, asked if we needed anything else.

Bailey shook her head. I asked for a menu.

I leaned in. "This is the twenty-first century. I know there's racism, but they hired him. Surely they think he can do the job—whether or not he's sleeping with me."

She spilled a little of her martini, pulling it toward her, something I'd never seen her do. "A public official is always a target. Always. You stand up in front of people and they start throwing things. The fact that they hired him doesn't make any difference. He still has to work twice as hard as a white man to prove he can do the job. It's like being a woman." Her hand shook a little as she raised the drink to her lips.

"Is this about your partnership?"

"You are crossing all kinds of lines with your relationship. People will watch you. You'll become as much of a target as he is. Are you ready for that?"

"You know I just love being a target. Favorite thing, hands down. So, no, I'm not ready to do it again. Not after that whole debacle with Mother in jail for murder."

"And not for nothing, Clara, but are you ready to deal with black culture? He's not a white man hiding in a black body."

"You seriously believe I would think that?"

"He's in a white town, working to fit in and meet the expectations of the people who hired him. But he will never fit in."

"Wow. Where is this coming from?" Why was she so angry? I'd never seen her like this, at least not about Kyle. When I first came home, she had been angry with me for leaving, for not respecting and nurturing the friendships of the people I'd left behind. We'd come to some accord on it when I'd decided to stay—or I thought we had. I couldn't really be as stupid as she thought I was, could I?

She said, "Think about it this way: you act a particular way at the office because people expect it. When you are alone or with your friends, you become a different person. It might be a big change, it might be little. The same is true for him. His real self is one he wears at home, with his friends and family. Don't you ever wonder if he feels annoyed that he's ended up here, protecting a bunch of white people?"

I stared at her, offended. "How are you such an expert?" It might have come out more sarcastically than I intended, given the twist of her mouth in response.

It was as if she suddenly had taken ownership of Kyle or of me or of what was between us. Had I really not thought any of this through? Kyle was just a man whom I was trying to get to know. I didn't think of him in terms of color, but maybe I needed to. Maybe our color defined us even if we didn't think about it, just because some people did define us that way. Certainly, some people in town thought of Kyle only in terms of his skin color. I'm sure a few of those people would think he was less capable of doing his job because of it, even if they never said so. They would keep their opinions to themselves, or they would share them with people they trusted, or post them anonymously on the town blog. If they ever wrote editorials for the newspaper, their hate would be carefully crafted to reflect their commitment to the values of honest discussion about race and tolerance. Was I being racist? What did it mean to be racist in this era? Should I notice color? Did that make me racist? Or did not noticing color make me racist? Was that some essential assumption that all people were really just like me?

I'd never assumed Kyle was just like me. In addition to race, he was a cop. He was from New Orleans. His worldview and mine had already clashed. He certainly didn't like me poking into police business, just as I wouldn't want him pretending to do landscape architecture. I could spend all night listing the things that made us different. But so what? Isn't that why we got to know a person? So we could find out about their differences?

"I don't know how to deal with race, Bailey, until I'm confronted with its results. We've never talked about it other than as an aspect of his job. He doesn't talk about his family, so how could I have any sense of what his 'culture,' as you put it, is? Maybe intersections exist. Maybe not. I guess that's why we are getting to know each other. That's what people do when they date, right?"

She shook her head. "You're not *thinking*. So much is out of your control."

"I almost *lost* him, Bailey, so I'm pretty aware how much is out of my control." I sipped my martini to give myself a second to calm down. A waiter ladened with a large tray came through the door. The professors had moved from cosmos to a bottle of wine and cheeseburgers. The tall one was showing the blonde something on her iPhone. Right now, I wished my life were as uncomplicated as theirs. "In a lot of ways, I wasn't ready for

Palmer's 'culture'; his way of living was to sponge off me for as long as he could. He's still trying."

"What made you complicit in that, Clara?"

I felt the shock of her question in my wrist and tried to rub the sudden pain away.

She drained her martini glass, bit into one of the olives remaining in its V. Tears formed along her lower lashes. "We're all complicit in something, Clara."

"Why won't you tell me what's wrong?" I begged her.

It was as if I hadn't spoken. She sniffed and brushed the tears away. "I really wanted to ask if you wanted to come to Hawaii with me to celebrate my promotion. I have ten days and the promise from the firm that I can go guilt free. Will you come?" She didn't look happy about issuing the invitation, more like she was doing it because she'd set her mind to it.

I couldn't leave right now; I'd promised Bianca I would try to clear Dom's name. "Can it wait until we figure out who killed Dom?"

"If you say yes, you need to mean it, Clara. You can't say it to placate me, then back out at the last minute because you have some crisis at the firm or Kyle needs you or someone gets shot in front of you or you're *dreaming*."

I supposed I deserved her sarcasm.

"I'm trying to be honest. If I answer your question right now with a yes—because I would love to go—I wouldn't be honest because I'm not sure I can. If I say no, that will seem like a rejection, but it's not. It's about timing. What should I do?"

She looked away, shook her head. Why couldn't she tell me what was wrong? Did it have to do with Dom and the gangs? The violence of the dreams rose up before my eyes, Dom lying bleeding on the grass, the thunk of the bullets hitting the ground, Kyle yelling at me to get down. He'd sheltered me. He cared for me. I might love him, something I wasn't sure I could even admit to myself. I wanted her to celebrate that with me, and I wanted to celebrate her new partnership with her. How did we get out of this argument? How could I get her to talk to me?

"Clara." She grabbed at my arm, lowered her voice to a whisper.

But I missed what she said. Suddenly, I saw green everywhere, lush and humid. Every shade from the turquoise green of a luxury swimming pool to crackling palm green to deep balsam flooded my vision. Bailey's hand on my arm steadied me, but visions and dreams always left a drugged hangover.

"Why am I seeing green, Bailey? Trees or sea or…" The green faded to yellow stringed with red. "…blood?"

Her sharp intake of breath yanked me free of the vision. She lowered her voice to a whisper. "I love you, and I want you to be happy, but you are doing things that are hugely complex, and you seem to be doing them without thinking about the complications, about what other people might do to prevent you from being happy."

"I think all the time, Bailey. It's not that we don't think enough, it's that we think we're the only ones doing the thinking. Tell me what's wrong."

Her eyes filled with tears. "I can't."

Helpless, I said as quietly as I could, "Because it got you the partnership?" It was the only logical conclusion.

She looked at me, stricken. "I betrayed her."

"Who?"

She shook her head.

"Come back to the house where we can talk." She nodded and we gathered our things, leaving the professors to their fun, but by the time we got to the parking lot, her steel nerves had returned. "I can't tell you now, Clara. Give me some time, OK?"

What could I do but say I'd be there whenever she needed me.

The house felt empty and cold when I got home. I put on some music, letting Miles Davis work on my worry, while I poured what remained of last night's bottle of wine into a clean glass. Leftover cooked chicken got tossed with a few snow peas, some canned water chestnuts, a couple of mushrooms, and some oyster sauce for a quick stir-fry that I took into the solarium. At least there, the darkness beyond the glass soothed me.

What had Bailey done? I couldn't help her unless she told me, and even then, there might be nothing to do but listen. The image of her worried eyes and all those various greens lingered as I brooded.

And was she right about Kyle? Was I just reproducing my same old relationship? Palmer would probably agree, suggesting I was jumping into something new to avoid dealing with him and giving him his proper payout.

I had left Palmer last fall, but it seemed like a lifetime. I rarely thought of him, and when I did, it was only in the context of wondering when the hell he was going to come to his senses. Perhaps the fact that I was no longer in Europe, no longer with his friends, no longer watching endless bike races, made it easy to let go. Life here was so different. I missed Europe, but I didn't miss Palmer. Not for one minute.

Was Kyle's race part of the reason it didn't feel like a rebound? Because he was so different from any other man I had dated, maybe I thought I was stepping well outside my usual pitfalls. But maybe no matter what, I chose the same man over and over, the one who would ultimately be unavailable to me—my first husband, whom I barely thought of anymore, because of his immaturity—and mine, to be fair; Palmer because of his infidelity; Kyle because of his race or his profession—and, therefore, I could justify retaining my independence.

Did I choose them because they protected me from having to commit? From coming to terms with my own shortcomings? Who among any of us was perceptive enough to see that far into the distance to know where our longings came from and the shape they would take in the world? Over and over we chose people and situations, trying to make some core thing right. If I had to play therapist to myself, I would say I was still looking for my mother's approval, still rebelling against wanting it. I didn't want to play therapist.

Maybe I shouldn't be in this relationship with Kyle. Maybe the healthiest thing would be to break it off, to let him stay in his "culture"—whatever that was—and me in mine. But wasn't stepping outside our comfort zones the way we grew?

Green, purple, gold waved lazily at the corners of my vision like a faint aurora borealis undulating in the night sky. I wouldn't be free of it until I solved this. For now, I needed to work with him. I cared about him. I didn't want him hurt. But maybe building a relationship meant growing up, divorcing, getting my head on straight. Then, if he was still around, maybe.

CHAPTER 16
Kyle

Jonah's parents lived in a gated community about twenty minutes outside the city. Kyle got the guard to let him through on his police credentials, but figured the guy picked up the phone the moment his wheels started rolling again. Wendy had probably already called, too. He would try anyway; he needed answers to protect himself, wanted to know if they'd seen their son, how he was doing, his state of mind. He wanted to see if they would let anything slip. Did they know Jonah had murdered twice to cover up his old sin? Had the trial and the prison time damaged him so much that he would take a hit out on Kyle? It was hard to imagine, but much else about the time after the storm was hard to imagine as well.

Grasses and flowers—Clara would have known their names—huddled in beds alongside the flagstone walk that led to Alec and Patsy Harris's front doors. The house backed up to the golf course, cleaved into sections by a winding river. A small bridge with an ornate railing made both sides available to the golf carts dotting the fairways. The house itself was over-large and modern, a quasi-Victorian design with etched glass windows and turrets. It was all a little ridiculous.

And why a gated community? Did the former police superintendent wish distance from his city? Did he feel safer with the dubious protection of a paid security guard, as if the felons he'd convicted over the years couldn't find him by Googling? Or was this a status buy, a way to placate his wife or impress his friends who would have to drive a distance to see him?

He caught himself and laughed, sad. Maybe they just liked golf.

It had been over a year since the trial ended, long enough for Jonah to think on things, and Jonah was the type to think on things. Even with his cases, he had taken his time, making sure every piece fit, so that when the defense attorney tried to take him apart in court, he couldn't find a crack to wedge open. He'd always been a by-the-book kind of cop, the kind others turned to when they needed to make the law work for them. Sometimes, Kyle thought Jonah would have made a good lawyer, except he didn't like arguments. He wanted the law black and white, clear-cut rules to solve clear ethical and moral breaches.

Kyle had appreciated that Jonah could be relied on to do it right, even if the guy's ambition to be superintendent, like his father, lurked behind every decision. Kyle didn't care, as long as the agenda didn't get in the way of the case. Jonah seemed to want to work his way up honestly, making sure the men respected and trusted him, but even though Kyle and Jonah had been partners, he thought friends, and their lives had intertwined outside the force, he'd never felt he could see past the curtain Jonah kept drawn against the most private parts of his mind. Even now, Kyle wasn't sure if his friendship with Jonah had been a genuine connection. Who had he been connecting with—the cipher Jonah presented to the world or the real man?

Kyle pressed the bell, heard a chime boom. They made him wait, then opened the door together, as if creating a body barrier to the rest of the house.

Alec Harris stared at Kyle. One hand gripped his wife; the other, a cane. Had he been injured in the line of duty? Kyle couldn't remember.

He had certainly aged, his full head of hair bright silver and slicked back from the strong forehead. But his body had thinned, so the golf clothes both he and Patsy wore hung on him as if he were a wire rack in a trendy department store. Behind them, prescription bottles and mail cluttered a hall table. Maybe he hadn't gotten away as scot-free as Kyle had assumed.

Patsy found her voice first. "Go away," she hissed, shaking off her husband's hand.

"Just a few minutes."

"You want to apologize?" she snarled. "After all this time? You ruined our son. Nothing you can say will bring him home."

Apologize? He'd never considered it.

"I did my job for the murdered man's family. Their peace comes from knowing what happened."

"My son will never have a life again!"

"Your son chose that, ma'am." *More than once,* Kyle thought, now that he'd heard Wendy's story. *Car fire.* Whose idea might that have been?

"You left us without any peace."

Alec's hand came up again, rested on Patsy's shoulder. "He was doing his job."

She turned on her husband. "You always supported this one," her hand flailed at Kyle, "even more than you supported your own son."

Maybe because Alec was trying to keep his job when everything around him had washed away in the flood, exposed like a scrubbing that takes the clean down to the bone.

"You know I love Jonah, but Jonah killed, and he is paying the price for that."

Kyle wondered what these words cost him to say, what it cost to watch his son be convicted of murder, perhaps even to know that if he hadn't paid off that girl, his son might have found his way back from his internal darkness. Kyle wondered how he himself would have handled it, when he had a son of his own someday, if he had a son of his own. Would he be able to let him suffer if he could stop it?

Alec said, "Why are you here, son? What do you need?"

Patsy threw up her balled fists, as if looking for something to pound, and stalked off into the house, leaving the two of them alone. Kyle tried to ignore that patronizing *son*. He hadn't ever wanted to be Harris's son, in any sense of the word. Kyle couldn't remember a single time he'd heard Harris address a white cop as *son*.

"I'm sorry," Alec said. "I'd invite you in, but…"

"I understand, sir." He swallowed his distaste at asking for a favor and from a man who had never done him any. "Someone has put a hit out on me, and I need to find out who."

"You think…Jonah?" Alec grabbed at the door, as if it could shield him from this new wound.

"Someone up north used the words 'car fire' and 'homeless' in relation to the hit." Memory flickered across the father's face.

"I see." He thought a moment, his hands doming the head of the cane. "I always thought you had a good head on your shoulders. It's why I gave you so much responsibility after the storm, and why I trusted you to investigate Jonah. I still trust you." He peered into Kyle's eyes, as if confirming his trust. Kyle kept his gaze steady, tried not to let his distaste show.

"I'm sorry I couldn't protect you better. I'm not sure anyone could have." He drifted off, caught in his own past.

Kyle had a few memories of his own about those weeks after Katrina, most of which he avoided. But he remembered clearly Superintendent Harris telling him to investigate Jonah. Then Harris told him to stop.

That afternoon after the storm, Harris had stood when Kyle entered. Thin and tall, he'd seemed somewhat emaciated even then. At the time, Kyle had written it off as the stress of Katrina, but now, he wondered if Harris was already ill. At least, he assumed it was Alec who needed all the pills on the table behind him. Maybe Harris had been waiting it out, doing his duty to the city until the aftershocks of Katrina receded.

Harris had gestured to the two upholstered captain's chairs facing his desk. "Officer DuPont, have a seat, please."

Kyle sat. Harris stayed behind his desk. The super's office was designed to impress. Polished walnut built-in bookcases, thick carpet, a shiny window view of the freeway.

"You've been working hard, son."

Son. As if white people were still plantation owners. "Just doing my job, sir."

"Yes. About that." Harris folded his hands on the desk, rubbed his thumb over a knuckle. "It's time to take a break." Harris looked up. "You've solved the case. My son will go to prison for what he's done."

For one of the murders he'd committed, but not both. Kyle felt the protest rise in his throat, but he choked it down.

Harris held up a hand. "You did the right thing. Jonah panicked, tried to save his career. It doesn't excuse the action, and it's appropriate he serve his time."

But "panic" couldn't account for the destruction Jonah had wreaked. Harris hadn't yet gotten to the reason for the meeting.

"I've seen this before, you know, an officer convinced some conspiracy lurks beneath the surface, or some bigger crime's been committed. Let me assure you, there is no conspiracy here."

Oh, yes, there was. "Sir, I still haven't solved the death of the first man, the one burned up in the car."

"Accident." Harris shrugged, dismissed it.

Kyle started to speak, but Harris held up his hand. "Your certainty is not my concern."

"The family—"

"Will survive. If they believe my son did it, they will have the satisfaction of seeing him imprisoned."

Yes, but not for the time he deserved.

"Meanwhile, I am concerned about your health and well-being, and that of my other officers. I've heard rumors the men feel you are investigating them."

Harris's lips twisted, and Kyle wondered if the real problem was a black man doing the investigating. He straightened his shoulders. "I've done only what was asked."

"You never know how a fellow officer will react to being put on the spot. More unrest could lead to danger for you or your family—especially since your father is so at risk."

He'd reached his point. Icy rage swept through Kyle like a blast of air conditioning, followed by despair. His father: the one person he couldn't protect.

"Take a couple weeks off on the department to clear your head, son. When you return, we'll call it a fresh start."

Kyle stared at him.

"That's all," Harris said.

"Yes, sir," Kyle had said back then, and, even now, though it didn't matter anymore—the man was dying, Kyle could tell just by looking at him—it still twisted bitter in his gut that he hadn't stood up to him, hadn't said that he knew Harris's actions that day had kept Jonah from serving the time he deserved for two murders rather than only one.

Some Katrina crimes would never be solved. Harris simply consigned that boy's death—the one burned up in the car, the one Wendy believed was the brother of the girl Jonah had raped—to the cold case file, while letting the homeless man's murder be solved. He had assigned Kyle the case, a token black officer investigating the bad white boy, given him a couple of weeks, let him solve the second murder, the cover-up murder. When he got too close to the first murder, the one that would have exposed Jonah's corruption, Harris called the investigation off, declaring the department's morale of more importance than a life.

Now, standing on Harris's doorstep, hearing him talk about trust almost made Kyle laugh. Harris didn't trust him; he just figured he could manipulate him.

"My son's ambition twisted his perspective, but I don't believe he has turned into a vindictive man. However, I have not seen him in some months." He lifted the cane off the floor, stamped it down again. "As you can see, I am unable to make the journey. If you would like to see him for yourself, I will arrange it. That's the best I can do."

"Thank you, sir. That's more than I expected." *And why offer this?* Did Harris hope sentiment would override logic or that Kyle might believe justice was done if he saw Jonah incarcerated? Kyle didn't pity criminals. Yes, environment made some, but Jonah chose.

"Do you have a phone number?"

Kyle gave him his cell number. Then, Harris turned and shut the door, off to placate his wife, no doubt. Kyle returned to his car, put it in gear, and drove out of the gated community toward the city, so absorbed in his thoughts that the green Honda behind him just looked like a shadow.

CHAPTER 17
Kyle

Kyle needed leverage. Harris would get him into the prison to see Jonah, but Jonah would tell him nothing if Kyle didn't have anything to bargain with, and only Jewel could give Kyle a bargaining chip. She linked Jonah inside to the Sunset Boyz outside, and even if she hadn't carried a message between them, she might know who had. Either way, he'd have something to use with Jonah, to find out if Jonah had put out a hit on his life.

Wendy had given him the address of the house where she sometimes sent girls in trouble, but he couldn't interview Jewel alone. He needed backup. Only one person in NOLA had the skills, but he and Lucas had history.

Sunday afternoons at Mama's ran on a predictable track. Everyone showed up after church, usually around one o'clock. The chicken would have been fried the night before and placed, along with plastic-wrapped salads, in the refrigerator. Cold beer chilled in a cooler on the porch, and as long as it didn't rain, everyone ate in the backyard.

He felt lucky Mama had this house. A small bequest from her father and some regular extra money from Kyle's father had allowed her to afford what she otherwise couldn't have. His father hadn't contributed much to the family over the years, but the little money he earned, he'd given them. In fact, the financial connection was the final thing that still linked his mother and father. They'd been divorced for years now, but he had insisted she use his military disability benefits to pay off the mortgage on their Garden District home.

In return, when he came by every couple weeks or so, Kyle's mama gave him food, a little money, a book or two. She cashed his checks and kept an account for him, hoping he might straighten up. Either way, he might need that money someday for medical care.

Years ago, when they were still married, she had tried to get him into AA or a VA program for alcoholics. His father just drifted back to the streets when the program was over, setting up his shelter under a bridge, making peace with other street residents, keeping to himself, mostly. Vietnam had not been kind, and his father accepted the damage as his penance for the suffering he had caused.

As a kid, Kyle felt both guilty and angry about his father, pestering his mother to *do something*. Maybe if they'd known more about post-traumatic stress or addictions, but none of that accounted for what his father wanted, which was to be left alone to numb his pain. Kyle had once thought, maybe, that becoming a police officer would provide a bridge to his father, but sometimes he thought his father might even consider Kyle's job a betrayal. Too many nights when the cops rousted them, forced them indoors, hauled someone off for a crime none of them had committed, their only crime being poor and isolated.

Kyle pushed open the gate and walked around the house to the backyard. On the porch, he pulled a beer from the cooler and twisted off the top, settling himself into one of his mother's comfortably padded wicker chairs.

They wouldn't be back for another forty-five minutes, and the peace of the garden soothed him. He hadn't had time to think for months now, not since he'd taken the new job, and had used every waking minute figuring out New England culture and Clara. It felt healing to be back in this slow rhythm. The insects buzzed, the damp slow-dripped from the leaves. Outside, a bicycle creaked by, and the neighbor's cat flapped through its pet door.

"Kyle?" He awoke with a start, his mother standing over him, her red-flowered Sunday hat still on her head. "Honey, you OK?"

"Hey, Mama." He reached up to flick her hat brim with his finger.

"What happened to your arm?" She brushed his fingers aside, gestured at the sling.

"Little dustup at work. Nothing big." She rolled her eyes. "So I'm in town on business, thought I'd stop and see the family."

"You couldn't warn us you were coming?"

Warn her? "Didn't know 'til yesterday."

"Isn't that what you have those fancy electronics for? So you can call from anywhere?"

He stood to hug her. Clara was right; there was no winning with mothers. "I know, Mama. I should have called. I didn't. I'm here now. Do I get any points for that?"

She turned toward the house. "You should have joined us at church. The others will arrive in a few minutes. Help me get these salads out."

Nope. No points. He smiled and followed her inside.

The kitchen looked the same as when he lived here as a young man, gleaming and spotless, except that the woman who ran it was aging. Something around her eyes had grown tired and softened, like a wilted leaf, and she moved as if things that didn't used to be connected on her—like her hip to her shoulder—suddenly were. How could it happen in a matter of months?

She set her hat on the counter, and dug a platter of potato salad and a bowl of coleslaw from the refrigerator. He brought them outside to the picnic table, then turned to go back for more, but she was standing behind him with a basket of rolls and the cutlery. "You're in trouble, aren't you? You said you wouldn't come back, that we would have to visit you up north, so you'd only come because you are in trouble." Her eyes and hands were steady. Too many crises managed.

"Nothing I can't handle, Mama." He said it to reassure himself as much as her.

She shook her head. "It's Jonah, isn't it? You want Lucas's help."

Mama always could read his mind. His sister's husband was a private detective. Lucas could carry a weapon.

"You might have to work for it," she commented, turning back toward the house for another load of goodies. He followed.

He hadn't been Lucas's champion, way back when. His brother-in-law was eight years younger than his sister, twenty-two when they married. Kyle hadn't believed a twenty-two-year-old knew his own mind well enough to know that he wanted to spend the rest of his life with an older woman. An older woman who wanted children right away. He had warned his sister, repeatedly. She hadn't listened.

Then, Lucas declared he wanted to be a PI. Fresh out of the military police, he had some investigative skills, but building a clientele at twenty-two with no extra-military experience and few police force contacts was a daunting task. Again, Kyle urged caution. Again, no one listened.

He had to give the kid credit. He'd worked hard, harder than many of the cops Kyle knew. He'd gone to every training he could find, joined all the organizations, attended the meetings. He'd built himself a slick-looking website, an 800 number, and an office sublet from a bunch of lawyers with a tony address. The lawyers had supported him at the start, paid for a lot of the training. Now he had a rep as the PI the best criminal defense firms wanted on their team. Kyle had been wrong, but he'd been too bull-headed to apologize, and it hummed like static between them.

"Any advice?"

She passed him a pecan cake and a basket of fried chicken. "That boy loves your sister more than I've ever seen any man love any woman. But I wouldn't appeal too much to family. You don't have a leg to stand on there."

They seemed to think he had abandoned them, left them to a police force unreliable because it was angry at one of its own: him—and by extension his family. He thought he'd gotten out of town so everyone could forget, so his family could be safe again.

"Yes, ma'am." She carried the cucumber salad and a stack of paper plates, then tipped a little and used the paper plate hand to balance herself against the counter. "You OK?"

"Just tired. I feel it more these days."

Before he could ask her what that meant, the front screen door slammed and small feet pounded toward them. "Grandmama! Guess what?!" The swinging kitchen door banged open and a small boy skidded to a stop in front of Kyle. His red shorts had a smear of dust and the matching red and white shirt hung untucked, like a tail.

"You remember your Uncle Kyle?" Kyle's mother looked down at her grandson, her affection like softly popping fireworks.

Kyle set down the food and squatted beside his nephew, holding out his hand. "Nice to see you again, Antoine." The boy shook, shyly.

"Kyle!" His sister dropped her foil-covered dish onto the counter and wrapped her arms around him. Over her shoulder, he saw Lucas watching, one corner of his mouth pinched in. He gave Mariam a good squeeze and then turned to shake Lucas's hand.

"You look good, Mari." Tall and lean, his sister epitomized one of those Egyptian goddesses, all bronzed elegance. She played it, too, wearing dramatic colors and graphic prints that sharpened her cheekbones like a knife on a whetstone.

"What are you doing here? Are you staying long?"

"I'm only in town for a couple days on business." He avoided his brother-in-law's eyes. "Had to come see my baby sister, though, and her handsome son." He put his hand on the child's head, but Antoine ducked away and wrapped his arms around his mother's leg.

"Haven't seen you in a while," commented Lucas.

Kyle wondered if it was a dig, like, *you say you care about your family, but then you move fourteen hundred miles away.*

"Starting a new job is challenging," Kyle countered, trying to moderate his tone. He couldn't afford to offend Lucas any more than he already had.

He picked up the cake and chicken. "C'mon, Antoine. Let's go see what else there is for lunch." The boy looked up at Mariam, who nodded.

Outside, they gathered around the picnic table, and Lucas said grace. The food was good; Mama's always was. They talked about the sermon and the weeks behind and ahead, the boy's school and friends. They caught him up on the family gossip—Uncle Roland's latest infidelity, Aunt Tisha's threats to boot him because this was the *last time.* All the while, Kyle felt Lucas's probing gaze, even as he ran possible approaches to getting his help. Finally, they all had a piece of pecan cake and Antoine was sent to play video games inside. Mama and Mariam were in the kitchen working on dishes, and Lucas wanted to know what was up.

"I need your help," Kyle said, appealing to his brother-in-law's competence.

Lucas leaned back in his canvas chair, draping one arm over the back. A shiny gold watch decorated his left arm. "Never thought I'd hear you say those words. Not sure I care at this point."

"I know you think I did the wrong thing, that I abandoned my family, but I'm protecting them, Lucas."

"Not from where I sit. With you in Connecticut, no one's watching. Those cops—if they wanted to harm us, who'd stop them? Mama said some thug came around last week, asking where you were."

"Who?"

"Officer O'Reilly. All professional. He wouldn't give a reason. You know what it's about?"

Buzz O'Reilly of the coffee shop, sniffing around his family.

So Kyle told him about the gang shooting, the loss of his officer, the words *car, fire, homeless, righteous;* he told him about seeing Jonah's parents, about Alec's willingness to set up a meeting with his son in jail. He explained that Jonah's sister Wendy was treating the pregnant wives and girlfriends of the Sunset Boyz, that she had given him the address of a safe house where she sometimes sent them. He wanted to check it out. He didn't want to do it alone, in case it was a trap.

"I've had a day to think on this, and my theory is Jonah's working with the Sunset Boyz. He's put a hit out on me from prison, using them to enact it, and he's paying for it in trade, by having Wendy take care of the gang's girlfriends."

"She's OK with that?"

"She's going to say no to the Sunset Boyz, when her brother is in the next cell?"

Lucas rubbed his fingers down the bridge of his nose. "Why now?"

"Don't know. Maybe it took him this long to get in with the right crowd, find someone willing. Maybe it took him this long to figure out how to pay for it."

"You think he held a grudge for that long?"

"That's why I need to talk to the girl, find out if she's carrying messages. If so, and she'll tell me their content…. You don't have to do anything but be there."

"In case some bad guy shows up."

"She came alone to Wendy's, but I'm not sure what Wendy told her. If the boyfriend's gotten wind of me, they might take this as an opportunity to finish the job."

Lucas shook his head. "I've got a son. I promised Mariam nothing stupid. This is stupid."

Kyle understood. If he had a son, he wouldn't want to jeopardize his ability to watch the boy grow up and become a man. Somehow, while Kyle had been gone, Lucas had become the man of the family. They didn't need Kyle anymore, but they needed Lucas to be the solid core. Kyle wouldn't jeopardize that.

But justice mattered. Whether people could sleep in their beds at night without fear mattered. His own life mattered to him, and he didn't particularly want to get shot again because he'd gotten surprised without backup seeing this unknown quantity of a girl—or because some idiot finally got lucky with his aim.

"You're right," Kyle said. "I shouldn't have asked." He leaned across and dropped his hand on Lucas's shoulder. "Thanks for hearing me out, though, despite our history. I appreciate someone here knowing where I'm going."

Lucas stared at him, long, thin fingers drumming on the canvas chair arm. "Lemme get this straight: You come here after trying to persuade your sister not to marry me, after not supporting my choice of profession—making it hard for me in every way you can. And now, your butt is on the line and you think it's OK to ask for my help?"

He deserved it. "Lucas, cops are trained to deal in evidence. You were young, untested. Lots of big dreams."

Lucas started to speak but Kyle stopped him. "I'm sorry I haven't supported you. I admit now that my judgment was wrong. It's taken me too damn long to get past my own prejudices to see it. I would understand if you won't, but someday, I'd like your forgiveness. Now, I'm going to get going. It's a long drive."

Lucas said, "I didn't say I wouldn't go."

"Nah. You shouldn't."

"Yeah, I should. In addition to never forgiving me if I got killed, Mariam would also never forgive me if you got killed. It's a no-win, man."

"Don't do it, I'm telling you. I'll be fine." Kyle pushed himself up from the table and looked around for his mother. The women and the boy had migrated inside where it was cooler. Maybe he could get to the safe house before dark, drive back, get out to the prison first thing in the morning. Late tomorrow afternoon, all things being equal, which they never were, he could go home to Connecticut and Clara, where he could get some distance from his past.

"There's a price."

Kyle looked down at Lucas. "What?"

"You gotta see your father."

Kyle hadn't seen his father since Katrina, when the old man had tracked him down, but Lucas knew where to find him. "I keep track for Mama."

Kyle wondered what he would say. He'd betrayed him. While he had tried to rectify it, he didn't know if his father had forgiven him. His own shame had caused him to turn his back on the man who created him.

He'd been fighting in Vietnam when Kyle was small, and when he came home, the streets took him—the streets and a country that didn't care. For a while, when he still lived with the family, his father liked to take him out in the Gulf fishing on his buddy's boat. The men drank a lot of beer and talked about stuff Kyle hadn't understood—gooks and *in country* and helos and flashbacks and dreams—scary stuff for a six-year-old boy. Those days were his fondest memories of his father, the days before he disappeared into his own guilt about whatever pain he caused in those jungles.

The other complication was his father's current state of mind. Would he be drunk or sober? Angry or peaceful?

Some days he still longed for a father, someone to show him how to live as a black man. How should he jog through a white neighborhood without being afraid? How should a boy forgive an absent father, keep himself from giving in to rage? What should a man do when he loved someone like Clara—white, privileged? How does a man negotiate his own emotions?

"He still come by once a month with his check, looking for books?" Kyle asked.

"Yeah, and she feeds him a big meal, gives him some food to take with him. Who knows how long he hangs on to it."

"He have any running buddies?"

"Couple, I think, but they're always changing. Last month it was some lady dressed all in pink, with pink hair and a little tiny dog. God knows how she manages to pay for the hair dye or actually dye it. I suppose public bathrooms work. Gotta be dedicated to pink hair to go to all that trouble."

Kyle wished he could laugh, but the idea of his father, a distinguished veteran of the Vietnam War, hanging out under an overpass with a pink-haired woman turned his stomach. He looked out the window of Lucas's Acura at the city streaming by and thought of the collection of his father's associates he'd met over the years. The faces blurred together, but the older ones always had haunted eyes, even before Katrina. Hank had served with his dad in Vietnam. Shelby's husband beat her; Lorna's child had fallen from their third-story balcony, while she'd been passed out drunk; Cleo, a man, loved other men and loved to dress as a woman, much to his family's horror.

Kyle had served at one of the soup kitchens for a while, and he'd returned to that kind of service up north. It helped. Made him feel as though he was feeding his father, even when his father was nowhere in sight.

The Acura smelled of new leather, and Lucas had music thumping softly in the background. "You nervous?" he asked. "I'm not even sure we'll find him. Last I knew he was living under the Pontchartrain overpass in a tent city. I thought they'd cleared that out, though no one ever really leaves; they just let the cops think they're going, and then they come back later, after all the fuss is over. City was threatening to put up fences, like no one homeless has ever seen a wire-cutter before." He shook his head.

They turned from St. Charles Avenue onto Calliope Street and started to scan. "He doesn't tend to wander too far, not when evening comes. He likes to settle in somewhere, read a little if he's still sober enough, fall asleep with his back to a wall." Lucas pulled into a makeshift parking place, even though he would be hard-pressed to justify it to any meter maid worth her paycheck.

"C'mon," he said. "We need to walk a little."

"You're just going to leave the car here?"

"We won't be long."

"How long do you think a car thief needs?"

"Trust me, Kyle. It will be fine. Your mama's got me out here about once a week, checking on him, so I know these guys."

Another thing Kyle should be doing himself. He tried to be grateful that Lucas had stepped up, but he could only see his own failures. Not that he'd visited much when he lived here: his father's choices felt dishonorable, something others could use against him, especially given his race. His father was just another homeless black vet who couldn't cut it with his family, which meant Kyle should be stronger, better, more responsible.

They stepped from the vehicle into the humid dusk. Heads turned to watch Kyle and Lucas, eyes glittering from the fires set up in trash barrels. Hands went up to wave, smiles creased worn faces. "Hey, El! Man, how are you?"

"What's up, Lucas?"

"You good? Family good?"

"Your dad's a couple rows over. He's pretty good tonight."

The voices rattled from the darkness like rain on a tin roof. A green Honda covered in dust rolled by.

"Guess you come here a fair amount," Kyle said, thinking how much more Lucas had seen of his father than he had. "How is Dad? Is he, I don't know, healthy? Does he have enough food and clothing?"

"Healthy as a homeless guy living under a bridge can be, I guess. He doesn't complain, unless somebody steals his stuff, which seems to happen about once a month. Then, he says, he doesn't sleep for a couple of days."

"How does Mariam handle Dad being out here? You ever talk about that?"

"Some. Your mama handles it best, suppose because she's been around it the longest. Your daddy isn't going to change. He'll even say that if you ask him. You just have to accept he's living his life the way he wants to, or the only way he can manage to keep on living."

"You think he's punishing himself? I've wondered that over the years."

"Makes a kind of sense—especially since he won't talk about it."

"Yeah, makes me nuts. We know so much more now. There's trauma therapy, medication. He could have a full life."

"That you think there are safer, healthier ways to live doesn't matter. It's his choice. Mariam tries to understand that, and some days are better than others."

"She see him at all? Does Antoine know his grandfather? Does he understand?"

Lucas stopped and turned to face him. "Those are some questions, coming from you. You ever think about your father up there in your plush New England town?"

"It's not so easy, Lucas."

He shook his head, but less in anger than frustration. "Do you think Antoine should know his granddaddy?"

"He's your son; it's your decision. I don't even know how I feel about it myself. I guess that's why I'm asking."

He ran his hand over his face. "We haven't decided yet. We've told him his grandfather is homeless, that he *chooses* to be homeless, but we haven't brought him here. Seems like a lot for a little kid to handle. Then again, kids tend to handle things better than adults. Mostly it's Mariam who's not ready, and it's her decision. Antoine will start to ask more questions soon, but for now, he doesn't get it."

Kyle felt his phone buzz. He pulled it out to find a text from Joe.

2 MORE DRIVEBYS

ONE INJURED

SB THOT 2B KILLING OWN MMBRS

COULD USE INPUT

SB. Sunset Boyz. *Dammit.* If the Sunset Boyz were doing drive-bys in his town, he needed to get home.

WILL CALL WITHIN HOUR, he texted back, then shoved the phone back in his jacket pocket.

"Where's Dad?" he asked Lucas.

"Everything OK?"

"I've got a situation developing. Honestly, I shouldn't even be in NOLA. If I don't get back, my 'plush' job probably won't be mine much longer."

Lucas nodded. "Let's get on it then. Dad's usually over here." He led Kyle toward a bridge abutment. At its base clustered some small tents and large cardboard boxes.

CHAPTER 18
Clara

I had the dream again that night, the dream about Vlad's grandson. Only Vlad didn't have a grandson. There he was in school, passing out drugs like doctor's office lollipops, pink for the little girl, purple for the little boy, each a color to match their outfit, to turn their tongues and lips into an unnatural rainbow. As they dropped the sweets onto their fragile tongues and I screamed, pounding on the invisible wall between sleep and consciousness, they swallowed and then fell into little rainbow-colored heaps, body upon body upon body, until the pile was as high as the St. Louis arch, and the pot of gold at the grandson's feet filled to overflowing.

I woke with my chest heaving and my hands curled in fists. Dark still curtained the window, with only a red outline on the horizon. Shaking, I put on my robe and slippers and went downstairs for coffee, which I took into the solarium for solace.

What did the dream mean?

Vlad didn't have a son or a grandson, as far as I knew, but maybe he treated someone as a son, perhaps even Evangelia's husband. Maybe I could probe a little when I saw her today; Ernie had vetted her landscape plans, but we'd adjusted some plant choices and dimensions, so I had to talk her through the changes. We had an appointment for nine; would seeing Lia and her daughter again reveal a connection some part of me had intuited?

I should also talk to Paul; he had helped with my dreams when Mother was in danger, and he'd asked that I apprise him of any repeating dreams. I'd ended up hospitalized before, the dreams about my father's death having driven me nearly to suicide. But these didn't seem so perilous for my own mental health. Sure, they cost me—in sleep, in worry, in not being able to protect Kyle because I couldn't figure them out—but I hadn't yet experienced any of the physical symptoms that sometimes assailed me: physical weakness, disorientation, hallucinations. Maybe I'd be lucky enough to escape those side effects this time. I couldn't afford to lose the time at the office; the economic downturn had undermined our client base. So I needed to talk to Paul. He would help me to stave off any symptoms; I made a mental note to call him later. I needed to apologize anyway. I'd left the rift between us alone for too long. And maybe after that, I would call Bailey again.

Mother always said that a woman should dress the way she wants to feel, not how she actually feels. Going to Vlad's provoked a desire for a suit of armor, but black jeans and boots with a black wool jacket and a pink and white striped silk blouse would have to suffice: professional, unafraid.

When I arrived, Vlad was there as well, in cowboy boots, black jeans, and a brilliant turquoise shirt with neon green suspenders dotted with pink and red stars. Only someone pretty scary could retain respect in that get-up.

We spent forty-five minutes hunched over the kitchen island, drinking Lia's heady espresso and going over the plans and the adjustments until I had explained everything to their satisfaction. I noted where we'd suggested border gardens, where the paths would go, how we would structure runoff, where we would build walls and put in trees for shade and anchoring.

Lia murmured her approval, adding a couple of minor changes, and finally sighed in delight. "It's better than I imagined, Clara. Thank you!"

"Does your husband also wish to look at the plans?"

"My husband doesn't care," Lia said. "He probably won't even notice the new garden for a year. 'Did you move a deck chair or something?'" She parodied a man's voice, laughed. Vlad didn't. His eyes followed her, and he frowned, a swath of tornado clouds across his features. He caught my eye, stared me down.

"You can start the job any time," she said.

The little girl played alone by the fireplace behind us, the television on low to a cartoon with brightly colored animals speaking in high-pitched voices. Once in a while, she would mimic one of the characters, making the dolls she was dressing and undressing speak. She seemed perfectly content; I wondered at her life in this house with the father who didn't notice things, imagined Lia doted on her, and Vlad too. I wondered if Vlad wished for a grandson; maybe that's what I was picking up on.

"Do you want children?" Lia asked, seeing me watch her daughter. Vlad turned from his granddaughter to wait for my answer.

"Your daughter is beautiful," I said, "but I wouldn't make a good mother."

"I'm sure you would," she said politely, but she couldn't know. I could barely keep up with the attention my friends and colleagues needed, never mind something small that needed me twenty-four hours a day.

"People want different things in their lives. Perhaps you want something other than a family." She smiled. "Some days I wish I didn't have one, to be as free as you are."

Even alone, traveling, doing as I wished, I hadn't felt free. I felt obligated to make my life meaningful, manage my loneliness, confirm my next hotel reservation. I understood how untethered I'd been. But now, my list of obligations stretched miles—to Ernie, my employees, Kyle, my mother, Richard and Paul and Bailey, my clients, myself. Sometimes, it so threatened me, I almost couldn't breathe. Perhaps she could see all that on my face, as she cocked her head in sympathy.

Vlad just watched.

I said, "At the moment, I run a business—but freedom is enticing." More days than I could count, I wanted to drop everything and buy an open-ended first-class ticket.

"Do you want more children?" I asked Lia.

She shook her head. "One is enough, although my father would like a grandson, right, Papa? His one girl had one girl."

There was my answer.

He was nearly tender with her. "I love my girls. Wouldn't trade them for anything."

Even I could hear the longing.

She hugged him. A woman, affectionate and pretty, hugged Vlad the Impaler and he smiled. Watchfully.

She said, "Boys are different. Boys carry your *name* forward in the world. Girls only carry your blood."

He tapped his finger on the counter, the nail softly clicking like a metronome. "Names mean something, little girl. Never forget that. We are who we are because of history, because someone before us did something that made room for us in the world. Made enough money to have another child, invented a drug to save a life, learned about cooking meat to kill bacteria." The tapping finger moved to the back of her hand, but gently, as if they'd had this conversation many times already. "You are a product of history—the world's and mine. It is not vain to wish mine to continue."

"Of course not, Papa." She smiled again, but seemed tired, and I wondered if she felt the need to resist him. Perhaps her trying for a boy had become a sticking point between them. A boy might be expected to take on the family business, and perhaps Lia wanted to save her children from that fate.

I looked over again at the girl. She turned then, and I saw in her face the face of the boy in my dream: big brown eyes, brown curls, sweetheart smile, pale soft skin. Could my feeling be Lia's fear that her daughter would grow up to follow in her grandfather's footsteps? Perhaps Vlad didn't care who took over the business, male or female. Perhaps he just needed an heir. Maybe Lia herself was involved in the business, though I found that hard to imagine. Or maybe the son-in-law was the heir apparent, and I was conflating the granddaughter and her father.

"What kind of work does your husband do?" In for a penny, in for a pound.

Vlad looked at me again, assessing. "My son-in-law owns a construction company," he said, "but he occasionally substitutes as a manager in some of my clubs. You met him the other night."

"Oh!" I hiccupped in air, coughed. The manager. This beautiful woman had married that sleazy, scarred man? Why?

The fire in the fireplace suddenly seemed to increase the room temperature ten degrees.

More disturbing was that Moscarelli had told Vlad about Paul, Richard, and me and, presumably, about our interest in gang members selling drugs.

"He knows when to bear down hard and when to go easy. I could hire him full-time, but he likes his independence. Most people do, until they find themselves in a difficult spot. Then they want help. You know what I'm saying?"

I willed myself not to step back. "I find it's best to allow my employees to try things first before I 'bear down,' as you say. They often find their way without my help."

He smiled, but it wasn't pretty.

I tried another tack. "It was a nice club, but I doubt I'll go back, sadly. It was rather young for me and my friends, and partying isn't my scene."

"Yet you chose to go out with your friends on a weeknight?"

"I was bored. Your daughter's project will prevent further boredom I'm sure." I held his gaze through this interchange while Lia watched us.

"Very good. It is bad to be bored. Sometimes it gets people in trouble."

"Sure." I nodded, pretended it was an abstract observation.

God, I hated these conversations, everything masked and cloaked like we were playing CIA/KGB games during the Cold War. Why had I agreed to help Bianca? Then the smell of Dom's blood on my clothes and hands came back, sharp and bitter, and I knew I wouldn't stop, no matter what anyone said.

I rolled up the garden plans, sliding them into a cardboard tube for carrying. Conscious of Vlad at my back, and wishing nothing more than to get away, I held my hand out to Lia. "I'd better run along. Crews and equipment should arrive by the beginning of next week. Let me know if you need to change the start date. I look forward to working with you." The professional phrases rolled rotely off my tongue.

Before long I was outside in the cool air, breathing, wondering if, even now, I could justify to myself getting out of this job. Vlad and I were fencing, and the little pinpricks stung. As I drove to the office, I tried to let the clean air blow my reservations away, but they clung, like smashed bugs to a windshield.

The third shock of the day, after the dream and Vlad's cloaked threats of violence, came in the form of Teo, twitchy and pacing back and forth across reception at Montague and Brown. Therese sat quietly in one of our black leather chairs, looking at a picture book. His hands were jammed in the pockets of his red hoodie, his jeans slung low on his hips. No kitten this time. The thick hair fell across his face, and he pushed at it impatiently. Something about him reminded me of a sheathed knife.

Shona looked relieved to see me. I knew I would get some static for my new class of "friends." She had standards, our Shona. I could see the middle-aged church lady forming in her already. Not that I blamed her. Teo arriving at my office made me feel like I was being watched.

"Teo. You here for me?"

"Oh, yeah. Yeah. You gotta minute?"

"Come in."

He hesitated, looking at his daughter, then at Shona, who allowed brief annoyance to flutter across her face. "Bring her with you," I said. "She was no trouble last time. Shona, perhaps you could get Therese a cookie. Anything for you, Teo?"

"We won't be long."

I gestured to my office door, and he picked up his daughter and followed me through. I shut the door behind him, wondering if it was a good idea, and let him choose a seat. He sat on one of the couches, his leg bouncing, his eyes rimmed red. Therese opened her book. It had photographs of animals, mostly large cats: panthers, lions, Siberian white tigers.

I sat behind my desk—using it as a protective barrier—and dropped my purse into a drawer and Lia's landscape plans onto the desktop.

"What can I do for you?" I looked up, caught my breath. How could I not have seen it? Pink and purple lollipops. Children. Schools.

Teo was talking. I tried to catch up.

"—and you just can't go doing things like that. You're going to get yourself in trouble." He tapped his fingers on his knees, as if the energy was so overpowering, he had to let it out, somewhere, anywhere, even in a drum beat on his body. I could almost feel it on my own.

"Back up. What are you talking about?"

"The club. Moscarelli is furious. He thinks you're going to rat us out to the 5-0." He pinned me in a glare.

Us.

"Moscarelli thinks I'm going to rat him out to the cops for what?"

"You accused him of dealing." He moved forward on the couch and I forced myself not to move back, toward the window.

I looked at Therese, wondering how much she understood. "Wasn't he?"

"Oh, miss. You just can't say things like that." He pushed his thick hair back off his face. It fell forward again.

"I saw you leaving, you know."

He leaned in suddenly, angry, his body stiff like a Magritte figure. "I'm an errand boy. I bring messages. That's it." He sliced his hand sideways, as if chopping a head from its body.

Unlikely, since at twenty-five, he'd been in the gang for more than ten years. "What message?"

"How would I know? It's done the old-fashioned way—a sealed envelope that they burn after it's read."

I laughed. "For real? That's so… pirate."

Startled, he grinned for a moment, a flash across his face, and I could see he was still a child, as if being part of the gang had both shot him into early adulthood and stunted his emotional growth. Therese poked him. "Look, Daddy. A lion. Grrr!"

He softened, calmed. "That's right, baby girl. Just like that kitten I brought you." He settled his hand on her head, but she twisted from under it, turned the page to the next beast.

"Mommy doesn't want the kitten," she mumbled, rubbing her hand across the lion picture. "But I *love* her."

I said, "OK, he's upset with me. Should I be concerned?" First Vlad, now Moscarelli. I fought to keep my hands and body placid, to communicate a lack of fear I didn't feel.

"He wants someone to send you a message."

"What kind of message, Teo? I don't know what that means."

"You know." He looked frustrated. "Send you a *message*. Put a scare on you."

"How might they do that?"

"Break into your house. Jack your car. Beat up somebody you love."

I stared at him. Bianca had *begged* me to clear her brother's name. Now, her boyfriend's gang was going to beat up my family and friends? Moscarelli had threatened Richard and Paul. Thugs like Moscarelli often targeted gay men. I felt myself start to panic.

"Jack your car," the little girl singsonged, turning the pages.

Teo looked momentarily disconcerted.

I forced my question through the red swirling in front of my eyes. "So who exactly thinks it's a good idea to hurt people who ask questions?"

He shrugged. "My boss."

"Your gang killed Dom. Your child's mother asked for my help clearing her brother's name. You've come to me today—at my place of business. What do you want if not to help me?" I paused, but he stayed silent. "So, Moscarelli? Is that your boss?"

"Sure." As if I would believe him.

"Moscarelli is the part-time manager, when he's not running his own company. So either the guy that runs that club full-time is your boss, or the guy you were bringing messages to and from is your boss. I'm guessing I know who he is. Am I right?"

He looked again at his daughter, and the pink and purple flashed in the corners of my vision. "You're talking in riddles, miss. I'm just trying to help you."

I let him sit with his lie for a minute, tapping out sixty counts on my knee, invoking the Montague spine. Then I snapped, "Oh, give me a break. You've come here—and why would you do that, unless it was to help Bianca?—so be straight with me."

The knife-edged rage contained just under Teo's thin skin hardened his features.

I held up the cardboard tube of plans. "Vlad Espejo is your boss. I was just at his house. He warned me off, too, although not in so many words."

How was bravado a good idea? I needed my head examined. I needed that appointment with Paul.

His tension shifted its focus. "You talked with Espejo?" He leaned forward, his palms open on his knees as if in supplication.

"Not my favorite experience."

He shook his head. "I've never met him."

Of course he hadn't. If Vlad knew what I now knew, what I had realized, it would change everything. Still, he hadn't answered my question about his boss.

"Count yourself lucky. What do you want from me?"

"Stop looking into Dom's death. No matter what Bianca says, Dom isn't going down because of me. Five-oh never think anything bad about themselves. Stupid of her to ask you."

I wondered why he'd suddenly decided that Dom's reputation was off the hook when, just a few days ago, he had been frantic to prove the opposite.

I shrugged. "How do I convince them I'm backing off?"

"Will you?"

He looked relieved, suddenly put his arm around his daughter's shoulders and hugged her, as if it were she who had been threatened. Maybe she had been.

How could he stay in the gang with that beautiful little girl to care for? I couldn't imagine Bianca wanted him on the streets. What must it cost her to love him? How would she feel if she knew what I had suddenly apprehended, that Teo was Vlad's son? And could I use that information to get Vlad to back off or to protect Kyle?

I needed time to think. Telling Teo might protect him from the threats to his family, if he'd received them. Did Vlad know Teo was his son? Who was Teo's mother and where was she? Was any part of Teo's story about his own parents true? Teo said he'd never met Espejo, but that didn't mean

Espejo had never seen his son. Even if he had, he might not have recognized the physical similarities unless he'd been looking for them. I hadn't seen it until the dreams put it front and center.

What about Moscarelli? I thought about his nasty red scar and his anger. If he found out about Teo, what might he do to protect his place in the family business?

"Will you?" Teo repeated, anxious.

I nodded in place of an answer. He could assume what he wanted. I refused to commit to any course of action, including backing off, until I'd had more time and more counsel. The moment the door closed, I called Joe and told him everything.

CHAPTER 19
Kyle

Unable to face his father, Kyle hadn't seen him since just after Katrina. Just as with the woman at the Rowayton car fire, he'd given in to stereotypes. How could a homeless man know anything useful? Now, as he approached the small cluster of tents, he wondered if he could see his father as a human being, forgive him for being absent, and forgive himself for acting out his anger.

Kyle noticed the smell first: old urine and body odor with some wet dog and rotting canvas thrown in for good measure. Over that lay a thin veneer of diesel exhaust, all packed into a space that should have been well ventilated but probably never really aired out.

The three faces in front of him didn't express any emotion at all, as if their quota had been used up, and only a blankness remained. Somewhere, they'd found some aluminum lawn chairs with most of the straps still intact and grouped them in a circle around a box, on top of which stood a bottle of cheap gin and some playing cards. Sure enough, the pink-haired woman sheltered her tiny dog in her lap, and a man with a grey baseball cap wore a faded green sweatshirt about three sizes too big for him. At least his father had friends. That comforted Kyle.

Then Kyle realized with a start his father didn't recognize him, and a spurt of shame zipped through him.

"Hey, Pop. Long time."

His father stared at him, then hopped to his feet to grab Kyle in a hug. "What happened to your arm, son? It's so good to see you."

"A work thing, Pop. No biggie."

Kyle smelled the alcohol on his father's breath, wondered how early in the day he started, if he was eating anything. His body still had some strength, not like those old drunks he used to roust who could barely stand because alcohol had wasted away their muscles.

Then he wondered when his father had last showered, and if his father's smell would stick to Kyle's clothes. His old anger took over. Sure, he'd let Kyle's mom have his money, but that wasn't the same as being around for questions about how to handle girls or the bully on the track team, or to protect his family. Wasn't that a man's job?

He tamped down the sudden attack of bitterness. What had Lucas thought this meeting would accomplish? It wasn't like their relationship was going to get better. They didn't even have a relationship.

His father stepped back. "Sit down, sit down." He gestured to his own chair, the only remaining unfilled one.

"It's OK, Pop. You sit. I'm good." But his father insisted, and Kyle realized it was the only gift he could give his son.

Kyle sat, and his father hovered. Lucas receded into the background, while still standing in the exact same space. Something about the quality of energy, as if he had dimmed his own lights, so the spotlight focused on Kyle.

His father introduced his friends, Joelle, the pink-haired lady, and her dog Titus, and Lawrence, the sweatshirt man. Lawrence was a veteran; Joelle had a mean old man. Same stories Kyle had heard a thousand times.

What was wrong with humanity that we still couldn't get it right, after all these centuries of trying?

"What you doin' in town? Visitin' your mama? That good woman still takes care of me, even though I don't deserve it."

"'Course you deserve it, Pop. Everyone deserves it."

His father shook his head, rubbed his finger down the front of the brown corduroys he wore. They must be stiflingly hot, Lawrence's sweat-shirt, too. Maybe you never got warm when you lived outside.

"Nice of you to come see me. You haven't done that in a long time."

"I know, Pop. I'm sorry about that, but you and me..." He shrugged. What was he supposed to say? That he forgave his father? He didn't even know if that was possible.

"I know," his father said softly, retreating a few paces. "I haven't lived up to my responsibilities. You right, but I can't explain it to you anymore. You're grown up. Gotta decide how you're going to live your life with me the way I am."

The shuffle, the hunched shoulders, the death grip on the bottle—all of it suddenly broke something in Kyle. Maybe he couldn't forgive his father, but he could see how much pain he was in because his son had rejected him. That impossible chasm. Neither of them could change enough to cross it, but Kyle could try to understand the horror his father had suffered in Vietnam, horror that bent his father's life in its claw.

Kyle reached his hand out. "I didn't come to make you feel bad. I came because I wanted to see you." A good lie. "And I came about that old case. The one you helped me with, remember?"

His father fixed his eyes on Kyle. "The one you didn't believe me about."

"I was an arrogant little prick." Kyle dropped his hand, smiled.

His father let out a snort. "That you were. You almost got me killed. Got a friend a mine killed too."

He felt the emotion rush up through him, steam through a kettle spout. "I'm ashamed about that. I don't expect you to forgive me, but I'm trying to do better." He was, wasn't he?

He tried to remember a moment when his father had been present, in the house. When they had been a family. He couldn't. It had always been just him and Mama and Mariam.

"Well, we both lost someone, didn't we? A toast to the lost." He picked up the bottle, held it out. Kyle hesitated, and his father smiled slowly. He pulled a none-too-clean rag from his pocket and ran it over the mouth of the bottle. Held it out again. "None of us is sick, but, you know. Just in case."

Kyle bristled. He wasn't a prig. "Lucas and I have to talk to someone after this, that's all." But he took the bottle and had a swallow. It was harsh and strong, and he had to keep himself from coughing.

His father laughed. "You outta practice." He held the bottle out to Lucas, who swigged easily, then grinned at Kyle.

"I'm not easy to love," he said. "I appreciate that your mama and you all still takin' care of me. It's more than I deserve. But I deserved more from Uncle Sam too, and just because I live on the streets doesn't mean I'm stupid. I've never been stupid. You should know that. When my friend told me that story, and then went missing, well, you should'a done something about it. You could have helped." He switched his weight from one foot to the other.

"It was already too late, Pop, to save him. You know that. At least we found out what happened."

"I know. I know. Barry saw that Jonah kill the boy. He was a witness, and Jonah didn't want no witnesses. I got that. But Barry's family—and we're his family too—" he waved his hand at Lawrence and Joelle and, presumably, the dog, "we worried for a long time. We shouldn't have had to wait that long, be treated as less important than those fancy people in their mansions who ended up with a little water in their basements and not much more."

"I wish we could have proved that part of the case. I wish I'd found your friend—Barry—sooner, that I'd known there was a witness. It would give justice to that young man's family; they've never had it."

"You know why Jonah did it?"

"I do now." Kyle told his father what Jonah's sister had told him about the rape.

Joelle stroked her dog and studied the cards. Lawrence disappeared into the tent.

"You can't get him for that because you have no evidence, right?"

"That's right."

His father took another pull on the bottle, wiping his mouth thoughtfully. "You know, my friend, he said something funny before he disappeared. He said he'd seen your cop friend down there a lot, poking around, almost like he was looking for something. Can't imagine what anyone thought they might find after that flood. She tore outta here with everything anybody'd ever owned."

Kyle sat up in the lawn chair, hoping none of the straps gave way. "You think he'd been searching for the man he killed? It wasn't a *wrong time, wrong place* kind of thing?"

His father nodded slowly. "Think so."

Kyle stared at him. It wouldn't change Jonah's punishment—he'd been given a long sentence—but it did reinforce Kyle's instinct about Jonah's hidden, darker self. It also made it even more possible that Jonah had put a hit on Kyle for revenge or for fun or just to even the score because he now had access to the kind of people who would kill for him.

The information shook Kyle. He'd accepted that he hadn't truly known Jonah— apparently, no one had. But what had all those barbeques and beers after work meant? Why choose Kyle as a friend? Had Jonah been working some agenda other than promotion?

Shame washed through him again. What a gullible pup he'd been, lapping up the attention of the superintendent's son, the little black plantation kid looking to make his master happy. His stomach twisted.

"That helps a lot, Pop." Kyle looked up at Lucas, who nodded. "We gotta get going. We have a long ride to talk to some more people." He stood.

"You OK, son?" His father shuffled toward him, put his hand briefly on Kyle's shoulder and then removed it, as if afraid his son would brush it off.

Kyle caught his hand and pulled his father into another hug. "I'll be all right, Pop. Thanks for asking." He stepped back. "You need me, Lucas will always know where I am, OK?"

He nodded. "I know."

Kyle patted his father's arm once more, and turned to follow Lucas to the car, feeling his father's eyes on his back and wondering how it felt to be left to drink under the freeway in a lawn chair by your only son—even if it was your choice.

The hour and a half to the bayou would give him time to make calls while Lucas drove. Work would help him put aside the anger he felt at learning Jonah had lied about something else, and the shame he felt at abandoning his father. Or was he ashamed about Jonah and angry at his father? He understood his father's reasons—in his head—but why choose a decrepit lawn chair when he could live in a beautiful home surrounded by people who loved him? Yes, he knew his father felt he didn't deserve it, but who did? No one deserved the universe's generosity, but what fools were those who didn't give thanks for all they'd been given.

"It's hard seeing him that way," Lucas said, reading Kyle's mind.

"It's been hard every day of my life."

"Hard to accept other people's choices, especially when they don't fit our own preconceptions."

Kyle looked over at Lucas, feeling himself ready for a fight. "You making a point?"

Lucas grinned. "No way, man. Just chatting." He took his hand off the wheel to wave at Kyle's phone. "Make your calls."

Kyle shook his head, pulled back from his anger. Blowing up at Lucas wouldn't help anything, especially when he was being more generous than Kyle had any right to expect. He turned on his phone. Joe first.

He looked at the text again: 2 MORE DRIVEBYS

ONE INJURED

SB THOT 2B KILLING OWN MBRS

COULD USE INPUT

So his troops thought the Sunset Boyz were killing their own? Why would they do that?

He dialed Joe after a quick scroll through Twitter. "Everything seems quiet on social media. What's up?"

"I don't know what feed you're looking at, but gang war is brewing in Stamford. It's not our patch, but SPD is convinced Dom's murder set it off."

"The shooting and car fire were payback?"

"SPD thinks it's some kind of internal spat."

"Where'd the shooting happen?"

"Stamford, thankfully, west side, south of I-95."

Not thankfully it had happened, but that it had happened in a town with better resources to handle it.

"They think our case is connected?"

"Trevor has seen cars cruising neighborhoods by the train station, and down the Post Road, late three nights this week."

"Did you put on an extra patrol?" The last thing he needed was the gangs invading his town. He could see the headlines: *New Top Cop Lets Gangs in Back Door.*

"Wasn't sure about the budget, but I will."

"I'll worry about the budget when I get back." The council would pay for this. Gangs scared rich white people more than almost anything except drops in the stock market. "You think they're looking to expand?"

"Maybe. Some want to, some don't."

"Why wouldn't they?" People always wanted more power and money.

"Too much territory to control effectively. New cops to figure out. Why branch out? People come to them. Stamford's not far."

"That takes us back to me as the target, Dom's death as a mistake setting off the war because someone had to pay for the mistake, and then the other idiots had to pay back for the payback... What a mess. Does no one learn from *Romeo and Juliet?*"

Joe laughed. "Do they even still teach that in school? *West Side Story,* maybe."

"Yeah." Kyle looked out the window and thought about family feuds, thought a family feud might cost him everything, felt fear drop some ice into his anger.

"How you making out down there?"

Joe's voice had a challenge Kyle didn't like, but maybe he was just pissed off at everyone. "On our way to talk to a source."

"You got backup?"

"My brother-in-law's a PI, Joe." But he checked his side-view mirror anyway. Green Honda, panel van, two semis—and about forty other cars. Too many to tell if they had a tail, but he should watch.

"Hey, just looking out for my job." His laugh sounded forced. Before Kyle could ask, Joe said, "Have you spoken to Clara?"

"Not recently. Why?" *What now?*

"She's been approached twice now by Teo Welles. First time, he told Clara he needed her help because no one would believe Dom was innocent if they knew he and Dom were friends. Second time, he told her to back off."

Kyle felt his gut jump. "He threatened her? She OK?" What could he even do? He couldn't leave New Orleans, not yet.

"Shaken, but fine."

"She agree to his demands?"

"What do you think?"

Kyle sighed. "Right. I'll call her, see if I can get her to quit looking into things." Like that would ever happen. And her dreams always complicated matters. "Is she muddying the investigation?"

"Not as far as we can tell. We're not even sure how much of a player Welles is. Sunset Boyz are definitely selling X and a couple other substances out of that club; Stamford's been monitoring them for a few months now, trying to trace the supply chain, see if they can nail some of the higher-ups. For the moment, Welles seems to be nothing more than a messenger boy, but he's a bit old for that."

Kyle could almost hear Joe shrug.

It meant they had nothing, which took Kyle back to the "car fire" reference. Even if no one in NOLA or at Jonah's federal prison had it in for him, even if Jonah proved to be oblivious, maybe Jonah had told the story of why he was in jail, and one of his new jailbird friends had talked. Maybe the gang wanted Kyle gone for reasons of its own. If he could figure out the beginnings of this telephone game, he could trace it all the way back home. All the way, maybe, to Vlad Espejo.

"Here's the thing, though. Clara thinks Welles is Espejo's son. She's pretty sure Welles doesn't know; he claims never to have met Espejo. Not sure there's anything there but some family drama, but figured I'd pass it along."

More family drama, as if negotiating his sister's anger, his mother's disappointment, and his father's neglect weren't enough. While Teo Welles centered the drama at home, how did he connect to New Orleans? Those words—car, fire, homeless, righteous—they formed the link, if he could only find it. What did "righteous" mean, anyway? A personality trait? Righteous, as in solid? As in virtuous or moral?

"You still there, boss?"

Kyle pulled himself out of his musings, thought about Joe's frustrated tone of voice. "You getting any pushback about my absence?"

"It's not great."

"Who's asking?"

"Not the guys. I told them it was a personal thing. But the Town Council? Mitzy Hellernan must have been in here three times already." He sighed. "That woman gives me hives."

Kyle laughed. She gave him hives too. "I'm sorry, man. Just a couple more days. Try to hold the hordes off for me? I really appreciate you picking up the slack; you know that, right?"

"Wish you'd tell me what was going on."

He couldn't, not yet. He didn't know anything for sure. "I'll call tomorrow."

Next up Oz for some background on the resident of the house where they were headed, but Oz didn't have any, other than the name Kyle already had, Fredericka Toussaint. No police record. She owned the place—not much to own—and she'd lived there a decade, give or take, on her own.

Kyle shut down the phone and tucked it into his jacket pocket.

"Everything OK?" Lucas stared into the dusk ahead. They'd exited the interstate twenty minutes ago, heading for the address Wendy had given him in Chauvin, on Highway 56.

"I don't know." Kyle leaned back in the seat. "It's complicated."

"Women generally are."

He ignored the dig. "It's more than that. I don't know if I'm doing the right thing. Maybe my officer's death has nothing to do with what happened after Katrina."

"Won't know 'til you check it out."

"Ain't that the way we always get into trouble."

"Trouble's what you signed up for. And you're not much for backing down."

"Can't."

"Right." Lucas spun the wheel, pulled off the road. "I think we're here."

CHAPTER 20
Kyle

The mustard yellow house sat up on concrete blocks, as if that would protect it from the water that glimmered flat and menacing in the near distance. The area around it lay empty, scrub trees and narrow little spits of land between washes of water. It was a poor area, given to shrimping and salt. Things looked pretty ramshackle against the majesty of the gulf, but then most working oceanfront communities looked that way.

The house hadn't seen any maintenance since whenever it was built, which could have been three weeks or fifty years ago. A four-wheeler sat in the yard, and a ladder leaned against the front window. A red plastic gas container, an old radio, and a garbage can hung around the wooden front steps like three guys on a lazy Saturday afternoon. A lawn mower was shoved partly under the front of the house. Shredded plastic waved from the windows, as if to ward off evil spirits, and a set of Tibetan prayer flags spun in the breeze from the porch to the lone tree in the yard. Next to the house, herbs and seedlings already grew in a substantial garden. Two cars sat parked haphazardly in front. Kyle wondered if one belonged to some-one who wanted kill him.

"You stay here," Kyle said. "No need to spook them more than we need to. I've got your number pulled up, like we agreed."

Lucas nodded, and Kyle got out, checking the distance for other cars, but the road was as empty as the expanse of water.

A dark-haired, dark-skinned woman opened the door cradling a shot-gun. She had the regal look of a healer, face in repose, waiting.

"I'm looking for Jewel," he said. "I'm not here to hurt her." He just needed her to tell him something he could use to get Jonah to talk.

"I'm looking for your ID, Mr. Cop-man." Her voice sounded like honey melting on gravel.

He sighed. He didn't hide who he was, but people were always so proud they'd figured out he was a police officer, like it was a special skill or some kind of second sight. He pulled his badge out slowly, held it toward her. She scanned it. "It says Connecticut."

"That's right."

After a moment, she handed it back to him, stood aside. Basically a living area and a bedroom, the shabby but clean space was well stocked with windows across the back that brought in the stern, unforgiving light off the water. The window frames were rotting along the bottoms; grey and green linoleum covered the floor. A set of sage-colored chairs crowded an oak table with a full napkin holder and a set of salt and pepper shakers to mark its center. Jewel sat on a nubbled green couch, a large cup of what looked like chocolate milk in front of her on the coffee table. She huddled, her elbows tucked over her rounded belly, her chin in her fists, as if to protect the child she was growing. The woman set her shotgun behind the door and pointed to the single chair opposite the couch with a caned seat and a high ladder back, guaranteed to make him uncomfortable.

He extended his hand. "You know my name." He knew hers too, but better if she introduced herself. He needed her to feel some control, so she wouldn't need the gun.

"Fredericka Toussaint." She gripped his hand hard, like a man.

He sat, addressed the girl. "How you doing, Jewel?

The girl studied the cup, acted as if she hadn't heard him, as if she could pretend he didn't exist. He felt exhaustion first, that this was how it would go, and then the part of him that had dealt before with reluctant witnesses took over.

Continue to address her by name. Appeal first to her better self. "Jewel, I need your help."

Fredericka guarded the door near the gun, glancing every so often out the window, as if she were expecting someone or just making sure Lucas didn't do anything sneaky. Kyle's antenna prickled. He hoped Lucas was checking his mirrors.

Jewel looked up from studying the cup of chocolate. "Why am I gonna do that." It wasn't a question.

"Good question."

"That's your pitch? It's a lame one, mister." Haiti whispered in her voice.

"What would make it better?"

"Not givin' you nothin'."

Give them at least part of the truth. "Here's the thing, Jewel. I think your boyfriend put out a hit on me, a police officer. You know about it, because you know that's the reason Wendy gives you free prenatal care. If you don't tell me what your part in it is, the state can convict you of being an accessory, and they will put you in prison. When your baby comes, someone in your family will need to take care of it, and—"

"Him. It's a boy." She rubbed her hand once over her belly, as if to assure the child she knew him.

"Yes, him. Someone in your family will need to take care of him, and if there's no one in your family, the baby will go into foster care."

She reacted to his tone, shoved her chin at him, defiant. "My family will take him."

He was coming on too strong. He settled back, let his hands fall open. The girl would never talk to him if he didn't soften his attitude, but the hard, angry part of him hadn't receded enough after seeing his father. Plus, the whole situation felt off—and he wanted out as soon as he could. Who was Fredericka looking for? Still, he tried to pull back. "You're willing to give him up?"

She shrugged the teenager shrug, the one that said she didn't care what happened to her, which was true as long as no one challenged her.

He tried a different tack. "Why are you in a gang, Jewel?"

"I'm not!" Indignant. "That's just my boyfriend."

"You never hang out with his friends? Listen to them talk about what they're going to do? You don't have girlfriends who belong to other gang members?"

He heard Fredericka easing toward him across the floor, felt his spine thread with ice. He turned his chair slightly as if he were crossing his legs, to get her in better view. She stopped, rested the butt of the shotgun on the floor between her feet, her hands wrapped around the barrel to keep it upright.

"Something wrong, Miss Toussaint?" He kept his voice steady.

"Don't like you threatening my girl."

"I am merely laying out the facts as they will appear to lawyers and judges and local police officers. I want Jewel to know exactly what she's doing if she refuses to talk to me, which is perfectly within her rights."

The girl went back to studying the chocolate milk. She dunked her finger into the liquid and sucked the brown sweet off.

"It's not even his battle," she said.

"What do you mean?" An opening. He held his breath.

"It was a favor for some guy."

"Someone inside?"

"Guess so. Who else?"

Surely, he had visitors. "But you carried the message to the gang on the outside."

She dunked her finger into the cup again. Kyle took that as a yes. "What did you tell them?"

"That they had twenty-four hours to do it. Your name and where you lived. Didn't matter anyway. Anybody with Google could track you down, you're such a hero." Her sharp sarcasm bit at him.

"And after the twenty-four hours?" Could she tell him if the hit was still active?

"No idea." She shrugged again, indifferent to all life but her own.

"The payment was the care for your baby."

She looked up at Fredericka, but her face was impassive by the time he turned.

"Why was I targeted?" This was what he had come all this way to find out. What had changed since Jonah had entered prison almost three years ago?

"Nobody tells me that. I'm just an errand girl."

He studied her, feeling the tension between his shoulder blades.

She didn't like the examination. "Maybe if Xerxes was out or whatever, you know, we'd be hanging out or something. Then they say stuff like we aren't even there, just invisible, but he's inside. Anytime I talk to him, we talk in code or whispers, and he's always watching the cameras." She shook her head. "I don't know nothing."

She probably knew more than she was telling, but with Fredericka standing over him with a shotgun, he couldn't pressure her or ask her the questions that might get her to rethink her position, like what she really thought was going to happen to that baby. What kind of life would gang money buy her and her child? If that boyfriend of hers got out of prison, would she take the child and live with him, while he dealt meth or heroin or guns? When he was killed in some shoot-out, what then? Was she out of her mind?

He felt trembling in his core from controlling his frustration. He didn't understand the short-term thinking. Her world boiled down to pain, and if she could control that pain, then maybe things would be all right, even if only for a couple of hours. It was how his father lived. Kyle sometimes wondered if his dad believed he *could* live pain-free. Maybe some people had so little experience of joy that expecting it—or even looking for it—seemed futile.

He considered Jewel's vulnerabilities. The baby, the money, the loneliness. If he could get her to a police station, he could make her understand how few options she really had.

"I'd like you to come with me, back to New Orleans. Tell the police your story."

That unhunched her quick as a small, startled bird.

"No." Her fingers crabbed at each other, knocking the milk over. Fredericka dropped the shotgun against the door and retrieved a roll of paper towels from under the sink. The brown puddle spread across the little table like lava headed for the ocean. Fredericka wiped at it until all the streaks were gone, then threw the towels away in disgust. Jewel hadn't moved, as if she simply didn't know how to fix the mess she'd made. Fredericka sat next to her and the girl curled into her like a small child.

"Jewel stays here."

"I need a written statement witnessed by a police officer." He made a fist. Fredericka saw and he relaxed his hand.

"You're a police officer."

"One with authority in this jurisdiction."

"No."

"My life is at stake."

Jewel cried, "And mine isn't? What do you think they'll do if they find out I told you about the hit?"

Fredericka stroked the girl's arm and considered him with her dark eyes. "I'll come, too. Would that work, honey?"

If, as Wendy suggested, Fredericka took in a lot of girls, she understood the risks for both Jewel and her baby—and maybe to her own self for sheltering Jewel or allowing a cop into her home. Jewel admitting her role could protect them both.

"I'm not going," the girl said. "I don't care how much you threaten me. Xerxes finds out I talked to you, he'll disown me or worse. I need that money for the baby."

"I'm not threatening you, Jewel, but that's blood money you're taking."

"It's blood money or no money. What kind of job you think I can get? I don't have no high school diploma. No one wants to hire a pregnant girl, figure I'm running off the moment the baby comes." She fidgeted out from under Fredericka's arm, sat up straight as if reclaiming her identity. Agitated, she picked up the cup and waddled with it to the sink, washed it and set it on the drying rack.

He felt her slipping away, along with his chance at resolving this, at saving his own life. Maybe that's why he stood suddenly and moved into her space, even though he could see she was frightened. He put his hands on her arms, up high by the shoulders where she couldn't easily escape his grasp. Even then, even as he spoke, he knew he'd done the wrong thing. He could see it in her eyes. "Listen to me, please. I can help you. I can keep you safe."

"No!" She twisted away and darted around him, grabbing the shotgun from where it leaned by the door. She raised it in his direction, the barrel shaking.

"No, honey," Fredericka shouted, standing up with her hands out in supplication. "You put that down." He saw Fredericka reach for a cell phone on the counter.

Kyle said, "You don't want to shoot that thing in here. You'll kill me and Fredericka and hurt yourself and your baby, too. Put it down gently, and no harm done." People who shook often shot without meaning to. Their fingers slipped on the trigger. Their fingers were slicked with sweat because they were scared. Sometimes their aim was off. Sometimes it wasn't.

He didn't want to be shot. Not with a shotgun, not at close range, not at all.

"Go away. Leave me and my baby alone." She stepped toward him, using the gun to motion that he should make a wide arc around her to get to the door.

"OK, I'm leaving." He raised his hands and moved as she'd indicated toward the door. He felt behind his back for the doorknob and twisted, opening it gradually and backing out, even backing down the steps to the scrappy front lawn. As he moved away, she followed, matching him step for step until she was at the top of the stairs and he almost to the car. Even from there, he could see the gun trembling in her hands.

Please let me make it, please let me make it, he chanted in his head. He'd seen Dom bleed out, and that was with medical help only a few minutes away. Here, there was nothing for miles. He didn't even know if there was a hospital within an hour. He would die for sure, with a hundred stupid small pellets lodged in his gut. If he didn't die, she could blind him—or a hundred other horrible things.

He hoped Lucas was making himself a small target. His sister would never forgive him if Lucas was hurt. He would never forgive himself.

"What's your problem?" she demanded. "Get in the car and get out of here."

Fredericka's silhouette darkened the door behind her.

His hands were still in the air. "I'm going. I'm just reaching for the car door." He lowered his left hand. Fredericka said something he couldn't hear and reached for the gun from behind Jewel.

That's when the gun went off.

Kyle ducked into the car, and Lucas hit the gas, spinning them out of the drive and back toward the highway.

"You hit?"

"Don't think so." He couldn't feel anything. Was that good or bad?

Lucas glanced over at him. "I don't see any blood." He checked the rearview mirror. "No one seems to be following us."

"Did you think that little pregnant girl was going to chase us down the road with her shotgun?" Sarcasm made him feel more in control.

"Never know. Cajuns can be crazy."

Kyle snorted, twisted to look back, still amped up on adrenaline. "Damn. She wasn't even Cajun. What was she thinking?"

A green Honda pulled out of a side street behind them.

"Not much, I imagine. She was all fear."

He tried to relax back into the seat. "What an irony—not shot by the gang, but by their little girlfriend. Pregnant girlfriend. Probably never fired a gun before in her life." He shook his head.

"You get what you need from her?"

"Not much I didn't know before. She carried the message to the gang on the outside from boyfriend Xerxes. Unclear why the boyfriend would put a hit on me. Twenty-four hours to do it. No idea of money or what happens after the time's up. She won't make a statement. Looks like I gotta go meet Xerxes." He sighed, moved in his seat to make sure there were no delayed pains, felt his arm twinge. "Anywhere around here we can get a Coke? I'm suddenly thirsty as hell."

"Sure," Lucas said, checking the rearview mirror with a frown. "We can stop in Houma."

CHAPTER 21
Clara

"Kyle's been shot," the voice said.

"What?" I surged out of bed, phone to my ear, half awake, looking for clothes on the floor and the bed, where I never left them. "When? How? Who is this?"

Oh my god. Oh my god.

"It's Mariam. His sister. You should come. Can you come?"

"I'll be there as soon as I can get a flight." I tried to focus on the clock, but the numbers were a fuzzy red blur. "Is he OK?"

"He's in surgery. We'll know more by the time you get here."

She told me which hospital. I gave her my cell phone number, said I would text her my flight information and meet her there. I hung up and started throwing things into an overnight bag with one hand while I dialed the limo company with the other.

When I arrived at the hospital in Houma, about an hour outside New Orleans, later that morning around eleven, half dead from lack of sleep and nerves, the nurse directed me toward a tall woman pacing in the waiting room. She wore a graphic black and white print dress, and looked exceptionally well-groomed for someone whose brother was in surgery.

"Mariam?"

"Clara?" Her eyes had passed over me when I entered, dismissive. Now, she appeared startled and paused to take me in, head to toe.

"Yes. How is he? What happened?" I used the full force of my New England reserve to keep from grabbing her arm.

She was brusque and turned partly away, as if she didn't want to tell me. "They stopped for Cokes on the way back from seeing some girl in the bayou, and a couple guys rolled up on them, shot Kyle in the chest. Punctured a lung." She stopped, as if her own breathing was impaired. Started again. "They were only a few blocks from the hospital. Lucas got him to emergency."

I touched her arm, tried to get her to face me again. "What do the surgeons say?"

"They've repaired the lung, put him on a ventilator. Now we wait."

My legs folded under me and I dropped into a chair. I'd been going on adrenaline and espresso since she'd called at midnight.

"Can we move him back to New Orleans?"

"Eventually."

"Won't he get better care there?"

"I imagine they'll tell us if that's needed, don't you think?" she snapped.

I pulled my overnight case toward me and plopped my purse on top of it, while I tried to figure out how to tell her I would pay for the MediVac, if need be.

She stepped away, then turned and sat next to me. "Kyle never mentioned you were white."

That was the problem? I said, "He never mentioned you were beautiful. Does that make us even?" I smiled, tried to keep the snark out of my voice, even if it was shouting in my head.

"There aren't any black women in Connecticut?"

"You will have to ask him why he chose me." My race was the most important thing to her? Really? All I wanted was to know he was OK, that he would be whole and healthy, and would come home.

"Why did you choose him?"

I felt my face flush with anger. Not the right response, but my emotions chafed only a millimeter under my skin. I knew it was a good question, the same one Bailey had asked me. Why did Mariam need the answer at this moment? I couldn't answer her properly. Not right now. But I wanted her to like me. If she liked me, maybe Kyle would let me in a little more. I smiled again. "Why do any of us choose our partners? Why did you choose your husband?"

It was the wrong response.

She seethed. "Oh, so Kyle's talked about me and Lucas. Well, that's just perfect. Like it's any of your business that Lucas is eight years younger than I am. We love each other, and Kyle just needs to get over it."

"I'm sorry?" What had I stepped into? "Kyle hardly ever talks about his family or New Orleans. He keeps telling me he doesn't want to discuss it, so I don't know anything about you and your husband."

"Oh." Unrepentant, she still simmered, barely controlled.

"Mariam? I'm here because I care about Kyle. It's not the way I wanted to meet his family. Please. I don't want to start out hostile to each other."

She rolled her eyes and flopped back in the hard chair, its straight lines framing her elegance. "Lordy, I'm a bitch, aren't I? And you came all this way. I'm sorry, honey; I'm just all wound up. It seems Mama and I have been waiting for Kyle to get shot ever since he joined the force, and now it's here and all we can do is yell at everyone, 'See we told you so.'" Her eyes flooded.

"It's OK." I rested my hand on her arm briefly, and she grabbed it and held tight. An orangey-red overwhelmed my senses—colors of vibrancy, determination, passion. This fierce woman would be reckoned with, one way or another. I let the color wash through me and was cautioned. "Can you tell me what he was doing down there?"

"Lucas can tell you when he gets back."

As though she'd called to him, a tall young man appeared, carrying two cups of coffee. Very young. It hadn't really registered when Mariam said her husband was eight years her junior. He worked to mask the difference by dressing professionally in a dark blue suit, white shirt, and dark red tie, as if he were running for president, but his unlined face and lightness on his feet gave away his youthful energy.

After Mariam introduced us, he apologized for not bringing me coffee and offered his own. "Please, ma'am. It's white and sweet; hope that's OK." I thanked him and took it; I was near collapse from fatigue. Mariam asked Lucas to tell me about the shooting.

"Near as I can tell, they'd been following us since we left New Orleans. I sent the cops out there after the girl, and if she's still there, they'll find out if she dispatched them after us. She couldn't be more than about seventeen and almost full pregnant by the looks of her. What she's doing with those guys…" He didn't need to finish his thought.

"What girl? Why did he want to see her?"

"She's the sidekick of a gangbanger imprisoned with Jonah."

"Who's Jonah?"

Lucas and Mariam glanced at each other, the kind of glance that communicated both a question and an answer. Lucas said, "Maybe we'd better let Kyle tell you."

"Maybe we shouldn't," I snapped, then regretted it. I modulated my tone. "I'm sorry. I got on a plane because he was hurt, and how badly I didn't even know. He won't tell me anything about what's going on, left Connecticut without even so much as a 'hey, honey, I'll be gone a couple days,' not even by text! Can I please have some information? He nearly died in Connecticut, too, or didn't he tell you that?"

Lucas gave a sharp shake of his head, as if I'd let out something he'd been trying to keep quiet.

Mariam saw it. "You knew? You didn't tell me?"

"He asked me not to."

I looked at her, reaching into that intense orange energy to align her with me. "He's keeping us all in the dark. Now he's hurt." It was a mistake.

"Little white girl telling us our family business." She glared at Lucas, her body upright and rigid.

He leaned back in his seat, lacing his long fingers with his wife's. "Maybe it would be better to hear the Connecticut part from you," he said.

So I told them about Dominick, the drive-by shooting, the subsequent car fire, the connections Kyle's officers had made to a local gang. I told them that the men in his department thought someone had put a hit out on Kyle, but they didn't know who, and about the connection to a local businessman whose legitimate clubs acted as fronts for drug- and gun-running. Finally, I asked how it all related to New Orleans and the convict he'd mentioned.

"Kyle thinks Jonah, his old partner, set up the hit as revenge because Kyle found the evidence to convict him for a murder he committed after Katrina. Jonah's in the federal pen, but he should have been the next NOLA police superintendent."

I sat back, stunned, as if being more stunned were even possible. "Kyle turned him in?"

"Kyle investigated him; his evidence put Jonah behind bars."

Any bravado I had maintained on my journey here, any hope that Kyle was just a cop in the wrong place at the wrong time, and that Teo was wrong, and the shooting was all about Dom was wiped away with that sentence. It seemed to be *all* about Kyle, and Kyle's past, something about which I knew almost nothing. I didn't know how Vlad fit into the attacks on Kyle, but whatever skills I had were useless to Kyle in New Orleans, where I knew nothing about his past, nothing about his family, nothing about this culture. I rearranged landscapes and built gardens for a living. What could I offer?

"I shouldn't have come." I felt tears building and straightened my spine. Not here, not now. "I'm just so afraid for him."

"Of course you should have." Mariam was immediately indignant. "Kyle would want you here. We want you here. You think he told us any more about you than he told you about us? No way am I going to miss out on a chance to get to know you." She paused. "Even if you are white." She let out a half-smile. Lucas looked disconcerted.

"Thank you."

"Lucas here is a PI. He can continue investigating while Kyle is laid up. He's going to be just fine, you'll see."

Lucas said, "Tell me about this businessman. What's his connection to the case?"

I gave him as much as I knew: who Bianca was, that she had claimed Vlad Espejo ran the gangs in southwestern Fairfield County, that I'd been warned off by Bianca's gangster boyfriend Teo and also by Vlad himself, who had hired me to do a landscape job for his daughter, presumably to keep tabs on me. Lucas already knew Kyle thought the car fire was the gang's retribution against its own members for killing a cop. Mistakes had to be punished.

I said, "If Kyle thinks his ex-partner Jonah hired the gang to kill him as revenge for putting him in prison, why now? He must have had opportunities to exact revenge before this."

"That's the question. Kyle hoped the girl Jewel knew a motive, maybe even the name of the guy who paid for it, but she claimed she didn't know—or she was too scared to say."

"He was lying there bleeding, telling you what that girl said?" Mariam shivered and her aura paled.

Afraid he wouldn't make it. Wanting someone to know.

Lucas put his arm around his wife's shoulders. "He's alive," he said.

Mariam teared up again.

"There's something else," I said. "I don't know if it's connected, but it's been eating at me." I wouldn't tell them I knew because my dreams had told me so. "I think one of the young men in the gang is Espejo's son. I can't tell if Vlad knows or not, but I'm pretty sure the boy doesn't know Espejo is his father."

"I'm not sure it's relevant, ma'am."

I sighed. "Does he call you ma'am, too?" I smiled at Mariam.

She raised her eyebrows at me. "We're probably about the same age."

Lucas laughed, an easy laugh, a little brash. "Am I making you feel old?" he asked me.

"I'm not, thank you."

"How do you feel about kids?" Mariam said. If her question was abrupt, her manner wasn't. She had relaxed into the plastic chair and watched me with a half-smile on her face.

"I like them just fine," I said, feeling it a kind of test. I wasn't about to tell her, just as I hadn't told Lia, that I didn't fancy having any of my own.

"Good." She sat up. "I have to go home and get my son Antoine when he gets off the bus from school. You'll come with me, and we can chat."

I felt my poor little nerves, already fully on edge, twitch in fear. *Chat? That couldn't be good.*

"I'd like to see Kyle when he gets out of surgery. I booked a hotel nearby."

"They won't let you into your room until four. Lucas can watch over my brother until then. After supper, I'll drop you at the hotel. You'll be fine." She grinned at me a little wolfishly. "And the ride back with Antoine will give you plenty of time to decide whether you truly do like children."

While Mariam had threatened a chat, she hardly talked on the hour ride from Houma to New Orleans. I found myself imagining Kyle out in the bayou, and wondering how I felt about being folded, suddenly, into his family. I knew I was in love with him. He understood, I thought, why I needed answers to my dreams' images and questions, even if he didn't understand the dreams themselves.

Unexpectedly, our relationship had shifted from slow but steady into a bullet train because he was in the hospital, suffering from gunshot trauma. Would I spend my life, as apparently Mariam and her mother did, worried every day? I had thought a lot about his getting shot since Dom's death, but the human mind has an incredible ability to lie: *Kyle beat death last time; he will always beat it.*

Like clockwork, the old me resurfaced, the me who wanted to hop on that plane and head north to connect out of New York to anywhere in Europe. I hadn't spent much time in Vienna. Maybe there next. Maybe if Kyle was well enough, he would run away with me.

I was so tired I could barely think, and I was not a girl who dealt well with sleep deprivation. I rested my head against the passenger side window, and as my eyes drifted shut, I realized that, if his family liked me as much as mine liked him, we would hurt other people if we ended it. At the least, they would be thinking about our relationship, evaluating how we interacted with each other, as Bailey had the other night in the bar. I hated standing on this kind of stage. That was why I didn't tell people about the visions; they looked at me differently, as if I were an object they could parse, dice, analyze.

Maybe I was being narcissistic. But I'd done this before. Perception mattered after all, even if I'd denied it before, not just for me but for Kyle too. It mattered at home, where he was a public figure, and it mattered here, with his family. I wasn't ready to lose his strong, steady influence in my life, but what would I do if he couldn't return to police work? Would he return to New Orleans or need long-term care or physical therapy? I hadn't thought to ask. How stupid.

As the emotions rattled their way to the surface, part of me felt suspended, as if it were no longer in the car. Slowly, behind my eyes, a vision bloomed of purple and velvet and gold. Gold center-pointed the image, like the iris in an eye, and purple radiated out from that in ripples, as if the iris were a rock in a pool. The purple menaced me, lapping at my chin like a lascivious kiss, staining me bruised. As I watched, a black curtain, like an eyelid, descended over the eye and then began slowly to open, a thin crescent of purple at first against the black, black sky, slowly expanding, like a cat's eye glowing in the dark. I started awake.

"You OK?" Mariam asked. "You jumped. Bad dream?"

"Uh, yeah." I pushed my hair off my face, sat up straight. A purple eye? What did that mean? Did the gang have an "eye" on me? On Kyle? Was he still in danger? I felt dead-stopped, unable to connect the pieces. How had I ended up as this person who solved other people's problems? I couldn't even solve my own. I felt tears come, and Mariam reached over and grabbed my hand.

"It's OK, honey. He's going to recover."

I hoped she was right.

We had left the highway and were pulling into a cul-de-sac. Mariam parked in the drive of a small house with a front porch and a lush rear garden that peeked from behind a fence. Someone had spent some serious landscaping money.

"Antoine should be home in about twenty minutes. Come on in and have a cup of coffee. You look as though you could use it."

I rubbed the sleep from my eyes. "Thanks. That would be great."

The interior of the house was scrubbed and fresh-looking. Surfaces gleamed white and shiny, and against these were bright red, turquoise, jewel green, and purple chairs, couches, pillows. I felt as though I'd been dropped into a particularly joyful pot of paint.

She opened the freezer to pull out a package of coffee. "Can you make it? I need to pack a bag."

I took the coffee. She left the kitchen, returning a few minutes later with two small, zipped duffels. I'd measured the coffee and filled the water reservoir.

"How did you know to call me?" I asked, the question just occurring to me.

"Kyle made Lucas promise."

"He was conscious on the way to the hospital?"

She nodded.

"He say anything else?" She hadn't dragged me all the way home with her just so I could sleep in her car.

"My brother is a serious man. I imagine you know that."

My turn to nod.

She checked the water well, then punched the coffeemaker's on button. "He doesn't take up with just anyone. He…" She leaned against the counter, grabbing it behind her with both hands as if she needed the anchor. "He didn't much like Lucas. Thought he was too young, not steady enough for me. It…caused some friction."

"I'm sorry." She was working up to something—and it could go either way for me.

She stared at me. "I don't want it to be the same for you. If he loves you, I want you to know that I will welcome you in this family. I can't speak for anyone else, but if you do right by him…" Her eyes filled with tears, and she turned abruptly to check the coffee, which had started to hiss. "He needs you to do right by him."

I almost couldn't hear her whisper it.

I came around the kitchen island to where she was standing, thinking about the eye in my vision, the purple and gold gang colors, the image of Kyle surrounded by knives, my fear that I couldn't put together what the visions were telling me about who wanted him dead. "I will do my best," I said. "I promise. I'm so sorry he's hurt. I'm scared too."

She opened her arms and we hugged, our fears for him confirmed in the tears that dampened each other's shoulders.

The front door banged, and we jumped apart as little feet skidded to a stop in the kitchen.

"Hey, Antoine. This is Uncle Kyle's friend Clara. Clara, meet Antoine."

The boy was what I imagined Kyle looked like at that age. Big brown eyes assessed me, and then a smile lit up his face. "I love Uncle Kyle," he said. "I'm so glad he came to visit! Is he coming over soon?"

Mariam looked stricken, and she knelt down. "Antoine, Uncle Kyle's been hurt. He's in the hospital in Houma, and your daddy's down there with him. We came to pick you up, to go see him."

"Is he going to be OK?" The boy looked first at his mother and then at me.

"Of course he is," she said. "I've packed some pajamas and clothes for tomorrow. You go choose what you want—a book, your iPad, whatever—because we're going to stay overnight, OK? When you're ready, we'll go."

Antoine ran from the room, and Mariam turned off the coffeemaker, pouring the remaining coffee into two travel mugs. She handed one to me. "Traffic might be bad at this hour."

Kyle wasn't awake when we got back. The hospital had him drugged up with painkillers. Maybe another day, the doctor said. Mariam looked about as happy with that as I was.

"What do we do in the meantime?" I asked of no one, of the hospital air, stained with bleach and that smell of death.

"Rest," the doctor said. "You'll need it when he wakes up."

"So he's going to wake up."

"Of course," he said, smiling, but only a little, his smile as cautiously optimistic as his tone.

Lucas had stayed with us for this pronouncement, his arms locked across his chest. After the doctor left the room, he said, "Listen, Mar—"

"I know, I know. You've got to get back to work."

"No. I mean, yes, but I was thinking… That girl, she might have called someone. Maybe she wasn't satisfied that she'd chased him off."

She looked at him, and in the look I saw both trust and fear. After all, her brother lay in a hospital bed with a punctured lung, swathed in bandages after visiting that same woman.

"It's not your fault," she said.

"Still have to make it right."

"It's Kyle who should apologize, you know."

"He did to me, sweetheart. Probably would have gotten around to you in due time."

Her eyes rimmed with tears, thick and sudden. "You're going back out to the bayou?"

He nodded. "I should go tonight."

"But the girl's in custody."

"Yes. But Fredericka Toussaint, the woman who was sheltering her, was questioned and let go. It's her I want to see."

"You're not going without me," I said. I had to make it right too.

CHAPTER 22
Clara

The bayou was dark at nine o'clock. The smell and weight of the water lay heavy in the air, but the only sound was the car moving through the night. Lucas didn't say much for most of the half-hour drive. Fine with me: I had plenty to think about.

I'd solved one of the dreams: Teo was Vlad's son. The other two dreams, the man lying on the ground with the tree of knives and the eye rimmed with purple, still eluded me. The tree of knives seemed to represent the threat to Kyle. But why so many knives? Did more than one person want him dead? Were multiple people poised to carry out the hit, one picking up if another failed?

Based on my research, and conversations over the years with Paul, knives symbolized vengeance and death. The shortness of the knife indicated that instinctive forces were primary—that is, whoever was wielding the knife tended to be guided by his aggression, ego, passions, rather than his intellect or spirit. While that fit gang members, why would they suddenly fixate on Kyle? Joe suggested his officers thought the attack was racially motivated, but I didn't see it. The gangs might hate him for being black, but I had a hard time believing they would go after a police officer without some reason.

Then how did the single eye rimmed with purple fit? Shiva, Indian destroyer god, sported a third eye, so it could connect to someone whose primary motive was ruin. Royal purple suggested someone with power, and people with power sometimes used it to destroy. The purple could also connect to something spiritual, in the same way that the eye did. But why? The motivation puzzled me, and I couldn't afford the delay. What if someone tried while he lay in that hospital bed? Why couldn't I see more clearly? I sighed. Lucas caught it.

"Y'all didn't have to come," he said mildly.

"It's not...no, I didn't mean that... Although this is getting remote and creepy. How much farther?" I changed the subject. As I said it, I realized he might take "creepy" as an insult, but then I didn't want to apologize, because it would emphasize something he might not have taken that way and make it into something bigger than I intended. Sometimes being inside my brain was very complicated.

"Lots of space between people is why they live here."

I couldn't help myself. "I didn't mean it as an insult, you know."

"I know." Again, that mild tone. It must be useful in his line of work.

I tried to look out the window, but I could only see my own reflection in the dim green glow of the dashboard lights.

"Kyle says you have dreams."

I felt a jolt. "He did?" Why would Kyle have done that? He knew how private I was about the gift. Did Mariam know too? She might have been more aware of my dream in the car than I thought.

"We had a lot of time to talk the last time we drove down here."

I brushed my fingers over my lips, as if to seal them. They were dry from too much time in hotels and airplanes.

He said, "I think Miss Toussaint can see things too. Maybe ya'll can, I don't know, connect."

I said nothing. He made me tired. The gift wasn't for sale.

He didn't press it and remained silent until we pulled up to a shack on the side of the highway. One lone outside light gleamed yellow against the massive dark pressed around it. It lit a small space of the front lawn, where it looked as though a tag sale had exploded.

"I'll talk," he said. Not a question.

For the first time, I wondered what I was getting into. I didn't know this man. I didn't know the woman we were visiting, other than she was the last person to see Kyle whole and healthy. She knew something about some girl. Lucas hadn't really brought me up to speed. How was I supposed to "connect" with her, if I didn't know what I supposed to be connecting over? Perhaps I was simply to intuit what was going on.

Men.

I was a cliché, blaming him for my failings.

He opened the door and got out. As I followed, the house's front door opened. A tall black woman stood there, silhouetted by the light behind her.

"I wondered when you'd show up." Her voice was soft, like the night air, with some threat like sandpaper in it. The yellow outside light barely lit her face, her eyes just two gleams in the cashmere shadows.

"Will you talk to us, Fredericka?"

The gleams passed over me, then paused and came back. "Do I know you?"

"Not yet," I said. "But I'd like to come in. Mosquitos and I don't really get along."

"A northerner. And…something else."

I held her gaze as much as was possible in the half-light. She collected herself and turned, leaving the door open for us to follow.

The room was small, decorated in mostly grey and green, and boasted an impressive collection of masks. They looked as though they had been hand-carved and painted. Along the kitchen wall were open cupboards containing not only plates and cups, but also jars filled with powders and leaves. Perhaps she did more than "see." A long row of windows across the back of the rooms were curtainless and staring.

Fredericka stood, waiting.

I saw Lucas take in the room, note the position of a baseball bat behind the door.

"We would like to sit down and talk to you. May we do that?"

"Who are you?" She probed me with those eyes. They were hazel, I could see now in the harsh light from the overhead bulb.

"I'm Kyle's…" I hesitated. "Girlfriend," I finished lamely.

She nodded. "You love him."

We locked gazes. Was she asking me a question? The more I studied her, the less I could look away, as if she could see through my eyes and into my thoughts.

"Hmph." She walked to her tiny stove, picked up a shining teakettle, and filled it from the faucet. She didn't ask what we wanted, but pulled down two of the jars, pinched out some of the leaves, and dropped them into a teapot on the counter. Cups, spoons, and honey followed, and finally, when the water steamed from the pot, she gestured toward the couch and we sat. She made us each a cup of tea, starting by dipping the spoon into the honey then resting it at the bottom of the cup, after which she poured the hot tea in to melt the honey. The steam smelled like roses and mint, and something else I couldn't quite identify.

Lucas introduced himself, explained he'd driven Kyle to see her and Jewel, that he'd been in the car in Houma when Kyle had gotten shot. "You took him to the hospital," she said. "I know who you are."

"Then you know what we want."

"You want that poor girl to tell you what she knows, so he can be safe. But maybe he isn't supposed to be safe right now. Maybe that girl is supposed to be safe, while her baby is growing." Her head was slightly lowered like she might charge, her eyes pinned to him.

She unnerved me and made me wary of crossing her.

I sipped the tea, felt it hum in my system. What *was* that other ingredient?

Lucas didn't touch his, which was probably smart, but one of us had to pretend to be polite and that was my role, Northern-girl fish-out-of-water and all.

"Did she call anyone after we left?" he asked.

Fredericka directed her answer to me. "She was frightened. Wouldn't you be frightened? Some man comes after you, and all you're doing is just coming out of an appointment for your unborn child, and there he is, big and wanting to know things you've been told to keep to yourself."

"Yes," I said, thinking of the night Kyle had waited in my garden's shadows.

Fredericka looked into my eyes and it was as if she knew all about that night. She kept talking, pressing her point. "Then he shows up again, in a place you think you're safe? A place where you think no one can find you. Your friend, he pushed too hard and scared her. She wasn't going to tell him anything after that."

"You might have been willing to scare her too, if someone was determined to kill you."

She shook her head, as if she couldn't believe that would ever be true. "How did he find her anyway? That nurse tell?"

Lucas said, "That nurse's job is to make sure Jewel is safe and healthy. She is afraid the girl is in trouble."

"Cops have her at the moment, so I imagine she's as safe as she can be, under the circumstances."

A light flashed across the windows. Headlights? Something out on the water? Someone in the backyard with a flashlight? What was outside those windows anyway? The black pressed in like dirt thrown on a grave.

"That girl doesn't know what to do. She's afraid that baby's father and his friends are going to be angry with her."

"His friends?" Lucas's mild tone slid into our exchange. "Why would his friends be angry? I thought this was a deal between one dirty ex-cop and one gang member."

"I don't know any more than you do, except I do know you get one gang member, you get them all. And the boys outside take care of what the boys inside can't."

"Like murdering a cop?"

"Or a badly behaving girlfriend."

"They would kill a pregnant girl?" I said.

"How sheltered are you?" Fredericka snapped.

"Pretty sheltered." I neglected to mention the fifteen years on my own, starting at nineteen. Money sheltered me.

She scanned me again, taking in the expensive bag, gold watch, pearl earrings.

And I thought I'd toned it down.

The scan told me there was something else, something she wasn't telling us. Was she herself afraid of the gang? Jewel knew where she lived. She didn't strike me as the frightened type, more the type to be frightened of. What kind of power would the gang have over her, other than violence?

Paul's voice thrummed in my head. *Just ask*. So I did.

She twitched her head away, in what I thought was an attempt to avoid answering, but then I saw she had laughed. "Those punks couldn't handle my kind of pain." She waved her hands at the jars. "They won't come anywhere near me. The girls who shelter here tell them I am a witch."

She paused, drew a finger in a circle on the table. "Like you," she said.

"A witch?" I laughed, but not because I found it funny. I'd never been called a witch before. Other names, yes, but not this one.

Lucas turned to contemplate me.

"Don't be fooled," Fredericka said. "It runs deep."

What was she talking about? I didn't deal in powders and herbs, chants and spells. I just had a few dreams. "What I am isn't important. Please help us. Just like you love that girl, just like you want to protect that girl, I want to help the man. I care for him, and it isn't right that he's in the hospital."

My mouth was suddenly dry, and I sipped more of her tea. "You're keeping something from us, something that could help." I knew it, as surely as my own name. "Why?"

"I wanted to see what you were made of," she said. "You mustn't deny your gift, you know. It's bigger than you think, not just a few dreams you can confine to the safety of sleep."

I hardly thought my dreams were confinable, nor did I think of sleep as safe. In fact, sometimes I was so frightened by my dreams that I didn't sleep at all. That she knew I had them, well, how did she know?

"They will seep into your daylight hours, into your thoughts, into everything you do."

Yup. Been there, done that.

She seemed to be chanting, almost trance-like. The light flashed again across the window behind her head. I put my hand out toward her, to ask her to stop, and as it moved through the air in front of me, it was as if it slowed down, floated through air that had become visible. Trailing from the ends of my fingers were purple waves, like smoke that swirled and dissipated. She could see it, too; I saw the satisfaction in her face, as if she had proven something to me.

Lucas looked back and forth between us. I bet he didn't see any purple smoke. It had to be purple? *Really?* I felt as if I were in some kind of Disneyfied after-school movie on New Orleans voodoo. Despite my disbelief—what had she put in the tea?—I still had to find out what she knew. Her voodoo charms were meant to distract, but I couldn't let them.

"I think someone else was here that day, someone the girl was even more frightened of than Kyle." I was sure of it the moment the words left my mouth, and I could see by the look on her face that she felt caught out. "She's more frightened of this person than her boyfriend. Is she afraid of the boyfriend?" I watched her closely and saw the flicker of impatience. "No, the boyfriend's afraid of someone. Is it this ex-cop?"

She ran a finger across the spotless surface of the teapot, moved the honey pot an inch to the right, then moved it back.

"Please," I said. She'd ripped me open, forced me back onto my intuition. I felt raw. If she didn't answer now, I had no more to give.

She settled back, looked at Lucas. "You weren't the only watcher. That girl came out that door, gun pointed at your friend, and you all were so busy looking at her you didn't see what was happening down the road. But Jewel did. That poor girl thought they'd believe she snitched on them, got to trembling so bad your friend could have been peppered with a lot of holes, if I hadn't gotten that gun away from her."

"They were following Jewel?"

"They were following you."

I could see Lucas thought that wasn't possible, smart, savvy PI like him riding around with a police officer next to him. They couldn't be fooled, not them.

How long had they been following Kyle, looking for an opportunity to take another shot at killing him? Who else had he put at risk? I thought about Mariam and Antoine at the hospital in the waiting room, exposed to anyone walking in off the street, and all the breath fled my body into the wide vastness of the dark outside the windows. Fredericka saw me go white, grabbed my hand.

"They're OK, honey. They're OK."

I shook my head but couldn't speak.

"Can you tell us what they looked like? Did you see the license plate? Anything?" Lucas pressed her.

"Green Honda. Old and ratty with a long silver scrape on the driver's side. Didn't see any plates. Too far away. But I've got something better."

Lucas waved her off. He'd seen Kyle get shot by that car's occupants.

She squeezed my hand and stood up, crossing the room to the tiny desk. She opened the middle drawer and drew out a cell phone and a paper that she handed to Lucas.

"What are these?" I asked.

Lucas looked a question at Fredericka.

"That's the note Jewel was supposed to deliver. It made her so scared, she kept it. Made out the message she was supposed to deliver was verbal."

I slid down the couch to read over Lucas's shoulder: *KDP. 24 HRS. 10K. A.M.*

"What does that mean?"

Lucas said, "Kyle DuPont. Job should be done in the next twenty-four hours. Ten thousand dollars for a successful outcome. What's A.M.? Morning?"

Lucas looked at Fredericka, who shook her head. "No idea."

"This came from someone at the prison?"

"From Jewel's deadbeat boyfriend Xerxes, to be delivered to another deadbeat outside named Pedro."

"So we talk to Xerxes," I said.

"We talk to Pedro. He's easier," said Lucas.

"Pedro doesn't matter. He's just an errand boy. Xerxes knows all the players, and he's a sitting duck."

"You want to visit federal prison?" He looked back and forth between me and Fredericka.

"Gotta give the girl points for guts," she said.

I said, "Why not? And then we can talk to Kyle's buddy, Jonah, right?"

Lucas sighed and shook his head. I couldn't be that naive. Didn't people visit felons all the time? Anyway, I bet Mother's new boyfriend, the politician, could get us in. All I needed was some privacy and my phone.

I slept on the way back, as if the tea had been drugged. Well, the tea was drugged, but who knew with what. I think my sleep had more to do with all the traveling and revelations than it did much of anything else. Lucas was kind and let me rest, not waking me until we reached Houma. When I opened my eyes, he was pulling into the hotel parking lot.

"You didn't have to do this. I could have taken a cab from the hospital."

"You seemed pretty worn out. Besides, I'm pretty sure Mariam and Antoine are back here by now. It's way past Antoine's bedtime."

He drove around the side of the hotel and pulled into a space. We stepped out into the evening, the stars above glazed with humidity and streetlights.

"What's next?" I asked as we walked toward the hotel entrance.

"I'll talk to some of my connections, see if I can get leads on Pedro and the green Honda. Since none of us saw a plate, I don't know if I'll be able to get a trace."

"What about visiting Xerxes and Jonah?"

"Ma'am. I appreciate your coming with me tonight. I think that Ms. Toussaint spoke more freely because of you. I even have Kyle's contact to get me into the prison. I can handle it from here."

"I'm sure you can, but I am not so easily dismissed. Until Kyle wakes up, I'm not going to stop trying to help him."

"Getting in my way is your solution?"

A doorman hovered, unsure what to do.

"Let's go to the prison together. People often open up to me."

"Because of your magical powers?" His face was a blank as he said it, and I wasn't sure whether he was serious. I nodded at the doorman and stepped through into the lobby.

"I don't have magical powers. No one does. Occasionally, my perception extends a little further than most people's. I do not practice the dark arts, no matter what Ms. Toussaint says."

"We have a lot of 'dark arts' practitioners down here. They're hard to tell apart from the regular folks." His voice was bitter.

I looked around the lobby. An oversize vase of flowers stood on a small marble table in front of a mirror, to make it seem as if the wall was covered in blossoms. "What's really upsetting you?"

He stuck his hands in his pockets. "My wife is devastated about Kyle, and a bit shocked you're a white girl, even if she told you it was OK, and I'm sure she did. She's going to be bouncing between the twin poles of her anxiety, and it'll be my job to calm her down."

I nodded, just wanting my bed. "Sorry. I am a nice person—most of the time—if that helps any."

"It won't." He looked at me and grinned. "She's tough, but she'll come around."

I was touched. Perhaps I had won over a second member of the family. Only Mama to go—if I didn't mess it up. "So…will you come with me to federal prison?"

He shrugged. "I can't get in touch with Kyle's contact this late at night."

"I can get us into the prison, no problem. Rich white girl has to have some use, right?" I put my hand on his arm, felt him start at the touch, got a whisper of grey across my vision. Guilt? Maybe that he hadn't protected Kyle? "I'll meet you tomorrow morning around eight," I said.

CHAPTER 23
Clara

"Fly?" Lucas said. He'd made the mistake of giving me his cell number, and I had called him a half hour after we'd parted ways in the lobby. I couldn't sleep anyway, too wired up after my short nap in the car.

I'd called my mother, who had put Chaz Hardison on the phone. He'd listened, in that way he had where you knew you were the only thing on his mind in that moment, and then asked for twenty minutes. Nineteen minutes later, he'd called back with the names of the prison officials who would meet us with passes for the next morning at eleven. We would have access to both Jonah and Xerxes. Thirty minutes each. I allowed myself one pirouette. Sophisticated girls didn't do fist pumps.

If we could confirm that Xerxes was doing Jonah's bidding, then maybe we could reason with Jonah, get him to drop the hit. I didn't really believe he would listen, but if we didn't try, then we couldn't know why *now*. Katrina was over, the trial was over, the conviction was over. He was a year or so into his sentence. Why would he suddenly decide on revenge?

Jonah was incarcerated in the federal prison at Pollock, about four hours north and west of New Orleans. As I had looked over the route on Google maps, I discovered a municipal airport a short distance from the prison. It looked to be mostly a grass strip between trees, but it was still an airport. Now, all we had to do was to find someone to fly us there.

"I can pay," I told Lucas, "if you can find a pilot. I hadn't realized it was so far."

He coughed, but it sounded like a laugh. "I think I can do that, but you're going to have to wait, girl. Don't call me again. You might wake up my son, and that's not going to endear you to my wife. I will arrange this, but I will not wake anyone up when it's not an emergency, you hear me?"

The people in the next room had the television on low. I could hear its rumble and the man sneezing as the woman talked, her voice pitched just so to be irritating.

I rushed my last comment. "We have to be there by eleven, or we lose our passes."

"I got it." He hung up. This time, I was sure it was laughter.

If only the laughter had permeated my sleep. Instead, I spent a restless night, waking every hour or so from dreams that left me sweaty and anxious. Purple and gold eyes followed me through mazes paved with knife blades. In the center of the maze, always Kyle, pinned to the ground as if for sacrifice. I saw him over and over, and when I woke in the morning, I felt the prickling of those knives all over my skin like tiny electric shocks. Putting on my clothes felt like laying a wool blanket over open wounds. I breathed deeply and tried to forget my own body. I needed courage, not distraction, today.

We drove the tense hour back to New Orleans to take off from Lakefront Airport, ten minutes north and east of downtown, along Lake Pontchartrain. The terminal building, made of a beautiful blond stone, sported a carving of Hermes, his wings outspread, over the main terminal doors. An auspicious symbolism.

Following Hurricane Katrina, when the airport had sustained formidable damage, the city decided to restore the terminal to its original art deco glory, removing the bomb-shelter-era concrete encasement that had been added to the outside and covered over the building's beautiful details.

Even in my current state of mind, I could see that inside the charm continued with terrazzo floors with an inlaid compass pointing to different cities around the world. One point read Peiping, the old name for Beijing. The ceiling glowed bright orange, pink, and blue—in a mural of old-fashioned planes among cartoon white puffy clouds. Three old-style wooden phone booths were tucked into a corner. Did people use those booths for cell phone privacy? For a moment of escape and fantasy?

Everything about this perfect little space lit up my travel bug, made me long for the freedom to *go*. It didn't matter where. I was content with a trip to the federal prison at Pollock even while my body vibrated with painful prickles from my dreams. How pathetic was that?

We were in the air by eight-thirty. All those clichés about flying in a tin can came to mind, but from the moment I set foot in the plane, I loved it. With all my travels, I had never before flown in a small aircraft.

The plane sported a bank of instrument panels—three rectangles filled with lights and gauges, which lined the front of the cockpit under the window. There were switches to flip and buttons to press and dials to look at. The seats were black leather. The plane looked as if it had just rolled off the factory floor—spotlessly clean and perfectly maintained. I was impressed.

Our pilot, a man of about forty with a Marine buzz cut and aviator glasses, introduced himself as Gray Porter. No accent.

"Gray and I know each other from the service," Lucas explained.

Neither of them said much of anything else, except to discuss the flying. No reminiscences. No backslapping. No good-old-boy stuff. Just business.

Porter sat in the front left seat and Lucas in the right. They stuck me in the back, but I could still see out the side window, and that was enough.

I might buck for the front seat on the ride back. We fastened our seatbelts and Porter taxied toward the runway.

The plane rose over the lake, and in that moment of heaven, I lifted free of my fears for Kyle and the terrors of my dreams. I loved feeling like a little buzzing satellite over the ground, all the small people and cars and buildings and trees a blur below our airborne feet. Joy was being suspended in mid-air, daily life a couple thousand feet below me. I would worry about the misery later.

An hour later, Lucas commented, looking out the right side of the plane, "There it is." The prison complex was huge, flat, and grey and white, spread out in the middle of the forest below like a sudden white blight. Just the size of it would have reduced me to slobbering terror, never mind the thought of being incarcerated there for the rest of my life. For the first time, I imagined the kind of men who would be sentenced here and the crimes they would have committed. Who was I to think I could talk one of these men out of his secrets? I was unwilling to let go of my own.

It was a sign of my privilege that I thought I was smarter than everyone else, that I could figure it out when no one else could. I started to open my mouth to say it was a mistake, that we should return to New Orleans, when Porter set the wheels on the ground and the plane glided to a stop. He turned it to head for one of the two buildings that studded the edge of the triangle of runways that constituted Pollock Municipal Airport. There wasn't much else, except the green trees and a sort of sandy ground covered with rough grass. Its loneliness morphed my embarrassment into fear, and I stumbled as I stepped from the plane.

I saw Porter roll his eyes at Lucas.

I'd been in enough situations in my life where men underestimated me—and regretted it. I was small and blonde and that was a drawback, but Kyle couldn't help himself, so we had to do it for him. The dreams certainly weren't going to let me off the hook. I was going to be scared to death for the next couple of hours, but I would live through it, and I wasn't going unprotected. Jonah and Xerxes would either talk or they wouldn't, and then we could get in this plane and go home. I stiffened my spine—Montague women knew how to do that—and drew on two hundred years of Connecticut ancestry, a PhD, and the current solidity of my bank account. Privilege had to be good for something.

I looked at the two men. "You ready? Porter, I can't imagine we will be long. Lucas, you've done this before, yes? Any estimates as to time?" Lucas gave his best guess, and Porter nodded, heading off toward the other building, presumably to trade flying stories with whoever ran this place.

Porter had called ahead for a car. The driver, a lanky redhead, introduced himself as MacArthur. It was the last thing he said to us. He rolled the car out of the airport and onto mostly empty and green Airbase Road. The verge had been kept wide, probably so any escaping prisoners couldn't easily hide to intercept unwary motorists. The roads off it seemed to lead to sections of the prison complex other than the main gate, service areas perhaps. No Trespassing signs and gates and fences and high-intensity lights littered the way. This stretch also appeared to be where the town dealt with its waste. Consolidated Waste Industries had an Airbase Road Pick Up Station, and we passed what was very grandly labeled the Town of Pollock Wastewater Plant. It looked, rather less grandly, like a group of prefab sheds and tractors next to a couple of big concrete holes in the ground. The water was well hidden. I imagined that much of the town's waste— and industry—came from the prison itself, likely the major employer and economic driver in the area. How thoroughly depressing. But maybe I was wrong—and wouldn't that be nice.

We pulled up to the gates and signed in with the guard. The warden would meet us once we passed through security. My panic returned as a new set of guards took our IDs, checked that we were on the visitors list, and then ushered us through the series of doors that let us into the visiting area. As each one slid shut behind me, I felt a little less air available to my lungs.

The slam of the doors, and that institutional smell of antiseptically washed concrete, vibrated past the defenses I kept erecting. I couldn't even take deep breaths because they only drew in the offending smell, which made my stomach clench. Lucas kept looking at me, as if to say, *keep it together.*

I shrugged and smiled. I could do this for Kyle.

We asked to see Xerxes first, thinking we might get information from him we could use in our conversation with Jonah.

Xerxes did not in any way live up to his kingly name. No more than five foot three, he swaggered into the visiting room, an open room filled with plastic furniture, and swung himself into a chair on the other side of our table. The guards watched from near the door.

"Who are you?" he snarled, scraping the chair closer. "Don't remember putting you on my visitors list. Maybe Goldilocks come to get herself some of the dark side?"

I recoiled and felt my face heat up, which only made him sneer. "I scare you, huh? That's good, little girl."

I kept my mouth shut, tried to keep my hands under the table from shaking. The prickles had subsided for the moment, so I couldn't even use them for distraction. Instead, I made myself notice what was going on around me. For starters, Xerxes wore a sort of dark beige top and pants that looked as though it had been washed too many times and would feel scratchy. The room smelled closed and toxic, like too many needs squeezed into a space that couldn't hold them.

Lucas said, "That's enough. We're here to help you."

"Don't remember asking."

"You got a baby comin', yeah?" Lucas leaned forward, crowding Xerxes' space.

Xerxes started to get up. "Don't got no time for this."

"You want that baby to have everything, right? Don't want it to get hurt?"

Xerxes glared at Lucas. I tried to make myself small and figure out what Lucas was doing. Did he think that threatening Xerxes' baby was going to get us information? Xerxes was tougher than that.

"Hurt that child and I will rain so much hell down on you—"

"Xerxes!" the guard called out. "No cursing. You know the rules."

The boy settled back into his chair, leaned in toward Lucas, and lowered his voice. "I'm listening. Better be good."

Happily, he seemed to have forgotten me. I rubbed at the sweat on my palms and set myself to considering his pulsing, muddy-green aura. I figured most criminals didn't accept much personal responsibility for their crimes so that fit. But I also saw, farther in around his solar plexus chakra, a dark blue: fear. Of the truth? The future? That chakra was all about personal power—which Lucas was challenging.

"We're not the ones you should worry about. It's your boys on the outside. They seem to think your girl has been talking to the cops. If you tell us who they are, we can keep them from harming your girl."

Oh. That was good. I never would have come up with something like that—which was why I wasn't an investigator. Repeat: I am not an investigator. Repeat, repeat, repeat. I knotted my fingers tighter and waited and watched.

Xerxes stared at Lucas. "Why would they think Jewel was talking to the cops?"

"Because she was. Out-of-state guy, no jurisdiction, but he could still make trouble."

His look got more wary.

"You might even know him," Lucas continued. "Guy by the name of Kyle DuPont. Used to serve in NOLA. Ring any bells?"

A red spike in his aura. Anger? Fear?

"How would I know some NOLA cop when I'm locked up in here?"

"Grapevine, I'm thinking."

"What the grapevine want with this NOLA cop?"

"Really?"

"You accusin' me of something?" he hissed.

"Just trying to protect your girl."

He fidgeted for a moment, rubbing his hand across the top of the table. "What you want?"

"Information on who might have wanted that NOLA cop to disappear and why. Names of the guys outside who your girl passed the message to."

We already knew the name: Pedro. Was Lucas going for corroboration? Or did he think he could get the names of Pedro's friends?

"Why should I trust you? Don't know you. Never seen you before."

"Because if you don't, there's no one standing between your girl and your gang buddies. At least with us, you've got a shot."

Xerxes rubbed his hands on his thighs, thinking. "She's OK now, right? Baby's OK?"

"Yes."

Did we even know that? Was she still in police custody? If they'd let her go, would she be safe? Lucas looked relaxed and confident. I clutched my hands together more tightly, glanced over Xerxes' shoulders at the guards. They were talking to each other out of the sides of their mouths, as their eyes roved over the men and women in the room. Misery throbbed in the air.

"Message came down cop was visiting, good opportunity to rid some Northern boys of a problem. I just passed it on. That's my job."

"Are you saying the idea for the hit didn't originate here?"

Xerxes cocked his head, looked puzzled.

Lucas tried again. "It's not someone in Louisiana who wants him dead?"

"Nope."

"You're sure?" I couldn't help myself; it escaped me before I could keep it imprisoned behind my lips.

"Goldilocks can speak!" he mocked. He made a face at me, probably trying to reflect back whatever he saw on mine, before saying to Lucas, "I'm sure." Jerk.

If the order to kill Kyle hadn't come from New Orleans, or hadn't come from someone inside this federal prison, then it wasn't Jonah, no matter what Kyle thought. Someone at home wanted him dead. Who could that possibly be? He hadn't been in Connecticut long enough to make enemies, unless you counted the bleached blondes who were now getting ticketed for driving through town too fast in their SUVs.

Lucas said, "Who gave you that message?"

"It's a long line back to the source, man. You won't ever get there."

"That's my problem," said Lucas.

Xerxes shrugged and gave us a name. Maybe it meant something to Lucas.

"Thanks," Lucas said. "Assuming you're telling us the truth, we'll take care of your girl."

"Not lyin'." Xerxes pushed his chair back and, without so much as a good-bye, sauntered toward the guards at the door. One turned and followed him out, as an escort back to his cell, I supposed. Five minutes later, that same guard returned with Jonah.

Unlike Xerxes, Jonah appeared relaxed. He sat with his hands loosely clasped on the table. His back was military straight, a remainder from his days on the force, I imagined. He had brush-cut, reddish brown hair, and dark eyes.

He nodded at Lucas, shot a puzzled glance at me. I saw him check me out, realized I was surrounded by male guards and was grateful for the prison dress guidelines. I'd chosen jeans and comfortable shoes. My black cashmere sweater was modest, if too pricey. In fact, everything I wore was too pricey, but even as I thought it, I let it empower me. I had come because I could, because we had connections that allowed us to ask questions. I couldn't let go of that power because the surroundings intimidated me. I wished I'd thought of it when Xerxes was making faces at me.

"Dr. Clara Montague," I said.

"Shrink?" he asked.

"Would that be a problem?" I asked.

"It would be tiring, ma'am." His voice held the tiniest sarcastic tease, a challenge, like I couldn't figure him out even if I were a psychiatrist.

"I'm sure it would be."

Lucas said, "We're here to talk about Kyle DuPont."

Wait, didn't Xerxes' assertion that no one in the prison had ordered the hit prove Jonah wasn't involved? Why did we need to talk to Jonah at all? Maybe Lucas didn't believe Xerxes. Maybe we were just covering all our bases.

"How is he?"

Was he laughing? I felt Lucas press his leg against mine in warning under the table. "He's been shot. We'd like to know what you had to do with that."

Jonah looked momentarily disconcerted, then snorted. "Look around you, man. What could I possibly do? I'm locked up in the middle of nowhere, a guest of the federal government courtesy of your tax dollars. I'm here for a long fucking time."

"Jonah! No cursing," the guard admonished.

They must say that five hundred times a day.

Our half hour would go quickly if we had to spar for every bit of information. I said, "We know about Wendy and Jewel."

"Know what?"

I saw his right thumbnail start to dig a line down his left thumb. His aura was black, consuming the light around him, in the same way his betrayal consumed some light in Kyle.

"You know: how Wendy is providing healthcare for Jewel during her pregnancy. In her home."

"She's a nurse."

"Yes, but why wouldn't she have Jewel come into the hospital where she works, or refer her to a clinic? Surely, she doesn't have the equipment she needs at home to make sure the girl and the pregnancy are healthy."

"Or the license," commented Lucas.

Jonah tensed. "What Wendy has or hasn't got available to her isn't something I know. Again. How could I?"

"But you know about Jewel?"

I could see him working over the possibilities, the thumbnail digging deeper and deeper into its companion's pad.

"There's a guy here. Asked for a favor and it was in my best interest to grant it." He shrugged, and I flashed on what his life must be like, surrounded by the people he had worked for years to put away. Now, he was trapped with them, an ex-police officer. I wondered if the prison kept him apart from the others, or if he was subject to violence or humiliation because of his former occupation. Somehow, it seemed a particularly inhumane way to treat him, and I had to remind myself that he had killed a man. He had killed a man, but he was someone who, if I had known Kyle in New Orleans before the storm, would have been part of our lives. A friend.

Lucas said, "Xerxes?"

He shrugged again. "Could be." He tapped his finger on the table twice, as if answering in Morse code.

Impatient, I demanded, "Kyle needs you to tell us what you know. Why would someone shoot him? Did you tell them to?"

He stared at me. "Who are you again?"

"Dr. Clara Montague."

He waved my words away, and it caught the guard's sudden attention. Abrupt movements were apparently not a good idea when one was an inmate. Jonah saw me looking and turned to see the guard watching. He jutted his chin at the man, and the guard nodded, but didn't drop his stare.

"I know your name, lady. Why are you here? What's your connection to Kyle?"

If I wanted information, I would have to give some, which might put me in harm's way. Anyone connected to Kyle could be in danger if Jonah was revenging himself for the perceived injustice of his incarceration. But was his vengefulness the truth? The black aura flashed tinges of red: repressed rage lurked in his shadows. Did I have the courage to risk that rage to help Kyle? It was, after all, why I had come.

"Kyle and I have been…seeing each other. In Connecticut."

"Right. His new gig as a police chief. Nice he got a promotion out of my incarceration."

"I get that you think you don't deserve to be in here—"

"Oh, I do deserve to be in here. If I had been him, I would have taken me down too."

I stared at him. His voice was carefully controlled.

"Then why are you so angry?"

He leaned back slowly, and I noticed the guard relax his vigilance. "Who says I'm angry?" The thumbnail continued to dig into his hand.

I must have frowned. Jonah said, "You haven't known him long, have you?"

A deft shift in topic.

"Since December."

"Plays his cards pretty close, our boy."

I nodded. He shook his head, as if I didn't know what I was getting into, his dark eyes never leaving mine. Then, as if he'd made a decision, he said, "I didn't set him up. I heard he'd been shot. I'm sorry about that, but I didn't have anything to do with it." One eyebrow flicked sardonically upward as if to ask if we believed him.

How had he heard? Wendy? His parents? The dark eyes studied me, looking for weakness. The thumbnail had stilled, but a red welt ran along his thumb.

"What about the girl?"

"The girl is a favor, I told you. My…friend here… Well… Jewel doesn't have insurance. I knew Wendy could help, so I suggested it. Whoever showed up with the girl scared Wendy."

Lucas said, "So Xerxes asked you to persuade Wendy to help his girl out, but nothing else? And no one else has asked about Kyle or perhaps… you traded favors? Wendy's services for Kyle's life?"

He shrugged, his shoulders lifting tightly. "I've got a lot of years ahead of me in here and I'm an ex-cop."

"Kyle's theory is that you used this friend's connections to set up a hit on him, for revenge."

"After three years? He should let it go or come see me so we can hash it out." He leaned forward, keeping his eyes on me. I felt Lucas tense but didn't break Jonah's gaze. He wouldn't win. "I just want to get out and start my life again. Hurting Kyle would ruin my chances of leaving, and believe me when I tell you that leaving is all I think about."

"Then who?"

"Who what? Who put a hit on Kyle? Maybe he stepped on some toes up there in Connecticut. Maybe somebody didn't like his style or his skin color. Maybe they didn't like him dating a white woman," he sneered. "Motive is a slippery beast, lady. Look for means and opportunity first; motive, if it comes at all, comes later."

When the plane rose into the air over the prison complex and the national forest, the joy had gone. In its place, I felt sick and weighted. Jonah's flickering dark rage provided motive despite his claim that he wasn't involved. His connection to Xerxes proved he could have used the Sunset Boyz to carry out his revenge, but why now? And if he were innocent, as he claimed, who did that leave? Kyle had just arrived in Connecticut. What enemies could he have? Could Vlad be the threat represented in the knife dreams rather than Jonah? Why would Vlad want Kyle dead?

Kyle had been convinced it had something to do with his past or with the events of Katrina. Was that true? Who in the prison had given Xerxes the message to pass on? And how did that person connect to Kyle's new life in Connecticut? How would we ever figure out all the connections in order to trace the threat to its source? Most important, could Kyle's injury have been avoided if he hadn't come home to New Orleans? What would happen when he returned to Connecticut, if that's where the threat still lay?

CHAPTER 24
Clara

We ate dinner in a small Houma restaurant about fifteen minutes from the hotel. Kyle remained the same, Mariam reported. She would go with me in the morning, if I wanted to visit him again. I couldn't tell if she was controlling my access or being generous, and I was too tired and confused to parse it. I'd done nothing on the flight back but think about what Xerxes and Jonah had said. Lucas hadn't recognized the name Xerxes gave us, his outside contact, one in a long chain from Connecticut to Louisiana. Kyle had been convinced Jonah was the connection between the gang and Dom's death, but Jonah claimed he wasn't responsible. Was he lying?

What about Kyle's safety in the hospital? Would they try again? He was defenseless just lying there. I felt keyed up, as if I should be doing more. I just didn't know what.

Porter joined us for the meal, still mostly silent. The man really should have an eye patch or a pair of mirrored Ray-Bans to complete his persona. After the day we'd had, we could have spent the entire meal in exhausted silence, but that was impossible with a small boy at the table. Antoine was filled with stories of a school science project that had something to do with mud and lettuce and turtles, and of his buddy Max and a game they concocted after school that seemed to consist of seeing who could poke the other the most times with a stick, and the fat bus driver who wouldn't let them stand on the bus, which his mother thought was a fine idea, but bugged Antoine because sometimes you had to talk to someone and they were sitting in a different part of the bus, and what were you supposed to do?

Porter, to my surprise, was wonderful with the boy, asking him questions, in particular about the bus driver.

"Does he yell?" he wanted to know.

"Only if we haven't listened to him," Antoine explained. "He always pulls the bus over first and waits for us to calm down. If we don't, then he gets up and comes down the aisle and if we're still not in our seats, then he yells."

Porter seemed satisfied at this answer, and I wondered what he would have done otherwise.

Being with this family made me think about Bailey's comments about black culture. Was I supposed to feel some distinction?

The accents were different and perhaps some of the attitudes, but I didn't know this family. Knowing them at all was at the heart of things. The only way I would learn about differences or similarities would be to start the conversation, by being in the game, rather than a watcher on the sidelines, isolated and safe.

And it did need to be a conversation. As much as I might carry assumptions about Kyle and his family because they were black, they might have assumptions about me because I was white. That, it seemed to me, was what white people forgot, along with the more basic common sense that everyone was different: one black person was not the same as another black person. One white person was not the same as another white person.

That said, I needed to save philosophy for another time.

I ate a simple dinner—some fish, a salad, spicy rice, fruit for dessert—feeling unsteady after the flying and the experience at the prison. I didn't want to encourage dreams, or maybe I did. I was desperate for a breakthrough, some way to connect all the disparate pieces banging around in my head. If Jonah hadn't ordered the hit, did Vlad have some agenda I hadn't discerned—that maybe I could have discerned if I'd stayed home instead of running off down here like some idiot girl knight?

Mariam said, "You look all done in, honey. Why don't you head back to the hotel? I know Lucas will want coffee, but you don't need to prop yourself up just to talk to us."

"It's only eight o'clock, Mom." Antoine piped up. "She's a grown-up. She doesn't have to go to bed yet, does she?"

Mariam gave him a look that indicated he had stepped over his bounds, and that he was already an hour late for bed. He shoveled another forkful of macaroni and cheese into his mouth, and slid his eyes in my direction to see if I had minded too.

I smiled at him. "Antoine, your mom is right. Grown-ups sometimes play a little too hard and need to go to bed early to catch up on their rest." I addressed Mariam. "I'll get the maître d' to call me a cab and get out of your hair."

"I'll take you," Porter said. I hesitated. He sort of scared me. "We can talk on the way about the law enforcement contacts you want me to use," he said.

I shook my head to clear it. What was he talking about?

He took my headshake as a *no*.

"Yes, you will ride with me. It's not very far, and I will save you cab fare." He stood, dropping his napkin next to his half-eaten plate of food.

I looked at Mariam, and she smiled. "He's really fine," she said. "I promise."

OK, I was transparent. I sighed and nodded. I didn't have a choice anyway. Once Mariam called my attention to it, I realized how right she was.

The middle-of-the-night phone call, the concern over Kyle, the dreams and prickling knives, the traveling to the bayou and to the prison—all had taken its toll on me. I felt pretty shaky.

"Sure."

Porter nodded once, yanked his keys from his pocket, and preceded me to the door while I said my good-byes and grabbed my handbag.

As he turned out of the parking lot, I said, "What law enforcement contacts? And do what with them?" It came out a little aggressively, and I saw his eyebrow twitch as we passed under a streetlight.

Perhaps I haven't been clear about how intimidating I found him. He was just... solid. All muscle—chest, legs, arms, neck. If his eyes had been warmer or he had smiled once in a while, it would have mitigated the effect of raw power, but he didn't. Plus, I knew almost nothing about him, other than that he was a pilot and liked kids. That last didn't help since I was a woman, and the jury was out on what Porter thought about women.

"Ma'am, I am in law enforcement. Lucas didn't tell you?"

"Obviously not." Still a little hostile. I had to back off.

"Right. I'm with the Domestic Field Division of the DEA in New Orleans. Lots of contact with gangs. Had the day off, like to fly."

"Oh." That killed the hostility. He had done us a favor, and he would know about drug offenders. "So you would know if Xerxes' contact outside, the person who asked him to pass on the message to Jewel, was a Sunset Boy and had connections up north."

"That boy ain't never left Louisiana."

I shook my head in frustration. "He said it was a 'long line.' Even if he himself doesn't know anyone up north, someone here connects to the gang in Stamford or the line breaks."

"You're going about it the wrong way. You're thinking too much about the gang. Gangs have connections; they use them. North, south, in prison, out. Doesn't matter. There are ways to get messages around, as you've seen.

It's not the gang that's the problem; it's whoever set the gang in motion. Someone has the gang doing his dirty work. You need to find that person."

"You don't think the gang itself is targeting Kyle?"

"Why would they? From what Lucas says, Kyle hasn't taken on the gangs in Connecticut. Besides, Kyle seemed to think that organized gangs, ones like the Sunset Boyz that have loose national affiliations, hadn't made it to *your* town, only to the next town over—what is it? Stafford?" He went on without waiting for me to confirm. "The only concerns he had were a couple of bad boys who liked to pretend. Sounds like he landed a pretty cushy deal."

"It's a quiet town," I conceded. Or it had been until I arrived home. "How do you know all this?"

"Lucas and I have known each other a long time."

Asking would have been pointless.

He said, "That takes you back to Kyle. Who are his enemies? Why now?"

"Couldn't it be someone in NOLA who's holding a grudge? What did happen, anyway, after Katrina? Do you know?"

He glanced over at me, then back at the road. "Homeless guy comes to the cops after Katrina, says he saw a cop kill a guy, stick him in a car, set the car on fire. No one believes the homeless. Officers write up a report, go back to the cleanup. Couple days later, Kyle's dad comes to him, tells him the same story. Says his buddy saw the murder. Kyle says all he can do, like the officers before him, is write up another report; too much else is pressing, but he'll get to it as soon as he can. Few days later, Kyle's dad tells him the buddy is missing. Kyle says lots of people went missing after the storm. Kyle's dad says the guy wasn't missing immediately after the storm, but he is now, after he reported the murder. Kyle reluctantly goes looking, finds the guy dead in a junk pile. Kyle takes it to the chief, gets himself elected to run the case. Black homeless guy, black cop."

"That's it? Why is that such a bad thing? He caught the killer, right? Jonah?"

"Turns out the first dead guy, the one set on fire, was the brother of a girl Jonah date-raped in college. Jonah told the girl no one would believe her if she went to the police because his father was chief. Told her he could do with her what he wanted. The girl had a child from the rape, eventually committed suicide."

I felt a little sick.

"Turned out, the brother knew what Jonah had done and had recently threatened to take the story public. He'd found some other girls Jonah assaulted. The brother—name of Shannon—he had friends in the media. Jonah and his sister's child were alive, so there would be DNA proof. The brother lived in the Ninth, and Jonah found him there, and, using the storm as cover, killed him."

"But why kill the homeless man? And how did he know which homeless man it was?"

"He saw Kyle's report, knew Kyle wouldn't act on it because of Kyle's issues with his father's homelessness. Jonah found the guy and eliminated him. No witness, no crime."

"How does Kyle feel about his father?" I said it, then wished I hadn't. What kind of *girlfriend* didn't know how her partner felt about his own father? I could answer that too: one whose partner played his cards so close to his chest that she couldn't even see he had cards. Maybe that's how cops operated.

"It's complicated. Don't feel bad," Porter said, reading my mind. "You're not the first to wonder."

Other women? *Stay focused, Clara.*

"Jonah and Kyle were close, though, weren't they?"

Porter nodded, the streetlights giving off enough incandescence that I could see it.

"He must have felt so betrayed when he found out what Jonah had done." Sort of like I had when I found out who my biological father was and what he'd done.

"Yes, and he felt he had betrayed his own father by dismissing him as just another homeless person—especially since he should have known better. He knew his dad was clear-thinking enough to tell the truth. He just didn't want to deal with it, thought he knew what was important."

"Why did he leave NOLA? Why not stay? He had a good career; he'd done a good thing getting Jonah locked up."

"Kyle's brothers-in-blue decided he was a rat, so they 'lost' files, played pranks, even graffitied his house. Buried in that was the threat that if his family ever needed police protection, they wouldn't get it. Kyle decided his family would be safer if he left town. No one to blame then. His family disagreed, afraid that once he was gone, they'd be targets of the department's lingering rage."

"Were they?" No wonder Kyle wouldn't talk about his time in New Orleans.

"Cops have long memories, but they prefer justice. Once the verdict came down, the hate went underground, and most of the department let it go."

"You don't think anyone's left who might want revenge?"

"For what? For putting away one of their own? Maybe. But it's been three years, Clara. That's a long time to wait."

"OK, if the shooting isn't related to his time in New Orleans, then someone in Connecticut initiated the hit. But who?"

"Seems like you would know more about that than I would."

"You think it's personal?"

"Could be he's stepped into some hornet's nest, because he's new. What this story about Jonah should tell you is that Kyle's a pretty righteous guy."

I thought about his resistance to becoming involved before my divorce was final, about his careful adherence to the rules, about his sharing only necessary information. Then I thought about my own unwillingness to settle with my ex-husband. My soon-to-be ex-husband. I was pretty high on the righteousness scale myself, something Joe called me on when I butted into an investigation.

"I guess Joe Munson, um, Kyle's second-in-command, might know if Kyle has crossed a line or made an enemy. But wouldn't he have said something?"

"Won't know until you ask. Maybe this Joe isn't making the connection. Maybe he already has, and telling you isn't on his radar. Not like you're a cop."

I ignored the dig, thinking. Was it coincidence that the Sunset Boyz were involved both in Louisiana and Connecticut? "I know gang task forces are sometimes federal because gangs don't care about state lines. You said you or your law enforcement contacts might be able to help me. I mean, it could be the Sunset Boyz in Connecticut, right? Shouldn't we ask your contacts to check for connections?"

"Ma'am, I needed an excuse to get you in the car before you planted your face on your dinner plate." Was he smiling? Maybe his face was cracking. "I recommend you head back to Connecticut. Seems to me you've asked every question you can here. Seems you shouldn't be the one asking the questions at all."

Was he trying to get rid of me? We wouldn't have gotten this far without my contacts.

My phone buzzed an incoming text message. I pulled it from my purse, saw Mariam's number: *Kyle is awake.*

CHAPTER 25
Kyle

When he woke in the hospital, at first all he could feel was the heaviness of the drugs they'd used to keep him under, as if he were pressed flat under a couch. He so rarely took anything, even aspirin; he could always feel it in his system, slowing him down.

At least they'd stopped painting hospitals shining white, substituting an unfortunate mauve, as if he were in the women's wing, having a baby. He listened, heard nurses chatting somewhere outside his room, the clicking and beeping of monitors, the squeak of rubber-soled shoes on the polished floor.

Slowly, it came back: the boy, the garden, the drive-by—but he hadn't been shot there; the girl, the bayou, the shotgun—no, not there; the convenience store, Lucas, the green Honda. Yes, that. But why? He turned to look out the window. The need to remember pressed at the back of his head, like someone's hand, light but insistent. He'd cheated death twice now. Whoever was after him would make damn sure to do the job the third time.

It finally registered that he was looking at Louisiana, not Stamford. The light shining through the window indicated midday, but he couldn't trust his eyes, not with the drugs lingering in his system. He wondered briefly if this was what Clara meant when she talked about the persistent effects of her dreams.

Oh God. Clara. He'd probably received about a thousand text messages from her. He'd mentioned her to both Lucas and Oz, but they wouldn't think to call her. She would be frantic, considering hopping on a plane to New Orleans. He hoped she hadn't done that. Mariam would tear her to shreds. And his mother suffered no fools. Not that Clara was a fool. Lordy, his head was muddled.

The door opened, and Clara and Mariam walked in.

He looked at Clara. "How did you get here?"

"United's six a.m. flight a couple of days ago. How did you get here?" Mariam laughed.

Kyle scowled. "Not what I meant, and you know it."

"Mariam called me. My question stands."

He looked at Mariam.

"Lucas thought it would be a good idea to call her, you know, so she didn't worry. Apparently, she cares for you quite a bit. She hopped on a plane before I could tell her otherwise."

Was that his sister telegraphing him not to mess this one up? If so, Clara had converted her in a remarkably short time. At least, he hoped it was a short time. "What day is it?"

They told him. He'd been out of it for three days. A lot could happen in three days. Did they know Clara was still married? Mama would never forgive him. Maybe he couldn't forgive himself. What difference did it make? He'd almost died, and he loved her. "Am I OK?"

"You have a punctured lung, but the doctor has now tentatively agreed you should be fine. They don't like to commit, you know."

He looked at Clara again. Her eyes held a lot of questions, fear too. From her dreams? He felt so tired, too tired to deal with what she wanted to know, but he could see determination in her jaw and shoulders.

Mariam stepped back. "How about I get some coffee?" She headed out of the room without waiting for an answer.

Clara sat down in the ugly chair. "Kyle…"

He reached for her hand, glad the movement didn't hurt. "I'm sorry," he said, but she started talking as if she hadn't heard him.

"I know I probably shouldn't have come because, you said, well… the whole pulling back thing. But you were shot…" She rushed it, maybe worried he would stop her. "It didn't seem right, staying in Connecticut and waiting around to hear…"

"What about work?"

"Ernie can handle things for a few days. It's not like he hasn't been running the company for the last fifteen years. Kyle, I need to know…" She paused.

"Dreams?"

"You're not going to like it, but I've been helping Lucas, along with some guy Lucas knows named Porter."

He laughed. He wondered how much effort Porter had put into scaring Clara, just for fun. She looked at him, her eyebrows raised in question.

"I know Porter."

She nodded, but he could see she didn't get it.

He sobered. How much of the Jonah story had Lucas told her? Clara had probably weaseled the whole sorry tale out, and maybe about his father, too. A hot rush of shame flooded him. Why couldn't he let that go? "Clara, there's stuff in my past… It's not pretty."

"I've been talking to your family and friends while you've been… asleep, and we've visited Jonah."

"What?" He struggled to sit up. That was *his* story. He could only imagine Jonah's bitterness.

"He was so controlled," she said, seemingly unaware of his distress. "I guess he feels a lot of rage, even if he keeps it tightly reined in." She laughed a little sadly. "I'm so sorry. He must have broken your heart."

He said, "Jonah and his gang buddies set up the hit, using Jewel's maternity care as the payment. She told me…" It started to come together, the pieces interlocking in his mind, but Clara interrupted.

"No, it wasn't Jonah, Kyle. Lucas and I are pretty sure." She studied his face. "You are still angry with him, aren't you? Is that part of the reason you came back here? You should know Jonah says you did the right thing, that if the situation were reversed, he would have put you in jail, too. He said you should 'let it go.'"

He felt a little stunned. Jonah wanted him to "let it go"? Jonah should be asking Kyle's forgiveness for betraying their friendship: righteous in public, a man Kyle believed would never break his oath to protect and serve, but corrupt underneath.

Besides, if Jonah wasn't trying to kill him, who was? He and Lucas figured Jewel called the gang guys who shot him in that Houma parking lot, but the gangs had no beef with him. They wouldn't randomly target a cop. Jonah remained the only person in his life that would want him dead. If it wasn't Jonah, he'd read all the evidence wrong, let all his old guilts cloud his judgment.

Clara was still talking. "Porter told me about the rape and the murder and the department here shunning you and threatening your family. I mean, not threatening so much as…. I'm sorry. It sounds as though you went through hell. No wonder you came north. I get it. I wanted a fresh start too, after Father died."

His chest started to throb. He moved to try to ease the pain, but that made the throbbing worse. "Clara—" She was rushing now, as if she needed to say it before she forgot.

"Anyway, what's most important, and what we all agree on at this point, is that since it wasn't Jonah at all, it has to be someone in Connecticut—"

The throbbing was worse. "Clara… call the nurse?" He started to sweat. He could feel it on his face and chest.

She suddenly looked up at him and ran to the door, calling. A nurse checked the chart, noted the sweat, listened as Kyle explained.

"Here." He showed Kyle the infusion pump next to the bed and explained that he could press the button whenever he needed pain meds. Then the nurse pressed it for him, and in a moment, Kyle drifted into black peace.

The second time he woke, Mariam sat in the burgundy chair, flipping through some fashion magazine. Had he dreamed the visit from Clara? Had he dreamed Jonah's desire that Kyle "let it go"? He must have.

Mariam put down the magazine. "Hey, bro. Feeling a little better?"

He tried moving and, while his chest still hurt, it seemed less painful to breathe. Maybe. "How long have I been out?"

"You lost another eight hours of your life. It's time for dinner."

"Oh joy. Jello and mystery meat."

She smiled. "We figured you might be hungry for something different. Lucas will be by in a little while with some of my cooking."

"Where's Clara?" He looked around, as if she might be hiding behind a door.

"Down the hall, calling her office."

He hadn't dreamed it. He looked at the clock over the door. "At seven o'clock at night?"

"One of her clients asked specifically for her."

He wondered who it was. "She's been helping Lucas?" he rasped.

Mariam handed him a cup of water and a straw. Grateful, he sucked some down.

"Yeah," she said. "You know Lucas. Once he gets an idea in his head, I can't stop him."

"It was Lucas's idea to talk to Jonah?"

"They're cooking it up together. Your girl, she's as much of a terrier as he is."

He took another draw on the water, felt it cool his throat, watched his sister. She liked Clara, he could tell, but Mariam wouldn't commit for a while, not until she saw how things were playing out.

Then Clara's comments came back: if it wasn't Jonah, then who? Who else would have the gang connections? And why now?

He let the images of his last few conscious days, the days before they had shot him, float through his mind, the drugs easing their flow: Dom's shooting; the car fire—who had ordered that?; the meeting with Oz; Wendy and her parents; the girl in the bayou. Which part was important? What had he seen or done that threatened someone enough to want him dead?

Clara entered the room, phone in hand. "Hey! You're awake again." She smiled and crossed to kiss his cheek. That felt awkward, but Mariam looked on, wearing their mother's approving face. How could Clara win his sister over so quickly, while he still felt disapproval from all those glaring white women in Connecticut, never mind from his own family? Now wasn't the moment for that conundrum.

"Did your sister tell you Lucas is coming soon with dinner? We thought, if you were awake, we could all eat together."

"Where's Mama?"

"She'll be here." Mariam flipped a magazine page, and his stomach flipped with it, considering his mother and Clara in the same room.

He nodded. "Everything OK at the office?"

"Sure." Clara didn't seem sure, but he didn't want to press her in front of his sister. He would persuade her to return to Connecticut. Lucas was a good investigator; he could help Kyle handle whatever came up on this end. She could get hurt, and anyway she needed to run her company. And maybe he could get her out of here before any disaster with his mother.

"You can go home, you know. I'll really be OK. My whole family is here."

Mariam's approving look disappeared. Crap. He'd said the wrong thing. He could see it on Clara's face, too, a quick flash of pain.

Mariam snapped, "You can't just send her away because you're awake."

He raised his hand off the blanket, let it drop again. "Sorry. I wasn't thinking—"

"Hey! You're awake!" Lucas walked in with Mama, Antoine trailing him. He was carrying a rectangular casserole dish that smelled of garlic, tomatoes, and cheese. The boy held a wooden bowl, leafy greens peeking out the top. Mama carried a pecan cake. Mariam crossed and took the bowl from her son, setting it on the table at the foot of the bed. She kissed her husband.

"Hey, Mama. It's good to see you," he said. If anything, his mother looked a little drawn.

She set the cake down and hugged him, gently.

"It's OK," he whispered in her ear. "I'm going to be all right." She hugged him again, but when she stepped back her eyes were dry and maybe a little angry.

Mariam said, "Kyle here has suggested Clara go home, says his *family* can take care of things."

His mother gave him a sharp look.

Lucas said, "Oh man. You don't want to do that. She's gotten you a bunch of answers. She tell you about Jonah?"

Kyle nodded.

"Made us fly all the way up to Pollock."

"I thought that was you."

"I just got the pilot. Your girl here put the fire under my butt, pulled some fancy strings to get us permission. He's pretty much back to his old cocky self. Says you should come see him."

That sounded different from Clara's interpretation. "Jonah?"

Lucas rolled his eyes. Kyle wondered if Jonah had actually said that. Wendy had suggested he needed to forgive himself for having investigated her brother and put him in jail. Lots of people seemed to have lots of ideas about what he should do.

No doubt trying to be helpful, Clara busied herself with plates and utensils, cutting hunks of lasagna from Lucas's pan, adding salad and dressing. She gave the first one to Antoine, then slid a plate onto Kyle's lap table with a fork and a napkin. When she had served everyone, she settled onto a chair by the door, refusing to meet his eyes. He would apologize, but still, here she was, in his hospital room, thirteen hundred miles from home, after he'd said they had to pull back.

He sighed. If she had been shot, he would be sitting by her side in her hospital room, hoping he was making a good impression on her mother. Maybe the drugs were making him seesaw between loving her for it and being exasperated yet again. Maybe that seesaw *was* love.

He knew she would always try to do right, especially since her dreams drove her to discern their messages. She couldn't walk away, no more than he could, even if he got paid to solve his mysteries and she didn't.

Maybe he was kidding himself. Maybe it didn't matter that she still wasn't divorced. He should understand that his priorities weren't her priorities. Wasn't that part of being in a relationship? It was her money, after all. She had the right to preserve it for her own future rather than handing a bunch of it off to an ex. He should just accept that he wanted her in his life no matter what, and he would stand by her until she had things sorted. That was the kind of guy he wanted to be, and he hoped she would hold up her end of things. If she didn't, well, he had been there before.

He shook himself out of his reverie.

Antoine was telling a story about a monster he had conquered on his way home from kindergarten. Apparently, it was orange and wore pink sneakers and liked to lick behind his ears. Kyle smiled, caught Clara's eye. She still looked hurt.

"Sorry," he mouthed.

She nodded then looked away. Maybe his family would give them a moment before visiting hours were over. Maybe he could explain.

Family. Jonah's family. He let his fork drop onto the plate.

Kyle hadn't just damaged Jonah's career. Alec Harris had retired as police superintendent shortly after Jonah was convicted, shamed by his son's behavior. He would have had the power to make Kyle's life difficult, just by putting the word into a few of his trusted associates' ears. Alec Harris, having worked his way up from beat cop through vice and narcotics to superintendent, would know guys he'd put away, guys who would do him a favor for some concession—a transfer, some credit in their prison account—guys who would know how to pull off a gang hit in Connecticut.

He'd suspected Alec had been involved in covering up his son's crime, but Harris had taken him off the investigation before he could confirm it. Did he have the cold, hidden anger to put this kind of revenge plan in place? On Kyle's recent visit to Harris, Harris seemed to understand and had tried to be helpful. After all, Harris had spent his life serving justice. But so had Jonah, and look where Jonah ended up. Perhaps Jonah had learned from his father.

Clara cocked her head, and he realized he was staring at her. *Why now?* she had asked. Maybe he could answer that, too. Maybe Harris's kindness had been a cover, perhaps just like his son's acceptance of his incarceration. Alec Harris was sick. Kyle had seen the pill bottles on the hall table, the loose skin on his face and neck as if he'd recently lost a lot of weight, the cane he used to support himself. Alec Harris was dying, and before he did, maybe he wanted vengeance on the man who had destroyed his life and his son's. What did he have to lose? Nothing. He'd already lost everything he cared about.

CHAPTER 26
Clara

Kyle was staring at me with a strange expression on his face. He had just whispered he was sorry, but sorry for what? I had a list. I was glad of the buffer of his family, in particular, Antoine and his adorable monster story. I wished I'd had the imagination at that age to make up a cool orange friend with pink sneakers.

Kyle interrupted. "Has the doc said when I can go home?"

"Are you kidding?" I snapped. "You've been shot."

That earned me a crisp nod from his mama, who hadn't said much to me. Since Mariam apparently liked me, perhaps Kyle's mother would too, although she appeared to be a woman who made up her own mind, and she appeared not to have made her mind up about me.

Kyle said, "The department won't run itself."

Well, that was a shot, the second one tonight, over my very frayed nerves. First, the crack about his family being able to take care of him, implying I could just toddle on home, as if I hadn't gotten us access to

Jonah and Xerxes, and moved our thinking in new directions. Now I was leaving my business to run itself? What did he know about that? He didn't know how much time I'd spent on the phone, online, on email to Ernie and the crew, trying to keep up with the office in between flying to talk to Jonah and driving down to the bayou. Really? He thought I was neglecting my responsibilities? I didn't know how many more responsibilities I could take on and still remain one whole, unfractured human being.

"Excuse me." I got up and walked out of the room, letting the door swing shut behind me. I heard Kyle's voice in a question, and Mariam's gentle remonstrance. Maybe Mariam got it. I hoped she did. I wanted someone here on my side.

I paced to the end of the hall, not really knowing where I was going. Kyle had said he wanted to pull back. Perhaps my coming breached some kind of wall he'd put up. But he'd been *shot*. Wasn't this what people who cared about each other did?

While neither Ernie nor I was happy about his handling the business solo, he understood. I had done the same for him when his daughter died. When he retired, I would hire a second-in-command for backup.

Meanwhile, Ernie said Evangelia needed more hand-holding than I'd anticipated. I wondered how much of that was her, and how much of it was Vlad, trying to keep track of me. I hadn't called Joe yet either, and I wanted to tell him about Porter's belief that someone at home was behind the attacks on Kyle. Since Joe already was investigating that angle, he might know something new.

A set of double doors led to a stairwell. I pushed through and started down the steps. Maybe cellphone calls were allowed on a lower floor.

My shoes clicked on the concrete, echoing in the hollow air. I felt myself spinning in a void. My dark inner voice told me Kyle didn't want me. His family didn't know me, as generous as they were in allowing me to see him. It helped that Lucas, an investigator, understood the need for answers, but even with him, I felt a gentle tolerance, as if he could find out more without me, and maybe better and faster.

Bailey was so far away, and I was still surprised and hurt at her questioning my relationship with Kyle when I felt unsure about it myself. While I wanted to celebrate our new closeness, his pulling away had confused me. I needed someone to talk it through with, someone to support me, but she used lawyer-mind on me instead.

My mother, a whole other story, was in Montana. I had long given up expecting comfort from her, but I did expect it from Richard and Paul, who still felt shocked and dismayed at my subjecting them to gun-toting drug dealers. I'd only spoken to Richard since that night—easy, since he worked for me—and he'd counseled me to give Paul time. Even Richard had been cool when he'd said it, and that was unlike him. Finally, Palmer and his demands for money. I had brought it all on myself. Why did trying to do the right thing always piss someone off? And how did I rebuild these torched bridges while the dreams kept flashing their nightly warnings? I was only one person.

Oh, poor me. *Get over it, Clara.*

I pushed through the door at the bottom of the steps. It opened onto another floor of patient rooms, a nurses' station along the right wall, and beeping monitors. It still smelled like something slightly fermented bubbled in the corners, even under all the bleach. Wheelchairs littered the hallway. A man with an IV on a rolling pole shuffled down the corridor, his gown and bathrobe flapping like dry leaves around his thin legs. He saw me and grinned, did a little two-step. I smiled back, heartbroken. Why did our bodies betray us? How, with all our research and medical know-how, were we still not smart enough to conquer these terrible pains?

A nurse stepped from a doorway, saw me. "Y'all lookin' for someone?"

"I'm seeing a patient upstairs, needed a little break."

"Not a problem. There's a lounge with coffee and things on the main floor though." She pointed through the double doors at the other end of the corridor. "Go through there, make a right and down the stairs. You can't miss it."

"Thanks." Coffee at this hour would have me up for the rest of the night. Still, I could see she wasn't comfortable with me on her floor, and when I reached the main doors, I realized it was a cancer ward. Minimizing traffic helped control infections. I pushed through the doors and dutifully walked downstairs toward the café. At the bottom, I paused. What was I doing? Kyle's family would wonder where I had gone and why I was taking so long to return. This was childish and petty. Kyle and I would work out our issues some other time, and in the meantime, I had come to support him.

As I turned to go back into the stairwell, I heard my name. Kyle's mother was exiting the elevator. Here we go, I thought with dread. I turned on my best Fairfield County smile.

"Shall we get a coffee?" She gestured toward the café.

"I'd like that. I haven't had any time to talk to you." I could do this.

When we were seated with our drinks in front of us, she said, "Kyle's not thinking right, you know. He's angry at being in a hospital bed. He doesn't like having other people do for him."

I nodded.

"How long have you known my son?"

"Four months, give or take."

"Not so long, then."

"No, ma'am." I stirred some sugar into my decaf and waited for it. It was coming, just as Bailey said it would. I wondered how I would answer, how she would phrase her questions, what she really wanted.

"How's he doing up there? In his new job."

That surprised me. I had expected a laying down of the law, her expectations for how I should treat him, me being a white girl and all. I expected some more stern and severe version of Mariam, who could be pretty stern and severe herself, even if she seemed to have left that persona aside for the moment. But maybe my expecting this to be about race was racism.

"Fine, I think. A new place is always an adjustment, but he has the support of the town council, and his officers appear to respect him."

"Does he have any friends?"

He didn't, and it worried me a little. He only talked about men on the force, his workouts, his frustrations. Did Joe count as a friend? I wasn't sure if they socialized or if it was even possible given that Kyle supervised him. "I think he's been too busy to make them," I hedged.

"He says it's a pretty white community."

"That's fair." I smiled. "Not everyone in Connecticut is white, although I can't imagine he's not making friends simply because he's black. I'd like to think we're a little more progressive than that."

"You don't feel your difference, honey. Kyle feels it every single day. He feels it even more deeply now that he's up north. He doesn't know that, but I do."

I wondered how much of this discussion was about her son being far away and how much was about race. My mother and Kyle's mother might have some experiences in common after all, although my mother hadn't known where I was for most of the fifteen years I'd been traveling. Besides, Kyle and his mother seemed to feel a closeness I still didn't share with Constance. Even now, as she was lecturing me—gently, but still—about my white privilege, I didn't feel anger from her. Only a kind of reserve, as if she would wait and see, as if she had spent her life waiting and seeing.

I said, "He's intelligent, good at his job, attractive, athletic. Black is only one component."

"My boy, he wants to be really good—at what he does, at being human. Those two things, they don't always go together, especially not when white people might think differently about what's good."

"Won't there always be differences among people about what's good? Why does it have to be about race?" I tried to keep my voice nonconfrontational, but the language itself was so weighted, I didn't know if I could succeed. "I'm not trying to be difficult," I clarified, or hoped to. "I'm trying to understand. One of my friends at home, she says I can't ever hope to understand his 'culture.' Her word."

"You don't think your cultures are different?"

"I think people are people—each one a little different, each one somehow created, enhanced, damaged by his or her particular circumstances. I want to know Kyle's particular circumstances, and I want him to know mine. I am not all white people, and Kyle is not all black people. Isn't that what we've been striving for?"

"But you see yourself as the norm. White is a blank canvas. White is nothing. White just is. Anything that *isn't* white is difference." She twisted the cup in a circle. "I'm not saying it's deliberate, or that you are consciously racist. Everyone carries racism around with them, even black people. But think of it this way. What if you grew up somewhere everyone was black. When you walked into a room, everyone looked at you. Everyone wanted to 'understand' you. Everyone wanted to introduce you to the one other white person in the room. They wanted to help you achieve success, that is, when they weren't calling you nasty names behind your back. And usually, they just want you to achieve something to make them look good: *Look at all these poor white people we've helped out of the gutter.* It rarely has anything to do with making lives better." She sighed. "OK. Now I'm just being bitter. Forgive me."

I wanted to touch her, to reassure her that I did understand, but I didn't want to be patronizing. These discussions made me feel frozen. I didn't know what to say. My background seemed to place me in a morally culpable position, yet no one chose her background. We were born as we were. What we made of it was what mattered. But in the midst of the discussion itself, I couldn't move forward or backward. I considered everything I said carefully, and then, when I said it, it usually came out wrong and I spent the next month kicking myself.

"It sounds a bit like being a woman," I said.

She smiled. "You got that right."

I said, "I care about your son. I want to be in his life, and I want him in mine. How can I ease your mind?"

"You're going to have to work harder than other people. You can't assume you understand. You don't. And you're going to have to give more room to each other than other couples."

I nodded. "It's challenging to love another human being."

"I mean like just now. I know he hurt you, suggesting you weren't his family. But you're not—yet. He's still making up his mind. It's riskier for him."

That got to me. Maybe it was one final judgment among many. Maybe I had reached the crack in the sidewalk where I always tripped. "I'm sorry, ma'am, but you don't know me, and you don't know what I risk by loving him. I don't think that's a judgment anyone can make about another person, regardless of skin color."

She rested her fingers on my wrist. They were cool and so slender they were almost weightless. "We're not arguing," she said, "and I am not asking you to stop seeing my son."

Did a silent *yet* hover in that sentence?

"I just want you to be aware of the challenges."

"Mrs. DuPont, Kyle and I have economic differences, we have race differences, we come from different family environments, and we chose different professional paths. We want different things in our shared community. I'm aware of the challenges. But we both care deeply about doing right. We laugh together. We support each other. We listen. If we have any chance of surviving as a couple, that last is the most important thing I can think of."

She released my wrist, tapping me once with her finger. "OK," she said, as if she'd let me win this round, would see how I did going forward. I had no doubts the jury was still out, but at least I hadn't alienated her, and I breathed out a silent prayer of gratitude to the god of conversation for saving me from myself for once.

She said, "We should get back. They'll be wondering if I chased you away. They think I'm meaner than I actually am, but it's good to keep them guessing." She smiled again. "Don't you think you can't talk to me. I'm not trying to shut you down or chase you off."

To my dismay, I felt myself tear up. "I don't want to lose him," I said.

"That's as good a place as any to start." She stood, used the table to steady herself. I ran my index finger under my eyes to flick off the tears and followed her back upstairs.

"There you are," Mariam said. "We were just about to send Lucas off to find you. We've got to clear out. I'm going home for a couple of days, taking Mama with me. It's easier with Antoine in school. Clara, will we see you again?"

I hadn't even thought about my next step. I needed to talk to Kyle first. I looked at Kyle, wondering if he wanted me here or wanted me gone, wondering if he wanted to get out of the hospital so he could come home with me. New Orleans was his home, after all. Maybe being here had re-kindled a desire to stay.

I said, "I'll probably stay a couple more days. I promise I'll get in touch before I go."

She smiled. "Good. I'll hold you to that." She kissed her big brother and shepherded her family out the door, Antoine dragging at her hand like a tiny anchor off a steamship.

Kyle held out his hand to me. "Come sit next to me."

I sat sidesaddle on the edge of the bed. He took my hand, tried to pull me in, but I resisted, still hurt.

"It's like that, is it?" he asked.

"One thing at a time, OK? Let's get you well and home, and then we can talk about us."

"But seeing you here with my family—"

I cut him off. "I'm not part of that family, remember?"

"I messed up, Clara. Don't I get any credit for drugs in my system? Bullet wounds in my chest?" He smiled.

"You didn't trust me. Your father a homeless man? Your sister and her younger husband? Your ex-partner a murderer whom you caught? The shunning by the police department? Your fear for your family's lives?"

"You didn't trust me for weeks after we met, while I helped you protect your family."

"We've known each other a few months now, Kyle. Some of this should have, I don't know, come up over dinner. *Heard from my mother today...* You know. What people talk about." I sighed and put my forehead on his shoulder, felt him stroke my hair.

"It's OK," he said. "I'm alive. We have time."

I sat up. "Will you still feel that way when you get home? Or will I go back to being someone to protect yourself from?" I shook my head. "That's for later. For now, why are you so eager to get out of here?"

He started to sit up, excited, then winced and leaned back gingerly against his pillows. "Jonah's father put out the hit."

"What? Why? No."

"Revenge for putting his son in prison."

I ran my fingers through my hair, pulling it off my face, twisting it into a ponytail. "Porter thinks someone in Connecticut is the puppeteer. Jonah claimed he wasn't involved, and wouldn't he have some idea if his father wanted vengeance?"

"Or he played you. That's what people learn to do in prison: manipulate. If they aren't already masters before they go in. Does Lucas agree with Porter?"

"Less convinced."

He tilted his head as if to say *see?* "Anyway, what does Porter know about it? I thought he just flew you up to Pollock."

I told him about our conversation on the way home from Mariam's.

"Ah. That's how you knew all about my life. I figured Lucas had clued you in."

"Lucas is almost more close-mouthed than you, but he gave me pieces."

He grinned. "He's figured out how to survive Mariam."

"For a guy laid up in bed, you sure like to live dangerously." I flicked the air by his shoulder with my finger. Sobering up, I said, "How do we figure it out?"

He looked at me, almost with sympathy, as if I were a second grader who wanted to grow up to be president. "You'll help me? I need to get home."

"Home?" Did he mean here, with his family?

"Connecticut. We've done all we can here."

But I shook my head. Was the father/son theme about Harris and Jonah rather than Teo and Vlad? Why would Harris use a gang? Kyle seemed to need the Harrises to be culpable, as if that justified his own actions retroactively.

CHAPTER 27
Clara

Two weeks later, Kyle left the hospital. The day after, he persuaded Porter, probably against doctor's orders, to fly him up to the prison to see Jonah. What they said to each other didn't take long, but Kyle told me he walked away feeling he had done his duty. All the brotherly awe he'd felt around Jonah had dropped away like the leaves in the Connecticut fall, exposing the raw, bare trees underneath.

He said he hadn't told Jonah he suspected Alec, but instead reminisced about Katrina, comparing notes over what he and Jonah had used for communication or who they'd been paired with or what Alec Harris had told his son about working the storm. Kyle didn't learn anything new. Kyle believed some sense of duty to his father would always keep Jonah silent—even if Alec had acted foolishly to help his son cover up a crime, if, in fact, he had.

The problem now was tying Alec Harris—or someone in Connecticut, as the rest of us believed—to Dom Ofiero's murder. Joe caught us up on the Connecticut situation on a long phone call that Kyle generously put on speaker. He had joined me in my hotel room after leaving the hospital. "Mama won't let me out of her sight," he'd complained, "and being safe won't find a paid assassin."

We'd spent a long time talking about Harris, Vlad, Teo and the Sunset Boyz, and the possible connections and motives. Nothing fit exactly right, which was worrisome since my dreams felt increasingly frenzied. Last night, I'd cycled through a new one in which glittering and feral eyes slithered among the knives, noses twitching at the smell of blood. I kept screaming, but the man couldn't hear me and I woke again and again, my voice hoarse and high in the night.

Joe said, "The burnt car in Rowayton matched the car you described leaving Dom's murder scene, so those dead home boys had to be the ones who drove by, guns blazing. Someone in the gang wanted you dead, but someone *else* didn't want any dead cops; blue-car guys acted against the second someone's orders and got burnt crispy for it."

I asked how he knew someone in the gang didn't want any dead cops.

"We pay attention when they start killing cops."

"But then why would they agree, at Alec Harris's direction, to killing Kyle?" I asked.

Joe said, "There's a faction that's risking it, but we don't know why."

Kyle said, "That witness, Miss Hilary—she got us plates on the second car. Any luck with those?"

"Yeah, I tracked down the owners, but said owners, a couple of boys in hoodies with jeans hanging off their asses, claimed their car had been stolen, even though they hadn't reported it—*aw, man, you know the cops don't never believe us*—and their buddies alibied them for the time of the murder. They claimed that if they'd *smoked that pair—which they hadn't, cuz they was miles away, in another county even, hangin' with girls*—they would have done it because those *sherlocks* totally f-d up."

It was close enough to a confession to close the case on Dom's murder, but not to solve who wanted Kyle dead. And with no direct evidence tying them to the scene, since Joe said Miss Hilary hadn't seen their faces clearly enough for a lineup, unsatisfactory. Somebody needed to end up in prison for killing that young man.

Joe continued, "Espejo's still worth looking at. Clara's told you Teo's his son, right?"

"Yeah."

"Wondering if there's a motive in that."

"You mean Teo commits the crime to catch Daddy's attention."

"Maybe," said Joe. "You never know with sons and fathers."

Kyle shrugged, but I could see he was agreeing. "Maybe we should approach Teo, see what he knows about his old man."

I shook my head. Introducing Teo to Vlad would only result in tragedy: the boy with no father suddenly gifted one who understood his choices—it ensured his future as a criminal. Bianca's little girl would have a fugitive or imprisoned father—everything Pops and Dom had tried to protect Bianca and her baby from.

But Kyle had already moved on. "Check out Espejo's financials too. The gang knew I'd traveled to NOLA. Who does Espejo know here? Or maybe who has he paid off? Include law enforcement in your search. Bribes."

Joe took a different angle. "What about campaign contributions? Espejo's got the money to buy serious influence."

"You think some politician wants me dead? Good god. Well, follow anything that makes sense. I'll be home shortly."

They hung up.

How shortly, I wanted to know.

He was still healing, he said.

What about the good people in Connecticut who paid his salary?

Just a couple days to rest and all. Couldn't hurt to look around during his remaining time in New Orleans, now could it?

I took him at his word and booked tickets home for two days hence. I needed to get home too. I had fences to mend—and my dreams were intensifying. I couldn't fall apart in Louisiana. I needed Paul.

We went to Mama's for dinner to talk things over with Lucas.

Antoine came speeding out of the living room to ram his head into Kyle's knees.

"Careful there, buddy. I'm an old man, and I just got out of the hospital."

Antoine looked up. "Not for your knees, silly."

Kyle smiled. "No, not for my knees."

His little face turned serious. "Are you going to be OK, Uncle Kyle?"

He nodded. "I'm tougher than the bad guys."

Antoine smiled and ran toward the kitchen, yelling for his grandmother.

Mariam said, "For now."

"Exactly," I said.

Kyle said, "Neither of you would run the other direction if the knife came for you."

"But it hasn't been coming for me," I retorted, then wondered when I had mentioned my knife dreams—or even if I had.

"Not this time." He gave me a pointed look, and I shut up. No reason for his family to know my family drama.

"We want you safe," his sister said. "Don't you get it?"

"I want to be safe too. That's why I solve crimes, so everyone feels safe."

She shrugged and took his arm. She'd lost for the moment, but she wouldn't give up. "Come on. Mama's made all your favorites."

He reached back to grab my hand. "Oh good. Clara, you can take notes, so, you know, you can make them for me in Connecticut."

I bumped his shoulder with my fist. "Unlikely. But I do a mean takeout, and I know all the best restaurants in Paris."

"Good to know for the next time we're in Paris."

I shut my mouth. I wanted very much to show Paris to Kyle.

His mama had set the table with fresh flowers, a shiny pink tablecloth, and napkins printed with roses. A ham, sweet potatoes, biscuits, black-eyed peas—she must have worked all day to make him this dinner. It would be hard when he left again. All mothers wanted their children close.

He said, "Oh Mama. You didn't have to go to all this trouble."

"I don't get to see you so often, so you don't get to tell me how to spoil my own son."

They sat and Lucas prayed, while Antoine, who had insisted on sitting between Kyle and me, fidgeted in his chair.

"Lord, we thank you we are all together, and that Kyle is healing from his grievous wound. We pray you will protect him as he returns home, and that you will bless Clara as she supports him."

Say what?

Kyle reached around Antoine to poke my shoulder with his finger and I stifled a laugh.

"Lord, we pray you will guide Kyle's investigations, and we thank you for this feast before us. Bless us, oh Lord. Amen."

It felt strange to be prayed over. Mother used to take me to church when I was a child, but I'd stopped after I left home. I wondered if Kyle missed church-going, if he'd looked for a church up north. Both Stamford and Norwalk had predominantly black churches, if that mattered. Then I wondered if my thinking he would want to be part of a black church made me racist. Or if Kyle's mama would think I was racist for thinking it. It was so confusing.

Mama cut thick slices of ham and passed the sides. Antoine bounced over his plate, his pleasure in eating surpassed only by the pleasure of asking his Uncle Kyle questions.

"Are there a lot of bad guys in Connecticut, Uncle Kyle?"

"A few."

"How do you find them?"

"We go and look, buddy. How do you think?"

"But where?"

"Under rocks and picnic tables. Sometimes behind trees. Wherever bad guys hide."

And so on. It felt good to laugh.

Mama said to me, "I'm sorry you had to meet New Orleans this way. You should come back to see her sometime in the spring, when she really shines. You could meet Kyle's pops."

He glanced at me. Sheepish?

"I'd like that," I said, grateful his family seemed to like me at the moment. An invitation to come back was good, right?

He said, "If Pops is still around. You know his lifestyle isn't likely to lead to longevity."

"We look after him, so no need for you to worry."

Mariam took pity on me. "Our father is a homeless Vietnam War vet. He lives under the highway." Her tone was kind, but her face had gone rigid.

Stricken, I said, "I'm so sorry. I didn't know." At least not the under-the-highway part.

She nodded, gave Kyle a look that could have put a hole in his other lung.

Kyle ignored her. "I'm not worried about his care; I'm worried about what can happen on the streets. It's a free-for-all. You do understand that?"

I saw him visibly rein in his sharp tone, force himself to sit back in his chair and sip some wine. Glancing around the table at their resigned, tense faces, I wondered how many times the family had listened to his concern. I cut another bite of ham, stole a look at Antoine, whose wide, worried eyes tracked his mother's every emotion and movement.

A moment passed. Then Mama said, "He knows you're sorry for not listening to him after Katrina. Even if you had listened, you might not have been able to do much. It was chaos."

"I was the reason his friend died."

"You couldn't control what Jonah did, Kyle. You didn't know. You put your whole self into figuring it out—it nearly split us apart as a family. But you've come home—even if it's only for a short while—and you'll be back again. We've made our peace"—she looked around the table as if trying to assure their agreement, despite Mariam's visible anger—"and there's nothing else you need carry back to Connecticut but the assurance of that."

Mariam looked at her brother, waiting. "You get what you came for?" she finally said.

"Absolution?"

She was indignant. "You want absolution for endangering our family with your pursuit of truth, justice, and the American way? You want absolution for making us terrified that if we called your brothers-in-arms, they wouldn't come? Me, with a baby? You want absolution for ignoring your own father? You want it for going up north and finding yourself a nice *white* girl? There is none. Get over it." She shoved her chair back and strode into the kitchen. Kyle leapt from the table in a flash and went after her.

My whole body had gone hot, the flush spreading up my neck and across my cheeks. I looked down at my plate, forked up a bit of sweet potato and tried to eat it. Tears prickled at the corners of my eyes, but I pushed them back. This wasn't my fight. It was between Kyle and Mariam, and had roots much deeper than my showing up here.

Antoine snaked his fingers across the tablecloth toward me, laid his hand on my hand. "I like you, Aunt Clara," he said.

That made suppressing the tears harder. I took an uneven breath and smiled at him. "Thanks, Antoine. I like you too."

"Don't take it to heart, Clara," I heard Lucas murmur. "This is an old argument."

Kyle's mama mm-hmmed her assent. "They've been at it since they were little. You're just a convenient target." But her face turned toward the kitchen's raised voices. I wondered if she thought I'd added fuel to an old fire.

Stiff Montague spine. I put on my best party face, brushing quickly at the stray bits of damp on my cheek. "It's fine. I'm fine." I smiled. "I just hope they work it out."

"They probably won't." Lucas smiled in sympathy. "They're pretty grown up to be fighting like cats and dogs."

"Cats and dogs?" Antoine giggled. I was grateful for his levity, but I still felt the hurt.

Kyle's mama got up and started clearing plates. Antoine popped out of his chair with a cheerful offer to help. When they stepped through the kitchen door, the voices were lowered. I started to rise when Lucas stopped me. "Mama has lots of experience at this. Let it be," he counseled.

I subsided in my chair. "Am I clueless?" I asked.

"About?"

"I don't know. What my whiteness means to this family?"

"Don't make yourself more important than you are." He smiled again to take the sting from the words. "This argument isn't about you. It's about Mariam's feeling that Kyle doesn't do his fair share in the family, and that he'll use any excuse to avoid it. Nothing more, nothing less. Her feeling isn't going to go away. She feels it with me. I think it's something women carry when they feel responsible for everything and everyone in the family."

I nodded, felt the flood waters recede. "OK. I'm a vehicle, not a road. Got it."

He grinned. "You betcha. Now, I'm going to rescue my brother-in-law so we can talk about some things."

"Not without me."

"I'll be back." And he was, in a minute, Kyle in tow. Through the kitchen doors came Mama's voice: "Don't think you're going anywhere until you've had pie," she said.

Lucas, Kyle, and I repaired to the living room, after Lucas had sent Antoine to help his mother dish up dessert. I kept an ear out for further rumblings from the kitchen, while Lucas told Kyle about what we had learned from Fredericka about the message Jewel carried from the prison gang to the guys outside. Lucas had turned the original note over to Oz, but showed Kyle a photocopy:

KDP. 24 HRS. 10K. A.M.

"So I'm KDP," Kyle said, setting the note on the rattan coffee table where we could all see it. "I assume the rest is 'within twenty-four hours with payment of ten thousand dollars.'"

"That's what we figured too," said Lucas. "Xerxes was really clear that message had come from someone in Connecticut—via some kind of gang telegraph."

"Could be a blind."

"Or you could be blinding yourself. You're stuck on Jonah and his family, but the evidence just isn't there."

Kyle looked at me.

"I've been trying to tell you," I said.

He sat back, rubbing at his sore chest. He didn't talk about pain.

"So someone in Connecticut finds out I'm in New Orleans, and activates the gang network down here to finish a job they couldn't?"

"Sounds about right," Lucas said.

"So either that person has direct ties to the boys in federal prison, or they're working through intermediaries. Most of them wouldn't know what they were passing on. Maybe Espejo in Connecticut asked Harris to get a message to Jonah, who passed it to the gang in prison, who then passed it out again to whoever was on the street and available for the job."

"Sounds excessively complicated. Why include the Harrises at all? Gang to gang seems simpler, less risky."

Kyle shook his head. "The Harrises knew me. Maybe the gang needed information, and the Harrises provided it."

Lucas said, "Could be, but in that scenario, they still aren't carrying messages. Having a conversation about someone you know isn't illegal."

I picked up the note. "What's A.M.?"

Kyle said, "Morning? Did the execution have to be carried out at a particular time of day?"

I looked at him.

"Sorry. Wrong word. Well, not the wrong word, but a poor choice nonetheless." He put his hand over mine. "All right. That's a dead end." His eyes slid toward me, just like Antoine's at dinner, to see if I got the joke.

"Very funny. So is there anything to finish in New Orleans? The Harrises won't tell you if they were passing messages, and we can figure out what 'A.M.' is anywhere, right?"

Lucas said, "Oz traced the plate on the green Honda. It belonged to a couple of local Sunset Boyz. Oz has arrested them on attempted murder charges."

"I could talk to Jewel again. See if she passed a message to the pair that owns that car."

"That's Oz's job," I said. "It's obvious someone with gang ties wants you dead. We just don't know who—or their motive."

The smell of peaches and sugar wafted in from the kitchen.

Kyle said, "Maybe Jewel could lead us to the Connecticut connection."

Lucas said, "Jewel's talking to the Houma cops. We don't need to get involved."

Kyle shrugged, then winced. "I feel like I'm leaving things undone."

I said, "What's left undone has nothing to do with the shooting. We need to go home and figure out who at that end wants you dead."

Lucas said, "Listen to your girl, man."

"Damn straight," I said, just as Kyle's mother came through the door carrying the pie. She looked at me a long moment, as if the curse word had changed her opinion of me, then set the pie on the table and walked back into the kitchen.

Lucas snorted like a ten-year-old. "Oh, Mama does not like curse words. You're in trouble now."

I sighed inwardly. It's not as if I could be in any less trouble.

CHAPTER 28
Clara

Once the airline found out Kyle had been wounded in the line of duty, they bumped us from business class to first. After all he'd been through—half of which I still didn't know about (like the backstory of a father on the streets?)—he needed rest.

I did too—I felt as if I hadn't slept for weeks—but the dreams reasserted themselves, perhaps because we were headed back to the source of the danger. Again, I stepped into the forest. Again, I heard cries. Again, I saw the man surrounded by knives. I called Kyle's name, and he shook me awake.

"Clara!" he hissed. "I'm right here." He held my hand so tight my fingers ached.

I put my hand over his and squeezed, then gently extricated it from his grasp. "Sorry."

"Dream?"

"Yes."

The woman across the aisle, impeccably dressed in a silvery blue dress and a long string of real pearls, looked over the top of her *Wall Street Journal* at me. I smiled and said, "Sorry," but she sniffed and went back to the business section. Ah, the joys of home. The flight attendant asked if I needed anything, giving me a pointed look, but first-class travel had its perks. She didn't ask, and I didn't tell.

"No, thanks," I said. "We land shortly, don't we?"

"Thirty minutes," she said.

Cold traveled through me, as if someone were pulling an icicle through my internal organs. I rubbed my hands as if to warm them and knew these pains were precursors to bigger ones developing over the next few days.

"Did I hurt you?" he whispered.

I shook my head. "It's the dream."

His fingers brushed my chin, gently turning my face toward him. "It's about me, isn't it?"

What should I tell him? It's not as if the dream imagery would help him solve the case. All it did was warn me of danger, and we already knew he was in danger.

"Yes."

"Will you tell me about it?" He studied me, as if trying to read my thoughts.

I told him about the woods, about the knives, about the purple and gold that matched the Sunset Boyz medallion. I told him the pain ricocheting through me now meant my body couldn't take the stress, and it would start to shut down.

"Like what happened with your mom?"

"Like that." I'd already started feeling dizzy; the world felt off-kilter, as if I had vertigo, as if those trailing purple clouds of smoke might reappear at any moment. I was afraid to talk about it, as if naming my pains would give them more power. Paul had saved me from the Swiss sanatorium after my father's death, but I was pretty sure he was still holding a grudge over the nightclub debacle. I had a list of things to make right.

"Is there anything else?"

"Dreams don't give me facts, Kyle; they give me archetypes. Imagery of knives and piercing is masculine imagery—father imagery—but your father isn't out to kill you!" The woman in pearls looked over her newspaper at me again, one eyebrow raised. I leaned back in my seat, avoiding her glare. Kyle looked at her and then at me.

"Then whose father?" Kyle lowered his voice and leaned forward to block the woman's view and hearing.

I thought about my dreams in which Lia's daughter turned into a boy and distributed drugs. "Vlad's the father. Has to be, right? Vlad the Impaler—knives? Vlad's only son is Teo and Teo doesn't know. Vlad doesn't know either, because one day he complained that he only had a daughter and a granddaughter. But in my dream, it's his *son* distributing drugs and hurting people. So could Teo be behind this? Could Teo have wanted you dead and Dom tried to stop him?" I whispered. "Maybe they were supposed to kill both you and Dom that day."

Kyle shook his head. "That makes no sense. If Vlad's the father image—knives, piercing, whatever—"

I could see he wanted to roll his eyes.

"—then he would want me dead, not Teo. How are you making the leap to Teo, who doesn't even know Vlad is his dad?" He smirked at the rhyme.

"Unless he does. We've theorized he's looking to attract Vlad's attention, right? If we assume he knows, then what better way to move up in the organization than to pull off something big?"

"Like killing a cop and getting the entire police force looking for ways to lock you up? I don't buy it. It seems more like someone is trying to take over. Add territory. Undermine Espejo's authority. Think that's Teo? Is he that kind of strategic thinker? Has he developed the contacts?"

"I think he's smart," I said slowly. "Assuredly manipulative. But…" I threw up my hands. "I've only talked to him twice."

The flight attendant's voice interrupted my train of thought. "Ladies and gentlemen, please make sure your seatbelts are fastened, your seatbacks and tray tables in their upright and locked position, for our final descent into New York's LaGuardia airport."

Kyle said, "Why would Teo come to see you to protest Dom's innocence? That makes him more visible, and if he did the killing, he'd want to be invisible."

The plane touched the ground, and just like that, we were home.

I slept alone that night and mercifully, the dreams let me be. Maybe they figured I had enough information for the moment.

Still, the next morning, when I resumed my ritual of espresso in the solarium, I felt woozy and headachy, as if the dream's patience was fraying. The coffee cleared some of the fuzz out, and I hoped we might learn something today that would push us closer to resolution.

After a shower, I armored myself in my favorite red dress and headed to the office to clean up the mess that had accumulated since I'd departed so abruptly for New Orleans. Ernie asked after Kyle, and then spent an hour going over jobs and billing. For once the numbers seemed better. Maybe some of our business-building efforts were paying off. Maybe I should go away more often. I suggested this with a laugh and got a glare in return.

"You need to take this business seriously or sell it. I can't keep stepping in like this, Clara. I'm not a young man."

I nodded, chastised. Remember the to-do list: *find a new partner, so Ernie can retire.*

Around noon, I headed out to see Paul. I needed his forgiveness, and I missed him. I hadn't heard from him, and Richard just kept shaking his head at me at work, so I knew Paul was still angry about the night we'd met Moscarelli. It was high time I apologized, plus he was my best shot for figuring out the dreams.

Paul's office was the ground floor of a sweet little Victorian a couple blocks off our town's main street. It had a garden in the back and a green painted door and no one in the waiting room. His receptionist nodded at me, and I took a seat; he didn't make me wait long. His grudges didn't run that way.

"Come on in, Clara."

I sat in my favorite plush chair, deep green velvet backed by a window filled with the geraniums and jacaranda Paul nursed through the winter. I set my bag on the floor. Crossed my legs. Uncrossed them again. Leaned my elbows on my knees.

I could hear the traffic outside; people enjoying the afternoon light were walking from shop to shop talking in the newly warm air.

Paul sat quietly, watching me.

"I'm sorry," I said.

"For?"

I thought about it. "It's who I am."

"You're sorry for who you are?"

"No. I mean, I'm sorry that who I am put you in jeopardy. I didn't think going to that club would be so dangerous."

"What did you think?"

"What I thought was that someone had put out a hit on Kyle, and I had some information that could help. I thought it was a dance club with lots of people, and that would keep us from getting hurt."

"You didn't think that kind of investigation might be better left to the police?"

"I didn't even know if a Stamford businessman dealing drugs from a dance club and running a gang was credible information, or just something Bianca said so I would take her seriously. She was desperate and angry. All I wanted was to confirm it was worth looking at before I passed it along to Kyle."

"You don't think the police have the ability to check out all sorts of information?"

I dry-rubbed my face with my hands.

"You're going to get hurt, Clara, or get someone hurt. Richard was ready to fight, and you know he can't do that. He's ill. You can't put him in a position where he has to choose between his own health and someone else's."

That put me in my place. Richard seemed healthy most of the time; the HIV drugs did their job. But I knew he had to be careful; around Christmas, a Lyme tick bite had wiped him out for several weeks, much longer than it would have taken someone healthy to recover.

"You also didn't think about how gay men stand out in straight clubs, even now. Some tough guy gets a few drinks in him and suddenly we're targets, Clara. You don't see us that way, and I love you for it, but the world still isn't safe for people who are different. That club manager—what was his name?—what kind of damage could he or his bouncers have done to us? You don't live in our world. You think you understand but you don't because your privilege blinds you."

First Bailey, then Kyle's mama, now Paul? "Wow. You've never played the privilege card before."

"I've never had to."

Was I really that clueless? Wouldn't Richard have told me if he weren't comfortable? Then I realized he would have been worried about me, would have needed to protect me, wouldn't have wanted me on my own. He did that a lot, despite Paul's pleas for caution. So not only had I endangered them, I'd ignored their vulnerabilities.

"I don't know what to do but apologize."

"You can change your behavior," he snapped. Paul had never, ever snapped at me.

I sat back, staring at him. He was flushed, and his hands gripped each other.

I tried to keep defensiveness from my voice. "I've come home, after fifteen years of running away. I'm taking over Father's company so Ernie can retire. I'm making up with my mother. I'm trying to rebuild my friendships, including with you, however erratically I kept in touch while I was away. I'm starting a new relationship. I have changed a lot."

"We could have been badly hurt," he insisted, unable to let go.

"You're still frightened."

"Part of me is wary all the time. It's a way of life."

"Sort of like being a woman," I said. "Or someone who sees visions."

He shrugged and his hands loosened, a concession, but tension still lingered around his eyes.

"What you're asking of me," I said slowly, "is not unreasonable. I didn't think about anyone else for fifteen years, but I'm working on that now. That's why I'm here."

More relaxed now, he body-scanned me. "You're also here because you need me."

I pushed his assertion aside. "I'll handle it. I don't want to burden you. I didn't realize how much of your anger was about Richard. I'm really upset about that, Paul. Please know that."

"I know." He rubbed his hand across his face.

"Is he OK? I mean, he seems fine at work, but I've…been away."

"Everyone in town knows you've been in New Orleans. Have you spoken to Bailey?"

I shook my head. *Oh god. My other problem.*

"She muttered some things about you last time I saw her, something about your relationship with Kyle being inappropriate and a promotion she'd gotten."

"I need to iron it out. I can't seem to get this friendship thing right."

Finally, he looked sympathetic. "Come for dinner. Bring Kyle. We'll catch up and you can judge Richard's health for yourself."

I reached across to squeeze his hand. After a moment, he squeezed back, and I figured that meant I was nearly forgiven. I would be better, I promised myself, I would.

"Now. What are you here for? Dreams?"

I told him the whole story, beginning to end: the dream about the man in the forest surrounded by knives, Kyle getting shot, the trip to New Orleans, Teo and Bianca, the dreams that followed: Kyle in the middle of the forest circle, pinned to the ground, blood oozing from his wounds. The dreams about Vlad's grandson dealing drugs. I would wake up two or three times a night, panicked, disoriented.

"The dreams haven't stopped?"

"I got some respite in New Orleans, but they started up again on the plane home yesterday. I irritated the society broad across the aisle when I woke myself up crying, interrupted her reading."

"So something is still brewing, and you want me to …what?"

"I thought maybe talking it through with you would give me some insight."

"You seem to know everything already, except the identity of the person after Kyle."

"Not knowing could get him killed."

He brushed his hair back from his forehead with long, graceful fingers. "There's nothing else?"

Then I remembered Fredericka. "Someone I met called me a witch."

He didn't laugh. "That's an old name for what you are."

"I'm not a witch," I protested. "Witches fly around on brooms and make potions and have warts on their noses."

"This is about beauty?"

"Of course not. It's about identity."

"How did you meet her?"

I told him about visiting her home, the tea, the purple smoke. "Do you know what she put in that tea?"

"Probably salvia divinorum," he mused.

"Salvia? Not the red stuff everyone forces me to plant in their gardens?"

"No, no. This is a white flower. Look it up. It's used in Mexico in shamanic ceremonies."

"How would she get it?"

"The internet?"

"Right. Dumb. Sorry."

"Did it help you? Did you see anything different as a result?"

"No, just the purple smoke—one of the Sunset Boyz' colors."

"Did the other man with you—what was his name?—did he see it too?"

"Lucas? No. He gave me a couple of funny looks, but he didn't drink any tea. Maybe she only drugged mine. Why?"

"I wonder if it was to make you see something, or to keep you from seeing something."

"You mean she wanted to blunt my perception?"

"You wanted information from her. Maybe she knew more than she told you."

"We got something significant from her, Paul—the note the girl Jewel passed to the gang that described the hit. There are just some initials we don't understand: A.M."

"Morning?"

"That's all we came up with."

"Maybe she knew what A.M. was. Maybe she knew you already knew what A.M. was and she wanted to keep you from finding out. Or keep you from finding out from her. The psychedelic drug distracted you, right?"

"But Lucas wasn't distracted."

"Maybe Lucas doesn't have a connection to A.M."

"How would she know who knew what?"

He shrugged. "How do you?"

He had a point.

"So A.M. is someone or something here, in Connecticut."

"Something to think about, yes?"

"What would the delay gain her? Do you think she was working for the gang?"

"She helped one of their girls."

"She shielded her."

"I don't know, Clara. I'm just offering possibilities."

"Wendy Harris sent Jewel there to protect her. Fredericka runs some kind of safe house."

"Maybe she wanted to see what you were made of."

"She was testing my gift?"

"Sure. Maybe she wanted to see if you would tell her something she needed to know. Maybe she wanted to know the level of your investment. She'd seen Lucas before. Maybe she needed to know you were genuine, so she could show you the note."

"She knew I saw the smoke."

"Maybe she wanted you to use your gift to figure out the note. I'm sure you denied you were a witch, but she wanted to shock you."

I leaned back. "She was very interested in how I felt about Kyle. In fact, she mostly talked to me and ignored Lucas. Still, it's pretty under-handed to drug someone."

"Granted." He paused. "Maybe using some kind of hallucinogenic could help."

"What? Me?"

He nodded. "Maybe it would provide greater access to your subconscious. We could try a small dose under controlled circumstances."

That sounded terrifying. How much control was I willing to give up to help Kyle?

"I would be with you the whole time," he said.

"What about flashbacks?" I asked. "Isn't that a risk with hallucinogens?"

"Salvia divinorum is pretty safe."

Had that been Fredericka's gift? Could I figure this out with a drug trip? God, my language was as outdated as my ideas. "When?" I asked.

"How about now?"

I shivered, nodded.

CHAPTER 29
Kyle

Kyle leaned back in his chair, twirling his pen on the blotter. Late afternoon light bleached a square out of the papers strewn across his desk. He rubbed at his chest, which still ached. He had to call for a follow-up appointment with his doctor here, just hadn't gotten around to it. If he didn't, he risked long-term pain, but he mostly wanted it to go away and leave him alone, so he could get on with his life.

In some ways, going home to New Orleans had been reassuring. He knew his city. Even the corruption felt familiar, as if somewhere so humid could only breed vermin and provide it moldy places to hide. His job had always been to clean.

Here, he wasn't so sure. Sometimes, in the glances he got from the prim white ladies on the street, dressed in their designer silk sweaters and diamond stud earrings, he thought he might be the vermin they wanted cleaned out. They always had this startled, wary look in their eyes, as if he'd snuck up on them or as if he might suddenly drag them into a dark alley to be ravished. And ravished was definitely the word, like a romance novel with a dark edge. Their imaginations couldn't stretch further than that.

Maybe Mama was right, and this wasn't the place for him.

He looked out his window at the parking lot behind the police station. The trees were turning that yellowy-green they got just before they leafed out, and the air smelled sweetly cool and fresh, like after a rain. Two women got out of a Range Rover, and walked toward the station's rear door, one of them blonde, like Clara. He turned back to his desk and the problem at hand.

Kyle had told Joe before he left for NOLA that he would talk to Espejo, but he hadn't. He couldn't put it off any longer. Joe had found nothing in his financials. Espejo stayed clean by delegating the dirty work to the gang. Now, Kyle needed someone who would turn on Espejo, someone who wanted to leave gang life behind.

Was that Teo? Perhaps his approaching Clara had been him testing the water. He had a child now. Then again, he was in his mid-twenties—more likely he was committed to the life until the law or violence ended his career. The complicating factor was whether Teo knew Espejo was his father. *If* Espejo was his father. Clara's dreams did not a fact make.

The bigger question, perhaps, remained Teo's ambition. Kyle regretted that he'd ignored his own father to further his ambitions. For Teo, discovering that his biological father headed the criminal enterprise whose ranks he was attempting to climb might push aside all other considerations. Teo had lost the father he knew early, and that left a hole in a young man's life. He'd rejected Pops, instead searching for power over his own life. Association with Espejo would be a potent motivator.

Either way, Teo remained his most promising lead.

He picked up the phone and called Bianca Ofiero. "I need to talk to Teo," he said. "Can you put me in touch?"

"What for?" Her voice came down the line harsh and challenging.

He shut his eyes, wondered about life as, say, a line cook or computer technician. "Mr. Welles has information useful to the police department."

"Teo's not just going to call you. Why should he trust a cop? Cop's girlfriend made trouble for me."

"I'm trying to solve your brother's murder. Have you already forgotten Dom?"

"Have you? I've heard from nobody for weeks. Like I've dropped off the planet. Heard you went on vacation."

He rubbed his temple. Maybe a job as a mall security guard. "I was hospitalized for a gunshot wound. Know anything about that?"

She gasped. "Are you OK?"

"The people who killed Dom tried to kill me. I think Teo knows something. I don't think he did it." Maybe. "I just need to talk to him."

She thought about it, her breathing whispery in his ear. "I'll tell him to call."

"Thanks." He doubted she heard his sarcasm. He gave her his cell number, so Teo didn't have to call the department. "Do it now, please? The matter is urgent."

He waited ten minutes, reading reports, until his phone rang. Teo refused to meet at the police station but agreed to a Starbucks in thirty minutes. Kyle beat him there by fifteen and found a table in the corner where he could watch the door, leaving a message about the meet for Joe while he waited, skimming Twitter.

When the boy showed up, he held the door for a blonde with a baby in a stroller, charming the child with a goofy face. No hoodie today, just a pair of jeans that looked as if they would slide off his slender frame, and a long-sleeved yellow tee under a grey flannel shirt that just about hid the tattoo creeping up his neck. He sauntered Kyle's way and slid into a seat, while Kyle wondered what the woman would think if she knew a gang member had held the door for her.

"Want something?" Kyle asked. "It's on me." Teo looked like he needed a month of good meals.

"Nah. You don't owe me nothin'."

"You sure? I'm having something."

He shrugged. "A muffin? Those chocolate chip ones aren't bad."

Kyle got him two and paid, navigating between the tightly packed tables to set the muffins and a cup of coffee in front of Teo. He sat down and pulled the lid off his own to let it cool. "If you give me information related to Dom's murder, I might need you to write it all down and sign it. I assume you want to catch your friend's killer."

"I don't know nothin' about Dom's death. I *told* you that."

Unlikely, but OK. "I'm not asking about that. I'm asking about the argument you had a couple of days before he died."

Teo looked up from the crumbs of the first muffin, pain etched into his face. "Bianca can't keep her mouth shut." He flopped back in the chair. "Dom and me didn't talk after that. We shouldn't have yelled at each other."

"What did you yell about?"

"Dom wanted me to, you know, quit the life."

"I bet he'd told you that before."

"Especially after the baby came. Told me it was bad for Bianca, bad for my little girl. But how'm I suppose to support them? Money's gotta come from somewhere and I don't have skills that go on a resume. I'm good at gang business." His spine straightened.

Kyle considered his strategy, thought about asking about Teo's father, left it for the moment.

"Why was Dom so mad?"

"I knew something. Told him he should tell you. Told him I was going to my boss to try to stop it."

"That someone had a hit out on me?"

He nodded. "He was mad the gang would try to touch you."

"Why did you want to stop it?" Kyle figured going against the express orders of the gang hierarchy couldn't be good for the kid's health.

"Messing with cops never brings anything good, especially you."

"Especially me what?" He blew again across the top of his coffee, watched the steam swirl up.

Teo said, "We know you put that cop in jail in NOLA. If you'll turn in one of your own…" He shrugged. "That's cold."

Righteous. He nodded again, broke a piece off the second muffin.

"Dom didn't want me to talk to my boss. He said it could get me in even more trouble—going against orders. Instead, he said he'd talk to you, if I would just tell him why there was a hit in the first place, who you'd pissed off."

But Dom hadn't. Why not? Was he waiting for Clara to leave that morning? Did he think Kyle wouldn't believe him, would think a hit a fanciful notion put forward by a new cop?

Teo said, "I said I had to tell him. Far as I could see, the only issue's my boss's big ego. Thinks he can run bigger than he is. Somebody gotta take that on, or we're all screwed."

"Vlad Espejo?" Kyle leaned back, his arm stretched along an adjacent chair.

Teo stilled, long fingers poised like spider legs above his food. "What about him?"

Kyle had thought about how to approach this. Espejo's penchant for punishing those who betrayed him was well documented. Joe had shown him the files: he'd earned the Vlad the Impaler label righteously.

"Does he want me dead?"

Teo shook his head vigorously. "You got it wrong. That's not the boss I mean."

"You have more than one boss?"

"Seems like I got dozens, some days. But Espejo," he whispered it, as if he thought one of the blondes or their spoiled children in this posh coffee shop would expose him, "he's in charge of everything. He's the guy to know." His voice held awe, and Kyle knew he'd lost.

"Did Espejo order the hit on those two guys that shot Dom?"

Teo jutted his chin at Kyle.

Kyle took this as a yes. "Why?"

His long thin fingers pried at the paper cup of the second muffin.

"Can't have fools acting on their own."

So someone other than Vlad had ordered the hit on Kyle. Progress. "Do you *know* who wants me dead? And why?" That was the real question, the one that kept him up at night. He now understood Clara when she complained of insomnia.

"Can't say." Teo cocked his head, as if waiting for another question.

Kyle thought quickly, said slowly, "Can't? Or won't?"

He saw in Teo's eyes that he'd found the right question. "It ain't Espejo." He shoved the last bite of muffin in his mouth and wiped his hands on the napkin. "And it ain't been called off."

Kyle sat up.

Teo shrugged. "Would have told you sooner, but you disappeared, and I don't trust middlemen—or girls."

He balled up his garbage in his fist. "Most of us don't want to cross Espejo, but there are always idiots. Watch your back, man."

Kyle dropped his arm to the table, leaning forward into Teo's space. "I can get you out," Kyle said. "Maybe you'd like to be with your daughter, be a true father."

Teo bristled. "I'm a good father. I take care of my daughter." A kind of raw power rose off him, like nearly invisible heat waves off a fire. Kyle filed away Teo's reaction for later use. It was helpful to know a man's weakness.

"Money, sure. But will you be around for her first play in kindergarten? Her soccer games? Her first date? To walk her down the aisle?" Kyle pressed a little harder. "Do you love Bianca? I bet she's scared every day that someone like me is going to tell her you're in the morgue. Do you want your daughter to grow up without a father, like you did?"

Teo's face hardened, and Kyle thought he'd pushed him too far.

"What do you want, man?"

"I want someone who has answered my questions to be safe."

"No way I can be safe. And I'm not your CI. Dom is special. Was."

"OK." Kyle held up his hands, acquiescing. "What's your future, then?"

276

"Only way I see forward is up."

"You want to get closer to Espejo?" Teo had found a hero to worship.

"He's the power. It's a business. I understand it. I've been studying. I know where product comes from, who handles it, where it goes." Not naming the product. Already careful. "I know who's reliable and who isn't. I know the suppliers, the shipment routes, everything I can. You leave me alone; I leave you alone. Stamford isn't your town."

Kyle itched for that information, but Teo was right. It wasn't his town, but he could cultivate Teo long term, one baby step at a time, favor by traded favor. "Are y'all going to stop shooting at each other any time soon?" he drawled.

"What do you care? More dead bangers means fewer guys for you to worry about."

"Really? That's how you think cops think?"

"It *is* how cops think."

Kyle sighed in acknowledgment of a partial truth, but he ached at the loss of so many young men, usually young men of color. How much greater could his country be if it learned how to tap that energy rather than wasting it?

"Are you going to tell me the name of the person who put out the hit?"

"You want a lot, man, but some things you gotta learn on your own." Teo leaned in. "Some things aren't worth telling. Get me killed." He looked down at his coffee. "Get someone I love killed."

Kyle thought about his brother cops in New Orleans, their threats toward his family. "Have you been threatened?"

"Don't need to be. I know how to keep my mouth shut. But you better figure it out soon, or your blood's gonna be all over the place." He shook his head and stood, grabbing his coffee. "That's all my loyalty to Dom buys you. Thanks for the food, man." He turned and loped toward the door, sinking his wrappers in the garbage pail on the first try—as if he were a normal kid with no cares.

CHAPTER 30
Clara

"You're sure you're OK with this?" Paul asked. "You could probably achieve the same effect with a deep meditation."

"But you know I haven't been practicing. I need a short cut."

The jacaranda by his chair rustled and a leaf dropped to the floor. Paul's eyes never left mine.

"I know," I said. "No shortcuts. But Kyle's life is at risk and I can help."

"And next time?"

"I promise I'll start practicing."

"You've promised before."

I felt myself start to shake. Not visible, but as something that began in my gut and moved outward, as if all the feeling I had suppressed had gathered itself into a ball and begun spinning, its energy flying apart in strands that vibrated in my every organ and muscle.

Paul's eyes were flat.

This is how we felt our anger at each other. I knew he could see the energy.

I didn't need to tell him how desperate I felt, how powerless if he wouldn't help. I was willing to fly back to New Orleans to see Fredericka and her potions if that would get me the answers I needed. Paul worried I would do exactly that, risk my gift to save someone I loved, and thus risk my health and sanity.

"You will come weekly for training," he finally said. "No excuses. And if you don't, you're on your own after this. I'll neither enable nor save you from your risky behavior."

I hated ultimatums, especially when I knew the action was the right thing. But I nodded. I couldn't handle my gift without Paul.

"Next week," he said. "Not after Kyle's safe. Not after you solve some problem at the office. Not after you figure out how you've hurt Bailey. Next week."

Still shaking, I nodded.

"Fine." He stood. "I'll get the preparation. While I'm gone, start with the breathing exercises you already know. That will center you and help you focus on Kyle." He left through a door behind his chair that led into his workroom. He kept all manner of herbs there, many he'd collected in his travels in an attempt to find medicines to ease Richard's HIV symptoms and suffering. It looked a bit like Fredericka's wall of glass jars, but with more laboratory components for distillations, freeze-drying, and who knew what else.

I made myself focus on the shaking strings of energy. I settled my hands on the velvety chair arms, let the feel of the fabric ground me. Breathed in deeply and felt the energy ripple out through my skin, wave after wave, like an electrical pulse, until finally it calmed to just my heart's beat.

Paul stepped back into the room, holding a glass mug filled with what looked like herb tea. He set it on the table in front of me.

"I will stay with you for the whole experience, which should last thirty to sixty minutes. Have you set an intention?" He sat in his chair and reached for my hand.

"My intention is to access whatever deep knowledge I'm carrying about the danger Kyle faces."

"Can you make you it more specific? What's the common thread in everything so far?"

I let my mind wander loosely through all I knew: the dream, the knives, Vlad and Teo, Vlad's desire for a son, my dream about Vlad's granddaughter becoming a boy, Kyle's father living under the highway and his guilt that he couldn't save him, my own lost father—and my inability to save him.

"Something about fathers, I think. Or sons. Family. How what we are lives on through another."

"Good. That's your intention then: to think on fathers and sons in all their different variations. Let's see where it takes you. Ready?"

It took a few minutes to impact me, as when Fredericka had given it to me in the bayou. I shut my eyes, leaned back in the chair, and let my fingers uncurl, so my open palms faced upward.

Fathers, sons, fathers, sons...

I let the concepts float like islands in the golden mist that rose before my interior vision, and images became attached to them. I remembered my own father first, a moment of his silliness driving the car a little too fast over a hilly road, feeling my stomach jump. My father watching me giggle. Then my partner Ernie with his daughter, whom he'd lost, his grief whirling like charcoal dust. I saw Teo with his daughter, his hand on her curls, Pops in his garden building that swing set. Lucas with Antoine, listening to his dragon story. Kyle meeting his father under a bridge. Then, the mist swirled upward, like candle smoke in a draft, exposing Kyle, knives, trees, animal menace. My body stiffened, my hands rigid and clutching at the chair arms. Then Vlad's face emerged, unrolling a feature at a time like a window shade, blocking the other images, before it snapped shut again, revealing the face I had been looking for.

I gasped.

The mist cleared.

CHAPTER 31
Kyle

Clara arrived at six for dinner, straight from the office and as rigidly tense as a pair of steel scissors. Kyle handed her a glass of wine as remedy. And what was her problem anyway? Someone wanted *him* dead. He'd been shot twice. It hurt to breathe, and his arm felt stiff. His officer had died *as a mistake.* In New Orleans, he'd felt that he could do something; coming home just made him feel useless again, at sea in his own questions.

They sat down in his living room. Clara took off her shoes and tucked her feet up under her. He didn't have much yet in his place: a charcoal couch fronting a polished wooden coffee table. Two burgundy chairs facing the couch across a grey and black carpet. Pale grey walls. Cabinets to hide magazines and books and clutter. Two coasters on the coffee table for the wine glasses.

"What's wrong?" he asked, even though she should be asking him. The painting over her head was slightly askew. He got up to adjust it.

She shook her head. "Tell me first about your day."

He summarized his meeting with Teo.

"He wouldn't tell you who put out the hit, even though he knew?" she exclaimed.

"Said it put his life—and his family's—at risk."

"What about yours?" She untucked herself, put her feet on the floor.

He grimaced. "Not his priority."

"How is the department keeping you safe?"

He shook his head. No one could protect you from everything.

Clara frowned. "No patrol car, no nothing?"

"Sure, a patrol car once an hour or so. Like that's going to do anything."

She tugged her sweater tighter. "I've been thinking. You know one of Vlad's lieutenants is married to his daughter, right?"

"Yeah."

"We met him when we went to the club. Scary as hell."

"I remember you accused him of dealing drugs." Someday she would push someone too far.

She picked up her wine, sipped, seemed to decide something. "He *was* dealing—at least, he allowed it in his club. No way he didn't know. But that's not the point. That guy is married to Vlad's daughter, Evangelia. You know, where I'm putting in the Versailles gardens." She rolled her eyes. "Could it be him?"

He leaned forward. "Are you suggesting Vlad's *son-in-law* is behind the hit on me?"

She shrugged a shoulder, almost coy. "It would make sense, right? Son-in-law is a kind of son, and Vlad won't let him be anything higher than manager, is even paying for the landscape redesign I'm doing. Why wouldn't Moscarelli pay for it himself? Doesn't he have the money? Or is this Vlad's way of rubbing Moscarelli's nose in the fact that he can't care for Evangelia in the same way her father can? That kind of stuff takes a toll on the ego. Maybe taking over the gang is his payback."

"Does the daughter know about her father's and husband's business dealings?" Was she a place Kyle could apply pressure?

"Hard to tell. She seems caught up in this garden project and taking care of her daughter. If I had to guess, I would say she knows but doesn't want to."

He thought about it as he got up to check the stew in the kitchen. Cumin-scented steam rose from the pot as he lifted the lid. Just a few more minutes. He grabbed the salad from the refrigerator. Espejo wouldn't take kindly to the cops using his daughter against him, but Kyle, at least in this moment, wasn't in the business of kindness.

"What's she like, the daughter?" he asked, leaning against the door frame between the two rooms, the bowl still in his hand.

"Nice. A good client. Thinks through the problem, can see multiple solutions. She's willing to talk out ideas."

"As a person?"

"Her daughter seems happy and well-adjusted. Other than that, Kyle, I've only seen her for about three hours total, and Vlad's always been there. He might affect how she acts." Clara stood. "Is dinner ready?"

"Yeah."

She picked up her wine glass and joined him in the kitchen. He set the salad on the table, next to the oil and vinegar, ladled stew from the pot into white china bowls. Bread and a knife lay on a board in the middle of the table.

"This is cheery," Clara commented, but her shoulders hadn't relaxed. She took an appreciative sniff, dipped her spoon into the gravy. "The stew smells great. Thanks."

"Any sense of her relationship with her husband?"

"None. I've never seen him with her." She scooped up some stew, made appreciative noises.

Kyle took a bite of stew then carved off a hunk of bread, handed it to

Clara and cut another for himself, slathering it with butter. "Do you think Teo knows Vlad is his father?"

"I think Teo would act a lot differently if he knew. He said his parents had died, his mother in a drug overdose, his father trying to exact revenge on the gang. Anyway, why would he lie about his parents? How would that serve him?"

"Teo has never met Vlad. That's what he told me. He's not important enough."

She suggested, "But he has met Evangelia's husband. I saw him leaving the club that night, the night Richard, Paul, and I met Moscarelli. Couldn't Moscarelli have seen the resemblance? He knows how Vlad feels about having a son. What if this gang war thing is about assuring his position in Vlad's organization?"

Something about her tone seemed off, almost as if she knew her suggestions to be fact.

"You mean, if Moscarelli learned Vlad had a son, he might also think Vlad would pass the business on to his son rather than to his son-in-law."

"Evangelia told me how much Vlad wanted a son to carry on the family name, that names meant something to him. Moscarelli would know how important Teo would be to Vlad."

"Why not just kill Teo?" He drew her out, trying to figure out the thread he heard in her voice, like a stream suddenly swelling in a storm.

"Too risky. What if someone else knew? Then Moscarelli's in the un-enviable position of having killed Vlad's son. Discrediting him is better."

"You're sure Vlad doesn't know about Teo?"

She shook her head. "He might. I'm not in his confidence."

Kyle shoved his chair back, picked up his wine, decided he didn't care about Clara's issue if he could get to the source of the hit. "Vlad's daughter never mentioned a brother?"

"I'm not in her confidence either. I'm the hired help."

Hired help. He thought of all the different ways that phrase had sudden resonance. He was the *hired help* in this town. Teo and Moscarelli were both Vlad's *hired help.* Clara was the boss and the people who worked for her were the *hired help,* but at the same time, she was the *hired help* of a gangster. The issue at hand: the difference between being the *hired help* and being the boss in terms of determining one's own future. Who had control? Who wanted it? What did one give up to get it?

He thought about how the people in this town wielded money to get their own way; even looking as if they possessed it earned them respect, a respect he had to cultivate individually with each person he met. *Hired help,* like all those other black brothers and sisters in this country. Suddenly angry, he said, "Doesn't it bother you, taking a gangster's money? Being beholden to someone so abusive?"

She dropped her spoon onto the plate. "Wow. Where did that come from?"

He shrugged, kept his mouth shut. It bothered him, and he didn't understand how she could be so blithe. Or was he angry because she was holding out on him again?

She wiped her lips with the napkin, thinking. "Of course it does. I cringe every time I walk into his house. But I promised Bianca. I saw Dom shot—and then you in that hospital bed… I can't walk away." She shook her head, tears forming in the corners of her eyes.

He grabbed her hand, surprised at his own intensity. "It's a compromise," he said, squeezing hard. She squeezed back, then took her hand back to wipe her face.

He sipped some wine. "That's where all this started for me, with a compromise."

"After Katrina?" she asked.

He nodded.

"Sending Jonah to prison doesn't sound like a compromise to me."

"I knew his father had shielded him. Conspiracy wouldn't look good for the superintendent of police, but I couldn't prove it. Then I got warned: back off or my family takes the consequences. Mariam? Baby Antoine? The consequences didn't even have to be overt… just the cops not showing up when you call, or when someone in your neighborhood calls. I couldn't put them in that kind of danger."

"So you did the right thing. We all make compromises, Kyle. No one lives a life free of reversals and questions and wrong-headedness. We make decisions based on values, and those values can change."

"Values shouldn't be circumstantial."

"Values are different from the law."

"Of course they are."

"Right," she said. "You value your family, so you let go of the investigation and moved north to protect them, figuring people would forget that you went after a brother officer, never mind that he was guilty. What options did you really have? You did the best you could under the circumstances. That's what we all do—and we hope, in the end, it comes out for the best." Was she admonishing herself or him? She picked up her spoon and scooped up some more stew.

Kyle had lost his appetite. He poured himself a little more wine. It burned its way down his throat. Maybe it was the wine that made him ask, "Why are you still married? Is it about money?"

Even to his own ears, he sounded like a pouting ten-year-old.

"You think my money is more important to me than you? You should know me better than that." She tapped her spoon on the side of her bowl. "Listen to yourself: you just said that you went after Jonah because of the principle of the thing. He did something horrible, and you couldn't let his profession and connections keep him from the punishment he deserved. It cost you and put your family in danger.

"I have principles too. One of them is that Palmer doesn't get to use me to enrich himself. I know I contributed to the dissolution of this marriage.

I'm willing to pay up to even that score. I'm not willing to pay the amount he's asking. Why does this bother you so much?"

"It's the principle of the thing." He smiled slightly to let her know he knew he was being a prick, but realized that his temper was rising because she was still concealing some secret. How did he persuade her to trust him?

She smiled back, but tentatively, as if she wasn't sure where this would go. "OK, what principle?"

"It *appears* you value money over people."

"Appearances matter to you, but appearances aren't the same as principles."

"My job as chief depends on my principled appearance to the people of this town."

"You're talking about reputation."

"Yes. My reputation is affected by your actions."

"So to make sure your reputation stays sterling, you want me to give up my principles and pay off Palmer, is that it?" She said it in a flat tone, but her eyes burned. "You are saying that your principles are more important than mine?"

He shifted his tone, trying to de-escalate. "That is the question, isn't it? How do we determine whose principle gets priority when we disagree?"

"I don't think we get to decide for each other. We only get to decide for ourselves."

"And if I don't agree with what you're doing?"

"Then, I guess, your choice is whether you want to stick it out or whether it's of such importance to you that you need to exit the relationship."

They had been talking with great intensity, holding themselves rigid and not eating. Finally, Kyle picked up his spoon and stirred his congealing stew. He still didn't have much of an appetite, but he had worked all afternoon on the meal. He took a bite.

Why did he keep pushing Clara's buttons? He knew she wouldn't back down. She would fight until she was covered in blood. It was one of the things he loved about her—and loathed. He couldn't keep her safe if she insisted on heading straight for the fight.

She watched him eat, finally picking up her wine. "Just so you know, my lawyer thinks we should have the divorce resolved within a couple of weeks. It's not as if I've forgotten about it or ignored it. One doesn't, you know. It hangs on to you with its nasty little teeth until you are finally free of each other."

A peace offering. He couldn't force her to say what was on her mind; she would come to it in her own time. All those years of hiding her gift, her guilt at her father's death—reserve had become a habit.

He reached for her again. "I'm sorry. This investigation has its nasty little teeth in me."

"I imagine it's pretty unsettling to be a target."

"Being a black man makes me a target. Being a police officer makes me a target. I thought I got it, but nothing prepared me for this. I'm taking it out on you. Stick with me?"

She lifted his hand to her lips. "Of course."

CHAPTER 32
Clara

I drove home after dinner with Kyle uneasy on two counts. First, I wasn't sure if he'd understood that Moscarelli put out the hit. I hadn't been able to bring myself to confess I'd learned it in a vision, never mind a drug-induced one. I supposed I could have said it was a vision and left out the drugs, but it seemed easier to avoid it. If he had problems with my "principles" around the divorce, god knows how he'd react to my taking drugs, even nominally legal ones. Too risky.

Second, I wasn't sure if he believed me about the divorce—or even if my getting the divorce would make any difference in our relationship. He kept coming close and then pushing me away as if he couldn't decide what he wanted.

I'd driven the Porsche, probably a mistake. Would he see it as rubbing in our differences? Well, whatever happened next was up to him—both as it related to Moscarelli and to us. I needed to focus on situations I could influence, like my friendship with Bailey. Once I had arrived home, and curled up under the cashmere throw in the solarium, I called her. I had some amends to make.

Weeks ago, I'd texted to let her know Kyle had been shot and that I'd traveled to New Orleans; now, I let her know I'd returned. She'd been so upset that night at The Swan—but about what? Why wouldn't she tell me? Up until now, we'd told each almost everything.

When she answered, I offered drinks and dinner to catch her up. She accepted. Progress. I would figure out what to say later.

My second amends: The next morning, I packed a bag of gardening tools, insecticide, fungicide, fertilizer, and rose gloves into the back of my car and drove to Dom's rental. I had promised him I would help him save the rose, and it seemed the least I could do to memorialize his death.

But when I pulled into the driveway, I couldn't get out of the car. I hadn't counted on the trauma of the shooting to unhinge me one more time. Sitting there, terror washed through me, as if I were experiencing Dom's death all over again. I gripped the steering wheel until my hands hurt and tried to breathe as steadily as I could, one breath in, one breath out, over and over until the terror eased. Eventually it had to. Everything changes.

Flashes of that day came back to me: Dom's delight in his flowers, how he looked forward to the trip to the nursery to confirm the rose problem and solution, the gentle, teasing relationship he portrayed with his father over their dueling garden preferences: Dom for flowers, his Pops for vegetables. How could that interesting young man be gone?

Then the blue car with its menacing rumble and the gun bursts. The dive to the grass. Dom's blood leaching into the pristine carpet of yard. His effort to say something that neither Kyle nor I could understand. Maybe something about Kyle being the real target? If he'd known, why hadn't he said so?

Slowly, I unhooked my fingers from the steering wheel and scraped myself off the car seat. The house appeared unoccupied: no curtains, no other car in the driveway, no personal touches like potted plants. Who would want to live where someone had been murdered?

I retrieved my supplies from the trunk and walked around back to the rose. Many of the canes had brown patches and appeared woody rather than fresh and green. I put on my rose gloves and started pruning.

It was tedious and sometimes painful work when the thorns penetrated the gloves' heavy suede. The long canes draped from the side of a deck, arcing over my head. Keeping my eyes, neck, and shoulders free of pokes and scratches was a challenge, but the pain seemed my due for being unable to keep Dom alive, for still not knowing who was responsible for his death. I had promised his sister, but I hadn't figured much out, unless my vision of Vlad's son-in-law as the instigator paid dividends. Meanwhile, each thorny stab reminded me of my failure. In the end, I piled the prunings into two large paper bags, which I would include in one of my company's dump runs.

The rose looked better, and I hoped it would survive. Keeping something alive was the least I could do for Dom.

Six o'clock that evening saw me at The Swan waiting for Bailey. For once, I'd beaten her to the bar and had my own martini poured before she arrived: Dutch courage. By six thirty, when she still wasn't there—she was never late—and hadn't answered my texts or calls, I called Richard and Paul to see if they wanted to join me for dinner.

"Come on over," Richard said. "We haven't seen you in forever. Dinner should be ready in about fifteen minutes. Can you make it by then?"

I said I would and paid my bar tab, mulling over Bailey's absence. It was unlike her not to call, but maybe she'd had a work emergency. On my way, I tried her office, but they said she'd gone. I did a quick detour to her condo, but the windows were dark and she didn't answer the bell.

Had she deliberately stood me up? Maybe she had decided she still wasn't willing to talk about whatever it was. What would I do if she wouldn't talk to me?

I parked in Richard and Paul's driveway. I loved their little cottage and its sweet garden. The irises were blooming, creating a purple sea to walk through. I knocked and Richard answered the door.

"Perfect timing!" He bear-hugged me. The best. "We're eating in the kitchen. Come on and sit. Paul can get you a drink."

"I'm fine. I had a martini at the bar waiting for Bailey, who didn't show."

He laughed. "Ah ha! We're second best."

"Never," I said.

"We are where you come when you're wounded," commented Paul, pouring wine at the counter.

"True enough." I sat at the little table, covered with a yellow cloth and centered by a vase of purple iris—the yellow and purple an odd, happy counterpoint to my dreams. A plate with a composed salad of Bibb lettuces, bright radishes, and toasted pine nuts already graced my place. Paul set a glass of white wine next to me.

"Thanks," I said.

Richard stirred something at the stove, and then sat across from me. "What happened with Bailey?"

I told them about the conversation we'd had about Kyle and race, how Bailey thought I shouldn't date Kyle because I was still married and because of our differences.

"She said that?" Richard asked, startled. "That sounds like racism."

"She thinks *I'm* being racist, by not considering Kyle's point of view."

"His point of view on what?"

"On… I don't know. I think she's saying that our cultures are so unalike that there's no way we can connect. She thinks that my assuming I can learn enough about his culture for it to be OK is racist, a position of privilege that white people take." I shrugged helplessly. "Maybe it is. I don't know. I told her the only way I could know was to pursue the relationship. Then, I didn't notice a diamond necklace she'd bought to reward herself for making partner. Overall, I'm a bad friend and person. I'm not paying enough attention." I stabbed at my salad and didn't tell them about her fear or the compromise she said she'd made to get partner. Revealing that felt like a betrayal.

Paul put down his fork. "I will neither confirm nor deny that sometimes you are distracted, but you try to be thoughtful, Clara. It sounds as though Bailey has a problem she's not ready to share."

"How am I supposed to be a friend if she won't even call me back? If she ditches me for drinks?"

"You wait. You keep trying. She'll finally learn that you aren't going to abandon her."

"Maybe." I shook my head sharply, as if to clear it. The dreams hadn't stopped, so the haze had thickened, and this new emotional distraction wasn't helping. "Tell me what's going on with you."

Richard got up and cleared the salad plates, returning with a chicken and rice casserole and a bowl of buttered carrots. Comfort food. He set them on trivets in the middle of the table and handed me a spoon. "Dish us up, would you?"

I took Paul's plate and began to fill it. "How are things at your end of the office?"

"Fine. Shona has a bit of an attitude, but she's calming down. At the moment, I'm working on getting all your customer files up to date, so you can follow up with clients."

"Isn't that mostly data entry? Shona can do that."

"We're getting there." He rolled his eyes.

"Do I need to get involved?"

"Not yet."

I forked up some chicken. It was fragrant with cinnamon and anise, and I savored the bite. "Paul, how about you?"

He talked for a few minutes about the challenges of his latest clients: the one with an opioid addiction, the one whose husband left her, the one whose husband was having an affair, the one who lost her mother to cancer.

"I don't know how you handle all that pain," I said.

He smiled. "They have to carry it. I just listen." Then he said, "You look tired, Clara. Are the dreams keeping you awake?"

His kindness would *not* make me cry. "Lots of things are keeping me awake. I'm worried about Kyle, and oh-by-the-way he's annoyed I'm not divorced yet and thinks it's because my money is more important to me than he is; I'm worried about Bailey; the dreams won't leave me alone; I'm worried about Dom's sister and her family and that gang boyfriend of hers. I can't figure out what to do next."

"Why is Dom's death your job?"

"No, no, you're right. Of course it's Kyle's job."

"But," Paul said, "you take everything on yourself anyway." He set down his fork to rest his hand on mine. "You need to learn to let go, Clara."

"How can I, when the dreams won't let me?"

"I seem to recall a weekly commitment from you."

"Right. Meditation." He had taught me, at my mother's behest, and after I'd used it to help her, I hadn't practiced it for one more minute. But I'd promised, so next week, my new round of lessons began. I stuffed my resentment in with the last bite of chicken in my mouth and pushed my half-drunk wine to the side.

My phone rang and I grabbed at it, hoping it was Bailey. It was Kyle.

"We need to talk," he said.

What had I done now? "I'll be home in a couple of hours." I checked the time—almost nine p.m. I would probably be home even sooner, but better not to give in too easily.

"It's about Vlad and Teo. Can you meet me now?"

I looked at Paul and Richard. "Mind another guest for dessert?"

"You're in luck," Richard said. "There's plenty."

I smiled and told Kyle to join us.

Kyle pulled into the driveway about ten minutes later. Richard greeted him at the front door, ushering him into the kitchen while collecting a drink order. Kyle touched my shoulder and sat next to me.

Richard handed him a glass of red wine. "Are you hungry? There's plenty."

"You sure? I'm famished. Didn't have time for lunch." Kyle took off his jacket, slung it over the back of the chair and rolled up his sleeves.

Richard made him a plate and brought it and the seltzer to the table.

"What's up?" I asked.

Kyle addressed Richard and Paul. "She's probably brought you up to date." He shook his head a little at the breach in protocol.

When they nodded, he explained, "Clara's insights last night about Lia Moscarelli and Vlad really helped, especially her reminding me about Vlad's desire for a son. I did some research on Moscarelli this morning; turns out his first name is Reynaldo, alias Aldo." He turned to Clara. "Joe and I believe the A.M. from the note that Fredericka showed you and Lucas is Aldo Moscarelli."

"I could have told you that," Richard said. "I've known him for years; the guy's a real sleaze."

Aldo. He had enough menace, for sure. "Why would he go after you?"

"The Stamford gang unit thinks Moscarelli wants my town as territory, but Vlad doesn't."

My town. Ownership was a good sign, right? "The first time I met Vlad he told me he was a territorial guy—like maybe he wouldn't expand outside his territory?"

"Could be. We believe Moscarelli decided to take out me so the gang could move in here and thus show Vlad he could handle bigger responsibility. A town in chaos is a town ripe for criminal activity."

"So it's not about Teo?"

"Doesn't look like it, Clara." He paused. "Maybe the dreams were… wrong?"

I looked at Paul. Of course, Kyle would want my dreams to be untrue; then he could ignore them. It's what everyone wanted, including me. Too bad. I smiled, but it was feral. "Could be."

Kyle didn't seem to notice.

"So how will you prove Moscarelli is behind the gang war and Dom's murder?" Paul asked.

"Espejo's not a man to tolerate betrayal, not even in a family member. From what Clara's reported about his relationship with Lia, it seems he doesn't hold Moscarelli in very high regard. If we provide Espejo with a substitute for Moscarelli—a new son—he might be willing to help us."

"Teo?" I looked at him, shocked.

He nodded.

"Are you kidding me?"

"What Teo wants more than anything is a family, but he wants to earn his living his own way. He thinks he can beat the system." He ran his hand over his hair, as if he were trying to rub it off. "You can't save him, Clara."

"Sentencing him to a criminal life is better?"

"He'll owe me. They both will. That keeps my town safe, your town. That's my job."

"What about Bianca? She's already lost a brother and now you condemn her partner to… to this life? What will happen to them?"

"She chose Teo freely, Clara, and she chose to have a child with him. What influence can you exert that Dom's Pops can't?"

I shook my head. "Teo loves his little girl. Persuade him to leave the gang life by using her."

"I tried. He's not listening. Besides, how does that help us catch Moscarelli?" He stopped to drink some wine, then set the glass down on the coaster, twisting it first right and then left. "Teo wants an audience with

Vlad. He's told me he wants to move up in the gang, wants a 'management position.'" Air quotes and another head shake. "Scoring a meeting with the big boss would give him a lot of credibility."

"Gang management? This is insane!"

"Gets him off the streets. It's a business."

The shaking began again in the pit of my stomach. Paul, ever aware, got up and brought me a blanket he draped over my shoulders.

Paul asked, "You think once Vlad knows Teo is his son, he will take him under his wing."

"Right. I need Clara to get Vlad in the room with me."

Richard leaned across the table to squeeze my hand. I couldn't believe Kyle would ask this of me.

"You're the police chief. You ask, they come, right?" Paul said.

"I want a friendly conversation."

"Friendly? With Vlad the Impaler?" I got up wrapped in the blanket and went to stand at the window, but I couldn't see past my own reflection in the glass. Kyle let me think it through.

What mattered more to me? My promise to a young woman to find out what had happened to her brother? My love for Kyle, who was under threat? My sense that all life mattered? Was I tribal or global, in the present moment or considering the long term? No matter what I chose, I put someone at risk.

I thought back to my dreams: Kyle in the woods surrounded by knives. Teo dealing drugs to small children. *He'll owe me.* Favor for favor. The possibility of preventing gangs in my town. For now. Of saving three young lives at the cost of losing Kyle. Was the future already written? Did it matter what I chose?

I turned from the window to face them. "First thing in the morning," I said, "I'll call."

CHAPTER 33
Kyle

The next morning, Teo and Vlad agreed separately to meet at Clara's office. Clara told Vlad she needed to discuss Lia's project. Kyle told Teo he'd solved Dom's murder. Kyle promised him this would be the last time they needed to meet. At least until he had to arrest the kid, an unavoidable future if Teo persisted in his choices.

He hadn't slept well, running possible scenarios over and over. What if he'd misjudged Teo's desire to be important in the gang? What if Vlad turned angry or violent? What if Clara had misjudged Vlad's desire for a son? What if Teo refused to tell Vlad who put out the hit? As he tossed and turned, struggling with the variables, he finally realized that Clara had been right about motivation all along. Sure, Moscarelli was motivated by power and money: why be in a gang if you weren't? But the reason for the mess right now was that Teo had started to push back. What had he said in the coffee shop? That his boss thought he could *run bigger than he is.* That someone had to take on his boss's ego. Teo had become a threat not only because he was Vlad's son, but because he was pushing his way up the ranks, literally threatening to push Moscarelli out. As for the encounter turning violent, well, he would just have to rely on his gut and his training.

Shona, with red-beaded braids, showed Teo into Clara's office. She'd already set up coffee and pastry.

"Miss." Teo nodded once at Clara, then stuck his hand out toward Kyle. "Sir."

"Please sit down," she said, not looking at Kyle, still angry.

He took a corner on one of her couches, as if he might spring off at the slightest provocation. He turned down coffee but took a large bite from a pastry before setting it carefully on his plate and wiping his fingers on a napkin.

Clara's intercom buzzed. "Dr. Montague, your other guest has arrived."

"Show him in, please."

Teo looked wildly from one of them to the other. Kyle crossed to the young man and put his hand on his shoulder. "It's fine."

The door opened and Espejo walked in wearing cobalt blue pants and a dark red shirt topped with a grey wool jacket and a green tie. Who dressed this guy? He scanned the assembled company. "Chief DuPont, Ms. Montague. Good to see you, but I believe you, Ms. Montague, may have shaded the truth regarding the purpose of this meeting."

"I believe a small untruth is worth a greater payoff—for you." Clara sat across from Teo in the one available chair. Asserting her right to dominate in this space.

Vlad looked at her a long time, and she looked right back. Tough girl. Kyle had to hand it to her. Not many women would stand up to Vlad the Impaler.

Vlad turned to Teo. "I believe you, young man, are the only person in the room I haven't met."

"Teo Welles, sir." Teo stood and stuck out his hand as if he were a Wall Street banker.

Espejo took it and covered it with the other, patting it. Fear flashed in Teo's eyes, and Kyle wondered if he'd suddenly realized his boss had found him in the company of the police.

"Please, everyone. Sit down." Clara offered coffee, gestured at the pastry.

"Why am I here, Ms. Montague?" Espejo wasn't ever going to use Clara's title. His way of keeping her in her place.

"We have some information," Kyle said. "We thought a trade might be in order."

"Ah. A negotiation. I excel at those." He settled himself on Teo's couch but near the door.

Teo pressed himself into his corner, his hands stuffed in his hoodie's pockets. Vlad glanced at him, assessing but not really seeing.

Kyle continued, "We know why a gang war has brewed on your turf. We think that your knowing this information will help you end that war, which would benefit the citizens of your community." He paused.

Espejo nodded.

Kyle said, "In return, I would like you to call off the hit on my life."

Espejo studied him. "I did not order a hit on you. Ordering a hit on a police officer is a declaration of war, and I am not interested in war, only business."

"We know that. But someone in your organization did and Teo here knows who it is."

Espejo turned his raptor's eyes on Teo, then looked again, as if he hadn't really seen him before.

"I'd like that person's name," Espejo said to the young man.

Kyle said, "We'd like to arrest him and allow justice to proceed against him."

"Just so I'm clear," Espejo said, "the deal is as follows: You will give me the person's name who is conspiring against me, and who put out a hit on you, Chief DuPont, and in return, I will allow this person to be arrested and prosecuted without interfering, as well as making sure that no other member of my organization acts rashly with regard to your health. Is that correct?"

Kyle nodded.

Vlad said, "Seems that mostly benefits you."

Kyle looked at Clara.

She said, "One other bit of information we think you'll find relevant: We believe Teo here is your son."

"I'm what?" Teo went white, then red. "No, ma'am. My parents died."

Espejo stared at Clara, then turned to look hard at the boy, perhaps seeing the resemblance, which was so clear now that they inhabited the same room. He leaned forward, gripping his own knee hard. "How old are you?"

"Twenty-five, sir."

"Your mother's name?" The same intense tone. Clara's insight about Espejo's desire for a son was suddenly on display.

Teo told him.

"Ah. That was a long time ago."

Kyle glanced at Clara. She was studying Vlad with a slight frown. What did she see?

Vlad expelled a controlled breath. "You willing to do a DNA test for me?"

"Yes, sir."

Kyle watched the boy take it in, wondered what it would be like to get your father back after thinking he was irretrievably lost, even this father. Thought of the joy he would feel if his own father came in off the streets.

Vlad nodded, then took in Teo's outfit, the purple and red. "You're a Sunset Boy?"

"Yes, sir."

Kyle watched Teo screw up his courage.

"I want to move up."

Clara sent an anguished look toward Kyle, but Teo had to make his own decisions. This one had been made a long time ago, and nothing they could say or do would change Teo's mind, especially not if his new-found father asked. Some of the hardness had crept back into Teo's face.

"I can always use trustworthy people," said Vlad.

And the die was cast.

Teo flexed his hands, calculations running behind his eyes, like a computer running code during a search. He sat up straight. "Does telling you who's trying to cut you out of your own business count as trustworthy, sir? No matter who it is?"

"Absolutely," Espejo said.

"Do we have a deal?" Kyle interjected. Kyle and Vlad locked eyes for a long moment, the equivalent of a handshake. Vlad nodded.

Teo said, "It's Reynaldo Moscarelli."

"My son-in-law." Espejo's voice was flat, but Kyle saw his hands stiffen.

Kyle said, "We believe Mr. Moscarelli saw the resemblance between you and Teo, and decided to preserve his place in your organization's hierarchy." He caught Clara's surprised look out of the corner of his eye but pressed on. "Dr. Montague mentioned your desire for a son or grandson whom you could train in the business, who would carry your name. We believe Mr. Moscarelli saw Teo as a threat, needed to push you out before you could push him out. If we can't get Mr. Moscarelli to confess, we would like your help in convicting him for Dominick Ofiero's murder."

Kyle saw Vlad do his own personal computations, fitting Kyle's information into a matrix that made new sense of things: the attack on Dom, the gang infighting, other incidents only Vlad knew about. Kyle saw the moment Vlad realized it all fit.

"I can get him to confess," Vlad growled.

Clara shifted in her seat.

"We can handle it, sir, but we would prefer you didn't provide him with counsel. Also, Teo will need to testify."

"Family matters are taken care of in the family." He was perfectly still, like a glacier.

Suddenly his outfit didn't seem so amusing.

"Not this one. Moscarelli shot a police officer, took out a hit on the chief of police. He needs to stand trial."

Vlad's head moved a fraction to the left, as if he intended to shake it in the negative. Instead, he said, "A favor," and Kyle knew some day that favor would be called in. Vlad handed Kyle a card, told him to let him know the arrangements.

"C'mon, son," Vlad said to Teo. He held his arm out to the boy, and Teo followed him from the office.

"That was wrong," Clara said as soon as the door had closed behind them, tears pooling on her lashes.

"It was a necessary *compromise*," said Kyle. "You know all about that."

She turned away, and he regretted his sharp tone. He'd already made his point with her. He knew better than to push. And he hadn't liked losing Teo either.

At ten p.m. the next evening, Kyle was in the passenger seat of Nate Jones's government-issued Chevy Suburban.

Kyle had spent most of the day after the meeting coordinating with the Stamford police and the Connecticut office of the FBI. Technically, since the bust would be in Stamford and the charge was conspiracy in Connecticut and Louisiana, it wasn't his operation, but it was his intel, so as a courtesy they allowed him to ride along. Shelly Epstein, Nate's partner, sat in the back seat, tapping something on an iPad.

That afternoon, Jones and Epstein had joined Kyle in the conference room in the Stamford police station where the rest of the team waited. The Stamford police chief then took over the meeting. Rosica Videz was fifty and tough, and she wasn't going to tolerate a cop killer in her town. She stood at a podium in front of a diagram of Vlad's club, pointing at the various entry and exit points.

"Our target is the club's manager. Mr. Espejo has assured us Moscarelli will be working this evening. This man is married to Mr. Espejo's daughter, so every effort must be made to take him peacefully."

She outlined where officers would be placed and identified a Stamford detective, Tom Robertson, who would coordinate on-site. Robertson looked as if he was about three doughnuts from a heart attack. Nate and Kyle exchanged a glance. The operation would commence at ten p.m., once the club was up and running, but before it got crowded. Chief Videz expected there might be some random drug busts in addition. Officers should wait on those until Moscarelli was in custody.

Now, Kyle and the two FBI agents were waiting for all the officers to get into position.

"So, Mess-yur DuPont. They kick you out of New Orleans for being too honest?" Nate asked.

Kyle shrugged. "Something like that." After the reporting on Katrina, everyone thought every New Orleans cop was corrupt. He was tired of the conversation.

The radio buzzed. "Ready when you are."

"We're on our way," Nate responded. "Let's go, ladies."

They stepped out into the cool evening air. Kyle could hear the rumble of eighteen-wheelers on I-95, and the click and hum of the train as it pulled into the station. There wasn't much of a line in front of the club. Probably too early. In fact, Kyle wondered if it wasn't just for show, a few people standing there to make it look as though getting in mattered.

The three of them flashed their badges at the bouncer. Shelly stayed with him to be sure he kept his hands off his shoulder mic. Kyle opened the door, and Nate preceded him down the slate hallway. In the main room, a long bar stretched down one side and a balcony provided a second-story overview. They flashed their badges again at the bartender, and he directed them past the end of the bar to a dark blue curtain, which abruptly parted and their quarry stepped out.

"Gentlemen," he said. "What can I do for you?"

Nate jutted his chin at Kyle, offering him the arrest.

Suddenly, Kyle was faced with the man who had ordered the hit on him. He hadn't really thought about what it meant all day, as he'd been fielding questions and listening to strategies. But now, after Dom dying in his arms, being shot twice, and worrying about his family, here he was face-to-face with the man who wanted to kill him because he was an inconvenience to his business, because he was a "righteous" cop who wouldn't take bribes.

Kyle said, "Mr. Reynaldo Moscarelli, you're under arrest for conspiracy to commit murder. Anything you say…"

Moscarelli let him finish before he said to the bartender, "Call my father-in-law, would you? Tell him I need a lawyer."

The bartender, a well-muscled kid in a black t-shirt with a tattoo of a cross on his arm, said, "He just called, said to tell you you're on your own."

Moscarelli looked startled. He glanced at Kyle from under hooded lids, a flash of hate. He said, "Then try my wife."

"Same message, sir. They called within five minutes of each other."

"They knew you were coming?" Moscarelli said.

"Sounds like it, sir. If you'd turn around, please?" Kyle held up the handcuffs.

When Kyle thought back, he figured that was the moment Moscarelli realized he had nothing to lose. None of the officers had their weapons drawn. The club's few patrons were cordoned behind one of those silky opera ropes. The lights still pulsed red and purple on the empty dance floor, and no one had thought to turn the music off.

Moscarelli turned to the crowd behind the velvet rope. "Who betrayed me?" he roared. "Who? You show your face!"

As one mass, the crowd pulled back. The club went silent, the music off.

"Who?"

Kyle tried to turn Moscarelli to cuff him, but Moscarelli shoved him and stormed across the dance floor. Before the cops could react, several young men, all dressed in gang colors, broke from the crowd and surrounded him. A moment later, the group broke apart as if it were a shattered glass. On the floor Reynaldo Moscarelli lay dead, stabbed through the heart.

So much for trusting a gangster.

They spent the rest of the night booking every single probable gang member in the club, all told around twenty. None would admit to stabbing Moscarelli. The knife, of course, had no fingerprints.

The next morning, believing she had a right to see the end of things, Kyle called Clara to ask if she wanted to accompany him to see Bianca and Dom's Pops. When she agreed, Kyle collected Stamford P.O. Iannotta and met her there.

The morning sported the bright damp chill that characterized New England springs and made him miss the south. He pulled his cruiser into the Ofieros' driveway, and they got out. Down the street, Kyle saw Clara step from her car and walk toward him. He thought again about how beautiful she was, how difficult this had been for them both. Maybe they could swing a weekend away, just the two of them, without all these competing demands. Finally, did it matter that she wasn't yet divorced? He knew he loved her and that she would do the right thing.

"Iannotta, you remember Dr. Montague?"

Iannotta nodded, and the three of them stepped toward the front door, which was just opening. Dom's Pops stood in its frame.

"Have you caught the bastard?"

"Yessir. May we come in? It's a complicated story."

Pops pushed the screen door open and moved aside, gesturing toward the kitchen at the back of the house. "Bianca's making coffee," he said. "Won't be a moment."

Sure enough, when they entered that sunny space, three coffees already sat on the scrubbed tabletop, while Bianca worked the espresso machine.

"Please, sit." Pops took the chair at the head of the table, and Bianca handed him the coffee she'd just made, then took the seat next to him.

Clara pulled a cup toward herself, sipped. "Thank you. This is lovely." He noticed she looked slightly ill, as if she wasn't sleeping.

Bianca nodded, her eyes fixed on Kyle.

"How is your daughter?" Kyle asked.

"Fine," she said. "She's down the street at a friend's."

That settled, Kyle said, "The man responsible for Dom's death was Reynaldo Moscarelli. We believe I was the actual target of the hit, but the gang members Moscarelli commissioned to carry it out missed and hit the wrong man. Those two were subsequently shot by the gang for their error." He left out the burning car. No one needed to carry that image around.

Bianca looked terrified.

"Why did they want to kill you?" asked Pops.

"I stood in the way of a family feud over a territory expansion."

"Moscarelli?" Pops asked. "He's going to jail?"

"He was killed as we were trying to arrest him."

Pops leaned back, satisfaction on his face. Eye for an eye.

"One more thing." Kyle looked at Bianca. "You should know our investigation revealed that Teo Welles is Vlad Espejo's biological son. Espejo has taken him under his wing, apparently intending to make him his heir now that his son-in-law is dead."

Pops looked from Bianca to Kyle. "My granddaughter's father is the newly appointed lieutenant of a drug lord?"

"Yessir."

She looked at her father, desperate. "He loves her, Pops. He wouldn't let anything bad happen to her."

"And us? What about us? What about when another gang decides to use her against him? You're a fool, Bianca. I've already lost one child. Do you think I want all my children dead? Do you think I want to die myself?"

She started to cry, and Clara reached across to rest her hand on Bianca's arm.

Kyle wondered what decision this family would make about their lives going forward. Teo wasn't likely to give up his daughter, and most people weren't capable of going into hiding. The Stamford cops would offer what protection they could, but memories were short, and new cases would consume their attention. It would be easy some long winter night for one of Aldo's faithful to make Teo feel some pain.

CHAPTER 34
Clara

After meeting with Kyle and Bianca, I wanted to curl up under the covers, let my shaky body recover. While it would take a couple days for the dream's effects to work their way out of my system now that they'd caught Aldo, I was a little surprised I didn't already feel better. Something remained unfinished, so I made myself drive to Evangelia's on the pretext of checking on our project's progress.

Iris gleamed in a yellow row down the edge of the driveway, backed by shiny green rhododendron leaves. The trimmed grass reflected the back-and-forth tracks of the mower, like vacuum cleaner marks in a pile carpet, a serene mask for a violent face. I parked by the front door and rang the bell. Lia herself answered.

"Hi, Clara. Come in! I'm so excited for you to see how the work is coming."

Dressed in her trademark jeans and flats, her face was perfectly made up, her hair pulled up in a neat ponytail, and her nails manicured in a spring-like shade of pink. She didn't appear to be mourning her husband. Maybe she was happy to be rid of him. Could she be that cold?

"I am sorry for the loss of your husband."

She glanced at me. "Not your fault." Then she changed the subject, and we spent a pleasant half hour, walking the grounds, making minor adjustments to the plans or plants, and talking to the men doing the work. Then Vlad arrived, carrying Lia's little girl.

She turned. "Hullo, darling!" Lia took the child from her father's arms. "Did you have fun with Papa?"

The little girl nodded. Lia carried her back to the house and set her on one of the high kitchen stools, then glanced at me sideways. "I hear we have you to thank for the newest member of our family—and the loss of another."

I said, "It must be hard to lose your husband so suddenly."

She glanced at her father. Was she angry at him? Had he consulted her before he had his son-in-law killed? Did she know how ruthless her father was? Certainly she must.

Vlad said, "My son-in-law led a high-risk lifestyle."

Was he being ironic?

"It was only a matter of time before it caught up with him." He ran his hand over the little girl's hair. She looked up and smiled.

Lia's laugh carried a note of disparagement. Did she agree with her father? I thought about Kyle getting shot. Then I thought about Dom, gunned down in front of us, the blood pouring from his chest, the green grass stained red. I thought about Vlad's reputation as Vlad the Impaler, then forced myself not to think about it. Kyle was right when he said the price was too high working for gangsters.

"My husband was a fool." Lia opened the refrigerator to pull out the peanut butter. "He thought he deserved more than he did. The folly of fools always catches up with them." Something hard flashed in her eyes.

Vlad nodded at his daughter, then excused himself and left the room. "So, about the plans. This walkway here." She pointed to my design. "I think making it curved would fit that hill a little better."

"That's a great idea," I marked the spot on the drawing, so I would remember to make the change. "It means we have to adjust this, though." I pointed at two of the beds.

"Sure. Can we get this finished for the Fourth of July?" She twisted the top off the peanut butter and purple smoke swirled out.

I laughed. "What have you got in that peanut butter jar?"

She looked puzzled. "Peanut butter?" She tipped the jar in my direction. The purple smoke had disappeared.

I tried to recover. "Sorry. Thought I smelled mint. Silly me. Must be something on my clothes from our walk." *A vision? Why now?*

She tilted her head, assessing.

Hoping to derail whatever her thoughts were, I answered her earlier question about timing and deadlines. "It's a lot of work, Lia. We might have the terrace mostly completed by the Fourth, if we don't hit any snags."

"Excellent." She popped a couple slices of bread into the toaster.

Purple smoke? What connected her to New Orleans? And how could I find out?

Just ask, said Paul in my head.

"Any vacation plans for the summer?" I asked.

"Not with this project on the table," she said. Then she turned, her eyes fixed on mine. "My late husband used to travel quite a bit to New Orleans." She nodded toward the shelves around the fireplace. "There's a picture over there of him with some of his buddies."

I walked to the shelves and looked. Wedged between a Chilhuly vase and photos of him with his daughter at the beach was a picture of Aldo with four men. Two I didn't recognize, but the third was Jonah Harris, and the fourth, behind the other three and with his arms around the entire crew, was a man I guessed to be Alec Harris. The resemblance to Jonah was strong.

"I think that guy on the far right was a cop," Lia was saying. "Aldo said something about having a buddy on the force that he fed information to, used to laugh about how he manipulated him. Aldo grew up in New Orleans, didn't come here until ten years ago or so. He considers it home."

"Who's the older man?" I asked.

"Cop's father. Apparently, he took a liking to Aldo, tried to get him to…what did Aldo call it? Convert. Go straight. As if."

I picked the photograph up and walked back to the counter. "May I borrow this for a few days? I'd like to show it to someone."

"You can keep it," she said. "I never want to see that SOB's face again in my life."

I dropped the photograph at the station, with a note to Kyle, then went home to bed. I couldn't have continued working, no matter the circumstances.

This had to be the end of it, right? No more revelations. Aldo must have heard Kyle was returning to New Orleans, and through the gang network gotten a message to his boys there to kill Kyle. Better to take the second shot in Louisiana since there would be fewer links to Aldo. Whether Jonah was a willing participant in setting Kyle up or not, he and/or his father had certainly passed along information to Aldo about Kyle's character—*righteous*—and his past—*homeless, car fire*—that the gang exploited. Kyle was right that the Harrises were involved. Everyone attached to this case was corrupt. Even me, I thought, as I drifted into dreamless sleep.

That night, after I'd woken from my afternoon nap, Kyle and I went out for dinner. He chose Pasquale's, a local place we both loved. Tony always tucked us in a corner of the bar and let us take our time.

"Martini?" he asked me. I nodded. Kyle asked for bourbon and water. Tony set our drinks in front of us and left menus.

"To us," Kyle offered, clinking his glass against mine.

"That's a nice toast. To us." I smiled.

The sunset washed the street outside with a yellowy-pink light. Headlights swept across the windows as the cars turned at the stoplight.

"Thanks for that photograph. It cemented the connection I knew had to be there—between the gangs here and Jonah Harris. Aldo would have understood the need to take care of nasty, lingering details like the brother of the girl you raped in college or the cop that put you in prison."

"Jonah's the source of the words Teo used in his fight with Dom, right? *Righteous, homeless, car fire.*"

He nodded.

"You think they cooked it up together?"

"Unlikely. Too hard with Jonah in prison. But I think they were still communicating, maybe through the gang telegraph Jewel was running. Jonah will never tell us, but it doesn't matter anymore."

"You feel vindicated."

"Vindication is good."

"Does it bother you that Espejo has gotten away with killing his son-in-law—and whatever else he's doing?"

"They'll get him. Just a matter of time. No one gets away scot-free."

Inside the restaurant, a family on the other side of the divider laughed. I felt as though I hadn't laughed in a long time, but before I could, I needed to bring up one final thing. "I've gotten a talking-to from both Bailey and your mom about whether I'm ready for a relationship with a black man."

He looked amused. "What did you tell them?"

"That everyone was different from everyone else, and we all had to accommodate those differences—race, religion, gender, preferences."

"How'd my mama take that?"

"She accepted my words, but I think she believes I don't get it, the whole race thing. I'm a white girl, so how could I possibly understand the black experience."

"Do you understand the black experience?" He seemed more and more amused, not at all what I had expected. I had expected I would have to defend myself, explain how I would try hard to listen, to do the right thing.

"Of course not. You don't understand my white girl experience either." I wrinkled my nose at him. "The point," I tapped my finger on the pristine tablecloth, "is that we're in it together."

He pushed his bourbon aside and reached for my hand, but I shook my head. "I still have to apologize for that terrible stereotype I invoked about black men and white women the night we, well, you know. Slept together."

"Ah, that."

"I was angry. I shouldn't have said it."

"True. Think you'll do it again?"

"I can't make any promises. You know me, I get mad, but I will try very hard to be better."

"That, Clara my darling, is one of the things I love about you."

I shook my head. "What did I do?"

"You're a fighter."

"Am I wrong? Do you think we're doomed because I don't understand what it's like to be a black man?"

"Your gift makes you a bit of an outsider, no?"

I nodded.

"Then you understand a little of what it's like to be me. Magnify that by thousands, by the looks you get from every woman on the street who doesn't know your job is to serve and protect. From every single person who sees you as a threat. From every shopkeeper who thinks you might be there to steal. From every TSA agent who thinks you are a terrorist. From every cab driver who won't pick you up." He suddenly looked tired.

"That's compounded when you're with me, isn't it? I feel those looks. It makes us a target."

"Yes. You wouldn't be targeted if you weren't with me. While we're here, in the Northeast, in cities, we're mostly fine. It changes in other parts of the country."

"Are you planning on moving?"

He squeezed my hand and let go. "Not if I can help it."

Tony appeared. "Ready to order?"

We got salads, chicken Marsala, lasagna, glasses of Chianti. Tony took the menus and left.

"Will your mother accept me?" I asked.

He shrugged. "Mama has a mind of her own, like you. You'll win her over if you stick it out, if she sees you're doing right by me, like most mothers. And your friends? You think they can put up with a cop?"

"You think that's the problem?"

"I know that's the problem." He laughed. "They couldn't care less that I'm black. It's the badge that bugs them, even Bailey, even if she couches it in lawyer-speak about race." He polished off the bourbon, set the glass to the side.

"They'll come around. They already know you're looking out for me."

"That I am."

Tony brought our salads, whisked away the drink glasses.

I changed the subject. "So when do you get some vacation?"

"Eventually. It probably wouldn't look appropriate for the police chief to vacation six months after arriving."

"But next year around this time? We could go somewhere together? If you still like me, that is."

In the measured look he gave me, I knew what he was thinking. "Right," I said. "There's that little matter of my divorce."

He didn't say anything. I had to give him credit. He'd said he was going to pull back, but he really hadn't. He'd been as steady as always, right there if I needed him.

I said, "I've been thinking about it, you know."

"You've been thinking about it for six months."

I said, "No, I mean I've been thinking about what you said, about my unwillingness to compromise."

"I don't think I worded it quite like that."

I flapped my hand at him. It wasn't verbatim, but it was close enough. And I had been thinking about it, about how I might have treated Palmer to make him feel the way he did.

When Palmer had first become interested in racing, we'd gone to the Tour de France. We'd stood on the side of one of the roads where the Tour would come through, and waved at the riders and hung out with other race fans. I couldn't see the attraction of sitting around waiting for a bunch of cyclists to ride by, but then I wasn't as entranced by the prospect of riding a bike up and down the hills, and I really didn't get Palmer's obsession. What was fun about putting on those shiny clothes and a helmet and getting on those skinny tires and pitting yourself against others who were riding so close to you that the slightest mistake could send you crashing to the pavement? People had died. It didn't seem sane.

Anyway, it wasn't my choice, but I wasn't about to spend my life hanging around bike races, no matter how much Palmer was interested. If he wanted to do it, he could do it alone.

At the beginning, he asked me to come along every time. When I kept turning him down, he asked less frequently, until he didn't ask at all. I suppose I should have known someone else would take my place, but I was so absorbed in my own world that I hadn't noticed. One of the local landowners had asked for my help in restoring his property, reviving an orchard and creating a walled kitchen garden. I spent ten hours a day on his land. Maybe Palmer thought I was having an affair with him, and that justified his own.

We would never talk about it. We were beyond that stage. But Palmer's pointed observations had made me aware that I had a responsibility here too.

I said, "What I mean, Kyle, is that it's about time for me to compromise."

He reached across the table and squeezed my hand again. "That sounds like a great idea."

The following morning I made an appointment with my lawyer, after which I texted Bailey, asking one more time if she was OK. If we could meet for drinks. What I could do to make it up to her.

I spent most of the day on a design for the renovation of the Stamford waterfront, a new client. At four o'clock, I closed the file and headed out for my four thirty with the lawyer.

Jasmine Queros worked from a high-rise not too far from mine. Rather than pull the Porsche from the garage, I walked. The daylight was dimming, but the days were slowly stretching out toward summer. The afternoon traffic had already started to build, and trucks and cars jostled for position along the feeder streets for the highway. I could feel the road vibrate with their passing.

Inside Jasmine's office serenity reigned. Her firm rented the entire fifteenth floor, which a decorator had covered in the requisite grey carpet, and burgundy and dark grey leather furniture. Black and white photographs, some huge, some tiny, graced the corridors and the partners' offices. Her secretary showed me in and asked about refreshment. I shook my head, and Jasmine shook my hand.

"So you want to settle?"

"Can we just get it done? I'm tired of taking his phone calls."

"He wants money."

"What can I get away with?"

She named a figure. It wasn't as bad as I had expected. In fact, it was downright doable. "Offer him half that. See what he does."

"Want to see if we can catch his lawyer now?"

"Palmer's in Madrid, getting ready to go out to dinner."

"His lawyer is in New York."

"New York? Why didn't you tell me?"

"I didn't want you storming down there and ripping his tongue out of his head."

"Why did Palmer employ an American lawyer?"

Jasmine looked at me a little incredulously.

"Oh. American law. Fine. Call him. Let's see if we can wrap this up."

Jasmine had her secretary put a call through and waited on hold to see if Palmer's lawyer was available. I stared out her window. The view was approximately the same as mine. I wondered if lawyers and architects all over Stamford compared notes on their views at cocktail parties. I wondered how it would feel to be divorced. I wondered how quickly the paperwork would be done, and if I would have to go to court. Yes, Jasmine said, there would be a court date. It usually took three months. No later than the end of the summer. Once the agreement was worked out, court was just a formality.

It was sobering to think of saying aloud before a judge that I no longer wanted to be married. Saying it in public made it more hurtful than if we just signed some papers. "The judge wants to be sure you're sure," Jasmine said. "Sometimes there's coercion."

My phone buzzed with an incoming message and I looked at the screen. Bailey wrote:

Sorry I stood you up. Flew to Hawaii solo to think. Don't mean it about Kyle. Talk when I get back. xo

I texted her back—*Here when you're ready*—and clicked off my phone, sad but relieved.

The lawyer came on the line. "Hey, Larry. I'm here with Clara Montague, and she's agreed to make an offer." Jasmine named the figure we'd decided on.

Palmer's lawyer blew out a breath. "Done."

"Really?" I was shocked. I figured we still had a couple of weeks of negotiating.

"Yeah. He wants to move on. Said he'd take whatever you offered, as long as it was something. He didn't think it was fair to leave with nothing."

"Didn't think it was fair?" I felt a sudden rush of heat.

"Clara." Jasmine raised her hand to calm me.

I shook my head and turned away. He should be grateful I was giving him anything. I should take my offer down by half. I should give him ten bucks. *As long as it was something.* Like I hadn't put up with his crap and paid for his bullshit for three years. He wanted more?

Jasmine said, "That's great, Larry. We'll draft the paperwork and send it along. As soon as you have his agreement, let me know, and we'll finalize this, OK?"

Once the connection was broken, she looked at me, a little annoyed. "Are you withdrawing your offer?"

"Should I?"

She tapped her pen on the blotter. The sun was setting behind her and I couldn't really see her face. "At this point, all you'll do is help me rack up billable hours and deplete your fortune. Just pay the man and get on with your life—and try to do it with a sense of honor."

Kyle and my life were waiting for me. It wasn't much money. Palmer was right that I hadn't listened well, that my needs had taken priority. I'd still been working out my anger and pain at Mother's needs having come first all those years when I was a child, and my needs should have been first. God, I sounded pathetic and whiny. If I couldn't get over this sense that I was still owed something, I might lose everyone in my life.

"You're right. I'm done."

She smiled. "Good girl. I'll draw up the paperwork this week."

She walked me out to reception. Sitting in one of the chairs was a tall, chic woman with dark hair cut into a pageboy. As Jasmine shook my hand, the receptionist said, "Mrs. Espejo, if you'll follow me, Larry can see you now."

I waited until she was down the corridor. "Espejo? As in Vlad Espejo's wife?"

"She's Larry Dodd's client. Why?"

"I've run into her husband in another context. Is Larry's specialty the same as yours?"

She raised an eyebrow. "Family law comprises a lot of things, Clara."

I walked out into the early evening twilight. I'd seen Larry Dodd's name in the paper, usually attached to some high-profile divorce. He always represented the wife. *No one gets away scot-free.*

I turned in the twilight toward my office and car. I had an appointment to meet Kyle.